T0156567

NUCLEAR ROGUE

ROBERT W. BARKER

NUCLEAR ROGUE

NUCLEAR ROGUE

iUniverse books may be ordered through booksellers or by contacting:

iUniverse
1663 Liberty Drive
Bloomington, IN 47403
www.iuniverse.com
1-800-Authors (1-800-288-4677)

ISBN: 978-1-4917-8510-2 (sc)
ISBN: 978-1-4917-8511-9 (e)

Library of Congress Control Number: 2016902083

Print information available on the last page.

iUniverse rev. date: 03/04/2016

1

THIS MEETING ON THE THIRTY-EIGHTH FLOOR OF THE WORLD NICKEL Headquarters in Toronto was a clash of worlds, a revival of old conflicts and past grievances. Serg Ochenko, CEO, and his visitor, Gregori Borodin, shook hands grimly, as though each one could infect the other with something deadly. Serg motioned to a chair, and the two men sat down, facing each other across the highly polished table.

Serg briefly focused on the memory, still fresh and sharp, that Gregori carried into the room. They had been so young. The Colonel had sent him with Gregori. It was a simple job: just place some incriminating letters in the man's apartment and leave. They miscalculated. The man returned too soon, and at the soft sound of the apartment door opening, Serg panicked. He couldn't move. In that brief moment, while Serg stood like a marble statue, Gregori, without hesitation, had raised his pistol with its heavy silencer and shot the man in the center of his forehead.

Gregori had turned to look at Serg. When he saw the petrified look on Serg's face, he had begun to laugh. He had continued to laugh as the two men cleaned up and made the murder look like a suicide. Gregori was still laughing when they left the apartment and disappeared into the dark Moscow night. Serg winced inwardly as he remembered Gregori's mocking laugh.

The physical contrast between the two men seated in the World Nickel meeting room could not have been greater. Serg Ochenko, president and CEO of World Nickel, sat quiet and subdued, with an air of sophistication and money. His hair was neatly trimmed and lightly gray at the sides, and his athletic physique comfortably filled the sharply tailored, dark-gray Italian suit. Gregori Borodin presented an old-world opposite: short, heavyset, and bristling with barely controlled energy. His thick, black hair sat heavily on his oversized head, and his bushy eyebrows seemed to defy any sense of control. His rough hands, ill-fitting suit, and short tie were a caricature of a blustering Russian Communist left over from the Cold War.

Maria Davidoff, Serg's personal assistant, turned away toward the adjacent tiny kitchen. She knew that Gregori was no joke. She sensed in him a familiarity with cold and vicious cruelty that left her profoundly uncomfortable. She was all too familiar with vicious men, and she did not at all like being around them.

The catering staff had delivered two meals. Before she served the meals, though, she poured a healthy glass of Ardbeg Uigeadail scotch whiskey for Serg and a nearly frozen shot of Stolichnaya vodka for the visitor. After she brought the drinks to the two men, they raised their glasses with a silent nod. Gregori threw back his vodka in one gulp. Serg drank his scotch with greater measure, swirling the amber liquid slightly in the glass between sips. Maria returned to the kitchen, but she continued to listen closely as the two men initiated their conversation.

"I am here to remind you of old commitments." Gregori spoke Russian with a raspy voice. Maria thought he spoke with a Moscow accent.

She heard Serg respond with a steady and flat voice, "I remember some of my old commitments. They were made a long time ago, when

I was young and in a different world. Those days are long gone. The world has changed. Those commitments mean nothing now, not here, not in Toronto." Though they both spoke quietly in rapid Russian, Maria could hear and follow most of the conversation.

"Do you remember the words?"

"I remember many words, most of them useless and a waste of memory."

"And the words 'A sleeping man walks with purpose', do you remember those?"

Maria continued to prepare the two meals, but now she listened even more intently. *What the hell is going on here?* she wondered. After a long pause, Serg answered Gregori's question. He spoke sharply. "Those words do not belong to you. They may have been words of action, but you have no authority to speak them now. When I first heard those words the world was a very different place."

Maria listened to Gregori's quick response. "The world has not completely changed. Some things never change, my old friend." The last word sounded metallic and harsh. "On the surface, things have changed," Gregori continued. "The President of Russia wants us to believe that the world has changed. The Americans, too, want us to believe it has all changed. There are some still waiting to act in Russia, and a few still waiting in small towns and cities around the world. They made solemn and unbreakable commitments long ago, like you did. They are still bonded to those commitments, and so are you." After a pause Gregori asked softly, in his grating voice, "How freely can I talk in this room, my friend?"

Maria stepped into the room carrying two trays, one for each man. She saw Serg's small smile and watched him raise his hand in a gesture that encompassed the entire room. The open drapes let in a ray of sun that settled on one of the two small Monet oil paintings on the otherwise-blank white wall. "This room is more secure than the Kremlin." He gestured to Maria. "I trust Maria completely, and you should do the same." Maria smiled.

Without a glance in Maria's direction, Gregori responded flatly, "I prefer that we talk alone."

Serg looked intently at his guest, and Maria glanced at him as she put the trays down. His face displayed no emotion, but she could see the tension in his hands as he gripped the arms of his chair. "Very well," Serg responded harshly. He turned to Maria and spoke in English. "Maria, perhaps you'd be so good as to bring the rest of the meal and then leave us for a while. Please make sure we're not disturbed."

Maria returned to the kitchen and brought two small desserts to the table, chocolate mousse with sweet whipped cream. Without a word she turned and walked out of the room, closing the door with a soft click of the latch.

Back at her desk, Maria felt a shiver when she thought about Gregori Borodin and the conversation she had just overheard. Gregori was not the first man she had encountered who seemed to personify evil and personal cruelty. She'd known her share of violent men. Nor was he the first man to undress her with his eyes. The walk with Gregori from the elevator to the meeting room had not been pleasant.

Maria possessed an attractive, solid, confident beauty. Her strength and her expertise in the martial arts could intimidate some men, and she liked that. It gave her a sense of confidence and empowerment. It also attracted the kinds of men she found enjoyable and exciting, relationships tinged with risk and perhaps even a little danger. This one, though, this Gregori, simply smiled his hard, thin smile and looked right through her. He came across as cold as the Arctic in winter. Gregori brought back memories of violent men and helplessness that she preferred to suppress forever. Maria looked down at Gregori's resume and picked up the telephone.

After an hour had passed, Maria knocked softly and opened the door. "Would you like me to clear away the meal?"

Gregori turned and focused his cold, gray eyes on her. The men had not moved from the table, but she could sense a change in the atmosphere. They sat with set expressions, and a thick and heavy tension filled the space between them. Serg had moved his chair back, but Gregori leaned forward, his arms tense, stretched out toward the middle of the table.

Serg turned his head slightly. "Yes," he said. "We are finished, I think."

As she picked up the trays, Maria looked down and saw that Serg's knuckles had turned white from his tight grip on the arms of the chair. She found that astonishing. Serg was many things, but he was always under control, and as far as she knew he was afraid of no man. She heard Gregori say, in English now, "Here is my resume, with four references." His English was excellent. There was a slight Russian accent, mixed with hints of the English of his British tutor. Briefly he glanced up at Maria. "I gave a copy to your assistant. You will find that the references are solid." After a lengthy silence, broken only by the sounds of Maria picking up the dishes, Gregori went on. "It's time I left. Here's my business card. I have an office on Bay Street, and I'll be back in one or two days, once the Germans have contacted you with their proposal on Randal Lake."

Maria watched as Serg made a special effort to relax. Both men stood up. As she carried the trays to the kitchen she heard Serg return to Russian. She strained to hear the words. Almost hissing, he said, "Let me give you a word of advice, my friend. You are on my ground now. It can be dangerous to be too arrogant." Serg spoke a few more words to Gregori, but so softly that Maria could not hear them in the kitchen.

When she returned to the table, Serg spoke to her. "Please show Mr. Borodin to the elevator, Maria." Serg and Gregori did not shake hands.

As Maria left with Gregori she noted that Serg was already walking the few steps to the bar and the hidden, digital sound recorder. When Maria returned from the elevator, she stepped into the room. She watched for a moment as Serg tapped the memory card idly in his hand. She asked, "Do you want me to make a transcript for you?" He was staring out the large windows that looked out over the city and onto the lake. Windblown whitecaps covered the bay at the edge of Lake Ontario.

As Serg turned away from the window, he smiled thinly and dropped the memory card into his jacket pocket. "No," he said. "It is nothing." Maria raised her eyebrows slightly. Pointing to the table, Serg continued, "However, I'd like you to take his resume and check his references."

Maria smiled as she replied, "I've already checked some of my own contacts. They say that Gregori Borodin has a good reputation as a German construction engineer, particularly in the area of sinking and rehabilitating mine shafts in permafrost. He's worked a lot in Russia recently, mainly in the northern nickel mines at Norilsk. He speaks German, English, and fluent Russian with a Moscow accent." She paused a moment. "It's strange, though. None of my contacts seem to know him firsthand."

Serg laughed. "I should've known you'd already have the answer." He shook his head. "He says some German company wants to make a proposal for a joint venture on Randal Lake, but I haven't seen any details yet."

"Well, that would be a surprise."

"Wouldn't it?"

They parted and Maria walked the short distance from the meeting room back to her office. The hold that Serg had over Maria was unusually strong. When her abusive husband had finally gone too far, Maria had simply pushed him off the balcony of their fifteenth-floor apartment. Serg made sure she had the best lawyers available in Toronto, and she won her court case. Acting in self-defense. That was the ruling. A lesser lawyer or less money for her defense might have produced quite a different outcome.

Maria had worked a little over six years for Serg. Sometimes she could anticipate his next move, and he had few secrets from her, far fewer than he thought. At times their relationship, in subtle and not so subtle ways, bordered on the abusive. Like it or not, she was bound to him, servant to master. She knew Serg too well. He valued people only so long as they provided something he needed, and he could be violent in his retribution if anyone crossed him. He had captured her, and she knew it.

Maria did wield more hidden power in the company than was generally known. Even Serg had felt her sharp edge on occasion. Her evolving knowledge of the mining business and the stock market had been very useful to her, actually making her a wealthy woman. Maria knew she had to escape, but she needed something to hold over Serg, and Serg was cautious about exposing himself to that kind of risk.

There's something more to this relationship between Gregori and Serg, she thought. She shook her head. She was sure Gregori was no German. She didn't know how Serg and Gregori were connected, but it had to go back to when Serg had lived in Moscow, before he had emigrated to Canada. They must have worked together or gone to school together. Whatever it was, Gregori had some sort of hold over Serg. Maria shivered. Serg would have to deal with Gregori on his own.

In the dead air of the secure, internal room at CIA headquarters in Langley, Virginia, Harold James, director of the CIA, completed his oral briefing. He waited for a few moments to allow the other three men to digest what he had just presented. Harold sat straight in his chair, in a crisp shirt and a navy blue, pin-striped suit. A tall, angular man, Harold's slightly graying dark hair gave him the appearance of a learned, very well dressed professor. In fact, he had been a teacher at an exclusive private prep school early in his career, before he discovered his true calling. Finally he said, "I think it presents a unique opportunity, but it carries with it a very high risk factor." He looked at the three men. "Your thoughts, G?"

G was a short, dark-complexioned man, and he spoke with a heavy German accent. Harold always felt uneasy around G's large intellect and even larger ego. "Let it be," G said.

Harold inhaled. "Just let it be? And the risks?"

"There are few risks to us. Let it happen. Let them burn in the fires of their own damnation."

Harold turned to BD, the second man, tall and blond. BD spoke with a private-school accent even more pronounced than Harold's. "This type of opportunity always comes with risk to everyone. We have no choice. We must let them run. I think even our silent friend here will agree."

Harold looked at the third man in the room. Even with all his resources, all his connections, Harold knew very little about this man. In all the years they had met, the four of them, in so many rooms like this one, Harold had heard this man utter no more than a half dozen words. This time the man silently nodded ever so slightly.

"And POTUS?" Harold asked. "Shall we include the President of the United States in this?"

"Absolutely not," G growled harshly, "and quash the intelligence. We don't need anyone that naïve involved in this."

Harold turned to the silent man, "And the Pentagon?" The question was met with a small shake of the head.

Harold nodded, and without another word the four men stood and parted company.

2

P ETER BINDER STARED IDLY OUT THE SCRATCHED AND YELLOWING window of the old plane. He was happy to leave the Inuit community of Kuujjuaq behind. He had to admit, though, that the place had grown and added some welcome improvements. The relatively new regional government for Nunavik in northern Quebec, including its parliamentary-style council and cabinet, was situated in Kuujjuaq. The government officials, like most officials everywhere, had demanded a few more creature comforts than Kuujjuaq had previously offered. A bit of ecotourism had helped, too. The place even had a couple of new restaurants, and the new hotel was a major improvement. Peter was impatient, though. He wanted to get to work, and his work was about three hundred and fifty miles north of Kuujjuaq.

Peter was ready for the short summer season of northern Nunavik, even if summer wasn't quite ready to arrive in this land. Besides his heavy sleeping bag, his pack held his clothes, field gear, a shotgun, and most important of all, eight bottles of scotch. Peter would drink very little of the scotch himself. Each of those bottles was a low-cost insurance policy. They bought a lot of good will, a lot of favors.

The flat light of the late winter day gave the landscape of northern Nunavik a shapeless, edgeless character. The horizon of the subdued, snow-covered land was lost in low, gray clouds. The empty fierceness of this land could make strong men weak and wise men foolish, but Peter embraced the emptiness.

Peter had survived the rigorous military training and his service time with the U.S. Navy SEALs with few visible scars, but the invisible wounds were still fresh and sensitive. He had loved his time with the SEALs, and he had believed that he was doing something important for the country and the world. Peter had been an instinctive warrior, able to make the right decisions in the fog of battle almost instantly. The admirals praised him for his quick action, but sometimes his abilities frightened him. He had saved lives, saved them from disaster, they said. Peter knew, though, that his quick decisions had also cost lives, and not always only the lives of the targets. He had seen his best friends die, when his decisions had been responsible for their deaths. His officers called him a hero. They gave him a medal. Peter had left the SEALs as soon as he could complete his commitment.

Peter needed the emptiness of the northern landscape. It was a place where he could lose his memories. He needed to be around solid people, people like Tom Grogan, his assistant, and Roland Leroux, the cook. Tom had grown up with hard work, on a small farm in Ontario. He always did what needed to be done. He just did his job. Roland cooked. He'd started as a cook on the railroad, and cooking was his life, except for drinking between jobs. He never touched a drop when he was working. Peter didn't worry about either of them.

Peter continued to look out the window. As a geologist he had been here before, exploring for nickel deposits, but now the metal of the day was gold. He liked gold, and he liked the search for it. As a commodity, gold had its own flavor and life.

He let his gaze wander over the interior of the aging DC-3. The gray padding matched the view from the window. The plane was certainly showing its age. The once-white stuffing showed through gashes in the fabric that covered the sides of the cabin. As the plane slowly droned on toward the campsite at Nuvilik Lake, Peter could almost feel the ghosts in the old plane. He shifted back into the well-worn seat. The faint, musty smell of age surrounded him. He smiled. It was an old plane, but he knew that it was a reliable workhorse, well suited for this work. Beside him and along the length of the plane, cables anchored drums of gasoline to the floor, and piles of other supplies filled the remaining space. Enough for a start.

The pilot, Pierre Jadot, called back, "Hey, Peter, the meteor crater's up ahead. Come up here and help us find your camp."

Peter unbuckled his seatbelt and grabbed a map from beside him on the seat. He squeezed his broad shoulders past the boxes of groceries and sacks of potatoes to the front of the plane. As Peter scrambled into the cockpit, the sight of Pierre reminded him, as always, of a rather portly Colonel Sanders. The white, wavy hair and goatee were a perfect match. Peter leaned forward between the copilot and Pierre to get a better view. The crater was a small circle of perfection in the endless white snow and jumbled, low, black hills.

"Pierre, I thought you had GPS units in all these old buckets."

"We do. This one's busted." Pierre glanced at Peter with a smile. "I figured you'd be able to find your summer home easy enough, and besides, those orange-covered tents are hard to miss."

"Yeah. That's true enough," Peter responded. Visibility was excellent. He pushed his hair back from his forehead and searched beyond the crater for the gravel bank at Esker Lake. That was his landmark, his guide to the camp on Nuvilik Lake. He had given Esker Lake its informal name a few years earlier when he was exploring for nickel. The esker was a narrow, meandering ridge of gravel, left behind by a glacier, perhaps 10,000 years ago, a long, black line across the white horizon. He pointed ahead and said to Pierre, "See that black line up ahead? Hang a left when you get to it. Straight west from there, thirty to forty miles, should get us to the camp." Pierre pulled back on the throttles, and the noisy clatter of the old piston engines changed to a lower tone as he initiated the slow descent.

"I wasn't up here last year, and I left the other loads farther down the lake last week. There aren't any rocks along the lake by the camp, are there?"

"I haven't seen any. We landed in the summer on floats, and on skis in the winter last year. Never had any problems. Just stay in the middle of the lake." Pointing at the map he held in his hand, turning it so Pierre could see it clearly, Peter added, "I want to end up near the small point halfway down the lake in front of the camp. When you were up here last week you saw the orange tarps on the tents we left set up over the winter. Assuming the tents are still in good shape, we should be able to unload all the food and equipment from the plane and store it away before night. Let's get as close as we can to the tents."

"I had a quick look when we flew by last week. The tents look like they're in good shape."

For Peter, the end of a trip always seemed to take longer than he thought it ought to. He looked over Pierre's shoulder to the south and west as the plane made a slow turn over the esker. He squinted to take a closer look. He couldn't believe that he was actually seeing the tracks of a large Bombardier tractor in the snow below. The large, tracked vehicles, the same type of vehicle that ski resorts used for grooming slopes, were the standard for ground transport in the trackless expanses of northern Canada in the winter. But who would be out at this time of year? He assumed his crew was the only outfit crazy enough to be starting work this early. They were much too far from the coast for any of the Inuit, who usually used snowmobiles. It was way too early for most of the mining exploration companies. He looked back to the west, toward Nuvilik Lake, and the plane completed its turn and left the tracks behind.

As they started to head westward, the plane lined up with long, parallel ridges that stretched out toward the horizon. Peter smiled at his first clear view of the geology. The rocks had been turned on edge by continental forces eons ago, and the glaciers had scooped out the layers of softer mudstones and left the ancient and harder volcanic rocks as low, dark ridges. One long lake, Nuvilik Lake, was Peter's home for the summer. Between the volcanic ridges, the lake filled one of the depressions where the glacier had scraped out the softer mudstone.

After they turned west, a few minutes passed before Peter pointed ahead as the orange tarps on the tents first came into view. "There's the camp, Pierre, straight ahead. You're right. It looks like it's still in one piece." He counted the tarps. There were still six of them.

Peter watched as Pierre shifted in his seat, squinted, and looked ahead at the long, narrow lake. He lined up for a landing on the lake with a light wind out of the west. Pierre had called ahead to the nearby Asbestos Hill mine for weather conditions before they took off and again as they approached the meteor crater. The lake looked smooth, but that was a trap for the inexperienced. Northern Nunavik was nearly a desert, and there was never much snow in the winter, but the extreme winds could and normally did pack the snow into drifts three to four feet high along the lakes. Peter knew from experience that the drifts could be as hard as rocks. Around the tents, the drifts would reach seven to eight feet, the full height of the large canvas tents themselves.

Peter didn't know the copilot, who was young enough that he still fought a nasty case of acne. He didn't look like he could have many flying hours, but Pierre was a different story. It seemed to Peter that Pierre had been flying these planes forever. Pierre was always a cautious pilot; that was probably why he had survived for so long in the barren lands. Peter liked flying with cautious pilots. "I'll fly by and see what it looks like," Pierre said to Peter. To the copilot, "Put the flaps and skis down."

Peter turned and squeezed his way back to his seat beside the pile of supplies. His eyes met those of the old camp veteran, Roland

Leroux, and twenty-three year old, square-faced Tom Grogan. "We should be landing in a few minutes." Roland and Tom nodded.

After flying by the camp, Pierre turned the plane back to the east and circled around to line up to land into the wind, about halfway down the lake. The old DC-3 slowly lost altitude as it approached the landing. Peter smiled. He could sense Pierre fidgeting, trying to feel the frozen lake as he slowly flew the plane down to the surface. Looking out the window, with the gray clouds and the white snow, Peter had no firm horizon and couldn't predict precisely when the skis would touch the surface. Nose up, flaps down, almost slow enough to stall, Peter braced himself for the jolt he knew was coming.

Finally, the old plane hit the slope of one of the nearly rock-hard snowdrifts with a resounding, almost explosive crack. Peter felt his body strain against the seatbelt. The door on the side of the plane flew open and banged shut again, but all the supplies, fuel, and equipment stayed in place. The plane shuddered and bounced its way noisily down the lake toward the camp. Peter smiled. He knew, in a way most people would not understand, that he was home again. Home, where the emptiness would let the headaches fade. Home, where he could sleep without dreams, where he could completely trust everyone around him, where he could lose himself in geology and listen to the earth softly tell her story. *No firefights here*, Peter thought with a smile.

As Peter stood up, he turned to Roland and Tom. With a grin he said, "Well, here we are, home again. Let's go. We've got a lot of work to do today."

On the ground, as the old DC-3 droned along at low altitude toward Nuvilik Lake, four men looked up from a Bombardier tractor. Dressed in white, next to a white tractor that pulled a closed, white trailer, the vast expanse of the barren, white land swallowed them in its emptiness. The light westerly wind blew a small amount of snow along the ground, and the distinction between the earth and the sky faded to obscurity. Leonid Andropov watched the plane with his binoculars. Except for the scheduled 737 flights to the gravel airstrip at the Asbestos Hill mine and Deception Bay, this was the first sign of life he had seen in this forsaken place. He was not happy. He did not want to be seen. He wanted no company for this little exercise. He had enjoyed the emptiness of the land.

One of his men, small and sharp edged, looked up and asked, "Who the hell is that? Should we shoot them down?" Vladimir Kazakov had worked for Leonid for many years, and he had proved his worth just as many times. His answer to any problem was always violent and sometimes extremely messy. Leonid made a special effort to keep Vladimir and his love of violence under control. Sometimes it could be very difficult to clean up after Vladimir.

"Don't be an ass. It's almost impossible for them to see us, and even if they did, why would they care? If you shoot them down, you won't wait long before you're answering some rather unpleasant questions." Leonid glared at Vladimir. "Keep your dick in your pants, damn it. We'll stay here and see if the plane comes back, and then we'll see if we can figure out where it's going."

The relationship between Leonid and Vladimir always carried a certain tension, and they were used to it. "Should I get the camouflage netting out of the back to cover the tractor?"

At least he's using his head a little bit, Leonid thought. "No. White on white's hard enough to see." Leonid stared after the plane as it disappeared over the horizon to the west. "Anyway, everything looks innocent enough, unless someone gets really nosy. We're supposed to prepare things. That's it." Leonid paused and looked back at Vladimir. "No. We'll sit right here and see what happens. We'll take turns outside, watching for the plane to return. I'll go first."

Vladimir hesitated. "I still think we should at least cover the trailer with the netting. There's too much black on it."

"Shit. Nobody will see us," Leonid responded, "but if you feel so strongly about it, get the netting. I'll help you get it over the trailer." In about ten minutes the two of them had secured the white-and-gray camouflage netting over the trailer with short bungee cords.

About an hour later, as the sun broke through a low opening in the clouds and illuminated the Bombardier, Leonid still sat patiently outside in the cold. He watched the plane drone overhead, headed northeast. He listened intently. He thought he heard the tone of the engines change, maybe slowing for a landing, and then the sound was gone, swallowed by the growing wind. Still he waited. About thirty minutes later he heard the plane again, headed southwest this time. Finally he watched as it headed south in the distance. His permanent frown didn't change as he climbed back into the Bombardier.

Two younger men dozed in the back of the Bombardier, but Vladimir jerked upright in his seat at the first sound of Leonid entering the cab.

"Where are the maps?" Leonid asked, and Vladimir thrust a fistful of topographic maps toward him. Leonid searched through them to find the one he wanted. He pointed to the north side of Nuvilik Lake. "I think they landed at this small camp to the west, near where we saw the supplies on the ice. The mining company must have reopened the camp." Unwanted visitors could be a real problem. "We'll stay here overnight. Tomorrow we'll travel a little to the west, and if the weather's decent I'll take the skidoo to the camp. I'm sure they'd like to know what the other mining companies are doing up here." He finished with a rare smile.

"Oh yeah, I can't wait to introduce myself," Vladimir responded. Leonid glared at him. "What? I want to say hello."

"Right," Leonid grunted. "Just shut up."

3

THE WORKERS AT THE TOPOL-M MISSILE SILO STRUGGLED IN THE biting cold of a late winter wind, straight out of the Arctic ice of northern Russia. This was ugly weather in an unhappy land. The spring thaw and the brief season of wildflowers in this endless land of forests and rivers would be a long time in coming. Whatever the weather, though, these men and women were all happy to have a job that paid a decent wage. With what they made on this job they'd be able to buy food for their families and heat their homes for at least another winter.

The relentless Siberian winter wind assaulted the few small structures and equipment around the silo, but the workers ignored it. Most of them were direct descendants from the first settlers of the Siberian gulag. Some of those original settlers had surprised everyone, even Stalin and themselves, by surviving. Only when the low moan of the wind increased to a savage, high-pitched scream would they flee to shelter.

Some of the workers grumbled at the extra work required at this particular site. As Nicolai Mikhaylavich looked around, he heard one of the older workers respond to a complaint. "Hell, I don't give a damn. The money's good, isn't it? They can do whatever they want with this missile. They can shove it up the President's ass, for all I care." He heard a ripple of laughter above the wind.

With his brown coveralls, stocky Nicolai earned the nickname of "Bear" from one of the workers. From his father, who survived exile to Siberia when so many around him died, and from his Mongol mother, Nicolai had inherited a strength and toughness that few challenged.

Nicolai had climbed out of the silo to see how the crews were managing with the two worn-out cranes he'd assembled. The cranes would barely have the power to lift the 20 tons of the main stage of the ICBM, and Nicolai still hoped he would have a newer and larger crane for that part of the job. He was not optimistic. Even these relics he'd acquired should have little trouble lifting the 2650-pound warhead assembly with its single, 800-kiloton nuclear warhead and six decoys.

He looked to the sound of the laughter as he heard it again, but he made no move to rebuke the men. Satisfied with the progress so far, Nicolai turned and walked back to the entrance of the silo. They would be ready, and he would only be a distraction if he looked over their shoulders. There was no power at the site except for what was produced by the small emergency generator. The power had been cut off when the military stopped paying the bills, and then, shortly afterward, someone had salvaged the transmission lines. Nicolai found it astonishing that no one had stolen the generator. There had always been a small military presence at the site to maintain and protect the missile, but Russian soldiers were not above selling hardware to make up for their pitiful wages.

The elevator for the silo had stopped working long ago. Nicolai slowly climbed down a narrow metal ladder to the living quarters and the command center. The frozen mud left behind from the workers' boots made for a slippery and dangerous trip. In a few places the steel bolts that held the ladder to the cement wall were rusted and broken, pulling away from the flaking cement. The chipped gray and light green paint, broken pipes, and dusty, obsolete equipment lent a sense of age to a structure that was actually less than fifteen years old.

Nicolai stopped at a door, sighed, and opened it. Igor Luchenko sat at the old command center, in front of the original bank of dusty computers, all of which were worthless junk. He had one small, Japanese-manufactured laptop for his work. His pale, almost translucent skin stretched taut over his bony face. He talked little, and he didn't mix with the other workers on the site. He was not a pleasant man. In an earlier life Igor had run the engineering group that developed the Soviet missiles. A grim perfectionist, Igor drove the crews to a rigid schedule, and he never lost an opportunity to make sure everyone knew that he was the boss. Igor turned as he heard Nicolai come into the quiet room. "Ah, Nicolai. When will you be ready to start?"

"Twenty to thirty minutes." Nicolai went to the battered coffeepot and poured himself a cup of thick, black liquid. It had an acidic, almost metallic smell, and he knew the taste would be no better. "We should wait until we have the new crane here, in a couple of days. We'll have to use that one to lift the main stage of the missile."

"There's no time to wait," Igor barked. "You have to get the warhead out this morning, Nicolai. No delays." He frowned, "Now, let's go over the procedure one more time."

Nicolai groaned inwardly. Taking a swallow of the hot and bitter coffee, he held his stoic gaze on the narrow, pinched face in front of him. In a monotone he recited, "When the train stops on the siding, the train crew will open the top of the special car, car number fifteen. We'll remove the replacement warhead from the railway car and place it on the ground next to the silo. We can start lifting the original warhead off the missile shortly before 9:17, but we can't set it down until the train arrives and the car is ready. We'll begin the process of opening the top of the railway car and removing the replacement warhead from the train no earlier than 9:17, and we must complete the process of loading the original warhead and closing the top of the car, by no later than 9:52. The whole procedure should be easy and quite safe."

Nicolai knew that in this weather, and with the equipment he had on-site, none of this would be entirely safe, but he knew better than to voice his misgivings. "Is the railway car ready for the transfer?"

"It will be here precisely at 9:17," responded Igor. "Do you have the cranes ready and the cables in place?"

Nicolai shrugged. "We're ready," he said, "but I'll be amazed to see anything come together on that fine a schedule." He regretted his remark as soon as he said it, and he focused on finishing his cup of coffee, grimacing at the bitter taste of the dregs. He turned away to return the cup to its place beside the coffeepot.

"Nicolai, you shouldn't doubt the ability of us as Russians, at least when we're all sober."

The comments made Nicolai feel chastised like a schoolboy. It was hard for any of them to be anything but sober in this godforsaken place.

"The train will be here when we need it." Igor continued almost wistfully, "We once had the finest military machine in the world. Soon the world order will change again. Soon we'll take our rightful place in the world again."

"You may be right, Igor," Nicolai replied, but he didn't believe this wishful thinking for a moment. He decided to try baiting Igor to see if he could get any more information out of him. "But what does this missile have to do with any of that?" He knew better. He shivered slightly, and it wasn't from the cold. Igor simply stared at him, which did nothing to ease Nicolai's discomfort.

"Where do you live, Nicolai? Somewhere in the east, isn't it?"

"Magadan," Nicolai told him for the third time in as many weeks.

"Well then, you don't need to know any more about this whole exercise. If you lived in Moscow, perhaps I'd say something more." He looked at his watch. "It's nearly time. This must go as planned, or all this is for nothing." Igor returned to his computer.

Igor reminded Nicolai of the political officers from the time when he was a young man in the army. He'd grown to hate them with a bottomless passion. He turned without a word and started out the door to climb up the ladder one more time to the surface. His crew had already opened the great, shielding door to the silo, and the cranes hovered in their places. He turned to the foreman, Dmitry Nikolaev. "Let's get started, Dmitry." He watched as the crew in and around the silo began to respond. Their movements were like a primitive ballet. They all knew the dangers inherent in handling nuclear materials. He heard the rumble of the diesel engines of the arriving train. The squeal of the wheels against the cold steel rails grew louder in the distance, but then he lost the sound of the train in the increasing clatter of the old crane.

With a few shouted commands, Dmitry wound up the slack in the cables and began to lift the warhead gently off the top of the missile. The top of the warhead slowly came into view above the lip of the silo. Nikolai could hear the train quite clearly now, even above the noise of the crane. *Right on time,* he thought. *Amazing.* Then he heard the crane's engine skip a beat. He was not surprised. Bad fuel, perhaps, or maybe a bit of water in the fuel line.

As the train crept along the seldom-used siding, metal wheels still squealing against the rusted tracks, the diesel engine on the crane shuddered and stopped altogether. Suddenly white-faced, Dmitry swore as the warhead began to sink back into the silo. He slammed on the worn brake and stopped the descent.

Nicolai jumped up into the cab. "Jesus Christ. This is just what we fucking need. Start the damned engine, for Christ's sake."

"Yeah, yeah. What the hell do you think I'm trying to do?" Dmitry shouted back.

Nicolai stole a quick glance at Dmitry. Dmitry was old, unshaven, nearly toothless, and, like most Russians in this part of the world, a drunk. At the moment, Nicolai thought, he looked extremely sober. Nicolai hoped he was right.

Dmitry moved quickly to restart the engine. It turned over several times, but without much enthusiasm. If it didn't start quickly, the battery would simply die. "Start, you goddamned bastard!" Nicolai shouted.

The train came to a full stop in the siding beside the silo, and the train crew looked on with little or no understanding of the urgency of the situation. The warhead was suspended, half of it showing above the top of the silo. After a moment that seemed to Nicolai to last forever, the crane's engine reluctantly shuddered back to life.

"Get it out of there," yelled Nicolai. The warhead quickly rose above the lip of the silo. Nicolai looked at his watch. It was 9:25. "Shit! Eight minutes gone already."

Nicolai jumped down from the crane and looked over to the train, a simple line of tank cars. Part of the train crew attended to a car immediately adjacent to the silo. As Nicolai watched, the top of the train car split open to reveal the replacement warhead. Nicolai waved at the second crane, and it moved over to lift the warhead out of the car. Then the smaller crane moved away, and Dmitry began to swing the warhead from the missile over to the railway car. He slowly lowered the warhead into the car, setting it down on the first try. The crew closed the top of the car and Nicolai looked at his watch. It was 9:49. They'd made it with three minutes to spare. Nicolai could hear a second train coming by on the main line.

Nicolai took a deep breath. No matter what happened now, the first piece of the missile was safely packed away. If they pulled this one off, Nicolai would actually believe the old men still had the power. He shook his head. *Igor's right*, he thought. *It's best if I don't know any more about it.* But he already knew too much. Igor's question about where he lived told him all he needed to know. He turned away from the cranes to descend the muddy ladder into the control center. He had been without sleep for nearly twenty-four hours as the project approached this critical phase.

As Nicolai walked by the old command center, he opened the

door just enough to stick his head inside. "We made it with three minutes to spare," he told Igor.

"Good," was the only reply.

Nicolai looked at the back of Igor's head for a moment, and then he turned and closed the door behind him. The dismal corridor made no impression on his exhausted mind as he made his way to his tiny room. Once the room had held a small desk and a chest of drawers, but someone had long since stripped away that furniture. The room's furnishings consisted of a small bed and a pile of his dirty clothes in the corner. He stripped off his coveralls, tossed them onto the pile, and collapsed onto the narrow bed.

Perhaps Nica would come to his room tonight. She was a mechanic, the only woman on Nicolai's small crew. Nicolai smiled. She was a good mechanic, a bit coarse, but she was also young, and she and Nicolai enjoyed each other. He could use a moment of pleasure tonight.

He stared at the peeling paint on the ceiling. *Soon*, he thought. *Soon I'll have to make contact. I've got enough information now.* "Tomorrow," he muttered. *Sometime when Igor slept.* Nicolai sighed. Another four weeks and they'd be done. The pay would be good, especially with his bonus for meeting the deadline. Of course there was the third payment, too, but what could he tell them? They'd never believe his suspicions. They'd think he was crazy. Nicolai sighed. He'd have to stick to the facts. That should be enough. That should keep them happy enough to pay him. Well, maybe a hint, too.

In spite of himself he smiled. If all this worked, he'd have enough money to keep his family warm and well fed in Magadan, at least for this year and probably through the next winter. After that? Nicolai grunted. He shut his eyes and let the waves of fatigue wash over him and carry him into a deep sleep. An hour later Nica stopped at the door to Nicolai's room and looked in. She listened to him snore. She didn't wake him.

4

ON THE EDGE OF NUVILIK LAKE, PETER AND TOM TRUDGED BACK down the little hill from the large wooden frame tents toward the DC-3, where the crew was still unloading supplies. The crunch of each step left its mark on the snow, and the rising wind stirred the loose snow along the lake. *This could be interesting*, Peter thought as he walked back to the plane.

When they got close to the plane, he called to the pilot. "Hey, Pierre, we checked the stove fuel. We need to make a quick trip over to Asbestos Hill. We should pick up some drums of winter diesel at the airstrip by the mine."

Pierre jerked his head around to Peter. "You didn't tell me about that. We don't have time."

"I know I didn't tell you about it. I didn't know myself that we needed fuel."

"We've got to get back to Kuujjuaq." Pierre pointed to the west and the thickening clouds moving toward them. "There's a front moving in, and the wind's picking up. Pretty soon we won't be able to see the ground."

"Look, if you leave us here without any fuel for the stoves and a major storm moves in, it could get really dangerous. It's a quick trip, maybe ten or fifteen minutes each way once you get airborne. We'll grab ten drums and get them over here on the ice. We'll move the rest when you can get up here again."

Pierre grumbled, but he agreed to make the trip to the mine to pick up the fuel. During the flight to the Asbestos Hill mine for the fuel drums, the plane passed over Esker Lake again, and Peter took a closer look at the tracks in the snow. They must be recent, he thought, or the snow and wind would have obscured them. He noticed one set of tracks that continued to the west. Peter wondered if the Bombardier was from the mine site at Randal Lake.

Peter had briefly worked for World Nickel at Randal Lake a few years earlier. "Tom, isn't the Randal Lake mine site still shut down?"

"Yeah. As far as I know. Why?"

Peter pointed out the window. "Somebody's been running around with a Bombardier. I wonder if it's somebody from World Nickel."

Tom stared out the window at the tracks. "Ah, it's probably just somebody from Kangiqsujuaq over on Wakeham Bay."

Peter thought about the isolated Inuit community. "I doubt it. Too far. I don't think they have a Bombardier or the fuel to run one." Peter continued to look down at the tracks, until the plane left them behind. "Maybe I'll call Maria at World Nickel when we get the telephone set up."

At the mention of Maria, Tom glanced over at Peter, and Peter smiled. Peter knew it was no secret that he and Maria had spent a lot of time together when he'd worked for World Nickel a few years ago. As Peter thought about their time together, he realized their relationship had probably been inevitable. Their shared dedication to physical fitness and their mutual interest in the martial arts had been only a small part of what drew them together. Like two exhausted and wounded warriors, each had found a way to bind the other's wounds.

After a few quiet dinners, one evening they had found themselves on the sofa in Maria's living room. They were thoroughly enjoying each other. Maria pulled back slightly and smiled at Peter. "Shall we move somewhere a little more comfortable?"

"Mmm. I was just getting used to this," Peter responded with a smile, "but I suspect you have a good idea."

They left their drinks behind. Still kissing, they moved somewhat awkwardly into the bedroom. A soft light filled the room. The view to the south, through the open glass door to the balcony, encompassed the bright high-rise buildings in the downtown and the dark lake beyond. With the glass door open it was almost like making love outside above the trees. They could hear the slightly muffled sounds of the city around them. Taking their time, they finished undressing each other.

Peter lowered Maria to the bed and lay down beside her. Slowly they explored each other, delicately at first, kissing, nibbling, licking. Peter found that his skin anticipated every touch from Maria. His arousal and sensitivity stretched almost to the point of pain, and he found himself almost panting for breath. When neither of them could stand the anticipation any longer, they came together. Maria kissed him fiercely. "Oh God," she said hoarsely, "You don't know how much I've wanted this."

Peter grunted in reply and pulled her down for another kiss. Slowly, slowly, then they were both swept away on waves of undulating, fierce pleasure that seemed to go on forever. They lay together for a long time, not moving, and then they fell asleep with their bodies cradled against each other.

In the morning Maria awakened Peter with a kiss, and Peter's body responded almost instantaneously. Maria laughed and whispered, "I think we should take up again where we left off, but only if you don't mind."

"I think you already know my answer," Peter responded softly, pulling her to him. He wrapped his arms around her warm, naked body.

This time their loving was more leisurely, and the sun streamed into the bedroom giving a soft, warm glow to the whole room. They ate breakfast together, sitting naked and smiling, across from each other at the kitchen table.

For some reason that Peter didn't fully understand they never moved in together, but for a year they were together as lovers and together most nights when Peter was not in the field. Then they parted. In retrospect there seemed to Peter to be no clear reason for the parting, though some of the reason had to be that he had decided he could no longer work for Serg. Some of it also had to be his long periods away from Toronto.

Maria had told him a little about her experiences with her husband. Eventually, Peter decided that Maria, knowing the violence of some men so well, could not quite trust herself completely with a warrior—and Peter knew that in his soul he was still living as a warrior. Sometimes he was a little afraid of what he was. Maybe they both just needed to find out how badly they wanted each other.

Waking from his daydream to the noise of the DC-3, Peter said, mostly to himself, "Yes, I think I should give Maria Davidoff a call." If World Nickel was already active again at Randal Lake, it would be good to know.

When Pierre landed the plane at the Asbestos Hill airstrip, the mine manager, Jim Wurtz, drove up in his truck, as usual, to make sure he knew what was going on.

"Well, Peter, I haven't seen you for a while. What are you doing up here? Are you responsible for all these fuel drums making a mess of my airstrip?"

Peter laughed. "Yes. That's all my fault, I'm afraid. I'm doing some work for a little company called NorthGold out of the camp at Nuvilik Lake. Have you seen anybody else up here lately?"

"Actually, we had a big Russian transport plane come in here the other day with some scientists on a research program. They took off in a Bombardier with a trailer, headed somewhere down south of here. Can you believe that the thing is actually white? Up here? Other than those nuts, I haven't seen any others, but we don't wander too far away from home."

"I can imagine. Everything going well at the mine?"

"The usual circus. You need any help?"

"No. We're making a quick stop to pick up ten drums of winter diesel for the stoves. I don't want to freeze to death if Pierre can't get up here again for a while. Anyway, hang on for a second. I've got something for you." Peter went back into the DC-3, pulled a bottle of Scotch out of his pack, and returned to Jim. "For past courtesy," he said with a smile.

"You're a good man, Peter," Jim responded with a smile. "Let us know if you ever need any help."

"I'll do that," Peter replied.

After helping wrestle ten drums of winter diesel fuel onto the plane, Peter rested back in his seat and stared idly out the window. There wasn't much sun, but the clouds in the south cleared enough that a low ray of sunlight suddenly glinted off something on the ground. Peter jerked up in his seat. It wasn't easy to see, but there was a white Bombardier in the tracks in the snow. Peter hadn't thought about it when Jim Wurtz mentioned it, but anyone with any sense would want a vehicle a little easier to see in the snow. Survival could depend on someone being able to see you from the air.

After Pierre unloaded the fuel at the camp and took off for home, Peter and Tom manually moved all the supplies up from the frozen lake to the tents. The skidoos and most of the other equipment had been dropped off about two miles down the lake with an earlier flight. With a struggle, they moved two drums of the winter diesel up to the camp. Exhausted, they left the other eight drums on the ice. It was long, exhausting work for Peter and Tom.

For his last job of the day, Peter attended to the case of dynamite, the rolls of fuse, and the box of caps. They'd brought the dynamite to blast trenches in the outcrops of rock, to help in their sampling. He carefully wrapped the dynamite in plastic and canvas and stored it in a crack in the rocks on the far side of the hill behind the camp. He wrapped up the fuse and caps separately and stored them in the rocks a few feet away from the dynamite.

Finally he and Tom relaxed with a cup of coffee at the table in the cook tent as Roland prepared a rough meal.

"I think the potatoes were the only real casualty today, Roland."

"They won't be worth a damn when they thaw," he grumbled.

Peter laughed. "And they're a buck apiece by the time we get them up here." He turned to Tom. "We'll start on a hole in the ice tomorrow for water. It's probably about eight feet thick, so it's going to be a pain in the ass."

Pierre had been right, and with the suddenness so typical of northern Nunavik, the storm attacked the camp in full fury as they ate dinner. The wind quickly increased to a high-pitched frenzy. The long day passed into a noisy night. Peter lay on his bed and watched in the evening twilight as the wooden beams that supported the top of the tent bent inward with each fierce gust. The lantern wired to the beam along the ridge of the tent bounced wildly. Peter had seen this sort of storm many times, and the tents always held together, but each time he had the slightly irrational fear of being skewered to his bunk with giant splinters. Sleep did not come easily.

Over breakfast all three could hear the wind still tearing at the edges of the tent. The canvas slapped against the plywood sides and against the roof beams. Peter raised his voice to compete with the background noise. "I guess our first job is to fill the drums for the stoves."

"Damn good thing we have something to put in them," Tom responded.

They tackled the tedious job, using a hand pump to transfer the diesel fuel to the drums for the stoves in the tents. Though the temperature was not much below freezing, the wind was still strong, carrying the snow along the ground in a blizzard that often reduced visibility to a few feet. They filled the fuel drums for the heaters in four tents about half full. They'd have heat for the office tent, where Peter worked and slept, the cook tent, the cook's own sleep and supply tent, and one of the bunk tents where Tom would sleep. The other two tents, one for the helicopter pilot and mechanic, and another bunk tent, could wait.

After a break and another cup of coffee, Peter said, "Let's get the antenna for high speed data transmission up on the side of the office tent. We need to get our communications up and running." It took a while to aim the antenna properly. Then they secured it in the metal bracket on the corner of the office tent.

An hour later Peter dialed the unlisted number for Maria's apartment. It was Saturday. With a little luck, she'd be home. At least they had the satellite telephone, rather than the old radio telephone that everyone listened to for their entertainment. The satellite telephone was certainly more private and reliable. The telephone rang six times, and the answering machine clicked on with Maria's voice. "Hi, Maria. It's Peter Binder calling. If you're not at home, you can call me at—"

Maria picked up the phone and interrupted him in mid-sentence. "Hi, Peter. Where are you? I haven't heard from you for a couple of months."

Peter smiled. "I'm working for NorthGold in Nunavik, up in northern Quebec."

"Are you near Randal Lake?"

"Not too close. We're about thirty to forty miles west. We're pretty much alone up here, other than the Asbestos Hill crowd. I was wondering if World Nickel has anyone up here, in case we run into trouble and need some help."

Maria paused, and Peter noticed a change in the tone of her voice when she did answer. "It's interesting that you should ask. We had a visitor yesterday, a real tough guy. He claims he's a German engineer, but I think he's Russian." She paused again. "What are you using right now for communication, anyway?"

"I'm on a sat phone."

"Can I call you back?"

"Sure."

"Give me your number and I'll call you in about ten minutes."

Peter thought it was a little strange that Maria wanted to call back, but he figured she was just busy with something at the moment. After he hung up the phone, he stepped over to his bed and sat down to wait for Maria's call. When the phone rang, he jumped off the bed and in three steps answered, "Nuvilik Lake, NorthGold campsite."

At the other end, Maria laughed. "Well, that sure sounds official. I feel like I ought to punch in an extension."

"Not too many extensions at this office," Peter laughed. "So what's up, Maria?"

Maria paused a moment before beginning. "Oh, I don't know. Maybe I'm being a little paranoid. It's, well, Serg had a visitor yesterday, a really hard-looking bastard. Serg actually kicked me out and shut the door. He almost never does that."

"So he wanted a private conversation. What's so strange about that?"

Maria sounded annoyed. "You're right, of course, but this was different. He didn't tell me anything about what they discussed, and he didn't want a transcript of the recording. He always asks me to make a transcript. And this guy, he says he's German but he's got a Russian name, Gregori Borodin, and he speaks fluent Russian. I'll guarantee he's not German. Anyway, he just looks mean." With a nervous laugh, she continued, "I obviously didn't hear the whole conversation, but one thing I did hear was that a German company wants to make a joint venture proposal for the Randal Lake property."

"Who are they?" Peter sat down on the small bench at the worktable. "Who would want to joint venture that project, with all the problems it has?"

"I don't know." Now she sounded nervous. "Serg won't say anything. That guy had a really vicious air about him, Peter. I wouldn't want to meet him in a dark alley, I can tell you that."

"I hate to tell you, Maria, but this sounds a little crazy."

"Well, you asked. We don't have anyone up there, but this guy might, and I'd be careful of anyone who works for him."

"Okay, fine. I understand that you really don't like this guy, but I don't see any problem with those guys having someone up here. Do you? You'd expect it if they're serious about joint venturing Randal Lake."

"Look, Peter, I don't like the feel of this." Peter could hear the exasperation in her voice. "This guy Gregori looks and feels like trouble, that's all." The telephone picked up a lot of noise in the background.

"Where are you calling from?"

"I'm calling from the little park down the street. I didn't want to call from home."

"Christ, you must be worried, Maria." Peter laughed.

Maria snapped back, "Listen, you didn't meet this guy, and you didn't hear what I overheard."

"Okay. Okay." Peter moved the telephone to his left ear and shifted his position on the hard plywood bench. "The only reason I called, other than to talk to you, was that I saw a white Bombardier up here. It's supposed to be for some group of scientists, but I wondered if it might be someone working with World Nickel."

"Well they aren't working for us."

Peter sighed. "I guess, when I get the skidoos working, I'll go and see what I can find out."

"Be careful. I know you think you can handle anything, but this guy is a real piece of work. If he has people up there, well, just be careful." After a brief pause, "Do you have the telephone on all the time?"

"Probably not. If you want to call me, try between six and ten at night. If I'm around the camp I'll probably turn it on during the day, but you shouldn't count on it." Peter took a deep breath. "Have a nice weekend, Maria, and don't let this guy upset you too much."

"That's easy for you to say. You haven't met him. You be careful, and don't try to save the world or anything, okay?"

"I'll try to restrain myself," Peter laughed. "Call if you hear anything more."

"I'll do that. Good-bye, lover."

"'Bye."

As Peter cut off the call, all he could think was that it had raised far more questions than it had answered. Maria was a good judge of people. Sometimes he had thought she could almost smell violence in a man. He got up from the bench, unpacked his shotgun, and rummaged through his pack for the shells. After loading the shotgun, he leaned it against the table at the front of the tent and put the box with the rest of the shells on the table beside it. The simple fact that there were other people near the camp, people who seemed to want to be unnoticed, made him nervous.

5

THE NEXT MORNING THE WIND GRADUALLY CALMED, AND THE CLOUDS began to clear over the lake. The sky turned a deep blue, and the snow was almost blindingly bright. It was cool, but the sun on the snow could be deceptive, and dangerous. Exposed skin could burn very quickly. After breakfast Peter and Tom walked several miles down the lake to the west to the pile of equipment that had been dropped on the frozen lake on earlier flights. They needed transportation. The four skidoos were basic, workhorse machines, nothing fancy, and all of them were a bright yellow with black trim. With a little persuasion, Peter and Tom soon had them all running.

"Damn things. They're a pile of shit. Nothing but trouble," Tom muttered.

"Yeah, but we've got a lot of ground to cover, and no helicopter while the snow's still around."

"Yeah, yeah, but they're still a bitch."

They each chose a skidoo, jumped on, and headed back to camp. Later they'd build the sleds they needed in order to easily move much of the heavier equipment back to camp. It was turning into a beautiful day, one of those times in his job when Peter felt completely at peace with the world. *What most people would give to do this once in their lives*, he thought, *and I get paid for it.* He couldn't help but laugh out loud.

Peter and Tom increased speed as they ran down the frozen lake to the camp. Not quite so intent on lunch as Tom, Peter was startled to see a dark, moving speck in the distance near the east end of the lake. As Peter ran his skidoo up onto the slight rise at the camp and stopped the engine, he could already hear the approaching snowmobile. "Who the hell do you suppose that is?" Tom asked Peter.

"I have no idea," Peter responded. He watched a moment longer, and then he stepped into the office tent. He picked up his shotgun, pumped a shell into the chamber, and placed the gun out of sight next to the door, just inside the tent. Then he opened the small plywood door and stood in the doorway, waiting.

Their visitor made an impressive entrance, roaring up on a high-powered, mostly black skidoo. He was dressed in an impressive white parka. By now Roland had come to the entrance of the cook tent, wiping his hands with a towel. Roland had seen everything possible in Canada's north, but he was still curious about unexpected visitors. Their visitor stopped his skidoo in front of the office tent and stood up. He was tall and, like Peter, he had a powerful build, with a large chest and broad shoulders. When he pushed his hood back, he revealed a bushy head of black hair above a sunburned face. He had the rough-edged features of a man who has spent a hard life, but when he got off the skidoo he moved with a fluid, catlike motion.

"I see you guys have started to set up for the field season. I'm Jim Brown. I work with the Canadian government, and a few of us are up here to look around and set up our research camp for the summer. We're part of a Russian–Canadian group that's planning to study the northern lights together. I saw your plane flying around over Esker Lake, and I guessed it might be you guys. We saw the pile of equipment on the lake when we flew over earlier. I thought I'd stop by to say hello." His introduction sounded almost rehearsed to Peter, like the opening lines to a play. What was the accent? Peter couldn't place it. And what was with the rifle case on the side of the skidoo?

"I'm Peter Binder." He gestured to his right. "This is Tom Grogan, my assistant, and our cook, Roland Leroux. You had a long ride. Do you have enough gasoline to get back to your camp?"

"Oh yeah. I should be fine. I dropped off an extra ten gallons along the way. That should get me back all right."

"So you're staying at the old camp site at Esker Lake?"

"That's right. It's not a bad camp site, actually."

"Well, I'm sure Roland can fix up a pot of coffee for us," said Peter. He closed the door to the office and gestured toward the cook tent. After a moment's hesitation, Jim responded with a smile, "That sounds like a great idea to me."

Roland banged around the stove and started a pot of coffee. "I'm ready to put out some sandwich stuff for lunch. There's enough for a fourth if you want to join us."

Jim looked across the table at Peter, who shrugged his shoulders. "Sounds good. I didn't bring food with me, and I've got a long way to go back to camp."

Peter watched Jim intently as he talked about the survey crew's plans for the summer. "The main group of scientists won't be coming in for a few weeks yet. Eventually we'll move over to the Raglan Lake mine site, but the scientists want their first measurements away from the metal buildings."

"Seems strange," Peter responded. "I'd think you'd study the aurora borealis in the winter, and farther north."

Jim looked at Peter for a moment before responding. "They want to study the lights at various latitudes, at both peak and off-peak periods of activity."

The arrival of lunch interrupted their discussion. In his usual unceremonial fashion, Roland slapped plates and utensils down in front of the four men. Serving plates followed just as noisily, heaped with thick slices of ham, Canadian cheddar cheese, bread, mustard, and mayonnaise. Two pies and a cake completed the delivery, and then Roland folded his arms and stood by the stove to watch them eat. Peter smiled. If nothing else, Roland was predictable.

Roland liked it warm in the cook tent, and after eating his sandwich Jim stood to take off his heavy white parka. In spite of the heat, he did not take off a bulky, oversized wool shirt. "So what's NorthGold doing up here this time of year?" Jim asked as he helped himself to a piece of chocolate cake.

Still watching Jim closely, Peter slowly put his coffee cup on the table and responded. "Well, I always seem to come back to the same old places, though the commodities do change. We have a concession that butts up against Randal Lake's western boundary at Esker Lake. We're looking along the volcanic flows for gold showings." Peter smiled. "I don't think much of our chances, myself, but I'm not the one who makes those decisions. I just go out, do the geological mapping, and beat on the rocks to see if I can find a gold mine." Peter took another swallow of the coffee before asking, "How many people do you have up here so far?"

"There's four of us right now," Jim replied, "but the number will grow in the next few weeks, when we'll be over at Randal Lake. Stop by to say hello if you get in the area."

"I might just do that, Jim, but I don't relish that long a skidoo ride just for fun. Of course, when we get our helicopter I might stop by Randal Lake to say hello. It's always good to have neighbors up here."

Jim laughed. "Yeah. I can believe that." He finished his coffee and looked at his watch. "Well, I should be getting on my way. Good lunch, Roland. That'll make my return trip a lot easier."

As Jim rode his skidoo out along the lake to the east, Tom asked Peter, "What do you make of him?"

"He's full of it," Peter responded. "We flew over Esker Lake three times in the last two days. There's no camp there and no skidoo tracks. A few Bombardier tracks, but no skidoo tracks at all. Anyway, it's a hell of a long ride to get over here from Esker Lake, and back again, for nothing more than a quick social call." He shook his head. "I don't know what this guy is all about, but one thing's for sure, he's either an idiot or he's lying through his teeth." He sure didn't look like any scientist Peter knew, riding with a rifle on the side of the skidoo and maybe a pistol under his shirt. The weapons seemed like a bit much for a simple scientist or someone who was building a camp for the scientists. "Let's build those sleds now, Tom. I want to do some scouting around tomorrow, and I'll want to carry some extra gear with me."

At around 4:00, after he and Tom had finished building the three sleds, Peter stepped back to look over their work. Though the sleds were crude, they were effective and nearly maintenance free. The runners were two-by-eight planks, covered with thin copper sheeting, with a gentle upward curve in the front to allow them to ride up on the snow. Simple and cheap, the sleds were quick to make and easy to tow behind a skidoo.

Peter turned on the telephone for the day. A little after 4:30, the telephone rang. Peter walked back to the office tent and picked it up. "Nuvilik Lake, NorthGold camp."

"Peter, is that you? This is Maria."

"Yep. It's me." He sat down. "As a matter of fact I was thinking I'd call you again tonight, but I figured I'd wait until you'd be home. I wanted to ask if you had checked at the office to make sure World Nickel doesn't have anyone working up here."

"No. Like I told you, we don't have anyone up there." She sounded a little upset.

"I know that's what you told me, but we had a visitor in camp today, somebody who says he works with the Canadian government, part of a Canadian and Russian team to study the northern lights." Peter took off his knit cap and put it on the table. His head itched from wearing it, and he scratched his scalp. "He said he was camped at Esker Lake but would move to the Randal Lake camp later. You're sure you guys don't have anybody up here?"

"We haven't had anyone up there for several years, except for a quick trip once a year to see how the buildings and equipment are holding up. We don't rent the place out, either." She paused. "I called to tell you that it's been confirmed that a German firm has made an offer to World Nickel to joint venture Randal Lake and restart development." She paused. "Will you be around all night?"

"Well, there isn't much nightlife up here, so I don't have any place to go." Peter laughed.

"Keep the telephone on. I want to talk to you again."

"Okay, but make it before ten. I have a long day planned for tomorrow, and I don't want to stay up all night."

"I'll call in two hours. Okay?"

"That's good. I'll wait for your call."

After she finished the call with Peter, Maria returned the telephone to Serg's desk. "Just so you know, Serg, I don't like what you're asking me to do. He'll talk to you, I think. You know how he feels about you."

"Yeah, I know." Serg smiled. "We've had our differences, but I think what I have in mind will appeal to his sense of adventure, and maybe to his patriotic, self-righteous approach to life." He laughed. "Peter doesn't like bad guys who try to get away with murder."

"You need to tell him everything, so he understands the dangers."

"I know how you feel about Peter. What we need right now is a very special person, with special skills, in a special place."

I know what you bloody well need, thought Maria. *As usual, you need somebody to do your dirty work.* At the door she turned to face Serg. She tried to keep the anger out of her voice. Softly she asked, "Since you've told me nothing about your meeting with Gregori, perhaps now you'd like to tell me what you think is actually going on with Randal Lake?"

Serg did not respond immediately, and Maria began to think he wouldn't answer her question. When he finally spoke, he didn't look at her. "I don't know, but they want the mine for something." He turned and looked at Maria. "Gregori likes to tell people he's German, but he's Russian, and he was with the KGB when he was younger. He has some crazy plan." Serg shook his head. "Peter's the only one around with a decent reason for being up there. Maybe he can find out what's going on."

Serg swung around in his chair to look out over Lake Ontario, and Maria continued to watch him. It might still be late winter in Nunavik, but in Toronto it was a beautiful late spring day. People were walking along the edge of the lake, enjoying the warmth and the peace away from the heart of the city. "I don't want to call him from this telephone or from your home. I'll pick you up at your apartment at eight. We'll drive out toward the airport and make the call from a throwaway cell phone. I don't want this one traced to the company."

"Someone can still trace it to Peter."

"Yes, I know that, Maria, but it can't be helped."

"Call me before you get to the apartment. I'll be at the front door waiting for you," said Maria, and she disappeared out the door to his office. *So Gregori's a KGB bastard, is he? So are you, Serg. In the bottom of your heart you're his brother.*

Serg sat quietly at his desk for a while after Maria left, his head cupped in his hands. He picked up the telephone and called a number in east Toronto. "Do you have anything interesting from the phone tap?" he asked.

"Actually, I think we do. She made a call today to a man in Toronto. Not much to go on, but it sounded, um, different."

"When did she make the call?" Serg realized that it was immediately after he had visited Tania's apartment. He said tonelessly, "Send someone over with a transcript, to me personally. Mark it personal and confidential, and get it here in the next thirty minutes."

"No problem. We've already prepared it. You should have it in ten minutes if the traffic isn't too bad."

Serg shook his head. Tania's arrival in his life had always seemed a little too convenient, and maybe a little too professional. As his toy she could be quite delightful, but the tap on the phone line at her apartment was a simple and elementary precaution.

Fifteen minutes later, when the envelope arrived, Serg ripped it open and read the transcript carefully. He noted the time and the telephone number. He looked at Gregori's business card in his desk drawer. The numbers were the same. The conversation was simple. Tania told Gregori that she had nothing new to report. Serg dropped the transcript into the shredder.

6

TWO MEN AT CIA HEADQUARTERS AT LANGLEY, OUTSIDE DOWNTOWN
Washington, D.C., looked at a large computer screen. It showed
a satellite image of a missile silo in Siberia. "It's a nasty time to
be out working on a job like that. Nice, clear morning, though. Good
for watching."

"Yeah, it's a great image. You know, those missiles are heavy. I'm
surprised they have the equipment in a place like that to dismantle
the thing and lift it out of the silo."

The older man focused on the silo and enlarged the image. "Well,
you can bet that most of the equipment that was originally at that site,
inside and out, is long since 'salvaged' and sold on the black market."

"Just keep track of the bloody thing. This is one of the Topol-M
missiles that they're supposed to be getting rid of, not replacing with
the new RS-24. Let's make sure they finish the job the treaty began.
I want to be sure that nobody 'salvages' a missile and sells it and the
warhead on the black market."

"It should be easy to keep track of this one. They'll move it by
train, I imagine. You can see one train on the siding next to the silo,

waiting for another to pass. I'll keep a close watch. This is one of the last missiles to go."

The younger man took off his glasses and rubbed his eyes. He was tired, too tired.

In Saint Petersburg, in a gray office in a gray and featureless Soviet-era office building, Colonel Zakhar Rostov and his team were looking at plans for the Randal Lake mine site. The plans showed the buildings, the mine shaft, and the road leading eastward to the port at Wakeham Bay near Kangiqsujuaq, a small Inuit community. The reports on the project had been filed with the permitting authorities and the stock exchange in Canada. The four men stood around a large oak table in Rostov's office, where the plans were piled in several neat stacks. The three engineers, all short and husky men, wore dark suits as shapeless as the building itself.

In contrast, Zakhar Rostov stood over six feet tall. He had his hair styled, not cut, once each week, and he was proud of his well-toned, athletic body. It was his unblinking, piercing blue eyes that startled people. He adjusted his well-tailored Italian suit, bent over the table, and said, "Okay. Where are we? What's the status?"

After glancing at his two companions, the first engineer pulled back several large sheets of paper. His heavy face was animated by a nervous tic in his left eyebrow. He shifted nervously and pointed at the detailed plans for the mine shaft. "The shaft is easy. It's cement lined, smooth walled, and, at a bit over eight feet in diameter, it's almost perfect." He looked up at Rostov. "From all the public reports there's no broken ground, no cave-ins or other problems, but it's been a while since there's been any work done on it. There's surely some ice at the top of the shaft, but that's no problem. I expect we'll have to smooth and polish up the sides a little bit. The only other thing I need to do is set a good plug at the right depth." He shrugged his shoulders. "It should be an easy job."

"The reconnaissance team is in place," Rostov responded. "We should have a report on the condition of the shaft within a day or two. You have all you need?"

"It's all simple stuff. Everything but the sand and gravel we need is already on board the ship, ready to go." Still looking at Rostov, "You don't plan on using the shaft more than once, do you?" The engineer's right cheek twitched slightly as he asked the question.

"No. Once will be quite sufficient."

"There's no way to hide what we've done, once it's all over." The engineer didn't carry the question any further.

Rostov waved his hand in a dismissive gesture. "Once we're finished, we're finished." Rostov turned to the second engineer. "What about the support facilities?"

The second engineer flipped through the plans to a vertical section showing the details of the shaft and tunnels off the shaft at various depths. Speaking quickly, he said, "We need to blast out the space adjacent to the shaft. It will be a simple mining job and shouldn't require any special materials or equipment." He pointed to the shallowest mining levels. "We'll use part of the openings on the first and second levels of the mine. All we need is normal equipment for work around a mine. We have to sink a small shaft beside the main one for ventilation and crew access." He glanced up at Rostov and then back to the plan. "There shouldn't be any problems with any of it."

"Fine," Rostov responded. Now he focused on the third engineer, a thin man, older than the other two, whose face seemed to show no emotion at all. "Now tell me how we get everything to the site without anyone knowing what we're trying to do."

Speaking in a monotone, the third engineer said, "It's not that large. Our contract to rehabilitate the shaft at Randal Lake clearly states we'll line the top of the shaft with prefabricated steel liners because of unstable ground. That's what the manifest says we're shipping, all covered in tarps." He looked up at Rostov. "It's all nonsense, but people don't understand mining, and the lie will be easy to accept." He continued his toneless presentation. "As long as everything's covered by tarps, there's nothing that should arouse suspicion."

Rostov interrupted. "How do you get it past the Canadians?"

The man droned, "It's simple. It's a shell game with rather large shells."

Rostov laughed. "I remember now. Yes, rather large shells in this case." Nodding, Rostov continued, "So, we have the equipment on the ship, and we get it to the end of the fjord near Kangiqsujuaq. We can get it to the mine site?"

The engineer rubbed his angular fingers together and continued. "The road from the port to the mine site is in good shape. The trucks are on-site and have been maintained."

Unlike the other engineers, this third one exhibited no nervousness as he stared directly at Rostov and presented his description of the logistics of the project. Rostov smiled. This engineer was as tough as the steel he handled, and Rostov liked him. "I hope," the engineer continued, "that you have the funding you claim. Our German shipping friends demand payment in hard currency and charge an extremely high price for their discreet lack of curiosity."

"You don't need to worry about the money," Rostov answered. He had found plenty of investors from some of the old men of the Kremlin. Rostov paused, and the others waited. With a crooked smile and a softer voice he continued, "It's amazing what went on in this country, and it's worse today." Then he spoke with a quiet intensity, "Ah well, perhaps Marx and Lenin will have their day at last. Maybe we can do a better job this time."

The "true" Communism of Marx and Lenin was Zakhar Rostov's religion, and his devotion was not new to this small group of engineers. All but the old engineer with the angular fingers seemed to struggle to avoid cringing at his words. Rostov saw that he frightened the men, and he liked keeping them afraid. They might all share a distaste with

Rostov for the new order, but they had seen too much greed in the powerful men in Russia and too much laziness and drunkenness in the common man. In Russia, the combination always seemed to foil the best of intentions.

Miles away, in the Kremlin, two men examined a satellite image on a large computer monitor. The main light in the large, high-ceilinged office came through the tall windows framed by dark-red drapes. "You see, at 9:37 in the morning we have two warheads at the site. One sits on the ground next to the railway line. A crane is in the process of removing the other from the silo. It was a freak chance that we saw this. We were adjusting satellite coverage, and I just happened to look at this image out of simple curiosity to see how the decommissioning was progressing."

"I don't understand. There's one missile in the silo, with one warhead."

"Look closely at this railway car." He zoomed in on part of the image. "It's not a tank car at all. It's designed to bring a second warhead to the site and then hide the original one and take it away." He switched to another image. "Look at the next image. There's only one warhead. The other has disappeared, and the strange railway car looks exactly like all the others." Ivan Dinisovich smiled with some satisfaction. "Very clever, and perfectly timed. It would have avoided our normal satellite coverage for the area, and that of the Americans as well."

The first man unbent his back and stood up, stretching. "You're right, of course. So get to the point."

Ivan looked at the President and thought about what he had to say next. "I think I know where one of the warheads has gone, Mr. President." Ivan picked up a single sheet of paper and handed it to the President. "I had a man on-site at the missile silo. This is his last report. It's quite short."

After a few minutes scanning the report, the President looked at Ivan again. "You think someone or some group actually plans to use the thing?"

Ivan shrugged. "It's a guess. I believe it's a good guess." Ivan was silent for almost a minute. "We're watching this very carefully, but we saw it too late to follow the warhead. I will have someone check on the shipment to the Urals, but I have to be cautious. I trust no one, except maybe you, and I'm not always sure about you." He said the last with a small smile, but he noticed that the President did not return his smile. "If necessary, I'll go to the Americans for help on this one. With a few hints, a few small but believable lies about New York as the target, I've no doubt they'll be eager to help us. I should be able to stir them up over the possibility of maybe thirty million dead."

"Yes. Fear is a great motivator. It can even build a desire for cooperation." The President looked directly at Ivan, "Listen, Ivan Dinisovich, you watch this one closely. Involve no one else. Do not involve the Prime Minister or any of his staff. Report to me immediately if you see any new developments." He looked away. "I think I smell some of our lovely fanatics, some of the old rats crawling around."

"Mr. President, you have my word that they will not get away with this."

"They had better not. I have the feeling that if they do they'll make Chernobyl look like a spring frolic in Gorky Park."

7

ARIA DAVIDOFF HAD ASKED TO MEET WITH CAPTAIN RICHARD "Dick" Durban from the Royal Canadian Mounted Police, and they had agreed to meet at her favorite restaurant on Front Street in Toronto, not far from World Nickel's office. Now she looked down at her plate and pushed bits of chicken and pasta around in the red, marinara sauce. At the moment she wasn't sure the meeting was a great idea. "Dick, I feel really uncomfortable about this, and a little stupid. You know I owe Serg big-time and I don't want to give him any trouble, at least not when he doesn't deserve it."

Maria looked across the table at Dick Durban. She didn't know whether to trust this man or run as fast as she could to get away from him. Her feelings with regard to him were still a complete mess, she realized. "Look, Maria," Dick responded, "you know we've kept an eye on Serg for years. It may sound trite, but your loyalty to Canada is a higher calling than your loyalty to Serg. Besides, we're trying to keep Serg from getting himself into trouble."

Maria shook her head and looked up from her lunch with a small smile. She would never be entirely sure about the details of Dick Durban's game. In some ways she knew him and his business too well, but sometimes she wasn't sure she knew him, or his objectives, at all. "So what you're telling me is 'Trust me. I'm from the RCMP. I'm from the Mounties, and I'm here to help you.' Is that it?"

Dick laughed. "Yep. That's right, but I hope, considering our past relationship … Well, as much as we may have, ah, had our differences, you should know you can trust me."

Maria looked hard at the tall and handsome man across the table. Once she had loved him, and she had thought he loved her as well, but in the end he had left her questioning all her relationships and all her judgment. *I suppose I can trust him. He did tell me the truth, even then when I didn't want to hear it.* Right now, though, the truth was that she didn't want to tell him anything, though she knew she would. "I'm not sure it's anything," she said.

Dick sat back in his chair, quietly waiting.

She continued to push the food around on her plate. "Serg had a visitor the other day, somebody he knows from the old days, when he was still in Russia. His name is Gregori Borodin, and he scares the hell out of me. He comes across as one cold bastard. His resume checks out as a mining engineer, and I wouldn't have thought much about it, except," Maria paused for a moment, steeling herself to continue, "except Gregori spoke a phrase, as though it was some sort of code, and then Serg kicked me out of the room."

Dick continued to sit quietly, waiting.

"When I came back in, about an hour later, you could feel the tension in that room. This Gregori character said that a German company would make a joint venture proposal on Randal Lake, up in Nunavik. Serg was extremely upset, and he almost threatened the guy." Maria speared a couple of pieces of chicken with her fork and chewed them slowly. "I've told you that Serg normally records meetings like this one?"

"Yeah, you've told me. Did he record this one?"

"Yes, and he always asks me to make a transcript for him. But this time he just put the recording in his pocket."

Dick waited for more, but Maria kept silent. "You're right, Maria. It's not much to go on. There's nothing else?"

"Well, Serg did tell me that Gregori is ex–KGB. I think Serg is afraid of him. There's one other thing, too. A geologist friend of mine is working near Randal Lake, for another company. He had a visitor who claims he's working for a joint Canadian–Russian research team. The visitor said he'd be staying at Randal Lake in the near future, but we, that's World Nickel, don't know anything about this. Serg thinks the visitor may be working for this guy Gregori Borodin. In any case, my friend figures this guy's no research scientist." Maria shook her head in exasperation. "I don't know, Dick. There's nothing here but a bunch of disjointed bullshit."

Dick paused before he answered. "I think we should find out a little more about this 'visitor' in Nunavik. What's your friend's name?"

"Peter Binder."

"Oh yeah. I remember you telling me about Peter." Dick smiled at Maria. "He's a capable guy. Perhaps he could take a closer look at the visitor's camp."

"I think Serg plans to ask him tonight to do the same thing."

Dick laughed. "Well, that's great. Then he has two reasons to look around."

"You're sure that's a good idea? Suppose these guys are armed?"

"Look, I'm sure Peter's visitor is nothing more than what he says he is. In the meantime I'll do a little checking around to find out if the government has any record of a research program with the Russians up there."

"Christ," Maria muttered. "I wish I'd never set up this lunch."

Dick laughed again. "You worry too much, Maria. Peter can simply look around, and then we'll know if we have anything to worry about or not. Right?" He reached across the table and refilled Maria's glass with the dry white wine he had ordered.

At seven that night, Maria called Peter. "I'm calling to warn you, Peter. Serg wants to talk to you tonight."

She could sense Peter bristling at the mention of Serg Ochenko's name. "Why should I talk to that manipulative son of a bitch. What does he want from me?"

Maria paced the floor of her living room. "I don't know what he wants. He isn't telling me much, but I think he wants you to check on the visitor who came by your camp. Ask him yourself. Maybe he thinks your visitor is related to the guy we had in the office. I don't know." Maria stopped in front of the small balcony and looked past part of downtown Toronto and beyond to Lake Ontario, a few blocks away. The setting sun reflected off some of the small waves on the lake.

"Look, if you're so worried about this guy, why don't you and Serg talk to the RCMP?"

Maria sighed in frustration. "I've already done that. I know a captain in the counterintelligence division of the RCMP, and I talked with him over lunch today. I felt like a total idiot."

Peter laughed. "So what did the good captain say?"

"He wants you to check out your visitor, visit his camp, and make sure he's what he says he is." Maria shook her head. The light evening breeze pressed her thin white dress against her and ruffled her blonde hair, tinted a dark bronze by the setting sun.

Peter laughed again. "It seems like everyone wants me to do the same thing, and here I thought it was my idea to check this guy out tomorrow."

"Well, if he's got something to do with this guy who visited Serg, you'd better be prepared for just about anything, and I mean anything. Anyway, listen to what Serg has to say tonight."

She waited for almost a full minute before Peter responded. "I know he's your boss, but I sure as hell don't like him, and I don't trust him. I'll listen, but don't count on anything more than that."

"That's all I ask and all he expects." Looking at her watch, she said, "We'll call you in a little less than an hour."

"Okay."

After he hung up the telephone, Peter busied himself with putting together the gear he needed for his reconnaissance the next day. He packed his shotgun with a box of assorted shells, and after some thought he packed the large flare gun he would carry later in the summer, in case the helicopter pilot had problems locating him at the end of the day. *Christ, am I paranoid or what?* He knew that he was just being cautious, trying not to be naïve or stupid. This business of Serg not calling from the office didn't please him at all. After thinking for a moment, Peter tossed three white sheets into the canvas duffel bag that contained a small tent, a sleeping bag, and some emergency rations. He added one of the small, single-sideband radios he kept for local communications. At this point he had no idea of how long he would be gone. At eight, he settled back on his bed to wait for the call.

At twenty after eight, the telephone rang. "Nuvilik Lake, NorthGold camp."

"Hi Peter. This is Maria. Can you talk freely?"

Peter shifted the headset to his left hand and sat down. "Well, we have a camp of three people here. Tents do have pretty thin walls, you know."

"Yeah. Well, I've got Serg here. He wants to talk to you."

Peter grimaced. "Fine. Put him on."

Peter listened while Maria handed the cell phone over to Serg. He could hear muffled conversation between the two of them and the sound of traffic.

"Ah, Peter, this is Serg. We haven't talked for a long time."

"No, we haven't," Peter replied tersely.

Serg ignored Peter's reticence. "I guess Maria has filled you in on the visitor we had here at the office?"

"Yes. But she doesn't seem to know much about the details of the meeting."

Serg paused before he responded. When he did, Peter thought he sounded nervous. Peter couldn't think of any other time he'd ever thought Serg was nervous. "Well, I don't know too much about what's going on. The guy who visited me is associated with a German group that's made a joint venture proposal to us on Randal Lake. It's a deal the board won't let me turn down."

"So if the deal's so good, what's the problem?"

"Look, let's say there are some parts of the deal I don't like. One problem is that I lose control of the project. Right now I want to know if that visitor you had the other day is part of the German crew. I want you to check him out."

"He says he's part of a Canadian–Russian research team, looking at the aurora borealis. He also said they'd be moving over to Randal Lake."

"If he is, that's great, but we haven't approved any group like that to stay at Randal Lake."

Peter closed his eyes and rested his head in his hand before he responded. "I was planning to go out tomorrow anyway, follow the guy's tracks and take a look around. Reporting to you on the situation is no big deal."

"That's great." For the first time in the conversation, Peter could sense Serg begin to settle down. Then Serg laughed. Peter always worried when Serg laughed. "There's one more thing I should tell you. I talked with George Babin, the CEO over at NorthGold. I've joint ventured the NorthGold ground you're working on in Nunavik. The terms were generous. I asked if he would let you stay on to run the program, and he agreed."

Damn, thought Peter. *I'm working for the bastard again.* Before he could speak, Serg continued. "I've arranged to delay the geophysical crew until the middle of next month, but I've pushed up the arrival date for the helicopter. It will be on its way first thing tomorrow morning, and it should be up there in a couple of days if the weather cooperates. That should give us time to figure out what's going on up there at Randal Lake before you have your main work crew to worry about."

Peter resented the concept of his services being bought and sold without any of his own input, particularly when the buyer was Serg. Peter's voice had an unpleasant edge to it now. "So I report to you now, is that it?"

Peter was sure that Serg would hear the disgust in his voice, and he would have been happy to bet his entire career that Serg was smiling. "Oh, not really. You still report to George Babin. I would like you to come down to Toronto, though, so we can talk more privately."

"Look, Serg, I won't hide the fact that I'm not overjoyed at the idea of working for you. At the moment I don't want to leave the guys here in the camp alone." Peter took a deep breath. "Let's see what I find out tomorrow, and then we'll talk about my coming down to Toronto."

"That's fair enough. Let me know what you find. Either Maria or I will call the camp every evening between six and eight."

"Okay. You want a short leash. Fine. Now put Maria back on the line."

In a moment Maria said, "Yes, Peter?"

"Can Serg hear what I'm saying?"

"I don't think so."

"He still hasn't told you any more about this meeting with, what's his name, Gregori?"

"No. Not a bit."

In a soft voice, Peter continued. "Listen, you told me you talked to a guy in the counterintelligence division of the Mounties. I want you to talk to him again. He may need to send someone up here from his group. If I find anything suspicious tomorrow, I want to have some official backup."

Maria didn't answer immediately, and Peter listened to the

background noises of traffic. "Yes, there's a mechanic with the helicopter pilot. There always is."

"Really? An RCMP helicopter mechanic?"

"Yes."

Peter paused. "You still have a key to my house up on the lake?"

Softly, "Yes."

"I know it's a long drive, but I want something sent along with the helicopter, if you can get it in time. Drive up to my house tonight if you can and get the gun case out of the gun safe in the closet in my bedroom." He gave her the combination to the lock. "The case has my Weatherby rifle with the scope. There should be a box of shells beside it. Pick up the rifle and the ammunition and see if you can send them up here with the helicopter. Talk to the RCMP if you need some help to get them up here."

"I'll take care of that." Peter listened to the background noise. Maria continued, "Now you take care of yourself."

Peter stared at the wall of the tent, seeing nothing but an image of Maria. "I'll be thinking of you, Maria. Good-bye."

"Good-bye."

In his tent, Peter looked at the pile of equipment and supplies he had collected for his trip, and he frowned as he thought about the helicopter mechanic. Too many players. "Damn," he muttered to himself. There were already way too many plots to this story, and with that many plots there were sure to be more that he didn't know about. *Nobody's telling me anything, at least nothing I believe*, Peter thought. Even Maria was holding something back, and he had no idea of what or why. He slowly put the telephone away, stepped across the tent, stripped off his clothes, and dropped into bed.

After Peter said good-bye, Maria handed the telephone back to Serg. She was not happy. She didn't like being used, particularly when good friends were involved.

"You still there, Peter?" Serg asked, but the line was dead. As he shut off the telephone he asked, "What was that last all about?"

"He wanted to make sure they sent a mechanic with the helicopter, and he wants me to pick up a few things for him." Serg looked at Maria, waiting for more, and smiled. "It's not what you think," Maria responded to his look. "We haven't been together for some time now. We're just good friends."

Serg laughed. "Sometimes, but only sometimes, Maria, you're not a very good liar."

8

TOM AND ROLAND HAD HEARD ALL OF PETER'S SIDE OF THE TELEPHONE calls with Maria and Serg the previous night. The slightly old-fashioned rules of politeness in a work camp dictated that they pretend not to have heard.

Sitting back from his scrambled eggs and bacon, Peter looked across the table at Tom and glanced at Roland. "I know you both heard my telephone calls last night. You must be wondering what's going on."

Tom smiled. "Well, they did sound a little strange."

Peter took a piece of toast and piled the remains of the scrambled eggs onto it. Between bites, he began his explanation. "First, some German outfit is making a proposal to World Nickel to joint venture Randal Lake, with the idea of putting it into production."

"That sounds crazy," Tom responded.

"Yeah. The nickel grade is low and the metallurgy is tough, but I guess they have some idea of how to make it all work. Closer to home, World Nickel has joint ventured this ground from NorthGold. As of now, we work for World Nickel, not NorthGold. I guess for now I'll pretend I still report to George Babin, anyway."

"Did they give us a raise?" Roland asked with a laugh.

"Not that I noticed."

"Well, I guess there's no real difference to me, then," Roland said and started to wash the dishes.

Peter pushed his plate away. "There's one other thing. The RCMP want to be sure our visitor yesterday is actually part of a research group." Peter paused. "I'm going out today to see what I can find out."

Tom arched his eyebrows in surprise. "The RCMP want you to do that?"

"Yeah."

Tom shrugged his shoulders and got up to take the dirty plates to Roland. "Sounds pretty dumb to me. Why don't they ask a few questions themselves? Somebody must know about this research job. If they want to know what these guys are doing, why don't the cops just get in a damn plane, fly up here, and ask them?"

Peter laughed as he put on his parka. "I suppose they want to save money." Turning back at the door, he added, "Roland, make up five or six sandwiches for me, please, and dig out a couple of cans of juice and some candy bars. Tom, maybe you can give me a hand loading up one of the sleds. I want some supplies in case I get stuck out there."

Later, when Peter sat on the idling skidoo, ready to leave, he turned to Tom. "Start digging that hole in the ice for our water supply, and if you have time, start digging out the snow where we want to put up the big bunk tent."

"You sure you don't want me to go along?"

Peter looked to the east, along the length of the snow-covered lake. "No. We've got too much work to do here at the camp." In a pinch Peter didn't want anyone to worry about on this trip. He agreed with Tom. This all seemed pretty strange, but he was too curious to refuse. With a smile he said, "Don't beat yourself up too much digging that hole in the ice, and don't fall through at the end."

Tom laughed. "Don't worry about me. Just be careful yourself."

"Well, I'm prepared for almost anything. I'll call Roland on the radio if I run into any trouble." Peter smiled. "See you later."

Peter made good time on the frozen lake with his skidoo, following Jim's tracks of the previous day, but once he left the lake he traveled extremely cautiously. He was slipping back in time, slipping into his warrior mode. It was like a first hit of a narcotic after a long period of abstinence. He was addicted. He knew it, and he didn't like it at all. Because of it he was doing something that the RCMP should have been doing themselves.

Every time he came to a slight rise, he stopped and walked to the top to carefully peer over before he continued on with the skidoo. He didn't trust the man he was tracking, and Peter knew the man was well armed. The wind blew steadily, pushing wisps of snow along the face of the gray day. The light wind and snow had not yet filled in the tracks he followed, but it would soon enough. The wind blew from the east today, directly into his face. It was uncomfortable, but the wind would help hide the noise of his skidoo as he approached the Bombardier. They'd never hear him inside the cab of the Bombardier, not if they had the engine running, nor were they likely to see him if he approached from behind.

Only a little over a mile east of Nuvilik Lake, Peter came upon the tracks of the Bombardier. There were signs of a lot of activity, and the skidoo tracks stopped there as well. Apparently, they had loaded the skidoo into the Bombardier. Peter shook his head. Jim had obviously lied about how far he had to travel by skidoo. Some number of men had waited at the Bombardier, but it was hard to tell how many in the jumble of footprints. A lot of yellow spots and bits of uneaten bread littered the clean white of the snow. With a frown, he continued to the east, following the tracks of the Bombardier.

As the day wore on, Peter's progress was continually slowed by his cautious approach, and he began to grow impatient. He'd been traveling for over three hours, and he still hadn't caught up with the Bombardier. Once again he left the skidoo below the crest of a small hill. He climbed slowly and cautiously up to the top of the ridge. Crouching as he approached the top, he carefully peered over. There they were. He quickly flattened himself on the snow behind a boulder. The white Bombardier stood still, engine idling, in a broad valley down the hill and six or eight hundred yards ahead of him. It pulled a trailer, also white. Peter remembered that Jim Wurtz had mentioned the trailer, but for some reason Peter hadn't seen it when he first spotted the Bombardier from the plane.

Peter quickly trotted back to the skidoo. Reaching into the duffel, he pulled out a white sheet, his camera and telephoto lens, and his binoculars. He jammed the flare gun into the pocket of his parka, and he took out the shotgun, pumped one shell into the chamber, and leaned it against the side of the skidoo. The skidoo sat beside a small rock outcropping, and out of habit Peter looked around for a good defensive position. It had to be close to the skidoo. His weapons were not effective at long range. If they came after him, he had to lure them into close range with the skidoo as his bait. *I'm being an idiot*, he thought. *I should just go down and say hello.* Still, all his instincts told him this was a good time to be cautious.

Two small crevices in the outcrop would provide some cover. Peter noted their locations and, leaving the skidoo behind, he worked his way back on the rocks to the top of the ridge. He tried to leave no tracks. For the last few yards, he crawled, using the sheet to cover his dark-green parka. Lying in the snow at the top of the ridge, he took out his binoculars and looked at the Bombardier. Little puffs of exhaust showed that the motor was idling. Three men stood at the open back of the trailer, which was filled with boxes. Peter looked for a fourth man, but he couldn't find more than three. The three men seemed to be fully focused on what they were doing and must not have heard his skidoo over the sound of the Bombardier engine. He took several pictures with his telephoto lens. As he watched, the men opened one of the boxes and pulled out four black items that looked like assault rifles or light machine guns. Peter grunted softly. Then Peter noticed the tracks leading away from the Bombardier.

Damn, he thought. *I'm really getting out of practice.* He traced the tracks to the left, up a small hill, a continuation of the same ridge he was lying on. There, about four hundred yards away, Peter saw a black skidoo and in the rocks the low silhouette of the fourth man. He was hard to see, dressed in white like the others. He had to be a lookout for the crew down at the Bombardier. Peter shook his head. *They're better at this than I am,* he thought. *They don't want any surprises either.* As Peter watched, he realized the lookout was watching him. Slowly, the man raised his hand and spoke into what had to be a small radio. Peter turned his attention back to the Bombardier, and the tall man, he was pretty sure it was Jim, picked up a radio. Peter looked back to the lookout. If the lookout stayed there, Peter figured it would mean that he'd not been seen, or at least the lookout wasn't sure of what he'd seen. He couldn't have seen Peter's skidoo, but he must have seen Peter climbing up to the ridgeline. He must have heard Peter's approach on the skidoo. The sheet that was now covering Peter's dark clothes might make detection less certain, but his movements had to have given him away.

Peter could feel his body shifting, slipping into a completely different level of awareness. The thought flashed through his mind that it had been a long time. *God help me*, he thought. *God help me.*

Suddenly, the lookout jumped to his feet, took one last look in Peter's direction, and started to run to the black skidoo. "Oh, Christ!" Peter didn't hesitate. He slid back down off the ridge, bundled up the sheet, got up and ran down the rocks to his skidoo. He grabbed his shotgun, put the key for the skidoo in his pocket, and walked backward to the shelter of the rocks. He had left enough footprints around the skidoo. Another set that appeared to walk toward the skidoo wouldn't stand out among the rest.

"Jesus Christ," Peter muttered as he took off his camera and covered himself with the sheet. He squeezed into one of the small crevices in the rocks he had noted earlier. He still felt uncomfortably exposed from above on the rocky ridge, or from behind. But if they came directly over the ridge, where the snow completely covered the rocks, and went for his yellow skidoo, he was in an excellent position. Peter could already hear the black skidoo's engine revving at top speed, the sound increasing quickly as it approached the top of the ridge. "Please let them be overconfident," Peter whispered into the wind, "and please let them assume I'm unarmed." He was back on old familiar ground. He let his instincts and the years of training take control.

The powerful black skidoo leapt briefly into the air as it came over the top of the ridge, right where Peter had expected it. The two men riding it saw Peter's skidoo almost immediately, and their skidoo slid to a stop about ten feet from it. Peter uncovered his head enough that he could see around the edge of his rock cover and watch the men. They stood twenty-five feet away. *Almost point-blank range*, thought Peter. Both were talking loudly in Russian, and though they looked around quickly they did not see him. Just as Peter had hoped, they were overconfident of themselves and their position. Each carried a heavy assault rifle. It looked like a modern version of the Russian AK-47. One of the men was Jim Brown, though Peter assumed that the name was a false one. The other was a small man with a hard look and quick, nervous movements. *I'd better watch that guy pretty closely*, Peter thought.

Jim Brown spoke loudly, turning his head to look around as he did so. "We know you're here, and we don't like being spied on. You're too curious for your own good. First we'll take care of your transportation, and then we'll find you. You'll be another unfortunate soul who got lost in the Arctic. A fool to be out alone in this place."

I can't believe they're that arrogant, Peter thought. They should have been flushing him out, not making stupid speeches.

Jim Brown and his smaller companion turned and, laughing, fired short bursts from their rifles into Peter's yellow skidoo. They faced away from Peter, and he took advantage of their preoccupation. He stood up and moved quickly a few steps closer with his shotgun. The firing went on for only a few seconds. Peter didn't think they'd emptied their thirty-round magazines. The yellow skidoo shuddered with the impacts but amazingly did not burst into flames. When they stopped firing for a moment, Peter shouted, "Freeze!"

Jim instantly froze in place, but the little man swung around to bring his gun to bear on Peter. The ingrained instincts of his old training didn't fail him. Peter fired. The full load of buckshot caught the man squarely in the face, snapping his head back violently. At nearly point-blank range, bits of flesh and bone flew off Vladimir Kazakov's face. His hands dropped his gun and flew to his savaged face and sightless eyes. A high-pitched scream erupted from his throat as he fell over backward in the snow. Peter dropped to a prone position in the snow as he pumped a second shell into the chamber.

After Peter's first shot, Jim turned to fire, and Peter's second shot caught him squarely in the chest. At close range the force of the shot made Jim stumble backward, and he fell to the ground, his rifle firing wildly into the air. Peter pumped another shell into the shotgun while he watched in amazement as Jim scrambled to his feet and dove behind the shattered yellow skidoo. "Jesus Christ," Peter muttered.

Peter hesitated for only a moment as his mind raced through possibilities. There were two more men waiting by the Bombardier. They could be on their way already. He had to end this now. The smell of gasoline was strong from the punctured gas tank on the skidoo. Peter took a deep breath. He pulled his flare gun out of his pocket and fired it into the skidoo. For a long moment nothing happened. Then the flare went off in a burst of burning magnesium, igniting the gasoline and punctured gas tank with a dull explosion.

In the momentary lull, Jim must have loaded a fresh clip. As he staggered back from the skidoo, his face and hands badly burned and flames licking at his clothes, Jim fired wildly in Peter's direction. Peter aimed at Jim's head and fired. The buckshot hit Jim in the upper chest and neck, and he staggered backward again. The next round was a slug, and it hit Jim squarely in the face, jerking his head back and leaving the back half of his head sprayed out behind him. He crumpled in the snow, dead before he hit the ground. The little man had stopped screaming. Suddenly the only sounds Peter heard were the snapping and popping noises of the burning skidoo and the pounding of his own heart.

Peter ran over to Jim's body. He pulled one arm out of the parka and flipped him over to pull the parka off. Peter grimaced at the gaping exit wound at the back of Jim's head, but he moved quickly to finish removing the white parka. It had a few holes, an amazingly small amount of blood splattered on it, and it was singed around the edges. It would do for now. He stripped off his dark green parka, put on the white one, grabbed one assault rifle, and ran to the top of the ridge. To his relief, the two other men were still waiting by the Bombardier. Both were looking in his direction, and each held a rifle in his hands. With the hood over his head to cover his hair, Peter held the rifle in the air and waved. Once he saw that the two merely waved back and had no intention of walking to the top of the ridge, he turned and jogged back down to Jim's body and slipped off the white parka. Peter's heart was still racing, but he felt no emotions, none. He knew that would change, but right now he had to stay focused.

Peter pulled off Jim's heavy shirt. The task was not as messy as he had expected, as long as he avoided the back of Jim's head. Peter found the .44 Magnum pistol he had suspected when he first saw him at the camp, plus a Kevlar vest. He thought for a moment, and, after rolling Jim over one more time, he pulled off the vest. He slipped on the vest, shrugged on the white parka over the vest, and zipped it up. He and Jim were about the same size. Peter reconsidered, took Jim's holster with the .44 Magnum pistol, and slipped it over his shoulder, under the parka. He went through Jim's pockets. In addition to a detailed topographic map of the area, he found a Russian passport. He stuffed the passport into his pocket.

Peter walked over to the little man. The buckshot had shattered both of his eyes. He continued to bleed profusely, but he had lapsed into unconsciousness. Loud gurgling noises accompanied his labored breathing. Peter reached down for his wrist, and he felt a faint and rapid pulse. "Well, I can't do much for you," he said softly. Peter looked up and spoke softly. "Right now I've got to get on with the next act of this little morality play." Because the man was beyond feeling any pain, Peter decided to leave him to die quietly. He went through the small man's pockets, but he didn't come up with much of interest. Peter rummaged through the supplies from his sled for another flare, loaded it into the flare gun, and put it into the pocket of his borrowed parka.

Peter stepped over to the black skidoo. Reluctantly, he propped his shotgun against a rock and picked up one of the assault rifles instead. He took a fresh clip from one of the pockets of the parka, and he replaced the partially expended clip in the rifle. He took a quick look at the rifle. An AK-101. Nice. With the standard NATO 5.56-millimeter cartridge, this was a light and extremely reliable weapon. The rifle had a firing rate of about 600 rounds per minute. Peter smiled, made sure there was a round in the chamber, and snapped on the safety.

He rested the rifle across his legs, started the skidoo, and turned it to head over the hill to the Bombardier. *This will be interesting,* he thought. The two guys at the Bombardier had to have heard all the shooting, but his reassuring wave at the top of the ridge must have satisfied them. At least now he was more evenly armed, and the number of people he was dealing with had been reduced significantly.

Peter took his time approaching the Bombardier. The two remaining men were obviously curious, seeing only one person returning. As far as Peter could tell, they didn't have any weapons readily at hand. They must have put the rifles in the Bombardier. Peter couldn't see anyone else. As he came closer he picked up speed and came up to the Bombardier at a good rate. Recognition finally dawned on both the men, and one started to run toward the cab. Peter jumped off the skidoo.

"*Nyet!*" he shouted as loudly as he could. The man stopped in half-stride. Peter trained his rifle on him and moved to keep both men within his field of view. The second had already raised his hands in the air. The one who had started toward the cab slowly raised his hands and turned around.

Both men appeared young, probably eighteen to nineteen years old, and frightened—their hands trembled in the air. Peter motioned with his rifle, pointing down to the ground. The men hesitated, and Peter repeated the motion more vigorously, until both went down on their knees. He kept waving with the rifle, and they got the idea and both lay down on the snow.

One of the men knew a few words of English and kept babbling, "No shoot! No shoot!"

"No," said Peter, "I no shoot." Peter cautiously stepped back to look in the cab of the Bombardier, keeping an eye on the two. He picked up the two assault rifles in the cab, dropped the clips in a pocket of his parka, and laid the rifles on the skidoo. The two men on the snow remained perfectly still, watching him intently.

Again he backed away to look in the back of the trailer behind the Bombardier. It had two sets of bunk beds, but otherwise it was filled with wooden boxes. One that lay open, labeled "Kitchen Supplies," held more assault rifles. Another, only partly open and labeled "Pots and Pans," held several surface-to-air Stinger missiles. "Nice kitchen," Peter laughed and shook his head. The Stinger was the best the U.S. had to offer to the infantry, a hand-held surface to air missile that could bring down almost any aircraft in the world. He quickly looked back at the two men on the ground. They hadn't moved. Apparently, neither wanted to be a hero today. Among all the miscellaneous supplies in the trailer Peter saw a new roll of gray duct tape, and he took it back to the two men.

He walked behind the two, and both began to tremble. "*Nyet,*

nyet," Peter said. "I won't shoot. Lie still." The one who spoke some English muttered to the other. "You understand English?" Peter asked the one.

"A little, no much."

"Lie still and I won't shoot. You understand?"

"I understand."

"And your comrade?"

"I tell him." He spoke a few words in Russian to the other man, and he responded with a few words. "He understand."

"What is your name?"

"Pyotr Barisavich."

"And his name?"

"Is Yegor Gaidar." After a pause, Pyotr added, "Soldiers, only soldiers."

"Any more soldiers?"

"No. Just us. Just us. We just soldiers," Pyotr repeated.

"I understand, Pyotr, but now I tie you up. I won't hurt you or Yegor. Put your hands behind your back." Peter crossed Pyotr's wrists and wrapped them tightly with the duct tape. Then he wrapped his ankles. "Tell him, too," Peter said. When Peter had both men immobilized, he turned them over and helped them sit up. He stepped back and took his time to scan the surrounding hills with his binoculars. He saw no one.

Peter decided to search the Bombardier trailer in detail. He opened a few more boxes. In one labeled "Melons and Fruit" he found a supply of hand grenades. "Cute," he muttered. In other boxes he found more Stinger missiles and some Dragon antitank missiles. The Dragons were another great U.S. product, a very effective, hand-held tank destroyer. In the final boxes he opened he found a selection of light- and heavy-caliber machine guns. The trailer also carried two drums of diesel fuel for the Bombardier and one of gasoline for the skidoo.

Behind the cab and in the back of the Bombardier, he found boxes of canned food, frozen meat, bottles of vodka, a bunch of supplies and equipment, and a briefcase filled with large-denomination Canadian and U.S. currency, mostly hundred-dollar bills. "Christ! That must be a million dollars or more," Peter muttered. Peter couldn't imagine why anyone would need a million dollars in the middle of the barren lands of northern Nunavik. A well-padded box contained what looked like a satellite telephone, but it was not a model that Peter had ever seen before. What Peter found most interesting was the box of detailed maps and diagrams, with English and Russian place-names and locations of various exploration and mining camps, including his on Nuvilik Lake. The map box also contained plans of the Randal Lake mine site, what looked like a list of equipment at Randal Lake, and detailed diagrams of the shaft and underground workings.

"I guess I've seen enough for now," Peter said as he shut off the Bombardier engine. These guys were set for a small war. He walked to the two men. "I'm going for supplies. I'll be back soon. You understand?"

"I understand," Pyotr responded. "I need piss. Yegor too."

Peter looked at the two men, shook his head, and laughed. This would be quite a production with the two men unable to help themselves. He helped each one to his feet, made sure they didn't wet their pants, and after a good bit of laughter sat them down again.

Once they were both sitting in the snow again, Peter said, "I'll go get some supplies, and I'll be back in a few minutes." Pyotr nodded. They looked like they'd keep for a while. Peter just hoped they didn't have any friends around. Neither of them seemed to want to be a hero, but they had enough firepower in the trailer to blow away half an army.

Peter turned the black skidoo and ran it back up the hill, balancing all three rifles on his legs. As he reached the top, he took out the revolver. He didn't need to bother. The little man had quietly died. The blood from the two men left red stains in the snow. Peter hitched the singed but otherwise undamaged sled to the black skidoo. He put two of the rifles and his shotgun into the duffel, and he kept one rifle on his thighs as he ran the skidoo to the top of the ridge, where the two men back at the Bombardier could see him. Extending the antenna for his radio, he called the camp.

After a pause, "Peter, this is Roland. What's up? Over."

"I'm going to have a couple of guests for you tonight, and I want you to call a number in Toronto for me." Peter gave him Maria's number at World Nickel. "Tell Maria Davidoff, and only her, no one else, that I want to talk with her and her captain friend tonight at seven. They should call from a secure phone. Make sure they know this is an emergency. You got that? Over."

"Yeah. I've got all that. Are you all right? Over."

"I'm fine. Make sure Maria knows I'm serious. I absolutely have to talk with the two of them tonight. Over."

"I'll make sure. Over."

"Okay. I'll be back by about five. Over."

"I'll have supper ready."

Peter pushed the antenna down and looked down the hill at the two men. How was he going to get them to the camp? The easy way would be with the Bombardier, but he wasn't sure he wanted to move it right now.

Peter ran the black skidoo down the hill to the two men patiently sitting and waiting for him in the snow. After taking more photos, he removed the sleeping bag from the duffel and unrolled it on the boards of the sled. He tied the duffel to the back of the sled and lifted Pyotr onto the sled, in a sitting position near the front, facing forward. He tied several lengths of rope around Pyotr's thighs and through the metal hooks on the side of the sled. Then he untaped Pyotr's hands and tied each hand separately to an outside plank on the sled. He dragged Yegor over, sat him back to back with Pyotr, and secured him the same way. Then he bound the two men together around the waist and chest. He went back to the Bombardier and took out two lengths of lightweight chain he'd seen earlier.

Peter looked at the two men. They looked reasonably comfortable. "That should keep you for a while," Peter said and smiled at them. "Hold on tight," Peter called, as he started the skidoo. Moving slowly in deference to his two guests, he pulled up the side of the ridge.

When he got to the two dead men and his burned-out skidoo, Peter stopped to top off the skidoo with gasoline from the ten-gallon drum he had brought along. The two men stared at the bloody scene. "I'm sorry," Peter said, looking at Pyotr. "I didn't have much choice."

Pyotr said softly, "Is okay. Both fucking bastards."

Peter didn't expect that response, but he nodded his head. "I guess I can agree with you on that." Peter shucked off the white parka, removed the clips and flare gun from the pockets, and shoved the parka down between the two men. After he got into his own parka and collected the flare gun and extra clips, he got on the skidoo and took one last look at the mess he was leaving behind. *You've done it this time*, he thought. *Try to explain this.* He shook his head and headed the skidoo westward, toward Nuvilik Lake.

9

IN SAINT PETERSBURG, ZAKHAR ROSTOV ASKED HIS SECRETARY, "HAVE you heard from the team in Nunavik?" Rostov sat behind a large dark-walnut desk with a glass top. It had once belonged to a minor official of the Communist Party who, when he retired, had sold it to Rostov to get enough money to buy meat for himself and his wife.

His secretary answered, "We haven't had a call from him for over a day. It's not like Leonid Andropov. Maybe his satellite telephone isn't working properly."

Rostov grunted. "Yes, I'm sure there are many reasons why Andropov might not make contact with us, but we need his report." Rostov turned sharply toward the secretary, who now stood near the door. "Get Gregori on the phone in Toronto. Let's see what he has to say."

A few minutes later, Rostov waited as the telephone rang in Gregori's office.

"Northern Mining Consultants."

"Gregori Borodin, please."

"May I tell him who is calling?"

"Just tell him Saint Petersburg is calling."

After a few seconds of silence, "Gregori Borodin here. How can I help you?"

"One, three, seven," Rostov responded quickly.

Rostov's secretary switched on the scrambler. She knew it would take longer for Gregori to do the same. He had to look up the scrambler settings that matched the code Rostov had just given.

"How can I help you?" Gregori asked again. The voice had a somewhat disemboweled sound to it, but it was quite understandable.

"This is Rostov. We've not had any contact with our man in Nunavik. It's long overdue. Are you absolutely sure about Ochenko?"

"Serg Ochenko's as scared as a flushed rabbit," Gregori responded. Even with the scrambler, Rostov could detect the tone of disgust in Gregori's voice. Gregori continued, "He's soft and easily frightened, as he always was. He'll do what we ask."

"Don't be so damn sure." Rostov swung his chair around to look out the window. "I have a feeling something is wrong. It's too late to change the plan now, but if Serg Ochenko has turned against us, we must neutralize him." Rostov's voice had shifted to a flat, metallic tone with his last statement. Killing had always come easily to Zakhar Rostov.

"Yes, but I don't think he's done anything." Gregori sounded annoyed by the interference. "If you wish, I'll make absolutely sure."

"Do that," said Rostov, and he hung up the phone, smiling. Gregori never failed him. Gregori could frighten almost anybody, even Rostov, and he had a particularly sadistic streak when it came to dealing with women. Rostov assumed that Gregori would use Serg's mistress to sort it all out. Tania, that was her name.

In the Kremlin, in the President's office, Ivan Dinisovich and the President bent over the table to look at satellite images again. Ivan flipped through the images on the computer. "This group of images dates from the first day of surveillance. These are from the second and third. You can see that three separate stages of the missile were loaded onto the railroad cars. As I assumed, they all headed for Germany to be held for shipment to Denmark for recycling."

The President looked up from the computer screen and straightened his back with a grimace. Ivan thought he rather looked his age these days. Some of his enemies probably thought he did not feel his age nearly enough. The President asked, "What do you know about the company that handles the salvage operations?"

Ivan shrugged. "The company is a glorified junk dealer and metal fabricator." He waved his bony fingers over another image. "As you can see here, the company has a large, open yard in Hamburg for the storage of the components it purchases, as well as storage of fabricated metal items, large culverts, pipes, and metal tanks. They can load directly onto ships in the Elbe River with little additional handling."

"And the oil shipment? And the extra warhead? Where do you think they ended up?"

"The train of oil tank cars arrived in Germany at a small refinery, adjacent to the salvage company." He pointed at the refinery on the image. "We inspected the train before it left Russian territory, but the inspectors reported that all the cars at that point were normal tank cars. With all the oil tank cars that are shipped around Russia every day, it's simply impossible to find a single, special car if someone wants to hide it. This refinery receives many oil shipments from Russia. Without a pipeline, we ship the oil the old-fashioned way, by train."

Ivan was confident that the second, replacement warhead was at the depot in the Urals where they dismantled all the retired warheads. Without any special orders, it would be months, perhaps as long as a year, before the workers would discover what he assumed was a fake warhead. He continued blandly, "The location of the refinery is convenient, don't you think, Mr. President?"

"Yes. Too convenient."

Ivan took his time to continue. "This is the most recent image of the supply yard in Hamburg. They've placed the parts for the missile with many of the culvert-like pipes. In the last three weeks, they've placed the culverts on truck trailers and covered most of them with tarps. They also move the trailers around, on a daily basis." He waved his hand at the image with a dismissive gesture. "The sections of the missiles marked for recycling are decommissioned in Russia and taken here for a short time before shipment to Denmark." Ivan laughed. "It's an old parlor trick, a little sleight of hand, and lots of movement. We can never be quite sure which are pieces of missile and which are only large culverts and pipes."

"You're telling me we can do nothing?"

It had always been dangerous in the Kremlin to leave a statement like that unchallenged, and Ivan's gray hair attested to his political acuity in the Kremlin. "I don't want to involve the German government, not yet. I've asked one of my contacts in Hamburg to maintain surveillance on the yard. It's possible that because the missile parts are heavier, he'll be able to tell the difference by how low the trucks ride when loaded." He quickly added, "I know it sounds very crude, but it should work. I haven't had a report from him yet, but I expect one later today. Until then, we're maintaining a close watch on shipping."

"You'd better do more than watch."

Ivan ignored the interruption. "As you know, each Topol-M breaks down into three pieces, plus the warhead and guidance system. If the three main pieces are taken by ship, they'll probably be transported on deck. We should be able to see any major shipments out of this yard in Germany with our satellite coverage."

"But they could make the shipment in pieces, at several different times, couldn't they?"

"Yes, they could. If they do, there's not much we can do, given that we have only remote-sensing images. I'm assuming the people behind this are in a hurry. Their haste should let us see their hand."

"I sure as hell hope you're right." The President looked at Ivan.

"Do what you must. There is no time for finesse or subtlety here. We must stop this madness and regain control of the warhead and missile."

"Mr. President, I promise you, we will be in control."

10

PETER RODE INTO THE CAMP ON THE BLACK SKIDOO, WITH THE TWO men securely tied to the sled behind him. "Christ almighty! What have you been doing?" Tom asked when Peter pulled up to the tents. Even Roland was curious.

"Give me a minute. Right now, I need a hand to tie these two guys to a bed or something."

Peter moved to Pyotr. "This guy's name is Pyotr, and he understands a little English. The other one's Yegor, but I guess he speaks only Russian." Tom and Peter undid the ropes around Pyotr and Yegor and those that held Pyotr to the sled. Peter took off Pyotr's parka, retaped his hands, and only then untaped his legs. Peter pulled out the pistol and handed it to Tom. "Take him into the spare sleep tent, and hang onto him for a minute," Peter said to Tom. "Shoot him if he gives you any trouble." Tom raised his eyebrows and stared at Peter as he took the pistol.

Pyotr started stammering, "No, no, no trouble. No trouble."

"Okay, Pyotr. No trouble, no shoot. Understand?"

"Yes, yes. I understand. No trouble," Pyotr responded.

"I think he's okay," Peter said to Tom. "Take him into the tent."

Peter picked up the two lengths of the lightweight chain he had found in the Bombardier and retrieved four padlocks from the office tent.

In the tent, Peter said, "Okay, Pyotr. I have to secure you somehow." He wrapped one end of a chain around Pyotr's neck and locked it, and then he locked the other end to the metal bedframe. Only then did he untape Pyotr's wrists.

Tom shook his head at the arrangement. "You'll have to tell me what this is all about," he said. He handed the pistol back to Peter, who dropped it into the holster.

"In a bit," Peter replied. Looking at Pyotr, he said, "Okay, Pyotr. Now we can make you a little more comfortable. I'm sorry, but this is the best we can do." Once he and Tom had lit the stove, they rolled out two sleeping bags, one for Pyotr and one, on the second of four beds, for Yegor. Then they brought Yegor in and secured him in the same way on the second bed.

Speaking to Pyotr, Peter said, "We won't hurt you, but we have to be careful. You understand?"

"I understand. Is okay."

"We'll get some food ready for both of you soon."

Pyotr nodded. "Thank you." He started talking with Yegor in Russian as Peter and Tom left the tent.

Peter grabbed a coffee in the cook tent and sat down at the table. Smiling, he said, "I've had a busy day." Tom and Roland both laughed.

"This should be a good story," Roland commented.

Peter was silent for a moment. He wasn't sure how much he should say. Tom and Roland both needed to make some decisions. If they thought about it logically, the most important decision was whether to stay or leave on the next available plane.

Peter took his time telling the story of his day. "They've got enough weapons to start a pretty good war," he commented. "If those guys are actually scientists, they have a strange attraction to assault rifles and antiaircraft and antitank missiles, and they're sure sensitive about any visitors." Peter shrugged and commented, "I was lucky. The two guys were really overconfident. Obviously, they thought I was completely unprepared and unarmed." He shook his head.

"Jesus H. Christ," Tom said. "This is fucking unbelievable. You just killed two guys, and we've got two more guys chained to their beds? If I didn't know you better I'd be afraid to be in the same camp with you. Are you sure you know what you're doing?"

Roland scratched his head. "This is sure getting more exciting than last year," he said with a nervous laugh.

"It's an ugly goddamned mess, and, no, I don't know what I'm doing. That's why I've got to talk with the RCMP tonight at seven. Hopefully, by the end of the call I'll know whether they'll arrest me or reward me," Peter concluded with a bitter laugh. He looked at his watch. "It's six now. Can we have supper ready, Roland, in time for me to make a phone call by seven?"

"Yeah. Supper's about ready now." Roland got up from the table. "Will those two be eating with us?"

"No, at least not yet." Looking at Tom, Peter said, "You can take supper to them, but be careful. I guess we'll have to escort them to the outhouse, too. They're a couple of kids, but the other two weren't exactly putting out the welcome mat for me." Looking over at Roland, he added, "Actually, I think both of you should take the food to them together, one of you with my shotgun." Peter was quiet for a moment, "I'll make my call down by the lake. I don't want those two listening to my calls tonight." *Or you guys either*, he thought.

At a little before seven, after a quick meal, Peter sat by the side of the frozen lake on a small black rock with the telephone beside him. Right on time, the telephone rang.

"Peter, this is Maria. I'm with Captain Durban in the RCMP offices in Toronto."

"Thanks, Maria."

"Peter, this is Richard Durban. I'm head of the RCMP counterintelligence division. You can call me Dick. We're talking from a phone in my office. Have you had a chance to get a good look at the group that's running around in the Bombardier up there?"

"Yeah." Peter took a deep breath. "I've had a pretty good look at them, and I've had a good look at what's in the Bombardier."

"Great. So what did you find out?"

"Well, I don't think you're going to like this. We've got a hell of a mess up here. I've got two Russians in the camp, chained to a couple of beds, and we've got two dead bodies about ten miles from here."

Dick interrupted, "What happened?"

"We, ah, had an argument when they didn't like me looking at their Bombardier with my binoculars. The Bombardier is towing a trailer. It's loaded with enough assault rifles, machine guns, Stinger missiles, antitank missiles, hand grenades, and assorted ammunition to start a small war. Do you have any idea of what's going on up here?"

Silence. Surely this news was not what Dick Durban had expected. In the moment of silence on the telephone, Peter could hear the small squeak of Dick's chair as he leaned back to think about what Peter had just told him. "Perhaps, Peter," Dick said finally, "you need to give me a more complete review of what happened today. Take your time."

Peter proceeded to describe the events of the day in as much detail as he could remember. Dick asked a few specific questions about the contents of the Bombardier and the trailer. When Peter finished, Dick asked simply, "How fresh is your combat training, Peter?"

"I hope you're joking."

"I assure you, I'm not."

"I guess I can hold my own up here, but the tracks of the skidoos lead right to our camp. If there's any backup for these guys, I'll bet it's professional. We can assume they're bloody well-armed. We're easy targets." The phone was silent. Peter continued, "Can you please tell me what's going on up here? I don't like people trying to kill me, and I don't like being in a shootout without knowing anything about what's going on or why it's happening in the first place."

Peter heard Dick's chair squeak again. "I wish I knew, but I don't, and I can promise you that the Canadian government, our Prime Minister in particular, won't want to make any of this public."

"Do you think this Bombardier has anything to do with Randal Lake?"

"Well, they're supposed to be a scientific research group, exactly as that guy told you. The Canadian government did sign an agreement to study the northern lights with a bunch of Russians."

"I never heard of scientists feeling like they needed enough weapons to hold off a small army, have you?"

"Nope. Can't say that I have," Dick responded. "Maybe a rifle or two, but not a bunch of missiles and hand grenades. I don't know what they're doing with all that stuff, but at the moment we don't have any clear connection between them and Randal Lake. The deal the Germans made on Randal Lake appears to be totally square and legal. All we can tell about it is that they think they know how to set up Randal Lake to make money, and they want to develop it as soon as possible." Dick paused. "The Germans plan to send a couple of shiploads of equipment to unload at the west end of the fjord, west of Kangiqsujuaq. They've got a pile of mining equipment, supplies, and a couple of big, Russian helicopters. The first ship should be arriving in three or four days. We know the cargo's legitimate because we examined it before it left Germany."

Dick Durban kept silent for a few seconds, and Peter fidgeted as he waited for him to continue. He shifted his position and realized with regret that he should have found a more comfortable place to sit. Finally, Dick continued. "With what went down at the Bombardier … I want to keep this as quiet as possible for the moment. If we send up a big squad of Mounties and Quebec Provincial Police, we can't keep this under wraps." He paused again. "We need to figure out what's going on, and I want the investigation to be as low key as we can manage."

"Look, I've killed two men, and we have two guys sitting here in camp chained to their beds. We're a little exposed at the moment."

"I understand that, Peter, but you'll have to trust me on this. I'll have a small crew come up to your camp. We'll clean up the mess. You won't have any trouble over this, I promise. Go over to the Bombardier tomorrow and remove all the weapons. Store them under cover in one of the tents. After my guys clean up, take the Bombardier to the Asbestos Hill mine with all the supplies intact except for the weapons. When the next group shows up, we'll see if they claim the Bombardier and what they say about the missing equipment. I don't think we'll hear a word."

Peter cut in. "That's fine for a start. I'm not sure, though, that my guys should be here at all, or me either, for that matter."

"Look, I just want to keep all this quiet, at least for a bit, until we're sure we understand what's going on over at Randal Lake. I know the Prime Minister will want no international publicity of anything like this. Right now it seems like we've rounded up some nasty guys and a bunch of their toys, and let's leave it at that."

Peter was frustrated by the conversation. This was far too easy. He'd have to see if Maria could help make sense out of this. Dick continued, "I understand you have a crew of only two guys up there for now, is that correct?"

"Yeah. There's Tom Grogan, who helps run the camp and does a lot of field work, and the cook."

"Good. Find out if they want to stay on. If they want to leave, I'll send up a couple more men, one being a cook. Maria told you that the helicopter mechanic is with the RCMP?"

"Yes. I hope he's a decent helicopter mechanic and not just another cop who knows how to use a pipe wrench." The wind was not strong, but as it flowed over and around the barren rocks it moaned softly, providing a low, monotonous background serenade.

Dick laughed. "I know this guy really well, Peter. He's trained as a helicopter mechanic. He's young, but he's fluent in Russian and German and well trained in the military. He knows how to use all that stuff in the Bombardier, and you may need a little help. Who knows?" Dick paused for a moment. "We need your local expertise, though. From what I understand from your past training and your work today, I suspect you can more than carry your weight."

Peter turned his back to the wind and pulled his parka tighter. "Assuming I decide to stay on, and I'm probably too curious and too stupid to leave, you sure as hell don't need to send any more weapons. What's in the Bombardier is enough to fight off a pretty well-equipped army."

Dick laughed again. "Good. Maria tells me that Serg delayed the arrival of the field crews for a while. Right?"

"That's what he told me. It'd be nice if I don't have to do a lot of geological work until we get this mess cleaned up and a few questions answered." Peter wasn't happy. "Make sure any planes you send up here fly in low and from the west. I don't know if there's anyone else out there by Randal Lake or Esker Lake, but I'd prefer that you don't attract any more attention to us at the moment."

"Understood. Everyone who comes up from the RCMP will be fully briefed. You don't need to hide anything from them, but let's not talk about Randal Lake at all, at least not for the moment. These guys won't be in the pretty red uniforms, but they'll all have Royal Canadian Mounted Police identification, and they'll respond to the question, 'How was the weather on the trip up?' with 'The weather was good, for June in Nunavik'. I'll also send up a scrambler for the telephone. The helicopter mechanic will install it, and I want you to use it from now on when you call me. Here's my number." Peter recorded the number on a small notepad.

"I'll talk with Tom and Roland and let you know what they want to do. I'll have to tell them almost everything that's happened." Peter wasn't about to tell Durban that he'd already done that.

"No problem, as long as they stay. If they leave, we may need to send them on a little paid vacation for a few weeks."

Peter shook his head. "I'll call you tomorrow. Is there a special time when I should call?"

"Call the number I just gave you at any time, any day, and you'll get through to me. Wait until you have the encryption device installed if you can, but regardless I'll want a report tomorrow. Anyway, when the RCMP crew's finished, I want you to fly out with the DC-3. I'll have a plane waiting for you in Kuujjuaq. I want you up to speed on what we know, and I don't want to do that over the telephone."

"Christ. Is that really necessary? We've got a hell of a lot to do up here."

"I'll have you back in camp in two days, weather permitting. Let me know if you have any problems."

"You can bet on that."

Durban laughed again. "I'm sure. We'll talk tomorrow, then?"

"Right."

"Jesus Christ," Peter muttered as he packed up the telephone. This little job sure was getting a lot more complicated than a normal geological consulting contract. This was like a war zone, except in this war zone it seemed that dead bodies would just disappear. Added to that, Captain Richard Durban sure wasn't telling him all he knew, and neither was Serg. He wasn't even sure Maria was completely leveling with him. Peter shook his head and headed back to his tent. He couldn't imagine how the RCMP could make the mess he'd made today disappear without a trace.

Later, as the northern lights blazed and crackled in full glory in the night sky, Peter lay back in his bed. He thought about his day. He felt the same old feelings that he always felt after action. He understood the depression, and he was used to it. He never felt fear during the action, so why did he always feel this fear afterward? He closed his eyes and tried to calm his mind. After twenty minutes he fell into a troubled sleep.

11

PETER AND TOM MADE FOUR TRIPS TO THE BOMBARDIER THE NEXT day. Early in the day, when the snow was hard, the trips were quick. On the first trip, Peter stopped at the top of the ridge, beyond the now stiff and frozen bodies of the two men by the burned-out skidoo. With a loaded rifle beside him, he took a long look at the Bombardier and trailer. With his binoculars he thoroughly searched the land for any signs of activity.

Tom stared at the destruction Peter had left behind. "Jesus Christ, Peter. You weren't kidding about what went down yesterday."

Peter lowered his binoculars, but he didn't respond to Tom's remark. "We might as well get on with our work," he said quietly. "It looks safe enough. I don't see any other bastards out there waiting for us."

Tom laughed. "I sure hope you're right. I'm not getting paid enough for this kind of crap."

"Well, let's get going. We've got a lot to do." Peter started his skidoo and headed down the hill with Tom close behind him.

They loaded Peter's sled first, and he went ahead back to the camp, leaving Tom to load up and follow. When Peter got to the camp he carried most of the load into Tom's bunk tent, but before he finished he drove up to the back of the hill behind the camp where he'd stored the dynamite. There, near the dynamite but in a separate and larger break in the rocks, he carefully wrapped five assault rifles and about 1000 rounds of ammunition in the large plastic sample bags normally used for rock samples. He wrapped four Stinger missiles, a few hand grenades, and four Dragon antitank missiles in a spare orange tarp. He used a canvas tarp to cover it all and weighted it with rocks. Finally, he concealed it with dirt and dry grass.

In the afternoon, when they loaded up for the last time at the Bombardier, Tom commented, "It'll be slow going this trip with the soft snow."

Peter stretched his back. "Well, I'd like to take it slow anyway. I've about had it for today."

Heading west with the last loads, even the lightly loaded sleds sank into the soft, afternoon snow, and the skidoos labored with the effort of pulling them. At the east end of Nuvilik Lake, Peter stopped and Tom pulled up beside him. Peter pointed at the camp in the distance, where an MD 500 helicopter sat at the small helipad. "Looks like we have some visitors, Tom, and some slightly faster transportation."

"Yep. Looks like it. Let's go and say hello to our new team members." With that, they both started down the small hill to the lake and headed toward the camp. Peter hardly thought of these additions as part of the team. "More like my keepers," he grumbled to himself. Peter rode up to the camp, shut down the skidoo, and walked over to the cook tent, where the new arrivals waited. As he entered the tent, Peter stuck out his hand to the one closest to the door and introduced himself to the helicopter mechanic. Charlie Sturm was stocky and muscular, with a hard though youthful face that held a look of worldly confidence. With his close-cropped hair and broad smile, he projected the image of a man to be trusted, a man a person could rely on in a difficult situation.

"This is Arnie Ward, the pilot," Charlie said, turning to the man sitting beside him. Arnie, short, thin, and wiry, moved with the slight swagger so common to helicopter pilots. Peter said hello and shook his hand.

Charlie pointed at a sheet of paper on the table. "You've made quite a collection of interesting munitions here in the camp."

"Well, these two loads have the last of it: two boxes of hand grenades, six more stinger missiles, twelve more assault rifles, and a few thousand rounds of ammunition. I'm pretty sure the rifles are AK-101s, and brand new. There are also a few light and two heavy machine guns, though I'm not particularly familiar with them. The missiles are all U.S., nice, new Stingers and the updated version of the old Dragon antitank missile." He paused for a moment, looking at Charlie as he poured himself a cup of coffee. "There's enough firepower here to neutralize a pretty serious attack, if you have enough trained soldiers to handle it."

As Peter sat down, he could see that Charlie was looking at him rather closely. *Perhaps I just said too much*, Peter thought.

Charlie responded, "You're right about the AK-101s. They're the best the Russians have to offer these days, and the missiles are all high quality, American made, export grade, you might say."

Peter thought about the case of dynamite, the rifles and missiles hidden nearby, and the briefcase full of cash he had under his bed. They were not on the list in front of Charlie, and he made no move to add them. Peter and Charlie continued to look at each other for a while, each silently appraising the other. Finally Peter said, over his cup of coffee, "Well, Charlie, perhaps we should take a walk and have a little chat? Have you met our special guests yet?"

"No, I haven't talked with them yet. I wanted to talk to you first." He turned to Arnie as he got up, "We'll be back in a few minutes."

"No problem, Charlie," Arnie responded with a small smile. "Take your time."

Peter and Charlie walked down along the edge of the lake, sinking a few inches into the soft snow with each step. A light breeze blew bits of snow along the ground, but in the relative warmth of the afternoon sun it had lost much of its powdery texture. "So, Charlie, how was the weather on the trip up?"

Charlie glanced at Peter before answering, "The weather was good, for June in Nunavik." They came to the edge of the frozen lake. It wouldn't be long before the ice along the edges would begin to melt. They sat down next to each other on a broad, dark rock. Charlie turned to look at Peter. "Maybe you should start by telling me what happened at the Bombardier."

"If Dick Durban filled you in, there's not much I can add that I haven't already told him."

"Yeah, but go ahead anyway. I'd like to hear it firsthand."

Peter sighed. He didn't want to talk about it. He always found that the rush of the moment of combat quickly faded, and the more he told the story, the more it would replay in his mind and in his dreams at night. He didn't enjoy those dreams. But as requested by Charlie, he ran through the events of the meeting at the Bombardier, leaving out only a few details. When he was done, he turned to Charlie and asked, "What about Arnie? He'll hear about all of this, at least anything major, if not from you or me, from Tom and Roland for sure. He's probably heard everything already."

"Don't worry about Arnie. He knows how to keep his mouth shut." Charlie stopped speaking for a moment, and Peter and Charlie looked directly at each other. Charlie had a penetrating gaze, and after a moment he reached over and put his hand on Peter's thigh. "I know this has been a little rough for you, Peter." Peter didn't move and didn't say anything. Charlie patted Peter's thigh lightly, and with a small smile he pulled his hand away. Still staring intently at Peter, he took a piece of paper out of his pocket and handed it to Peter.

"Let me tell you what we plan to do," Charlie said quietly. "First, you need to call the number on that piece of paper and report that you found two dead men near a Bombardier. You think someone shot both men. The number's for the RCMP in Ottawa. We already have a team in Kuujjuaq. They're up there taking care of a rather minor, local problem with the Quebec Provincial Police. They'll be up here within a few hours after you call, if there's enough daylight." Charlie turned around and looked back at the camp. "I guess now I need to talk with your two guests to figure out how to handle them. What do you make of them?"

Peter shrugged. "Oh hell, they're no more than a couple of young kids who got caught up in something way bigger than either of them. The one, Pyotr, speaks a little English. When we stopped by the two bodies, I apologized for killing them." Peter laughed softly. "All he said was, 'Is okay. Both fucking bastards.' I don't think either Pyotr or Yegor got along particularly well with the two older guys."

"How'd they behave otherwise?"

"Once they realized I didn't plan on shooting them, they cooperated well enough. All I need to remember next time is to tie their hands in front of them so they can piss without help." Peter shook his head again.

They both looked back up the little hill to the camp. The orange tarps on the tents were the only bright bit of color in the black-and-white landscape. "You found a passport on the guy who called himself Jim Brown? Can you show me that?"

"Sure, it's in the office tent."

They headed up the hill in the snow to the camp and went into the office tent. Like most of the others in the camp, it measured twelve by fourteen feet, with a plywood floor and a wooden frame. Plywood on the sides gave six-foot sidewalls, and the canvas of the tent was stretched over the frame. The stove was running on low, and the space inside the tent was comfortably warm as they entered.

For the first time, Peter saw his gun case leaning against the side of the tent, with a small box that presumably held the ammunition. He felt better already. The rifle was one of his prized possessions, a bolt-action .460 Weatherby Magnum rifle, carefully maintained and with a fine scope. No longer the most powerful rifle in the world, it was still powerful enough. Frankly, Peter felt more comfortable with the rifle at long range than with any other weapon, including all those he and Tom had gathered from the Bombardier.

"What's in the gun case?" Charlie asked.

"It's my Weatherby."

"Well, I am impressed," Charlie responded with a smile.

There were two beds in the back of the tent, but Peter slept in the office tent alone. His sleeping bag was rolled out on one of the beds, diagonally across from the small worktable. Charlie, familiar with the etiquette of field camps, sat on the empty bed.

Peter waved his hand at the tent. "Anyway, welcome to my humble home, Charlie." Peter stepped over to the table and took the passport from a pile of papers, along with a small memory card, and sat next to Charlie. "Here's the passport I found on the supposed Jim Brown. I also took a bunch of photos of the Bombardier, the two bodies, and the trailer. You might want to look at them sometime."

Charlie went through the passport carefully, taking his time. He looked at Peter when he was finished. "His real name is Leonid Andropov. Why any scientific expedition would employ him is completely beyond me. I suppose he would find it difficult to find work in Russia these days."

Charlie looked back at the papers in his hands. "He is—well he was—a real bastard, one of the KGB's best black operators in the old days." Charlie focused on the far wall of the tent and sat quietly for several minutes. Finally he spoke again. "He was probably responsible for the death of at least twenty-five of the west's best agents, in Berlin mostly, maybe more than that. He normally tortured his victims before he watched them die slowly, unless they agreed to turn and be doubled and spy for the Russians. Even then, he'd let them live only if he trusted them completely."

Charlie focused back on Peter. "For one of his milder tricks, Leonid suspended his victims above a sharpened steel rod. They survived as long as they could hold onto another rod above their heads. When they could hold on no longer, they impaled themselves on the steel and slowly bled to death, screaming the whole time." After another short silence, "A few Canadians, French, Brits, and West Germans, along with quite a few Americans, ended up in Leonid's trophy case."

Peter watched Charlie. There had to be more to this story than Charlie was telling him.

Charlie continued to look directly at Peter, and his hand found Peter's thigh again. "Lovely fellow, this Leonid. If you killed him, you did the world a great service, Peter." Charlie took a deep breath. "You didn't get any ID off the other guy?"

Peter shook his head. "No. There might be something in the Bombardier, but I didn't look particularly thoroughly. He was a small guy, and he looked nasty and nervous. I thought he was the one I had to watch. He did turn first to try to shoot me, but I think it was only because he didn't understand English."

Charlie shook his head before responding. "If he's who I think he is, or was, he's worse than Andropov. He sounds like Andropov's right-hand man, a guy named Vladimir Kazakov. They always worked together. Vladimir liked to kill people just for fun."

Both Peter and Charlie sat in silence for several minutes. Charlie finally moved his hand and spoke again. "Let's go meet with the two you're holding. We should put off our call to the RCMP until I've talked with them." Once outside, Peter led Charlie to the tent where Pyotr and Yegor were captive. Walking in, Charlie looked at the two men, who stared at him silently. "I see what you mean, Peter. These guys don't belong in the same world as Leonid Andropov." Turning to Peter, "I'd like to talk with them alone for a while."

"If it's no difference to you, Charlie, I think I ought to stay, at least for a while. They seem to trust me a little. It's silly, but I feel somewhat responsible for them. If you're talking in Russian, I won't understand anything anyway, but if I'm here they might feel more secure and open up for you."

Charlie frowned. "I guess it's no problem for me. Let me frisk them, and then you can take the chains off while we talk."

"No problem." After Charlie asked them to stand up and frisked them, Peter unlocked the chains around their necks. Both men smiled with the release.

Peter spoke briefly to Pyotr. "This man's name is Charlie Sturm. He wants to ask you and Yegor some questions. I'll stay here for a while." Peter stepped over to the fourth bed in the tent and sat down. Charlie looked mildly annoyed, but Peter felt a little sorry for the two Russians, and he wasn't sure he trusted Charlie completely, or the counterintelligence arm of the RCMP for that matter. Peter wanted to watch this interaction. This was a time to watch and listen, even if he didn't understand the language.

The two Russians sat beside each other on the same bed, and Charlie sat down across the tent from them. Charlie began to talk softly in Russian. At first the two Russians said nothing, except for an occasional yes or no. Slowly, though, they started to talk a bit more. Since Peter could not understand more than a few words from time to time, the session soon became an exercise in boredom. Peter's mind started to drift off a bit, and he thought about Maria. He would see her again soon. Finally, after about thirty minutes, Pyotr startled him by pointing at Charlie and asking, "Is he spy?"

Peter laughed. "Are you a spy, Charlie?"

Charlie showed a small smile. "I suppose it depends on how you define spy. The simplest answer is yes."

"Pyotr, he works for the Royal Canadian Mounted Police, what we call the RCMP, or the Mounties. His job is to protect Canada from spies from other countries. Do you understand?"

"Yes. I think so." Pyotr turned back to Charlie and began to talk rapidly to him in Russian again. There was a lively exchange among the three of them, which lasted some time. After a while, Peter broke in and asked Pyotr if it was okay for him to leave.

"Yes, is okay," Pyotr said with a smile, and Peter left them to continue their conversation alone. There was nothing more to be gained by watching.

By the time Charlie came into the cook tent, Peter and the others had finished their supper. As Peter drank his second cup of coffee, he pointed to the list of weapons he and Tom had dragged from the Bombardier to the camp. "I guess we could do some real damage with this lot if we wanted to."

Charlie sat down, and Roland immediately slapped a plate of steak and mashed potatoes in front of him. Charlie helped himself to what salad remained on the table. That little luxury, the salad, was courtesy of the arrival of the helicopter. "It's interesting, though," Charlie commented as he ate. "Most of these weapons are best suited for defense. It's an interesting mix of Russian and American equipment, too. Like I said earlier, it's all really high quality. Somebody had connections or a lot of money, or both."

"Well," Peter asked, "what's up here that you would want to attack anyway, except maybe us? What is there for them to defend themselves against, for that matter?"

Charlie looked up from the coffee he was pouring for himself. "Funny you should ask that. Pyotr told me that Leonid insisted you were all heavily armed and ready to attack within days." Charlie sat back down at the table with his coffee. "Then they told me that they never knew anything about the weapons until Andropov opened the boxes."

Peter laughed. "That's a little hard to believe."

"They claim they're only a couple of soldiers who signed up for a scientific expedition, figuring it'd be easy duty."

"I never trusted any damn Russians," Roland grunted as he got up from the table to clean up from the meal. Tom just sat at the table shaking his head.

After sipping his coffee, Charlie continued. "You know, those two are poor country boys. Pyotr is from Ukraine. He grew up on a collective farm. You ever seen one of them, Peter?"

"Nope. Can't say that I have. I've never been in that part of the world, except for some time in Kyrgyzstan and a little bit in Kazakhstan."

Charlie shook his head. "If serfs still exist anywhere in the world, that's one of the places where you'd find them. It's a tough way to live. Yegor's from Siberia. His father worked on a gold dredge. His mother died when he was twelve, and he went to work with his father. Life on a gold dredge in Siberia probably makes life on a collective farm in Ukraine look easy. I think they both joined the army to escape." Charlie downed the last of his coffee.

"Anyway, I left them untied and told them to stay in the tent. I don't think they'll cause any problems."

"I don't know where they can go, but there's sure a lot of guns and ammo around here, and none of it's locked up." Roland had started to wash the dishes, and the noise of clattering dishes and clanking utensils filled the tent. "I don't think we should leave them unrestrained unless somebody's guarding them."

"Yeah, I suppose you're right." Charlie looked at his empty coffee cup and seemed to think about getting a refill, but he simply put his cup down on the table. Looking up at Peter, he said, "I suppose we should restrain them during the night. They insist that the four of them were the entire advanced team for the scientists, and I believe them."

"Did they give any details about their work?" Peter asked the question quietly.

"I don't think they had a clue, or really cared. They were promised good pay, a small fortune for them, for easy duty with a scientific expedition. That was enough to get them here, no questions asked." Charlie raised his hands from the table and gestured in the direction of the tent where the two were staying. "I guess I can't blame them. I told them that we'd take them south tomorrow at the latest, and they'd be completely out of the situation up here."

Peter said nothing. The plan seemed a little too simple, too quick and easy, but he guessed he didn't need to second-guess the RCMP on this issue. Peter looked at Tom and Roland. How much did they understand of what might be going on here? And Arnie, the pilot? If Tom and Roland thought about it, they should be terrified.

Finally, leaning back from the table, Peter asked, "Should I make the call now, to report the Bombardier incident? If we don't do it right away, we won't be able to get a plane up here from Kuujjuaq tomorrow morning. It's already too late for today."

"Yeah, I suppose it's time." Charlie pushed away his empty cup away. "Let's go. We can do it right now."

Peter and Charlie got up from the table as Roland's dishwashing activity reached a noisy crescendo, as he shook the utensils in a dish towel to dry them.

Charlie stood behind Peter in the office tent, with one hand on Peter's shoulder while he made his call. The conversation with the police seemed almost routine, something like reporting a minor robbery. It was over in less than ten minutes, and then he and Charlie returned to the cook tent. Roland, having finished with cleaning up, sat down at the table for his after-dinner smoke.

Charlie said, "Arnie, the plane should arrive at about eight in the morning with the RCMP crew. We'll have to take them to the Bombardier and pick up the two bodies and Peter's skidoo. They'll probably spend quite a bit of time there cleaning things up." He paused for a moment. "We need to get the Bombardier to the Asbestos Hill mine sometime."

Charlie looked over at Tom, who seemed preoccupied by a small remnant of his dessert. "Can you drive the Bombardier, Tom?"

Tom looked sideways at Charlie, with his fork still in his hand. With a shrug he said, "I guess so. I've ridden in them enough."

"What about you, Peter?" Charlie asked.

"It's not a problem. They're easy to drive, particularly in open country. Tom can handle it with a few minutes of practice."

"Do we have the maps I'll need to get to the mine, Peter?" Tom asked.

"We don't have any detailed maps, but we've got some large-scale ones, and they should be enough." Peter rubbed his eyes before he continued. "Anyway, there's a GPS in the Bombardier. It's Russian, but it should operate the same as our GPS. Charlie can help with the input. It should locate you to within a few feet. We can put in the coordinates for the Asbestos Hill mine. With the maps and the GPS and still lots of ice on the lakes, you should be able to get there with no problems."

Charlie broke in, "Look, we need to get this done, but I guess it can wait a while. You're leaving tomorrow for a couple of days, aren't you Peter?"

"Yeah. But it should be a quick trip, as long as the weather cooperates. I should be back in two days at the most." Tom, cocked his head to one side, surprised by the news, and looked up at Peter.

Charlie continued, "Okay. We need to move the Bombardier, and I need to get over to Wakeham Bay. I'm supposed to check on the equipment the German partners will be unloading for the work over at Randal Lake." Charlie glanced at his watch. "Look, let's wait on both of those until you get back. It'd be good to have another set of eyes along on the inspection, and the ship hasn't arrived yet. Anyway, I'm a little uncomfortable at the idea of leaving you alone at the camp, Roland."

"Don't worry about me, Charlie. Show me how to use one of those fancy rifles, and I'll be fine."

Charlie laughed. "Okay. We'll do that. A little weapons training would be fun for everyone. Maybe we should even have some missile practice." Charlie laughed again and looked back at his watch. "Right now, though, I'm ready to turn in." He nodded at Peter. "I'll make sure our two friends are secure. Hopefully we'll get rid of them tomorrow."

In a few minutes everyone drifted off to their tents, and the camp was silent except for the light slap of canvas against the wooden frames and the creaking of the ropes on the sides of the tents. In the quiet Peter turned in his sleeping bag to face the side of the tent. With the RCMP ready to handle the two dead Russians, with an RCMP officer as the helicopter mechanic, and with enough weapons in the camp to start World War III, Peter knew beyond any doubt that this wasn't going to be a normal summer. Too many hidden agendas. And who was Charlie, really? Peter frowned in the growing twilight. "Damn," he muttered. He knew he wouldn't sleep well.

12

THE AIRCRAFT DESCENDED INTO THE GRAY AND HAZY SKIES OF Toronto. It had been an uneventful flight in the small, Gulfstream jet, courtesy of the RCMP. Peter wondered what Charlie had told Pyotr and Yegor to make them so happy to get on the old DC-3 that morning. He had left them in Kuujjuaq, still happy, still smiling, still with their RCMP escorts.

Tonight he planned to stay with Maria at her apartment. Christ, he was horny, and he'd been in Nunavik for no more than a couple of weeks. All the way south on the plane he had thought about Maria. He was amused by his almost-painful condition. He laughed. He assumed that would be resolved soon enough.

Tania's call annoyed him. Serg did not mix his work and pleasure, and her call to Gregori Borodin had been an unpleasant reminder that he did not actually control her. Serg assumed now that Gregori had arranged for Tania to come to Toronto from Russia, but Serg had a weakness, and he knew it. His annoyance and displeasure melted instantly at the sound of Tania's husky voice.

"Come to me tonight. I want you."

"I don't think I can."

"Please. I want you. I really want you."

With a sigh, he said, "I'll be there. You know I can't resist you. Someday … someday I know you'll take advantage of me." *Probably right now,* he thought.

Tania giggled over the phone. "You're the one who's taking advantage of a helpless little girl."

Serg laughed. "Tania, you're probably the least helpless of anyone I know. I'll come by as soon as I can get away."

"It will be special tonight."

"It's always special with you."

It had been another extremely unpleasant day for Serg. The Germans had made their offer for Randal Lake. It was heavily weighted in World Nickel's favor. Both the Germans and his board had demanded that he sign quickly, and he did so, as he had known he would. He had no choice. He was unhappy and angry, but he couldn't explain any of his misgivings to the board. The arguments in favor of signing had overwhelmed any arguments he could muster publicly. If there was ever a night when he needed the release that Tania provided, this was the night.

When he arrived, Tania greeted him at the door in a blouse sheer enough to hide nothing, and skintight pants. Serg almost laughed at the more than normally blatant display of sexuality. His concerns regarding her calls to Gregori faded with the scent of her perfume. After all, he was careful. He rarely discussed anything about World Nickel with her, at least not in detail. What could she possibly pass along to Gregori that would be particularly damaging?

Tania pushed the door shut behind him, held him tightly, and kissed him fiercely. "I've missed you so," she whispered. "Your Ardbeg is on the table," she said with a smile.

"Thanks. I need a drink." Serg moved slowly to the living room and sat down, his fatigue showing. He took a long swallow of the scotch.

"How are things going with your Russian friend?" Tania asked softly.

Serg stiffened. "Well, the Germans made their offer early today, and the board approved it. I guess the bastards are already on their way to start work, but we aren't even allowed to have any of our engineers visit the site." Serg stopped and took several more swallows of scotch. He was feeling old, tired, and no longer in control of his life.

Tania sat down beside Serg, put her arm around him, and kissed him on the ear. He felt the caress of her soft auburn hair against his cheek, and her musky perfume softly filled the room. She rubbed her leg against Serg. *To hell with Gregori,* Serg thought. *I really do want her tonight, and if she doesn't love me she sure does a great job of pretending.*

"Come to the bedroom," she said. "I want you to be an animal tonight," she whispered in his ear. "I want you to take me by force."

He turned and looked at her with a smile. She was beautiful, but her voice was what always got him started. He kissed her hard and stood up, pulling her to him. He carried her into the bedroom, kissing her along the way.

Tania fell back onto the bed. She closed her eyes for a moment. Serg started to pull off her clothes.

"Quickly, quickly!" she cried. She sat up and started to pull at his shirt. A button popped off. He helped her with his shirt and undid the fastening of her pants and pulled them off. He pulled off his undershirt and dropped his pants on the floor. They both kicked off their shoes, and then they lay facing each other, naked, breathing hard, both feeling the rush. His heart raced with the building passion. All the problems of the day, all his frustrations, all his fatigue, all his concerns over her phone calls, all of it, even Gregori, faded from his mind.

He knelt between her legs and bent over to kiss her. He moved down her body to bite her nipples lightly, and then he grasped her breasts roughly with his hands.

"God," Tania cried, "I want you so much." She clawed at his back with her hands. As he sucked her nipples, she reached down and grasped him with her hands, and he grunted and moved against her. He backed away and moved down with his tongue along her stomach. He probed with his tongue, and she cried out with delight. "Oh, god! Oh, god!" she cried. "Come to me. Come to me now!"

He pulled away slightly, and then he entered her with a single thrust. He growled, "Is this animal enough for you tonight? Is it?"

"Yes! Yes!" she cried.

He kissed her fiercely. The bed squeaked and banged against the wall as they came to a wild climax together, crying out and digging their fingers into each other.

"Oh, god, Serg! That was wonderful," she panted.

"Oh yes, that was wonderful," growled a voice from the door to the bedroom. Gregori stood there with a hard smile and cold eyes. Serg pulled suddenly away from Tania. She screamed and tried to cover herself with a sheet.

"Suddenly modest, Tania?" Gregori asked, with a crooked smile.

Serg made no effort to cover his nakedness. He jumped off the bed to confront Gregori. The smell of their sex filled the room. "What the hell are you doing here? Get out of here!"

Gregori pulled a long, thin knife out of his waistband. "You will not tell me what to do," he said coldly. Serg hesitated, and in that moment Gregori took two quick steps and pulled Tania roughly out of bed by her hair. She screamed again, hitting the floor with a thump, struggling and grabbing at his hands.

Gregori jerked hard on her hair. "Shut up, bitch," he said coldly. After that she was still, except for a small, whimpering sound, and she hugged herself, shutting her eyes. Her wet skin glistened in the light.

Gregori looked directly at Serg, standing sweaty and naked. "You will answer a few questions, and if you are a good boy and answer my questions very quickly, your little tart won't get hurt."

"Let her go."

"No," Gregori said with his little smile. His voice was flat and metallic. "If you don't do as you are told, I will carve her up into little pieces while you watch, you little prick. Now, first question, what have you been up to in Nunavik?" Gregori's knife pressed against Tania's neck as he held her tightly by the hair. Tania continued to cross her arms tightly over her breasts.

"We haven't been doing anything up there, for Christ's sake."

Gregori jabbed the knife into Tania's neck, just enough to draw blood. She jerked her head in response, but he simply tightened his grip on her hair, and she was quiet again. "I can read the papers. You signed a joint venture with NorthGold on their properties in Nunavik. You have someone up there, and I want to know what they're doing."

"Oh, god," whimpered Tania.

"Stop it! Leave her alone!" Serg shouted. Gregori laughed. Serg quickly considered his options. He might be fit, but there was no way he could take out Gregori. Too many years had passed. He wasn't a killer, not anymore, and Gregori most certainly was. "Look," Serg said, "we don't have anyone up there, but you're right. There's a geologist, Peter Binder. He works for NorthGold in a camp a few miles west of our Randal Lake property."

Gregori jabbed his knife into Tania's neck again, and a little more blood trickled down, slowly running across her right breast. She moaned, but she closed her eyes even tighter and held herself absolutely still. "You're getting better. Tell me more. Quickly, you bastard, or this place will get extremely bloody."

Serg threw his hands up in front of him, in some vain gesture to make Gregori stop. "Okay, for Christ's sake! Maria and I talked with him yesterday. A man called Jim Brown visited him, and Peter saw a white Bombardier tractor near Esker Lake. Jim told him he worked for the government, but I don't think Peter believed him." Serg paused. "Maria told Peter we don't have anyone working up there, and that's the truth."

"That's it?"

Serg sagged a bit as he made up his mind. Peter could take care of himself. "Peter planned to follow Jim's skidoo tracks and take a look around." Serg stopped and looked pleadingly at Gregori.

Gregori jabbed Tania again. "And what else?"

"Stop it! There isn't anything else. I haven't talked with Peter since that conversation with Maria. I have no idea of what happened, if anything. If you have people up there you should have told me!"

Gregori looked at Serg for several seconds. He pulled Tania to her feet and moved the knife away from her neck, but he didn't let go of her hair. He wiped the bloody knife on her sweaty thigh, leaving a red smear. Looking back at Serg, he said quietly, "You're pathetic. I think you're scared shitless and couldn't lie to me if you tried." He laughed. "Nothing has changed from the old days." Gregori continued, "Has Maria talked with this Peter the geologist today?"

"I don't know," Serg pleaded.

"Where does this Maria live? She's the bitch I met at your office, isn't she?"

Serg stood slightly slumped, like a defeated old man. He meekly gave her address. "I don't know if she'll be there."

Gregori laughed unpleasantly. "Yes. Well, I will find her or wait for her, and she will tell me what I want to know." He laughed again. "Now, you two behave yourselves. I can be quite nasty, but I prefer to do no lasting damage to such, ah, quality goods."

Serg watched Gregori look at Tania, who now had her eyes open, staring at Gregori with cold hatred. Smiling, Gregori reached up to her breast with the hand that held the knife, and she tensed. Still with a smile he squeezed one nipple between his thumb and forefinger. "You will heal. Perhaps Serg will kiss it to make it well." As he started to move away behind her, he pushed her, and she stumbled toward

Serg. Serg grabbed her to keep her from falling. "A pretty sight," Gregori hissed. "Two lovers embracing."

Gregori laughed his cold laugh again and backed quickly out of the bedroom. Serg and Tania stood, holding each other, and listened as the front door slammed shut behind Gregori.

"Tania!"

"Oh, Serg. I'm such an idiot."

"Stop! Stop! Don't say anything." As she sobbed, he held her close. He found himself wanting her again. He felt strangely guilty about his desires, but his lust let him forget about Gregori. It even let him forget about what he had just told him. He thought for a moment that he should try to warn Maria. Then he inhaled the smell of Tania. *There's no hurry*, he thought. *There's plenty of time.*

The blood on her breast mingled with the sweat on Serg's chest. He felt himself getting hard again, and without another word he led her back to the bed. She was on top of him, more frantic than before. Their sweaty and slightly bloody bodies slapped against each other, and their fear was forgotten as they surged to their noisy conclusion.

"Oh, god!" Serg cried, and he held Tania with all his strength as her whole body quivered.

Once outside, Gregori looked along the street. He focused on a truck for the telephone company parked up the street at an open manhole, where two men were working under the street. He wondered for a moment, but neither man had appeared to pay any attention to him when he went into the townhouse. It looked innocent enough, but Gregori was vaguely uneasy. He had never worked in Toronto before, and he was not as well prepared as he would be normally. He got into his car and slowly pulled away from the curb. The darkened side windows in the car calmed his nerves somewhat, but still he was tense.

He knew he was taking a huge risk, but he couldn't waste any time. He had to find and confront Maria Davidoff as quickly as possible. In spite of the urgency, or perhaps because of it, he smiled. He looked forward to this visit. Women were so easy to deal with in the West. In his mind, the occasional opportunity for violent and sometimes bloody sex made his job worthwhile. He had enjoyed threatening Tania, and thinking about what he would do with Maria gave him an instant erection. He laughed.

Maria arrived home at her apartment building at the same time that Gregori pulled his car into a parking space across the street. He recognized her immediately and watched as she carried two small bags of groceries to the front entrance. The doorman, an elderly gentleman dressed in a fancy livery costume, smiled from his position at the entrance and talked with Maria. Gregori rolled the window down just an inch. He could just make out the conversation. "How are you today, Ms. Davidoff? Do you need any help with the groceries?"

"I'm feeling great, Frederick," Maria replied with a smile. "I'll be fine. I expect a visitor later on, Frederick. Peter should be by, and you can just let him come up."

"Very well. It will be nice to see him again. When do you expect him?"

"Not for at least an hour or two."

"I'll let him right up when he arrives. You have a good night." He held the door for Maria as she entered the lobby.

Gregori smiled at the conversation. He wondered if this was the same Peter that Serg had told him about. It seemed unlikely. It didn't matter. Even with one hour, Gregori had plenty of time, but he had to find another, less public way into the building. More cautious now, he pulled out into the street again and parked about a block away from the building. The busy street left him feeling exposed. Any one of the many cars and people could be watching him. He shook off his concerns. He didn't need to worry about these stupid and complacent Canadians. Americans, maybe, but Canadians? They were all clowns.

After he parked, Gregori paused for a few moments, watching.

Then he got out of the car, carefully locked it, crossed the street, and turned quickly into a side street. Taking time again in the shadows to watch, he could not see any obvious followers. Anyone watching him was extremely skilled or was standing off a good distance. Gregori turned into an alley that led to the back of the apartment building, to a delivery entrance. The door was locked, but in the growing darkness the simple lock yielded easily to Gregori's persuasion with his picks. He smiled at the ease of entrance. Not even an alarm or a camera.

Gregori took the fire stairs. With his quick, light steps, his rubber-soled shoes made little noise against the metal stairs. He arrived at Maria's door on the fifteenth floor, breathing only slightly harder than normal. *Wait,* he told himself. The hallway was empty. No need to hurry. He focused on his breathing and willed it to a slower pace, and he listened intently. Faintly, the sound of running water came to him through the door. Gregori studied the lock. He took out his picks, and the door opened after only a few moments' work. There was no deadbolt, no chain, no alarm. "Fools," he muttered.

Carefully, he closed the door behind him without a sound, and he slid into the entryway of the apartment. He could hear water running. He smiled as he thought of confronting Maria in the shower. He paused for a moment and then he stepped to a chair and quickly removed his clothes. He folded them neatly, stacked them on the chair, and left his shoes on the floor by the chair. Most men feel vulnerable naked, but Gregori liked it. He had the physique of a serious body builder, and he was, as some would note, well endowed. He had found that his physique often frightened people, and it gave him a slight advantage with both men and women, but particularly with women. *This will be fun*, he thought as he felt his erection growing harder and felt the special tingling sensation that always came with the imminent promise of forced and violent sex.

The bathroom door was closed but not locked, and he opened the door without a sound. The hot water and steam fogged the glass enclosure for the shower. Gregori watched the vague shape of Maria as she soaped herself.

Maria hummed softly, and she luxuriated in the feel of the hot water washing the soap off her body. She closed her eyes as she thought about Peter and how much she was looking forward to his spending the night. It had been far too long. She played with her nipples and ran her hands over her taut, wet body.

Maria opened her eyes with a start as she heard the door to the shower jerk open. Gregori filled the shower door, and before she could say or do anything he punched her two inches below the breastbone. She didn't have the time and then didn't have the breath to scream. With a little squawk, Maria crumpled to the floor of the shower. Gregori stepped into the shower and closed the door behind him.

He stood with his legs spread apart over Maria. She looked up. Water ran down his chest, across his flat stomach and past his throbbing erection. He laughed. "Let's have a little fun, shall we, Maria? Perhaps you can make me happy and I won't hurt you."

He laughed again as Maria regained her breath. She gathered herself back up to her knees and looked up at him. The water ran off her breasts in little rivulets, but she didn't notice the water anymore. She realized that Gregori would mistake her intense look as a look of fear. Maria's mind raced. Even when they're bigger and stronger, all men have a special weakness. As Gregori reached down to grasp her head with his hands, without warning Maria punched him as hard as she could in the balls.

Gregori doubled over, hitting the side of the shower with a loud thud. He gasped with pain, and Maria shot out of the shower. She knew that one on one, without some sort of equalizer, she'd be no match for Gregori's strength. She ran out of the bathroom looking for a weapon, anything, as Gregori quickly recovered and roared, "You fucking bitch! I'll kill you, you bitch!"

A decorative glass bottle with two small tree branches stood on the floor just outside the bathroom door. Maria grabbed it, threw out the branches, and crouched low beside the bathroom door. As Gregori ran out of the bathroom, she swung the bottle with all her strength across his shin. There was an audible crack as the large bone broke in Gregori's lower right leg. Gregori roared from the pain and stumbled, nearly falling to the floor.

That stumble gave Maria all she needed. She leapt to her feet and delivered a quick kick to the midsection. The moves came naturally to Maria, flowing from years of practice and competition and driven by a visceral hatred of abusive men, and this one in particular. As he started to recover and straighten up, she moved quickly to deliver a hard upward blow to Gregori's face, and blood erupted from his broken nose, splattering across the clean, white wall and onto the light-gray carpet on the floor.

The blows staggered Gregori. Through the fog of pain he tried to respond to this totally unexpected demon he was facing. He found it hard to stand with his broken leg, and he reached out to keep from falling. Maria took advantage of his confusion and instability, and she kicked him again, as hard as she could, in the crotch. That kick took Gregori to his knees with another shout, and the next kick from Maria, to the side of Gregori's head, laid him out cold on the carpet. Blood flowed freely from his nose, making a little puddle on the carpet.

"You son of a bitch," Maria panted. "I knew exactly what you were the first moment I saw you, you bastard."

Gregori moaned and started to stir. Maria looked down and kicked him in the jaw. She heard a distinct snap, and he passed out again. She went to the kitchen, brought back some cord, and rolled Gregori onto his stomach. She tied his wrists and ankles tightly. Then she rolled him onto his side, looped the remaining cord between his legs and arms, and pulled his feet up to his hands and tied them there. He lay still, completely exposed and vulnerable. He would be in a lot of pain from his broken bones, but she couldn't have cared less about that.

Maria stood up and surveyed her work. Gregori was trussed up like a calf in a roping contest, still bleeding from his nose. Part of the broken shinbone protruded through the skin. Maria began to relax. She still dripped soapy water from the shower, mixed with sweat and splatters of Gregori's blood. Looking down, Maria allowed herself a small smile. "I bet you thought I'd be an easy job, didn't you? You should have done your homework better, you bastard." Maria returned to the bathroom, got a glass of cold water, and splashed it in Gregori's face. He opened his eyes and instinctively struggled against his bonds, only to cry out from the pain. He looked up at Maria, standing naked over him, his look now one of pure, unabated hatred mixed with more than a trace of fear.

"You damn bitch. I'll kill you," Gregori's broken jaw caused a slur in his speech.

Maria looked at him, helpless and exposed. She kicked him in the crotch. Gregori grunted loudly. "I don't think you're in any position to threaten me. If you tell me what I want to know, and if you behave like a good little boy, I might not cut your nuts off, you bastard."

Gregori said nothing. "What's the matter, big boy? Can't think of anything to say? Maybe I'm not just the pretty face you thought I was?" Maria laughed. "Well, I've had to deal with a few assholes like you in the past. I've got a few questions for you, and I expect some answers." She looked down at Gregori. "Why do you want the mine at Randal Lake? What are your plans up in Nunavik?" Except for his heavy breathing, Gregori remained silent. Maria was still angry, and she went to the kitchen, took a broom out of the closet, snapped the head off on the granite counter, and walked back to Gregori with the broken broom handle in her hand.

Gregori looked up at Maria but still said nothing. Maria hit him in the crotch with the broomstick. After a rather loud grunt, Gregori still remained silent, and Maria felt her anger moving to the edge of control. "I doubt I have your subtlety in encouraging someone to talk, but I'm running out of patience. I'll bet I can be effective enough to make you regret you haven't told me what I need to hear from you."

Gregori spat clumsily at Maria. The red streak of spit and blood ran slowly down her left shin.

With that, the remaining dam of self-control burst inside of Maria. Gregori's face merged with that of her dead husband. With deliberation she tightened her grip on the broomstick and began to beat Gregori methodically, along the ribs, up and down the legs. At first she avoided his face, but she kicked him in the stomach, in the crotch, and in the chest. When her right arm grew tired, she switched to her left. In the beginning the beating only seemed to arouse him, and that just focused Maria's fury. The beating went on for a long time. Eventually, Gregori's eyes rolled upward and he passed out. His erection slowly subsided, along with Maria's fury.

Maria stepped back and dropped the bloody broomstick. She looked at Gregori for a long time, and then she shook her head at what she had done. She hadn't killed him, but she realized she wouldn't care if she had. She knew that feeling of rage, and feeling it again made her a little sad. She thought she'd moved beyond all that.

Maria checked to make sure Gregori's hands and ankles were still firmly bound, and then she went back to the bathroom to complete her shower. As she toweled herself off, she stepped out of the bathroom and looked down at Gregori. He had risen to a painful consciousness again, but he remained silent. "I think you'll be a little sore tomorrow," she said with a smile. "Have you changed your mind about answering my questions?"

Gregori was silent.

"That's what I thought." Maria continued to look at Gregori as she dried her hair. She thought for a minute, and then she retrieved a wide role of surgical tape from a first aid kit in the kitchen. She ripped off a generous piece and taped it firmly over Gregori's lips. He winced and grunted from the pain of the pressure on his broken jaw. She ripped off two more pieces to make sure his mouth was firmly taped shut. "That should keep you quiet." Maria smiled at him. He was breathing with difficulty because of his broken and bloody nose, and in near panic he exhaled forcefully. Small gobs of partially coagulated blood spattered onto the carpet. "God! You're making a real mess, Gregori, and I just had the carpet cleaned."

Maria went into her bedroom, pulled on a shirt and blue jeans, and returned to the hallway. "I'm going for a little walk, Gregori. Don't get into any trouble while I'm gone." Maria shook her head. "You know, you really should try to be neater in your work." She turned and stepped into the living room. She saw the carefully folded pile of clothes and the thin, stiletto knife on the chair, and she put them on the top shelf of the coat closet. She needed time to think.

As Maria touched the door, she heard someone insert a key, and she jumped back as if the doorknob had burned her hand. She watched and stepped back a bit more, to give herself some room as the door started to open. Then she heard the familiar voice. "Hello? You home, Maria?"

"Peter!" Maria jumped forward and pulled the door open. She fairly jumped into his arms, embracing and kissing him fiercely. "Oh Peter, thank god you're here." The greeting was even better than anything Peter had imagined on the long flight down to Toronto.

13

STANDING IN THE HALLWAY BESIDE GREGORI, MARIA RESTED HER head on Peter's shoulder. Two men from the RCMP stood with them. After seeing Gregori and hearing Maria describe what happened, and knowing the connection between Gregori and Randal Lake, Peter had insisted that they call Dick Durban. To Peter's surprise, the two men arrived within minutes of the call, both dressed as telephone workers but with all the appropriate RCMP identification. *If they've been watching Maria's apartment,* Peter thought, *they're not doing a very good job.*

"Jesus!" one of the men commented. "What did you do to this guy, anyway?"

"I guess I got a little carried away," Maria said with a slightly embarrassed smile.

"A little? This guy's a bloody wreck."

Gregori did not look pretty. The bruises that covered his body were swelling and turning a reddish purple. One eye was nearly swollen shut. Dried blood from his broken nose covered his face and lay in dark red smears across his chest. His broken lower jaw jutted to one side, and the broken end of the large bone in his lower leg protruded through the skin. Most of his crotch had already turned a hideous combination of red, purple, and black. In spite of his injuries, he remained conscious and alert. With his mouth taped shut he could only groan. One of the RCMP men felt his pulse and stepped back. "At least he's conscious, breathing, and has a strong pulse. He'll live. He may not want to, but he will." He pulled out his cell phone. "I'd better call Captain Durban again." Peter and Maria listened as he described the situation to the captain.

"Okay," he said as he finished. "Captain Durban wants us to turn him over to the Toronto police for breaking and entering. We'll hang around until it's all taken care of."

Almost before he finished, the apartment buzzer sounded. "Toronto Police department, Ms. Davidoff. We understand you caught an intruder in your apartment. With your permission, we'll come up and take care of this matter for you."

She almost laughed at how politely they asked her permission. "Of course. Come right up."

Maria let the police into the apartment. The two Toronto policemen had worked with the two men from the RCMP before. "Hi, Sam," the senior policeman said cheerfully. A short man with a rosy flush to his face and an impish smile, the senior policeman had seen almost all the dark corners of humanity in his years on the Toronto Police Force. "So, what special little package do we have this time, Sam? How do you want it handled, special delivery or just special handling?" They both laughed at their old joke. They discussed Gregori, and then the policeman suggested he have a look at his suspect. "Goodness," he said as he looked at Gregori. "Someone was rather thorough in subduing the perpetrator, weren't they? And that would be the little lady, I presume, acting in self-defense?" He chuckled again.

Maria said nothing, but Sam spoke up. "You may not believe it, but you're right. I think she did a fine job of protecting herself and her home, don't you?"

"Yes. Quite admirable, I suppose." The policeman looked at Maria with his eyebrows raised. "Well, I need to go through the formalities and ask you a long list of questions, Ms. Davidoff." He started with whether Maria knew the intruder. The RCMP man answered that with a negative. The policeman raised his eyebrows again but went on with his questions. When he asked about Gregori's clothing, Maria explained some of the scene in the shower and told him where she had put the clothes. Sam got them and gave them to the policeman, but with no wallet or identification. The policeman smiled as he searched, without success, for any identification.

The policeman motioned to his younger associate. "Call an ambulance, and we'll take this mess to the hospital just as he is. That should keep him quiet. You go with the ambulance crew. When you get to the hospital, I want full restraints and no clothing allowed. We also want a twenty-four-hour, armed guard on the room. We don't want this one to get away, do we now?" He laughed.

After the ambulance took Gregori away and the Toronto police had left the apartment, Sam turned to Peter and Maria as he prepared to leave as well. "I suggest you bolt the door for the rest of the night, Maria. I left the little knife in the closet, a souvenir for you, to remember our friend Gregori." He started for the door but turned back before he opened it. "I'll have someone come by tomorrow to clean up and improve the locks on your door. I'll make arrangements. You don't need to be here." Wishing them both a good night, he left and firmly latched the door. Peter reached over and bolted the door behind him.

Peter turned to face Maria. "You've certainly had an interesting day."

Maria kissed him and held him tightly. "That, Peter Binder, is an understatement if I ever heard one." Looking up into his eyes, she moved her hand down below his belt and squeezed lightly. She smiled and said, "I think I still have a little energy left. I'd like to see what we can do with it. Anyway, you seem to be ready for what I have in mind." She tugged lightly at Peter's hand, and they started toward the bedroom. Peter's whole body responded quickly, as his anticipation on the flight down to Toronto rekindled to a new level of intensity.

For a fleeting moment, before their frantic sex reached its wild and inevitable conclusion, Peter thought about the men who had been watching the apartment. *I wonder who's watching us now?* He held Maria tightly, and he realized he didn't care at all. *Let them watch*, he thought with a smile.

The German ship was proceeding slowly into Wakeham Bay. Guenter Liedtke, the German captain, had not been happy on the trip. When he was annoyed and unhappy he had little patience and he tended to work his crew hard, harassing them over minor failings. He was feeling much too old to still be doing these odd jobs for the Russians. These trips were never quite what they seemed, and these days the drones that occasionally flew over the ship were unnerving, to say the least.

Guenter paced the bridge as they approached the west end of the bay, watching the depth chart as it showed the sea bottom starting to rise. His ship carried two large helicopters as well as mining equipment and supplies. All legitimate, or at least it seemed to be so on the manifest. He could see the end of the fjord now, and he would set his anchors soon.

"Ahead slow. I don't want any unpleasant surprises." He stared ahead at the narrow end of the fjord. "Get the crew ready to drop the anchors, and tell the engine room to prepare to shut down."

"Ja, mein Kapitän," replied his first mate, as he proceeded to relay the massages.

In Hamburg, the second and third ships were beginning to take on their cargo. Both ships would load nearly identical mining equipment and supplies, one destined for Randal Lake in Canada and the other for the iron mines in Narvik, Norway. Deck cargo would be four large, steel pipes on the ship headed for Randal Lake, and the three missile stages and one large steel pipe on the ship headed to Norway. The second ship would stop at Copenhagen, Denmark, to unload the missile stages before completing its trip to the mines at Narvik. They were sister ships, built by the same firm, identical in every way but their name. They were expected to depart for the Atlantic the following night.

In Saint Petersburg, Rostov fumed. "We're ready, and now we hear nothing from either Andropov or Gregori? The ships are already loaded. They're ready to leave. Do we have any alternatives?" he growled, looking at one of his engineers.

"Not if you expect us to do all this on schedule," the engineer replied flatly.

Zakhar Rostov stared silently out the window of the office. The special glass, with its slight greenish hue, would withstand almost any attack, except a missile or heavy artillery. He could see some people preparing to find a place to sleep in the park. Turning back to the engineer, he continued, "Besides the main cargo, what do we have on the second freighter? Do we have any backup supplies? Any weapons?"

"Supplies are no problem. We have enough food and supplies for the job, and the mining equipment on the two ships is all we need to get the job done. Weapons are quite another issue. We will have a modest supply, but it's not enough for any attack by a well-equipped armed force." The engineer seemed to shrink into the fabric of his chair as he talked. He was never comfortable around Colonel Rostov.

Rostov's explosive temper rose close to the surface, but with a deep breath he controlled himself. "Perhaps Andropov had an accident." Rostov paused. "We can't send anyone to investigate on the ground at this late stage without exposing ourselves too much. We can hope he just had an accident."

Rostov's secretary entered the room, wordlessly delivered a sheet of paper to Rostov, and left the office as quickly as she had entered. The paper showed an image copied from the website of the morning newspaper in Toronto. Rostov glanced at it, and then he took a much closer look. The article reported on an accident in a remote part of northern Nunavik. A geologist had found two men dead beside their Bombardier. Both had been shot. They were part of a scientific expedition, in cooperation with the Russian scientific community. Authorities suspected that two missing companions shot the men, and they were searching for the two suspects. The article stated that the identities of the two dead men were being withheld, pending notification of next of kin and scientific authorities in Russia. Next of kin, indeed. Scientific authorities. Rostov almost laughed.

He turned to the engineer and handed him the piece of paper. "Call Gregori's office in Toronto again and find out what the hell is going on." The engineer read the paper quickly. He arched his eyebrows as he looked back at Rostov, who simply shrugged his shoulders. As the engineer left the room, Zakhar Rostov turned again to look out the window. This had to work. He wouldn't have a second chance.

Minutes later the engineer returned, clearly apprehensive. "Colonel Rostov, the secretary in Toronto says she has heard nothing from Gregori. She called his apartment, but no one answered. She says he has simply disappeared."

"Damn!" Rostov muttered. It had always been a mistake to have Gregori working alone, and Rostov knew it, but he had so few people he could trust completely. Gregori must have done something stupid. So long as Gregori didn't talk, didn't tell anyone their plans, he presented no threat. But what if the RCMP had him in custody? No one, not even Gregori, could resist modern interrogation techniques. In a similar situation Rostov would use all available resources, and he assumed other interrogators would do the same.

He sat down heavily at his desk and said to the engineer, "It makes no difference. Tell the secretary to keep us informed and to notify the police." Rostov laughed. "What a joke, but it must look like normal business. Now leave me. I've got work to do."

Once he was alone, Zakhar Rostov searched for a phone number in his computer, a number he had not called for years. It was a Toronto number for a middle-aged sportsman and former rugby player named Brian Mitcham. Brian owned a construction company and a large chain of sporting goods stores. The latter had once been a convenient front for dealing in illegal arms. Not too many years ago, Colonel Rostov and the KGB had been major clients. When Rostov was still with the KGB, he had managed to help Brian avoid a criminal conviction and a long prison sentence. Rostov smiled. Time to call in the debt.

Mitcham's receptionist answered the telephone and asked for Rostov's name and reason for calling. "Tell him it's an old friend, someone he knows very well, from Saint Petersburg. I have a business proposition for him." There was a pause as the receptionist put him on hold. Rostov leaned back in his chair with a small smile of anticipation.

"This is Brian Mitcham. How can I help you?"

"This is Colonel Rostov. Can you talk?"

"It's not convenient at the moment. Give me your number and I'll call you back in ten minutes." Rostov gave him his number, settled back into his chair, and waited.

When Brian called back, Rostov answered on the first ring. "Returning your call."

"Is this secure?"

"It's a throwaway cell phone that I'll get rid of as soon as we're finished. I'm in my car. What do you want?"

"We have, or at least we had, a man in Toronto. He was working for us to set up a deal with World Nickel. His name is Gregori Borodin. He has an office on Bay Street, in the name of Northern Mining Consultants." He gave Brian the address and a telephone number.

"Unfortunately, he seems to have disappeared. I'm concerned that he's been picked up by certain, ah, officials of the Canadian government. This could be extremely inconvenient. You understand?"

"What is it you want me to do?"

"I want you to find out what's happened. If he's dead, simply report that to me. If he's alive and in the hands of the authorities, find out where he is and eliminate this little problem for me."

Brian did not respond immediately, and when he did his words came slowly and carefully. "Look, I'm a legitimate businessman these days. I got out of the black stuff years ago."

Rostov leaned forward in his chair, as if to get closer to Brian Mitcham. "I'm sure you still have your contacts. Perhaps you forget the prison sentence you never served. What would the police say if I handed them all the details that they never found during their investigation?"

There was a longer silence on the other end of the line. "That was a long time ago. Things were different then."

Rostov's smile broadened. He could feel the man's discomfort even across the many time zones. "Yes, it was a long time ago, and it was a very big favor from us to you." Rostov paused to give the next statement more emphasis. "Do this one job, Brian, and the debt is cleared. That I promise." Rostov waited for an answer. An amusing thought, his promise. If a promise became inconvenient, well, in Rostov's mind it was no longer a promise.

When Brian responded, he spoke with a quiet intensity underlain by deep anger. "I'll see what I can find out. I can call you at this number?"

"Yes. That's good. I'll expect your call."

Brian Mitcham sat in his car, furious. He opened the door and dropped the cell phone into a storm drain beside the car. Zakhar Rostov was right, though. Brian still knew the right man to call.

14

IN THE SOMBER KREMLIN OFFICE, IVAN DINISOVICH WAS BACK, LOOKING at the satellite images one more time with the President. "You see here," he pointed to a small area on one of the images, "the missile sections were shipped as expected to the yard in Hamburg. They were moved around the yard with the other large pipes. I think it was done just to confuse anyone who might be watching the storage yard."

Ivan pulled up another image on the computer. "I believe these are the missile stages being loaded onto this ship." Ivan pointed at the leading ship. Then he pointed at the second ship. "A set of large pipes, the same size as the three stages of the missile, are loaded on the second ship. They're to line the mine shaft at Randal Lake. The ship also has a large cargo of spare parts, mining supplies, and equipment, all bound for Wakeham Bay in Nunavik. The same shipping company already has a ship unloading a cargo of mining equipment and two large helicopters at Wakeham Bay. Everything headed toward Wakeham Bay and Randal Lake appears to be entirely legitimate. The missile is on the first of these two ships here in Hamburg and is on its way to the approved recycling company in Copenhagen,

Denmark, along with a large shipment of mining equipment destined for Narvik."

The President sat back. "Then all is correct?"

Ivan looked at the President and slowly responded, "So it seems."

"But you don't believe it?"

Ivan took a moment before he answered. "I have nothing. No proof." He paused. "It's just that I don't like any of this. I'm not sure it's safe to assume that all these shipments are actually as they seem."

"Now I think you may be getting too paranoid, even worse than I am," the President sighed.

Ivan grunted. "Perhaps. But I do have some other interesting information. You remember Zakhar Rostov, of course?"

"How could I forget that bastard?"

"I don't suppose you could. As you know, he's a so-called legitimate businessman in Saint Petersburg these days. Because of his reactionary thinking, I have kept a close watch on him." They both pushed their chairs back from the table. "He does have a number of legitimate business interests, and as you also know, they have made him extremely rich. He generates a large income from a number of mining interests in Siberia, Kazakhstan, and Kyrgyzstan. He also exports cobalt and nickel and imports mining equipment. He even holds an interest in a contract mining company based in Germany."

Ivan bent over the polished table and turned off his computer. "One of our people is an accountant for Rostov. I asked him to find out if Rostov has any contracts with the companies in Hamburg."

The President sat back in his chair. "I'm not sure I want to know, but what did he find?"

Ivan hesitated. He slowly picked up his computer and put it into his briefcase. "He found certain contracts between a German mining company and Rostov's contract mining company in Germany. The German mining company and World Nickel, the owner of the Randal Lake mine, have agreed to a joint venture to refurbish the Randal Lake shaft in northern Quebec and put the mine into production.

Rostov also has contracts with the shipping companies in Hamburg to deliver the supplies and equipment to northern Canada for the mine rehabilitation. It includes the large steel pipes for shaft liners. It's all legitimate, but my accountant admits he doesn't see all the agreements or transactions."

The President got up from the table and sat down at his desk. "So what do you think is going on?"

Ivan turned and faced the President. "There's one more thing. I asked one of our people who works in the Urals, on the program that recycles the deactivated warheads, to check on the warhead shipped from the missile silo in Siberia." Ivan's eyes always had a sad and tired look, but it seemed deeper than normal as he looked at the President. "He said it was received as expected. He assured me that everything appears to be normal. Frankly, I don't believe it." Ivan watched the significance of what he'd said sink in with the President.

"You must be joking. No, I suppose you're not. You never joke." He leaned back and shut his eyes. "What are your conclusions, Ivan? If the warhead isn't at the plant in the Urals, where the hell is it?"

"Please understand. My comments are highly conjectural. I have no proof at all."

"Yes, yes. I pay you for your conjectures. Get on with it."

"First of all, why go to all the subterfuge with more than one warhead at the missile silo if you're planning to ship the warhead to the Urals anyway? It doesn't make any sense. I know Zakhar Rostov has some sort of deal with the Danish company that recycles our missiles." Ivan shrugged his shoulders. "There's no evidence that our missiles aren't sent to the company in Denmark. Everything looks legal and correct." He sighed. "It's just that I don't trust anything about Zakhar Rostov. I suspect anything he's involved in, regardless of appearances."

"Yes. He rails against the government and shouts that he's going to destroy us. He conveniently forgets that his old-line Communists bankrupted the country with their corruption and inept central planning."

Ivan made no comment except to continue his explanation. "From here on, I'm mostly guessing. I think somehow Rostov is involved with our discovery of two warheads where there should be only one. And I have a nasty feeling about Rostov's relationships to the German and Danish companies. I suppose it's possible that he might be handling everything according to our contracts, but that's not the Rostov you or I know. That inactive mine site up in northern Canada, Randal Lake, might have something to do with it." Ivan paused. "An old, abandoned mine shaft could make an excellent missile silo."

The President rose from the table, looked at Ivan for a moment, and walked over to the window. After a moment, without turning back he asked, "Did you get anything more from your man at the silo in Siberia?"

"Not much that we don't already know or suspect."

"Have you rounded up the people who worked at the missile silo?"

Ivan sighed. "We've questioned all the workers. They haven't told us anything new either. They confirmed the delivery of a second warhead, and they told us about a man named Igor Luchenko. He was the one in charge. He set the time for the transfer and directed the whole thing."

"So what did you find out from him?" the President asked as he returned to his desk.

"Nothing at all." Ivan shrugged. "I can find no trace of the man, or anyone by his name, with any involvement with missiles or warheads. He simply disappeared once the missile and the warhead were shipped off-site."

"I don't believe this." Ivan could see that the President was losing his patience, and he didn't blame him. "Sometimes I think we'd be better off to be back in Stalin's day. People didn't simply disappear in those days unless Stalin made them disappear."

The President drummed his fingers on his desk. "Okay. So you're telling me that you believe Rostov will end up with a complete, working missile with a fully functional nuclear warhead. If he sells it, that's bad. If he decides to blackmail us or the world, that's worse. If he decides to use it himself? Christ, I don't even want to try to imagine what a madman like him would do with something like that."

The President looked at Ivan. "This is crazy. I don't know why I'm talking to you. You have no proof. It seems to me that the only issue to watch carefully is that the decommissioned missile is properly destroyed."

Ivan responded quickly. "Canada will examine the cargo on the ship headed for northern Canada, and they'll do it in Germany before it sails from Hamburg. The trouble is that such examinations are usually cursory at best, and I don't want to tell the Canadians to try to find a missile or a missing warhead."

Ivan continued with growing intensity. "I want your permission to talk with Watson MacDonough at the United States embassy. He's their CIA station chief. I know him well from the old days. He's an old hand, and he knows how to keep a secret. The Americans have a lot of eyes and assets, and I think we can use them without giving away too much. I also plan to tell the German government that we're concerned about possible smuggling of refined uranium and plutonium out of the country and that I'd like them to search the ship in Hamburg that's headed for Wakeham Bay in Nunavik. That should get them excited."

"If you're so worried, why don't we sink the damn ship before it gets to Canada?"

"I'm not sure we have the resources to do that and do it cleanly, and a messy sinking could create a worse mess. After all, it is a German ship. Besides, as you point out, I have no evidence for my concerns."

"True. You sound like a madman."

"When I talk to MacDonough, I'll say the target is Washington, or perhaps New York, to destroy the financial base of the West." Ivan gave a sour laugh. "They may not take me seriously, but I think they'll start watching things."

"Christ! I hate going begging to the Americans, Ivan." The President glared at Ivan. "Fine. Go ahead. Talk to your American and German friends, but be sure that when you talk to the Americans you make it sound like we're doing them a favor. They need to think we are certain that the U.S. is the potential target."

"Yes."

"I assume you're not trusting anyone with any part of this project?"

"I have to trust some people, but only with small bits and pieces, never with the full picture."

"Keep it that way."

They stared at each other for a long moment before the President waved his hand to indicate the meeting was over. Ivan nodded, stood up, and turned to leave. As he got to the door and put his hand on the doorknob, the President spoke softly. "You listen to me, Ivan. If you're worried, I'm worried. Zakhar Rostov is capable of almost anything." The President continued firmly. "You will sort this out. You will get a definitive answer. If a warhead is missing, you will recover the warhead. You will ensure that the missile is properly destroyed. You will find out if Zakhar Rostov is attempting nuclear blackmail. If he is, we will destroy him." The President pointed his finger at Ivan. "If you fail in this job, I swear that before I'm done I'll have your head in a basket."

15

IN THE LATE AFTERNOON, PETER AND MARIA SAT IN RICHARD DURBAN'S simple and sparsely decorated office, listening to his attempt at an explanation for the events of the previous evening. The earlier, unstated relationship between Maria and Durban contributed a palpable sense of tension to the meeting. In appearance, Dick was a near caricature of the upper-class British officer, though he had long lived in Canada, having emigrated as a child. Tall and thin, with a close-cropped moustache, he had the requisite dry sense of humor and a wry wit.

Peter wondered how much information hid behind Dick Durban's cheerful explanations. Finally, Peter spoke up. "Does this have any connection to what I've been involved with in Nunavik? If it does, I don't think Maria should stay around Toronto. These guys are absolutely crazy."

Maria laughed and said, "I thought I handled the situation pretty well."

"You did," Peter said, nodding, "but the next time they might shoot first and ask permission later."

"Thanks a lot for your vote of confidence." Maria laughed again.

Stroking his moustache, Dick spoke quietly. "Peter's right, Maria. I think you should put some distance between yourself and Toronto. I've already talked to Serg, and I, ah, persuaded him to give you a month off. I think he's feeling a little guilty."

"He bloody well ought to feel guilty, for Christ's sake. Anyway, you don't need to worry about time off. I quit right after lunch. Any debts between Serg and me, after what he did last night, are canceled." *Damn well paid in full*, Maria thought.

With a jerk, Peter turned to look at her. "You quit? You're kidding. You didn't tell me that."

Maria smiled back at Peter. "You didn't ask."

"I guess that takes care of one concern, and it sure makes me a lot happier," Peter responded and turned to Dick. "What about making sure you know what Serg is up to? You're losing your major contact in his office."

"I wouldn't worry about that." Dick leaned back in his chair with a big grin. "We persuaded him to keep us well informed, and in exchange we won't do anything about a few, shall we say, questionable contacts he's had recently." Dick stood up. "Well, I think that about covers everything we needed to discuss. Keep in touch if anything develops in Nunavik, Peter, and let me know how to get in touch with you, too, Maria."

As Peter and Maria left the office, Peter asked, "So where are you heading on your vacation?"

"Oh, I'm planning to go to a little camp I know about, to stay with an old boyfriend." Maria looked at Peter and laughed. "Don't look so miserable. I'm going to Nuvilik Lake, you idiot, to stay with you."

"What? Jesus Christ, Maria, you can't do that. That's like going to hell to stay away from the devil."

Maria stared straight ahead as they continued walking. "Look, this is long overdue. I've finally managed to make the break with Serg, thank god. By literally feeding me to Gregori he made it easy, the bastard. Now I want to be with you, and Nuvilik Lake happens to be where you're going to be for a while. I can be your geological assistant, and I'll try not to distract you too much on the nicer days." She finally looked at him and grinned.

Peter shook his head, stopped, and faced Maria. "You're absolutely crazy." Then he pulled her into an embrace and kissed her on the busy King Street sidewalk. "I still think you're crazy, but how about we eat out tonight?"

"I like that idea," she said with a large smile. "After last night, I'm not sure I'm in the mood to cook."

"How about the fish place over by the TD Bank?"

"Sounds great to me." They turned and walked to the west, hand in hand. Over a long, relaxed dinner they talked about nothing of importance, held hands between courses, and generally tried to put the previous night behind them.

As they finished with a cappuccino, Peter turned serious. "I do think you're a little crazy to come up to Nuvilik Lake with me. Maybe you're not safe here in Toronto, but you might be jumping right into the fire by coming with me."

Maria looked down at the table and responded softly. "I know." Then, looking up, she smiled. "Don't you realize? I want to be with you. It's time we tried to be together again."

With a smile, "Well, I don't quite know why we broke up in the first place." With a broader smile he added, "You know, sex in the camp is against all my rules."

Maria laughed and kicked him under the table. Then she reached across the table to hold his hand.

They spent the remainder of the evening at her apartment, which was neat and newly cleaned. Frederick, after apologizing profusely for the previous night, gave Maria a set of keys for the new locks. The pleasure Maria and Peter felt from being together smothered, at least temporarily, any other fears and concerns. They made love slowly and quietly. They tried to make the feeling last.

Early in the morning, after she had packed her clothes and other essentials for her time at Nuvilik Lake, Maria called Dick Durban. "Dick, I'm calling to let you know that I'm going with Peter up to Nuvilik Lake."

"Really?"

"Really. We got the okay from NorthGold, so there's no problem there."

Dick hesitated. "Ah, Maria, could you stop by my office before you go? Alone? If you're going up there I need to talk to you. There's something I'd like you to do for me in Nunavik, and anyway, you should have a letter to give to the pilots. They need to know that your travel with Peter is official and approved."

Maria looked at her watch. "I could come by in about ten minutes."

"Great. See you then."

She called to Peter, who was drying off after his shower. "I'm going out to pick up a couple of things. See you in half an hour or so."

"Don't take too long. We should head to the airport pretty soon."

"I won't be long."

That same morning, shortly after Peter and Maria left Toronto, a man walked along the corridors of Toronto General Hospital. Dressed in light green scrubs, he looked just like all the other doctors in the hospital. His stethoscope hung around his neck, and a surgical cap covered most of his dark, curly hair. Passing nurses and orderlies going about their tasks, he approached a guarded door.

"Wait a minute, doc." The young, fresh-faced policeman at the door challenged him. "I need to see your ID."

"Sure. Sure. I understand." The man showed his hospital authorization with its photo ID. He was more muscular than most of the young interns, but the hospital was full of new doctors from eastern Europe. His appearance was nothing unusual, except for his large, black, bushy moustache and unusually large eyebrows. The young policeman glanced at his ID. All appeared to be in order.

"Okay, doc. I haven't heard a peep out of him. You must have him so drugged up he's feeling no pain."

"You're probably right, but we still have to check on him," the doctor said with a smile. He put on a pair of latex gloves, opened the door, and stepped into the room. He closed the door behind him and walked over to Gregori. Gregori Borodin lay on the hospital bed. His muscular and battered body struggled in a restless, drugged, and troubled sleep. His wrists and ankles were strapped to the metal rails of the bed. His nakedness revealed all his injuries. He was covered with deep purple bruises, and a large bandage wrapped around one leg. In spite of his background, Gregori's visitor had rarely seen a man this badly beaten and still alive. There were no monitoring machines in the room and no connections back to the nurses' station. Gregori's injuries were not considered life threatening. The man smiled.

He bent over the bed, as if to start an examination. With one hand he placed an iron grip on Gregori's mouth, and with the other hand he held his forehead. The intense pain from the pressure on his broken jaw broke through Gregori's morphine haze, and his eyes opened wide. He looked up, confused. Suddenly his eyes filled with unaccustomed fear. He struggled, but with the restraints his struggles were useless. In one quick movement, the visitor broke Gregori's neck. He kept his hands over Gregori's mouth and nose to make sure that he was dead, and then he arranged Gregori's head carefully on the pillow. He smiled slightly. Gregori looked very peaceful.

Shutting the door softly behind him, the doctor removed his gloves, dropped them into his pocket, and said to the young policeman, "No problem. You were right. He's feeling no pain. As beat up as he is, though, he sure will if he ever wakes up."

"That's for sure. Have a nice day, doc."

Gregori's visitor walked calmly down the corridor, turned the corner, and stepped into the fire stairs. He pulled a plastic shopping bag out of his pocket, stripped off his scrubs and hat, and stuffed them and his stethoscope into the bag. He was now dressed in running shoes, shorts, and a dark blue tee shirt. He pulled a small mirror and clippers out of his pocket and clipped off his moustache and closely trimmed his eyebrows. He made sure all the clippings were collected in the shopping bag. His dark, curly hair fell partway over his forehead. On the next floor down he walked out into the corridor. There were no security cameras in the stairway, and those in the corridors now recorded a visitor leaving the hospital. He walked out, unchallenged, unnoticed, and disappeared into the crowd on the street.

After he left the hospital, he walked along the street and took a pathway that led to a park. He watched the woman step away from the bench under the large tree, leaving a backpack behind for him. He had examined the area carefully, and he was quite certain that no security cameras covered the area. He sat down on the bench, by the backpack, and waited patiently until he was sure no one was watching him. Finally, he removed his blue tee shirt to reveal a dark maroon tee shirt and pulled on long running pants that were in the backpack. He removed his dark wig and pulled a baseball cap out of the backpack to cover his close-cropped hair. He stuffed his clothes, the wig, and the shopping bag into the backpack and zipped it closed.

He sat back on the bench and waited again, this time for an appropriate crowd to walk by. After a few minutes a large group of university students walked past the tree, most with backpacks. He stood up, shrugged on his backpack, joined them, and walked out of the park. The doctor, the last visitor Gregori would ever see, had disappeared completely.

16

PIERRE JADOT LANDED THE DC-3 AT NUVILIK LAKE IN THE EARLY afternoon with Peter and Maria, along with a fresh supply of groceries, fresh fruit and vegetables, and, of course, beer from Kuujjuaq. After they settled their packs into the office tent and helped with the supplies, Peter and Maria went to the cook tent. Everyone showed at least mild surprise to see Maria in the camp. *It might not be good for camp morale in general,* Peter thought with an inward smile, *but it sure is good for my morale.* He introduced her and said, "Maria will help me with the geological mapping and sampling." Whatever thoughts the others had about the arrangement, they kept them to themselves. One thing was certain, Maria's presence would have a salutary effect on their normally foul vocabulary.

After Peter and Maria finished a late lunch, Charlie said, "Peter, I promised before you left that we'd have a little target practice with the assault rifles. It's all set up behind the camp. If you and Maria want to join in, feel free."

Peter watched as Tom, Roland, Arnie, and Maria all fired the AK-101. Arnie, with his time flying for the U.S. military, had used similar rifles in basic training. At first the rest of them used at least half of a thirty-shot clip at each touch of the trigger, and their shots were pretty wild. But there was plenty of ammunition, and Charlie made sure each of them gained some degree of comfort with the rifle. Soon the targets were well shredded. Peter took a skidoo across the frozen lake and set up several flares on the opposite shore to provide a heat source as a target for the Stinger missile.

Charlie held the Stinger in his hands and briefly explained its capabilities. "These are easy to use. They're designed to be used in combat by harassed and distracted soldiers. They're about thirty pounds complete. They have a range from as little as seven hundred feet to five miles. Their effective range is probably more like two to three miles. They don't care about elevation and will accept a target on the ground and up to about two miles high."

Charlie continued. "A good operator will take about ten seconds to assemble the second round and about one minute to power up the unit, lock onto the target, and fire. The missile flies at a little over twice the speed of sound, so there's not much around that can outrun it. These are fire-and-forget weapons. Once you've fired at a locked-on target, you can drop the empty tube and run like hell if you have to."

Charlie looked across the lake. The two burning flares lay on the black rocks a short distance up from the opposite shore. "Well, Maria, there's your target." He held out the missile. "Give it a try. I'll guide you through the process of targeting and firing."

Maria laughed a little nervously, but she accepted the firing tube from Charlie. "Once it's powered up and you have it aimed at the two flares, you'll see the indication that it's locked on the target." Peter watched closely as Charlie began to lead Maria through the process of using the Stinger.

Maria sighted the missile. Charlie showed her how to power up the unit and explained how to tell when it was locked onto the target. "Once the power is on, the batteries don't last too long. You've got to lock on target and fire within a couple of minutes. Does it show you're locked on?"

"Yes."

"Fire away, then."

It was over in a few seconds. The missile completed the complex process of ejection from the launching tube. The main engine didn't fire until it was far enough away to avoid injury to the operator. Its sensors never lost sight of the heat source of the two flares. In the short distance to the target, the missile didn't even reach full speed before it hit the target and exploded.

"Not a big charge, but it's enough," Charlie commented dryly.

"Jesus Christ," Tom said softly. "That's impressive."

Charlie laughed. "Yes. Well, I don't think we should fire off too many of those. Somebody will probably want to collect these later, and they might object if we used them all up having fun. It's pretty easy, isn't it Maria?"

Maria shook her head, still looking at the dying flames of the explosion across the lake. "Standing and aiming at a couple of flares seems easy enough, but I'm not sure it would seem so easy if someone were shooting at me at the same time."

"That's the beauty of fire-and-forget missiles like these," Charlie responded. "Like I said, once you fire it, you can throw the launcher away and run. Right now, I think we should walk to the cook tent for a cup of coffee. What do you say, Roland?"

Peter picked up the rifle and the expended missile tube. Maria watched him while the others walked to the cook tent. Peter smiled. "Nice job, Maria. Now I know at least three of us can use a Stinger."

Ten minutes later, pausing over his coffee, Charlie said, "We should deal with the Bombardier this afternoon, and I need to visit Randal Lake and Wakeham Bay. The supply ship for Randal Lake is unloading. I'm supposed to have a look around." He looked over at Peter. "You need to come along to make sure Tom gets started okay with the Bombardier and headed to the mine at Asbestos Hill. You may as well come along, too, Maria."

Turning to Roland, Charlie asked, "Do you have any food prepared for Tom?"

"No problem. There's lots of sandwich stuff here, all ready to go."

"Well, get some food for your trip, Tom, and then we'll get going." Charlie got up, and Arnie followed him out the door to start the helicopter. Peter and Maria arrived at the helicopter a few minutes later.

The weather was beautiful, clear and brilliant. Peter knew that it could change all too quickly. The snow cover, beginning to melt now, still masked the edges of the lakes. The ice wouldn't completely melt on the lakes until August. Once, it had been easy to get lost in the barren lands, but GPS systems had solved most of that problem. Peter gave Arnie the coordinates of the Bombardier, and they picked up and headed east. After a while, Peter leaned forward, tapped Arnie on the shoulder, and pointed to the Bombardier. Arnie nodded, made a slight adjustment to his heading, and began his descent.

After all that had happened there, Peter marveled at the emptiness of the landscape. Already, with the moderate wind of the last few days, drifting snow filled most of the skidoo tracks. No evidence remained of the confrontation with Andropov. The RCMP had done a good job of cleaning up the mess. Peter could almost imagine it had been a dream, but he knew it was real. It was a little too convenient, the way it had all disappeared. That still bothered him.

The helicopter set down by the Bombardier with a little bump. Peter keyed the microphone in his flight helmet, "You'd better shut down. We'll be a while."

"No problem," said Arnie, and he started the process of reducing fuel flow, cooling the engine, and shutting down. Peter and Tom followed Charlie out of the helicopter. They bent their heads, as the blades of the MD 500 were not far off the ground, and walked over to the Bombardier.

"Well, Tom, this is your game," Peter said. "Let's see if the thing will even start." They walked over to the cab and Tom climbed into the driver's seat. Peter climbed in through the other door and sat down in the front passenger seat. The Bombardier started on the first crank, and the fuel gauge registered full.

Peter opened the door and called to Charlie. "Can you put the coordinates for Asbestos Hill into the GPS? I don't think I can follow the Russian directions."

"Sure," Charlie responded. He leaned into the cab, and after Peter gave him the coordinates, he punched them in. "See how it's giving you a bearing, Tom? That'll change if you get off course."

"Yeah. That looks good."

"Thanks, Charlie," Peter said. Charlie backed out of the cab, and Peter shut the door.

As the engine idled, Peter took out a map and unfolded it. He pointed along a proposed route he had sketched on the map. "It's pretty much a straight shot from here, Tom, so the route given by the GPS should be pretty good." It wasn't far to Asbestos Hill by normal standards, less than forty miles, but Tom would drive at about five to ten miles an hour, and the actual distance traveled, with detours, would be more like fifty or sixty miles.

"You won't get there this afternoon. I don't know how long we'll be looking around at Wakeham Bay. You might get about halfway to the mine. If you don't see us before eight or nine tonight, stop and give us a call on the radio, okay?"

Tom nodded. "If you don't mind, let's give this a little practice run before you leave."

Peter opened the door, leaned out, and called to Charlie and Maria, "We're going to check it out. We won't be more than a couple of minutes." Once Peter shut the door, Tom put the Bombardier in gear, grabbed the steering levers, and let out the clutch. At a low gear, they moved at a crawl, but everything seemed to work fine. Tom shifted to a higher gear and continued for a few minutes before turning back.

Peter contemplated Tom as they headed back. Finally, "Listen,

Tom, I don't really know what's going on here. If you don't see us tonight and can't make contact, keep going and get to the Asbestos Hill mine. You know Jim Wurtz. He'll give you a place to sleep if you need it. If you have to spend the night in the Bombardier, you've got four beds in the trailer, along with the four sleeping bags." Peter reached into his pocket and gave Tom a sheet of paper. "Call Captain Durban in Toronto if you don't hear from us for another day." They were back at the helicopter, and Tom stopped about twenty feet away.

Tom turned to face Peter. "I think you'd better watch your ass, Peter."

"Yeah, I plan on it," Peter responded as he shook Tom's hand. He got out of the Bombardier and headed over to Charlie and Maria beside the helicopter. Tom turned the Bombardier and began his slow trip to Asbestos Hill.

Peter watched the back of the Bombardier as it pulled slowly away. "I'll get the map," he said as he turned back to the helicopter. "I guess you should stay in the front for this part of the trip, Charlie. I'll try to show you some of the sights of the area." He unfolded the map and held it against the Plexiglas of the helicopter. He pointed at the Randal Lake mine site as Charlie, Arnie, and Maria looked over his shoulder. "Here's the mine site and camp. This doesn't show the buildings or the shaft. The map's too old. The road down to the west end of the fjord at Wakeham Bay goes along this line." He traced the route with his finger. "The road's raised and generally clear of snow in the winter, but we always had drifting problems near the bay." He pointed at the bay. "There's no dock, so they'll have to unload by barge." Peter folded up the map.

"We can stop at Kangiqsujuaq," Peter said, "the little community on the south side of the bay, if you want. I know the priest, Father Donovan. The last time I visited I needed some fuel. The church has the fuel concession, and he was up on the hill, building a pad for a new fuel tank with the church's bulldozer." Peter laughed. "You have to know a lot more than how to save souls to be a priest up here. I know the Hudson Bay guy, too, if they haven't brought in somebody new. If we talk to the two of them, they can tell us what's been going on in the bay." *And they might even tell me the truth*, Peter thought. At the moment, Peter thought truth was a commodity in very short supply.

17

THE AMERICAN SECURITY TEAM SEARCHED HIS BRIEFCASE, RAN HIM through two sensitive metal detectors and a full body scan, and swabbed his briefcase, laptop computer, and shoes for explosives. After a final x-ray of all he carried and after he turned on the computer, the Marine guard grudgingly allowed Ivan into the American Embassy in Moscow. The guard handed him off to an escort.

Ivan Dinisovich put up with the delay and intrusion. Visitors to his offices went through much the same. Finally, a young woman greeted him. "Mr. Dinisovich, please come with me," she said in excellent Russian. "My name is Sasha Karpov. Mr. MacDonough is expecting you." She smiled at Ivan. "Would you like some coffee or tea?"

Watson watched on the security cameras as Ivan reacted to Sasha. Her cheerful American manner and good looks forced a rare, slightly lecherous, smile from Ivan. She was probably too thin for Ivan's preference, but Watson didn't know of any women in Ivan's office who even knew how to smile.

"Yes. I would enjoy a cup of coffee, black please." Sasha led Ivan briskly to a small, windowless conference room. She gestured toward the oak table and four high-backed leather- and fabric-upholstered chairs. "Please have a seat. Mr. MacDonough will be with you shortly, and I'll have your coffee in a few minutes." With a parting smile, Sasha turned and left, closing the door slowly and softly behind her.

Watson MacDonough had reserved a secure, internal room for their meeting. Watson watched as Ivan smiled at the camera in the corner of the room and gazed around at the bare, cement walls. "He's probably wondering if any of the old KGB bugs still work," he muttered. "Well, they don't," Watson said louder. "But mine do." It was incredibly stupid and naïve to use Russian labor to build the new embassy, and Watson had argued long and hard against it. It had taken a long time to make the embassy secure.

As Sasha entered his office, Watson turned away from the image of Ivan. "What do you suppose he's up to, Sasha?"

Sasha shrugged her shoulders. "According to the guards, he's carrying a laptop computer in his briefcase. He also has a few small reports. Nothing else." Sasha moved closer to Watson's chair to see the image better. "When he called he said it was urgent that he talk with you, and you alone. I turned off the microphones in the room. Do you want the camera off as well?"

Watson looked back at the image of Ivan waiting patiently. "Leave the camera and the recorder on. He knows we'll record the meeting, even if we promised not to do so." He smiled and turned to Sasha. "It's time to find out what our friendly Russian wants from us."

As Watson entered the room, he let the heavy, soundproof door close itself behind him with a sigh of air and a dull thud. Speaking in Russian, he greeted Ivan. "Ivan Dinisovich, it's good to see you." They shook hands. "We should try to meet more often, I think." Watson waved his hand, encompassing the entire room. "Not very palatial, but we are used to that, no?"

The door opened again, and Sasha entered with two pots of coffee and two cups. "This is the decaffeinated coffee," she said to Watson, pointing to one of the pots. Then she quietly withdrew and left the two men alone.

Ivan poured himself a cup of the strong black coffee, and Watson poured the decaffeinated. "I'm getting old, Ivan. I can't drink real coffee anymore. It makes my heart do back flips. It's a good thing I'm past doing stakeouts."

"You probably don't drink enough vodka with your coffee," laughed Ivan. "You know, there's an old Russian saying, actually perhaps not so old, that coffee without caffeine is like a honeymoon without a bride." They both laughed. Ivan raised his cup, "To new allies and old comrades."

"Yes. New allies."

The two men looked at each other and sipped their coffee. Watson was remembering. He didn't want to open the discussions too quickly, but he was impatient. "You said you have something important to discuss with me, Ivan. Perhaps we should begin?"

Ivan nodded, pulled his laptop out of his briefcase, and switched it on. He pulled up the first satellite image of the silo in Siberia with the workers removing the missile. "As you know, we are nearly finished dismantling the missiles and silos as required under the treaty both presidents signed a number of years ago. This image shows what is referred to as Site 422A."

Watson stood up and moved to a chair adjacent to Ivan. "Yes, I've received a report that the missile, the last one in this series, has been removed and that the silo has been destroyed. The satellite surveillance has helped both of us verify that the disarmament treaty is being honored."

"Yes. The satellites helped. In this case, though, they may be telling us much more."

Watson did not respond immediately. "Exactly what do you mean by that, Ivan?"

Ivan sat down and waved his hand at the image. "You may not have noticed, but the salvage crews at this site took longer than normal to dismantle the missile. The three stages of the missile were carefully handled for their trip to Denmark for recycling."

Watson raised his eyebrows, but he decided to remain silent. He got up and moved back to the end of the table and sat down.

Ivan raised his hands in a pleading gesture. "Please understand. I am telling you this off the record. I have suspicions. I have no proof. But like the so-called 'Patriot Militias' in your country, we have some crazy ultranationalists in this country. Some of them have become extremely wealthy, and some have many, many connections to the old-line Communists of past days. One such person is a man named Zakhar Rostov." Watson raised his eyebrows again at the mention of the name.

"I remember him well. A real bastard, that one."

Ivan chuckled at Watson's comment. "Time has not mellowed his opinions or his nature." Ivan brought up a second image on the computer screen, which showed the port of Hamburg, Germany. Again Watson moved next to Ivan so he could see the image clearly. "We traced the missile to this storage area." He jabbed at the computer screen with his long, thin fingers. "The storage yard belongs to a company in Hamburg that manufactures large culverts and steel pipes. You can see that once everything is covered with tarps, a practice taken up not long before this missile arrived, no one can tell the difference between the pipes and the missile stages. When the missile arrived, the three stages were unloaded from the train and put on truck beds."

Watson leaned closer to get a clearer look at the image. Ivan zoomed in on several of the loads that were covered with tarps. "You can see that all the loads look the same."

After a few minutes Watson leaned back and faced Ivan. "Why have you shipped the missiles out of the country? I seem to remember that we all agreed to try to avoid that."

Ivan shrugged. "When we started the program, we needed the hard currency, wherever and however we could find it." Watson nodded. "We sell the missiles for recycling, after removing the guidance and targeting systems and the warhead."

Ivan continued, "The German company says they received the missile sections as usual and plan to send them on to Denmark for recycling. Here in Hamburg I have a man who watched the trucks in the yard and those coming out of the yard. He noticed that three loads were heavier than the others. So far, those three are still waiting to be loaded onto a second ship in the harbor." Ivan switched to a third image. It showed two ships being loaded in the harbor facilities adjacent to the storage area.

Ivan jabbed at the screen again. "This ship is loaded with mining equipment, construction supplies, and four sections of steel pipe, all destined, according to ship's papers, for the Randal Lake mine site in Nunavik, Canada. The second ship is destined for Denmark to offload the missile stages and associated electronics. It carries an almost identical load of construction materials and mining equipment for Narvik, in Norway. They are sister ships. From these images I cannot tell them apart. However, we know that this second ship is the one scheduled to head for Copenhagen, Denmark, and Narvik, Norway. It has one large, covered pipe on its deck, and what we believe are the three sections of the missile are still waiting on the dock to be loaded."

Watson took his time. He asked Ivan to enlarge the image of the two ships. Satisfied, he turned to face Ivan. He gestured at the image. "From what you say then, everything seems legitimate."

Ivan nodded. "That's true." He closed the laptop and nodded again. "On the face of it, I agree. But Zakhar Rostov appears in the picture at this point. He owns a contract mining company based in Hamburg, with an office in Toronto. His company has a contract to rehabilitate the Randal Lake mine shaft in northern Canada and to prepare the property for development and production. The companies in Hamburg, this pipe plant and the shipping company, and the recycling company in Denmark—they're all related. The shipping companies are well known for their reliability and notable lack of curiosity, for which they charge astonishingly high prices. No one would use them unless they have no other choice."

Watson leaned back in his chair and shut his eyes. After a moment, "Are these the same companies the KGB used before? To take the original missiles to Cuba?" Watson cocked his head to one side and looked at Ivan.

Ivan let out a short laugh. "Yes, the same." They held a momentary silence, as if in memoriam. "Rostov has strong connections with all of these companies, and he's using them for purchase and shipment of his supplies and mining equipment for the Randal Lake job."

Watson leaned back again. His chair creaked slightly in protest. "It seems simple enough to me. You watch the two ships and make sure the cargoes go to the right places. Search both of them when they arrive."

"That's easy to say, but cloud cover presents a problem over the North Sea and parts of the North Atlantic this time of year. Satellite coverage will be somewhat limited. And Denmark, Norway, and Canada are all quite sensitive about their sovereignty. None of them would be particularly happy about Russian agents searching cargo ships in their ports."

"Well, suppose Rostov does have a missile. Without a warhead, what can he do with it except sell it? He's going to have to move it again, I imagine, to sell it. You still have time to sort it out and make sure it's actually recycled."

"There are two problems with what you just said. First, this is an advanced ICBM, a Topol-M, not some short-range piece of crap from North Korea. It's an older version, ready to be retired, but it's still operable. Second, so what if he doesn't have a warhead? Suppose our defense systems detect a missile launched at Russia or the United States? What do you think the reaction would be?"

Ivan's questions hung in the air. Both of them knew what the reaction would be to any launch, regardless of what was on the top of the missile. Finally, Watson responded softly. "What do you want me to do?"

Ivan suddenly became more animated, his voice brighter. "I only want you to be aware of my concerns. Watch. Tell me if you see anything suspicious."

Watson, in contrast, slumped deeper into his chair and asked, almost dully, "Why don't you simply ask the Canadians to examine the cargo when it arrives at Wakeham Bay, and the customs inspectors when the ship arrives in Denmark and Norway?"

Ivan dismissed the idea with a wave of his hand. "We have already asked the Canadians, and they're content to examine the cargo before it leaves Hamburg." Ivan shrugged. "Denmark will rely on cursory customs inspections and the report from the recycling company. I doubt Canada would be willing to have us visit to look at what's going on in Quebec."

"Nor us, I'm afraid, at least not formally." After some moments of thought, Watson straightened up in his chair and continued. "As you are aware, our best satellite coverage is occupied these days, but I'll alert Washington to watch these two ships. Along with the Canadian inspection, it should be enough." He paused and then added as an afterthought, "By the way, what are the names of the ships?"

"As I said, they're sister ships. The one headed for Denmark and Norway is the *Hamburg Frau*. The one headed for Canada goes by the name of the *Hamburg Liebfrau*." Ivan handed a memory card to Watson. "This contains the satellite images I showed you."

After Ivan left, Watson returned to his office where Sasha joined him. He sat behind his desk, with his fingers together under his chin. "Well, Sasha, nothing with Ivan Dinisovich has ever been as it seems. He's hiding something." He picked up some reports that lay on his desk and began to read. "See if you can arrange for someone to get a good look at the cargo on these two ships."

Sasha knew it was time to leave. She was already used to Watson's absentminded dismissals.

Later that afternoon the telephone rang on the desk of Hans Britmeister, a former member of the East German Stasi secret police and now a high-level officer of MAD, the German military counterintelligence agency. It was no surprise that the Russians were worried about losing track of some enriched uranium and plutonium. The Russians could lose anything, so long as it was worth something to someone somewhere.

Hans quickly bumped the report up the chain of command. They'd recently caught the Americans snooping far too much on German turf, including some extremely embarrassing phone taps of high-level politicians. Should they bring the CIA into this exercise? He received a quick and firmly negative response.

18

WATSON MCDONOUGH READ THE REPORT HE HAD RECEIVED FROM the agent in Hamburg. With no explanation, German customs officers had completed an examination of the cargo and ship's manifest for the *Hamburg Frau* in much more detail than was normal. German intelligence officers of the BND and the MAD also made a thorough search of the *Hamburg Liebfrau*. Once asked, the Canadians confirmed that they had asked the Germans to check the manifest. The Germans were silent on the matter.

Watson swung around in his office and looked out the window to a gray day in Moscow. Zakhar Rostov was on his mind. The possibility, however small, that a man like Rostov might have one of Russia's best ICBMs in his pocket was an unpleasant thought. He turned back to his desk and sent a notification to Washington that he would be calling on a secure line later in the day.

Late that afternoon, Watson shifted in his chair to find a more comfortable position. The conversation with Andrew Boyles in the Washington office had already gone on for far too long. "Look, Andy, Ivan wouldn't come to me with this sort of story unless he had major worries. He'd be too damn proud, unless his balls were in a wringer."

"But seriously, I don't see it." Andy's petulant response was beginning to annoy Watson. "Like you say, everything is on the up and up, as far as anyone can tell. So what the hell is there to worry about?"

"Come on, Andy." Silence.

"Okay, Watson. Look, I can't guarantee full coverage. We're rather busy in the Gulf and over in Afghanistan at the moment." Silence again. Watson kept his mouth shut and waited. "I'll do what I can, but give me a break, for Christ's sake. This has to be another red herring your friend Ivan cooked up. If he's trying to divert our resources for some reason, it's not going to happen."

"I have a bad feeling about this, Andy. Whenever that guy Rostov's involved in anything, I don't sleep well at night."

"I think you may be getting a bit obsessed, Watson."

Watson ran his fingers through his thinning hair. "Yes, I am. I don't deny that. This is really important, and the consequences are too frightening to ignore. Being obsessive has kept me alive." The comment was a not particularly subtle dig at Andy, who had never been a field operative. "The other thing that bothers me is that business with the German intelligence teams that were crawling all over the *Hamburg Liebfrau* today. I asked our embassy boys to find out what was going on, but the Germans clammed up and wouldn't say a damn thing."

"Ah, they're probably looking for weapons. Almost anything in the Russian arsenal is for sale on the black market, if the price is right."

Done with his hair, Watson massaged his eyes. *God, I'm tired*, he thought. "Do me a couple of favors, Andy. Talk to the Canadians. See if they have anything going on up around Randal Lake in Nunavik, and have our satellite team look at some recent images from that area. If there's nothing to see, and our Canadian cousins are all happy and smiling, maybe I can relax. See if you can get anything out of your contacts with the Germans about what they were looking for on the *Liebfrau*, and keep a watch on those two ships, okay?"

The response finally came, curt, annoyed. "I still think you're goddamned obsessed with this situation, but I'll see what I can do."

Watson felt too tired to enjoy Andy's grudging offer of help. "Thanks, Andy. I owe you one."

"Pay for it with a beer when you get to Washington next time, okay?"

"No problem. Thanks again."

Christ, Watson thought, *it really is time for me to retire.* The word was that Harold James, his ultimate boss at the CIA, thought Watson was dangerous, a relic of the Cold War, maybe even of World War II. Watson shook his head. There was no way anybody in the Company would be willing to put his ass in a sling for any of Watson's ideas. The director would have them for breakfast. Watson toyed with a pencil. Maybe they'd watch the two ships for a while, maybe even Randal Lake. Watson realized that for anything else he was entirely on his own. He called his contact in Hamburg and asked him to watch the two ships.

Later that night in Hamburg, heavy, dark clouds covered the stars, and the new moon still lay well below the horizon. The tall man stood in the doorway of a darkened warehouse and watched the two ships. The shipping channel cloaked itself in an almost-liquid darkness, with only the running lights of ships indicating any activity. The *Hamburg Frau* and the *Hamburg Liebfrau*, fully loaded, quietly slipped away from the docks. With a little help from the harbor tugs, they slid into the shipping channel and headed northwest along the Elbe River toward the North Sea. Occasionally they used their searchlights to find the marker buoys for the channel. The man lit a cigarette as he watched the ships go, shook his head, and turned away.

As the two ships crept along the pitch-black shipping channel, no one noticed the men near the bow of each ship. Quickly they loosened the bolts, removed the nameplates, and replaced them with new ones. The old nameplates joined others in the Elbe with two small splashes that no one saw in the dark or heard above the sound of the ships' passage. At the mouth of the Elbe, after a brief exchange between the two captains, who were old friends, the two ships headed their separate ways, one to Wakeham Bay in Nunavik, Canada, and the other to Denmark and on to Narvik, Norway. All was well. The customs inspections had been completely uneventful.

Later in the week, Watson called Andy again. "I guess you were right, Andy. The *Hamburg Frau* landed in Denmark today. The company that handles the recycling of the missiles for the Russians accepted the deck cargo. Maybe I am getting paranoid. Too many years chasing ghosts."

Andy laughed. He sounded satisfied with his small triumph. "That's two beers you owe me then, Watson. I did have the satellite guys keep an eye on the ships when they left Hamburg. As best we can tell, the two ships departed normally and went their separate ways. No stopping to exchange cargo or anything like that." He paused. "I assume I can shut this one down for now?"

"I guess it was a false alarm after all."

"Don't forget the beers you owe me next time you're in town," Andy finished with a chuckle. Watson knew that Andy Boyles was happy. He had avoided looking the fool.

Watson hung up the telephone, still troubled. Although he didn't believe it was, he'd have to report to Ivan that everything seemed normal with the two ships. He picked up the telephone again. "Sasha? Please come here for a moment."

Sasha entered the office and Watson looked up from his desk. He liked Sasha. She was young, bright, and quick, and she tolerated his grumpiness. Watson reported on the ships' movements and shrugged his shoulders. "I guess I was too quick to take Ivan's bait, but I still have a bad feeling about this. Keep a watch on the Randal Lake area for me, will you? Let's see if we can get someone to check on the missile shipped to Denmark. It'd be good to confirm that it actually got there." Watson gave Sasha a half smile, and then he returned to the papers on his desk.

"I'll see to it," Sasha said and turned to leave. Watson doubted she would expend much energy on these tasks. She'd focus on things she thought were more important, more exciting. Like most of the newer staff, she preferred the remote-sensing gadgets to any real field work.

The next afternoon Watson's official car lumbered toward Ivan's office. Upgraded with armor plate and the latest in composite windows, it could withstand most small arms fire, even survive a modest-size bomb or IED attack. His driver carried a sidearm under his jacket and a light machine gun under the seat. Normal procedures and overlooked by the Kremlin security, so long as the driver didn't leave the car.

Watson got out of the car on the side of Red Square. His long tour as station chief, out of the field and away from any physical work, had left its mark. He was working on a second chin and had gained nearly thirty unwanted pounds in the last two years. He puffed a little when he climbed stairs. He had lost most of his hair, though the moustache he had first grown in Moscow remained in good form, thick and bushy, if rather gray. Even the thick eyebrows that met over his nose were turning gray.

For the first time in his life, Watson was thinking seriously about retiring. He and his wife were long divorced. He had spent far too many unexplained nights away from home. He rarely saw his two sons, which was not much of a change from earlier years. He had missed most of their growing up. He thought about that with a pang of regret. Perhaps if he retired soon he would be able to enjoy his grandchildren, if he was welcome. He finished his second flight of stairs and stopped to catch his breath. Then he walked down the hallway, through another metal detector, a body scan, a thorough examination of his identification by the guards, and on to Ivan's office.

"Hello, Mr. MacDonough," the dour receptionist said in excellent

English with a slight British accent. She ushered him into the outer office. "Mr. Dinisovich is expecting you. I will tell him you are here." Watson watched the woman leave. Her sour and well-worn appearance mirrored the drabness of the office itself. In a few moments she returned, with Ivan leading the way.

Ivan shook hands with Watson. "Good of you to come. Please, come with me. You would like some coffee, of course? I'm afraid we have none of your decaffeinated coffee here." Turning to the receptionist he said, "Two coffees, please, in the meeting room. One black with no sugar, correct?" Watson nodded and followed Ivan into a conference room, similar to the one in which they had met at the American embassy. As they sat down, Ivan said, "I have turned off all the recording devices, so we can talk freely." Watson did not believe it for a moment.

The receptionist closed the door behind her after delivering the coffee. Her grim expression never varied. She really was depressing. As usual, Watson opened the discussion. "There's not much to tell you, Ivan. We kept track of the two ships in Hamburg. We shadowed the *Hamburg Liebfrau* in the North Atlantic, and it is indeed on its way to Wakeham Bay. The *Hamburg Frau* unloaded most of its deck cargo in Denmark. The Danes tell us that the deck cargo includes the three stages of the missile for recycling. The ship's on its way to Narvik as we speak. The Germans, on the request of the Canadians, examined the cargo of the *Hamburg Liebfrau* in Hamburg, and the German intelligence teams were all over the ship. Everything appears to be in order."

Ivan nodded. "I'm not surprised. What do your people in Washington think about all this? I assume you told them."

"They think I'm an old man with paranoid delusions." Watson laughed. "They don't take me very seriously most of the time."

"And you? What do you think?"

Watson thought how strange it was for the two of them to be meeting and talking in this way in the Kremlin. *The world changes,* he thought, *but Ivan has not changed. Ivan is still hiding something.* "I think you know more than you're telling me. I hope we'll find a way to tell each other the truth before it's too late." *And the real problem is that you don't know the truth, or perhaps even what you're hiding from me.*

Ivan bent over the edge of the table across from Watson, his face as close to Watson's as possible. Watson was used to Ivan, and he did not move. Up close, Ivan's face bore the small scars and marks of poorly treated childhood diseases. "We have much in common, you know, though I have not played this game as long as you. Neither country believes they need us anymore. We are anachronisms. We're not modern enough."

A heavy silence permeated the room. Then Ivan thumped his chest with his fist. "Believe me, Watson. Zakhar Rostov wants something extremely badly. He wants power that comes from controlling the government, and somehow that missile will end up in his hands. I don't know when, and I don't know how he'll use it, but he will use it." Ivan grunted. "You should pray that you die before the new order rises."

Watson did not change his expression, but he felt cold. He could feel the growing frustration of the man across the table, the man who once could move mountains and imprison thousands, if needed, to get to the truth. Quietly he said, "You give me little to work with. You tell me stories about an old, hard-line bastard like Rostov, who's now a legitimate businessman that I can't even get close to. You tell me stories of suspicious ships and cargo, and they all go to the right places. They laugh at me in Washington."

Ivan pushed his chair back from the table. With a note of disgust he responded, "I have given you all that I can give, all I have to give. I am asking you to watch. Perhaps together we will find something. I will tell you that the news you bring should help me sleep at night, but I will not sleep. When I think of Rostov I don't sleep." A pause. "You should go now. I have already said more than I should."

The two men shook hands and the receptionist let Watson out. He left his coffee untouched. It was probably just as well. Ivan's coffee was terrible, and Watson knew he shouldn't have the caffeine anyway.

As Watson walked down the corridor and down the stairs again, he felt the gloom of the office building begin to seep into his mind and body. He realized that no matter what was happening, he would have to fight on his own. He might get some help from Ivan, but Ivan would never tell him the whole truth. He would get no help from Washington. His driver, who waited for him, unlocked the door as he arrived. Watson let himself in and settled into the back seat. "Let's go home," he said to the driver, and they pulled away from the curb. It wasn't the first time he'd battled alone, not by a long shot.

"Sorry for the inconvenience," Harold James said. "I hadn't planned on meeting again quite so soon. However, there have been some developments, and I need to give you some background."

G, with his German accent, asked, "Does the death of the two men in Nunavik have anything to do with this?"

Harold did not answer directly. "They were taken out quite effectively by a geologist working in a little camp for a mining company. He's a former Navy SEAL. He obviously hadn't forgotten all his training." With a small smile, Harold continued. "It's not an issue of any importance."

"If it's not important, why did you insist on talking with us?" G responded, obviously annoyed.

"This program has attracted the attention of Ivan Dinisovich in Moscow, and he has in turn alerted Watson MacDonough of our Moscow station. As you can imagine, this is a dramatic increase in risk. Do you still support it?" Harold looked at each of the three men in turn.

BD responded first. "Can you contain the situation?"

Harold shrugged. "Ivan is out of my reach, but I suspect some actions can be taken there to minimize his impact. Zakhar Rostov has some very powerful connections. I don't think either Ivan or Watson has much more than suspicions. Watson is an old fool, but a dangerous old fool. It's time he retired. I may be able to hasten that event."

"Why don't you sell him?" BD asked.

Harold smiled thinly. "There's not much of a market out there for tired Cold War spies. Some sort of early departure from the Company is an easier approach."

"What about that damn geologist?" G asked. "He's very annoying."

"As is the case with Ivan, that is not entirely under my control. There are some ways to minimize his impact as well."

"Eliminate him. He's your biggest risk," G growled.

Harold smiled. "Possibly, but at the moment it's too much force. It adds too much risk. It would bring unwanted attention to a remote part of Canada. We already have two dead men to explain."

"I disagree. Eliminate him."

"I appreciate your opinion, G, but that's not going to happen. Not yet."

BD spoke up. "He's right, Harold. This geologist is the only one on-site who can really stir things up. He has enough weapons, and he knows how to use them. He's completely unpredictable."

"No, gentlemen. That's a decision I have to make, and I've made my decision. He's not an immediate threat. We don't need any more bodies right now."

"You're making a big mistake." This from G.

Harold stood up. "I think the meeting's adjourned." The silent man looked at the other three and smiled.

19

AS THEY LIFTED OFF, ARNIE CIRCLED THE BOMBARDIER. TOM GAVE A wave, and Arnie banked and turned to the east. In the back, Maria reached over and ran her hand up the inside of Peter's thigh. He shook his head and smiled when he saw her broad grin. He looked out as they approached the Randal Lake mine site. This trip triggered a lot of memories from when he had worked at Randal Lake. He pulled his camera from his pocket and took some photographs.

There hadn't been this much activity at Randal Lake for several years. Two cranes worked around the mine shaft. Two or three graders cleared the remaining snowdrifts from around the buildings, and exhaust plumes showed that the big generators were running. Twenty or thirty people worked in the vicinity of the shaft. Two large Russian helicopters, Mi-17s, sat to the side on a large helipad not far from the headframe. Peter raised his eyebrows in surprise. Each would have three men for a crew, and each could carry about thirty additional men. The helicopters could also carry an impressive array of rockets and machine guns. *You don't usually see machines like those at mine sites,* he thought.

Peter triggered his mike. "Lots of activity, Charlie. They didn't waste much time if the ship landed within the last couple of days."

"Yeah. Well, let's go in and say hello, Arnie. Land at that bare spot, left of where those two graders are working. That shouldn't bother anyone." As Arnie turned to land, Charlie said, "Arnie, I want you and Maria to stay with the helicopter. You can shut down if you want, but I won't be long. We'll make a quick hello and go on to Wakeham Bay. Let's use NorthGold as our corporate name, Peter, rather than World Nickel."

Arnie was careful, as always. He made sure of his wind direction to ensure a safe landing. As they approached, Peter took a closer look at the headframe. Workers appeared intent on dismantling it, which seemed odd to Peter. Essentially a heavy lift, stationary crane, the headframe offered the only easy way to hoist the heavy mining equipment needed to work on the shaft or any of the other underground workings. The workers had already removed the main hoisting cable from the giant pulley arrangement at the top of the headframe, removed the wheel itself and much of the framework and cross members at the top, and were busy removing the sheet metal siding. It was beginning to look as though it could collapse in a high wind.

After they landed and Arnie settled the machine on the ground, Charlie and Peter stepped out the side doors. A small welcoming party met them near the helicopter: several impressively large men and one smaller man; the latter appeared to be in charge. He and Charlie seemed to know each other and immediately struck up a conversation in rapid German. Peter could follow only a little of the discussion. No one asked Charlie to provide his RCMP identification.

Charlie turned to Peter. "This is Shawn Schmitz, the project manager. He says he's glad to know that there's someone else up here, just in case. They're getting ready to cement in large steel liners, to eliminate some caving problems near the top of the shaft. I told him that you'd worked up here before, and he says it's okay if you want to look around a bit, but don't go far. I want to get off to Wakeham Bay in a few minutes." When Peter didn't leave immediately, Charlie went on. "Ah, I'd like to talk with him for a few minutes. See what you can find out by looking around."

Peter shrugged. "Sure." Charlie nodded and turned back to continue his conversation with Shawn.

Peter walked a little closer to the shaft. Charlie and Shawn had to speak loudly to be heard over the noise of the helicopter, and Peter could still hear bits of their conversation, though he understood very little. Peter was fascinated by what they were doing at the headframe. Putting in steel liners didn't make much sense to him, and tearing the headframe apart didn't seem like a great idea either. He heard a shout from Charlie and turned to see him waving him back toward the helicopter.

"Let's take off," Charlie said when Peter approached the helicopter. Charlie shook hands with Shawn and thanked him in German for his patience. Peter nodded and shook hands, but he didn't try any of his schoolboy German.

Charlie turned to Peter as they walked over to the helicopter. "They're sure getting a lot of work done."

"Yeah. They're tearing the hell out of the old headframe. If they do much more the whole bloody thing might fall down."

Charlie looked over at the headframe and back to Peter with a shrug. "He told me they're pulling off the top of the headframe so they can lower the steel liners into place. Then they'll put it all back together at the end of the summer."

When they got into the helicopter, Maria leaned forward and asked Charlie, "Well, what did you find out?"

Half turning, Charlie said, "Not much. They're pretty busy getting the shaft ready to put in some steel liners. I asked about the men with the Bombardier. He said they never had any advance team up here. They claim to be the first workers on-site. I guess those nuts you confronted, Peter, had nothing to do with Randal Lake at all."

Peter didn't respond. At that point Arnie had the helicopter at full power, and they lifted off to fly the short distance east to Wakeham Bay. Peter looked out the window. He continued to be amazed at how quickly the RCMP had swept the whole Bombardier incident under the rug and ignored it altogether. He realized he'd never told Charlie about the maps and plans for the Randal Lake site that he had found in the Bombardier. He didn't think he would, either. With all the secrets around him, it was time to keep a few himself. One of his secrets was that he could understand a little of the German conversation between Charlie and Shawn.

The group completed the remainder of their inspection trip without any surprises. In the last few days, the stronger sun had melted much of the snow, and the bulldozers and graders had already cleared the few remaining drifts along the road from Randal Lake to Wakeham Bay. The German ship rode high in the water a few hundred yards offshore, and a large pile of containers, heavy equipment, and construction supplies were gathered on shore, ready to be moved to the mine site. The ship's crew was busy unloading the last of the cargo onto the barge. Like every big project, this one was clogged with equipment and supplies.

Bored with the uneventful examination, they all clambered back into the helicopter and flew the short distance to Kangiqsujuaq. The Hudson Bay proctor, Bill Spence, was still in residence, as was Father Donovan. Father Donovan was getting old, but he was still thin and active. With a smile behind his bushy red moustache, Bill expressed his deep gratitude for Peter's gift of a bottle of Scotch, as did Father Donovan. It could be lonely and extremely dry at times in a place like Kangiqsujuaq. Neither Bill nor the good Father gave them any news of interest.

On the way back to Nuvilik Lake they detoured to the north and picked up Tom at the Bombardier. He could finish moving it tomorrow.

After Arnie landed back at Nuvilik Lake and they all had a late supper, Peter and Maria relaxed, stretched out on their sleeping bags reading before heading to bed for the night. The telephone rang.

"This is Richard Durban. Is Maria there, Peter?"

"Yes. She's right here. Do you want to talk with her?"

There was a moment of silence on the phone. "No. Not right now. Gregori died in the hospital at about the time you were flying out of Toronto."

Peter grunted. "Well, I can't say I'm surprised, considering his injuries." Maria looked up from her book.

"He didn't die from his injuries. Somebody murdered him in his hospital room. I think they killed him to silence him, to make sure we couldn't interview him."

Peter sat down. "In Toronto General Hospital? You've got to be kidding me."

"I wish I were. We don't have any autopsy reports yet, but it looks like somebody broke his neck. We had him under restraints, so it would have been easy. Some guy dressed as a doctor got past security, broke his neck, walked out, and disappeared. Neat as could be."

Peter looked over at Maria. "Things are getting a bit nasty, aren't they?"

Peter could hear Durban exhale before he continued. "Yeah, well the body count is mounting." A moment of silence, then, "I want to warn you. The Prime Minister has decided that he doesn't want any international involvement, so he wants the Bombardier affair to stay quiet. He's prepared to accept that this was an unfortunate incident. I'm concerned that you and Maria may be targets. Stay alert. Don't trust anyone too much. Talk to Charlie about anything, particularly if you see anything that looks strange."

"Okay, Dick. Thanks for the warning."

"Yeah. I'll talk to you later."

After Peter hung up the phone, Maria asked, "What was that all about?"

Peter turned to her and said, "Let's take a walk along the lake."

Maria looked at him for a moment, marked her place in her book, and swung her feet over the edge of the bed. She started lacing up her boots. With a laugh she said, "That sounds like a great idea. A nice stroll through the neighborhood before we turn in for the night." A sense of peace at the end of the workday had already settled over the camp, though the sound of the small gasoline engine for the generator would be with them for at least another hour, mainly to charge batteries for radios and the telephone. At the edge of the lake they walked over to the little point that formed a small bay in front of the tents.

"Durban told me that Gregori died in the hospital today."

Maria stopped. "So that's what that conversation was all about. Well, I can't say that I'm too upset about that."

Peter looked out over the lake, which was still covered with ice. "Perhaps you should be upset. Durban thinks he was murdered." He looked at Maria. "But that's not what I want to talk to you about. Durban told me that we should be careful and not trust anyone too much." Maria raised her eyebrows, but she didn't comment. "You and I have to trust each other and watch each other's back. I don't think there's any problem with Roland or Tom, and Arnie seems to be a straight shooter. I'm not so sure about Charlie."

They had arrived at the end of the point and sat down on the rocks. "I don't know," Maria commented. "He seems like a fairly typical helicopter mechanic to me, except that he's also part of the RCMP."

"Well, he works for Dick Durban, but I don't know in what capacity normally." Peter looked out over the lake. "How well do you know Dick, Maria?"

Maria laughed. "Oh, I know Captain Durban pretty well. I did work for him part time for a year or so, and we were lovers for a while, or at least I thought we were." She laughed again, seeing Peter's startled look. She leaned over and kissed him on the cheek. "Don't worry, he left me for a younger man."

"A younger man? You must be kidding."

"Nope. I'm not kidding at all. He doesn't seem to be too partial, one way or the other. Anyway, he's our great Canadian spy-chaser. Maybe that's why he's so good at his work."

Peter shook his head. "That's a real surprise. Times really have changed."

"Yes, times have changed, but it was still an extremely unpleasant surprise for me." She smiled. "To be honest, I don't seem to have the best track record in my relationships with men." She laughed. "Present company excepted, I hope."

Peter didn't know how to respond, and they sat in silence for a while. Finally he commented, "I still have some doubts about Charlie and I guess the whole RCMP, for that matter."

"Like what?"

Peter paused. How much should he say? His common sense told him not to worry, but his gut told him something different. Peter wanted to have someone covering his back, but he wasn't happy about making Maria that person. He began to tick off the points on his fingers.

"Think about it. First, our two Russian friends, who should have been extremely worried about prison or deportation and probably punishment at home, left with big grins on their faces. Whatever Charlie told them sure put their minds at ease. I can't imagine what it was, and Charlie's not saying a word. I wish you had been here to listen in on their conversations."

"I think I'm glad I wasn't."

Peter laughed. "Well, second, everybody wants to sweep the whole thing about the Bombardier and the two dead Russians under the rug. Whatever they were doing, you'd think the RCMP would be all over that Bombardier, but they never touched it, as far as I can tell. Third, I understand a little German. When Charlie was talking with that guy at Randal Lake, they mentioned the German word for missile, *Wurfgeschoss,* several times. Why would they be talking about a missile, and why wouldn't Charlie mention it when we asked him what he'd learned?"

"Maybe Charlie was just asking about the Bombardier and all those handheld missiles."

"Perhaps," Peter responded. They were both silent for a while. Then Peter said, "It's just that when something like that incident at the Bombardier happens, I start to get a bit wired. I start seeing things differently. Sometimes what I see isn't real, but most of the time it is." He looked at Maria with a small smile. "It's a gift or a curse. I don't know which."

Maria looked at her watch and then at Peter. She hesitated before she said softly, "Let's head back." After they had walked part way back to the camp she said, "I think you've got to trust the RCMP on this, Peter."

They heard the generator sputter to a stop as it ran out of fuel. With the wind calm, the land fell silent in the long Arctic twilight. Their feet made little squishing sounds with each step in the tundra where the snow had melted. "You're right. But let's make sure we both watch each other's back, particularly when we're around Charlie, and particularly if for some reason the going gets tough. I'm still not convinced that someone isn't ready to sell you or me to the highest bidder. Hell, Serg already has."

They came around the end of the bay, back to the main shore, and turned to the east, toward the camp. "Well, Peter, I think you're getting a little crazy." She smiled at Peter. "But I promise to be careful." She gave his arm a squeeze. "Right now, though, I think it's time to turn in for the night."

She took his hand, walked backward facing him for a few moments, and then they both quickened the pace and walked together to the office tent. Contrary to all his better instincts about camp life, they were sleeping together at least for part of most nights. Their sex was quiet, almost silent, which was not easy, especially on the squeaky beds, but they managed. He knew that camp sex could cause major problems, but he couldn't help himself. So far, the camp had survived.

Later, after Maria had moved back to her sleeping bag and her own bed, Peter lay awake thinking. He thought a lot about Charlie, about the fact that until Maria arrived Charlie had made a series of silent but not particularly subtle sexual advances. He wondered about Charlie's preferences and how they might fit with what Maria had told him about Dick Durban. Still feeling the afterglow of their slow and quiet sex, he decided to stop worrying so much.

20

WATSON FLEW TO VISIT AN OLD FRIEND IN COPENHAGEN, DENMARK. Though he had asked Sasha to check on the actual cargo carried by the *Hamburg Frau*, she had been unable to find out much of anything beyond the fact that the recycling company had signed for the shipment of the three missile stages and that the customs inspectors had cleared the cargo. Watson assumed she wanted to distance herself from his obsession. She had a whole career in front of her. "Well, I'm not quite ready to retire," he muttered to himself. Not quite yet.

Watson's friend in Copenhagen, Willem Philip, had been a real legend in his youth. Early in the Second World War, when Willem was still a teenager, he had stolen the plans for the improved Enigma machine, enabling the British to crack the German codes for first time since the Poles had done so on the simpler machines in 1932. Though a quite elderly man, Willem was thin and active, with a bright, rosy complexion. Willem still had a full head of dark-brown hair, perhaps aided by a bit of hair dye. His home and lifestyle gave little hint of his earlier exploits. Now he presented the perfect image of a solid if slightly vain citizen, elderly, conservative, and perhaps even a little dull.

In spite of his age, Willem still handled the occasional odd jobs for the CIA, and Watson could hire him discreetly from his unreported "black funds." When Watson showed up at his house, Willem answered the door with a broad smile and a burst of enthusiasm. He fairly pulled Watson into the house. "Watson! We haven't talked for more than a year, and now you visit. Still fighting the evil Russian bear these days?"

Watson laughed as he allowed himself to be thrust into a chair. "Haven't you been reading the papers, Willem? We're all happy allies. The bear and Uncle Sam dance together at the fair these days." They both laughed. After a moment of silence, Watson continued. "I do need you to do a little job for me, though." The heavy furniture and dark wood paneling of the room provided a balance for Willem's unbridled enthusiasm for life.

"You disappoint me, Watson." Willem puffed on his old pipe, putting up a fog of sweet-smelling smoke. "I thought you came to visit to hear my new jokes." Willem laughed. "I don't know, Watson. I'm getting old, you know. I'll be seventy-five this year, and I'm pretty much retired."

Watson laughed and shook his head. If Willem were seventy-five, he would have still been sucking on his mother's tit when he first stole the Nazi secrets. He had to be over ninety. Anyway, Watson knew that Willem wouldn't do anything himself. He never did, even in his younger years, but he always found a good operative to get the job done for him. Watson leaned forward in his chair, facing Willem. "Look, Willem, this job isn't much. No tough work. No black stuff, and it can be done in one night. I'll pay double the usual fee because I want it done right away." Watson didn't add that he didn't know anyone else he could use who wouldn't report this little exercise to Washington. "It's a simple get-in-and-look-around job. If it looks like it's going to get heavy, get out as fast as you can, with as little evidence left behind as possible." He paused for effect. "You're the best around for this sort of thing."

"Ah!" Willem grinned broadly. "You flatter an old man, and flattery will always get you somewhere. Well, I'm listening. I won't promise you anything, but I'm listening." The pipe smoke created a blue haze around Willem's head, softening his angular features.

Watson settled back into the oversized cushions of his chair. "There's a company down in the port that's recycling Russian missiles, and they recently received a shipment of three large, tubular items. They're supposed to be sections of a decommissioned missile from Siberia." Watson gave Willem the name of the company.

"Yes," Willem replied. "They're often on the shady side of the law, but nobody's ever caught them entirely on the wrong side. A lot of scams run out of that company, you know. Some were created by our old friends in Moscow, and some, I think, by our old friends in Washington." Watson laughed dutifully. Though he would never say it himself, Willem was always delighted to be part of the action again.

Watson took out a small copy of a satellite image of the storage yard for the recycling company. He pointed to three elongated objects covered with tarps. "A ship left Hamburg with deck cargo consisting of one large steel pipe, destined for Narvik, and the three stages of a Russian missile out of Siberia. Everything was covered with tarps. The company here signed for the delivery of the missile, three large pieces, but I want to make sure that the missile got here." He leaned forward and spoke more softly. "I need to have someone get inside the storage area, lift up the edge of the tarps, and directly confirm that the missile stages are there. That's it."

"Ha! So you think the Russians are playing hanky-panky with one of their missiles. Fantastic!" Willem puffed on his pipe. "You know this is a job for a younger man, Watson." Willem paused and increased the smoke around his head yet again. "You say the pay is double the normal?"

"Yes."

"I could probably get my brother's grandson, Teunis Kwak, to get in there and take a look around. It's never been well guarded, you know. A few guard dogs, but that's all. You can always take care of them with some good steaks laced with tranquilizers."

Watson waved his arm. "Look, Willem, I don't care how you do it or who does it, so long as you get the information I need."

Willem stood up. "Well, then, I'll see what I can do. I'll call you tomorrow morning. Your usual hotel?"

Watson nodded and handed Willem an envelope with half the money in it. "The other half will come to you in the mail, as usual, when I have the information." Willem nodded and happily pocketed the envelope. It was an old and comfortable system, and they parted company, each pleased with himself.

Watson took a cab back to his hotel to have an excellent if somewhat heavy meal that he didn't need. He walked through the neighborhoods around the hotel after supper for some exercise. He didn't see anyone following or observing him, but he really didn't expect any problems in Copenhagen. He went to bed early. At six in the morning, a call from Willem tore him from a deep sleep. Instantly alert, he picked up the telephone. Willem sounded extremely distraught, his voice high and cracking.

"You killed him, you bastard. You killed him." Willem slipped in and out of English and Danish.

Watson could not follow what he was trying to tell him, but Willem's tone was enough on its own to bring a surge in adrenaline. "What are you talking about, Willem? Who did I kill?"

"Good God. My grandnephew, damn you. He went to look around the lot, lift up the tarps, a simple job like you said. A few minutes ago a car stopped in front of the house."

Willem made a noise Watson could not fully identify over the phone, and then it sounded as though he blew his nose. "Oh, God forgive me," he said. "I sent him to do what you told me was a simple little job, you bastard, and they sent me his head in a box!" The end was almost a scream, and Watson pulled the receiver away from his head.

"My grand-nephew. My youngest brother's only grandson. Damn you. Damn all you devils. He was just a child." Willem stopped as suddenly as he had begun. He blew his nose again. "You're a fucking bastard, Watson."

"Willem, I didn't know. Believe me, I didn't know."

Willem's cold voice gave way to anger, "Get the hell out of here, Watson. Leave me to try to explain this to his mother and father, you bastard. Don't ever come back here again. Just go!" He slammed down the telephone as he shouted out the last words, and Watson was left holding the receiver in silence.

Watson quickly took an envelope, already addressed and stamped, out of his briefcase. He dressed and packed in a few minutes. This early in the morning few people were up and about, and he checked out of the hotel without a wait. He dropped the envelope in the postbox at the corner of the lobby and went to the front of the hotel. Two taxis waited by the curb. Watson walked to the next hotel down the street and took a cab to the airport. He didn't need to be told to leave. *I'm getting too old for this shit*, he thought.

At the airport, Watson changed his reservation to an earlier flight. After takeoff, as the plane leveled off and the pilot turned off the seatbelt sign, Watson thought about Teunis Kwak's head in a box. He unbuckled his seatbelt, walked to the toilet, and quietly vomited. *Ivan and I make a great team*, he thought as he cleaned up. *Both of us are emasculated, worthless old bulls. No teeth and no balls.* Then he walked back to his seat and signaled to the young lady serving breakfast in the cabin. He ordered a scotch, to wash the taste out of his mouth.

21

EVERY MAJOR EFFORT IN DECEPTION HAS ITS VULNERABILITIES, AND Zakhar Rostov knew it. The larger the project, the larger the number of people involved. With more people, there is always a higher potential for blackmail, betrayal, and simple human error. The Nunavik affair was no exception to this rule. Success would rest upon the ability of Rostov's countermeasures to deal with the unanticipated but inevitable attacks and simple failures.

First there was the loss of Andropov and Kazakov, along with the bulk of the weapons to defend the site. That loss increased the risk, but Rostov thought the remaining security force was still robust enough. The Nunavik affair moved forward, thanks to a little bit of naïve help from the Prime Minister of Canada.

Gregori Borodin's capture in Toronto had been a potential disaster. For a while Rostov thought he would have to cancel the entire project. Gregori knew far too much. But thankfully, his elimination was quick and clean. Gregori's demise, like Andropov's and Kazakov's, was due to a combination of overconfidence and bad luck, but the most recent incident in Copenhagen was far more serious. For the first time, someone was looking for answers, and that was a dangerous development.

Rostov began to circulate rumors around the edges of the Kremlin and the Russian leadership, rumors that Ivan Dinisovich was not quite as loyal to the Russian President as it seemed. Dropped into the caldron of paranoia that was the Kremlin, they assumed the first shreds of credibility. Ivan would feel them.

In Moscow, Ivan Dinisovich once more pulled up in front of the American embassy in his large, black official car. It had not run properly for several days. Occasionally it punctuated its uneven progress with a loud belch of black smoke. His driver looked around carefully before he stepped out to open the door for Ivan. The Marine guard, forewarned, waved Ivan through with fewer questions than normal, though he still had to endure most of the normal security checks.

Ivan's guide shepherded him into the same bare conference room as before. Watson watched him arrive, sit down at the simple table, and light a bad Russian cigarette. Ivan scowled, most likely due to the foul taste of the cigarette. Ivan preferred Winstons. Watson let him wait for five long minutes before he showed up at the door. In the middle of another cigarette, Ivan stubbed it out in deference to his nonsmoking host. Watson frowned as he greeted Ivan.

"You need to turn off any recording devices, Watson. For your own good, if nothing else, this should be between us alone."

Watson studied him. Ivan was not usually so direct. Then he turned to the telephone. He spoke softly for only a moment. "The room is closed down now, Ivan. I won't guarantee that you don't have an active listening device in here, though." The last was stated with a hint of a smile.

"We don't have anything that works in this part of the building," Ivan responded, "and that's the truth."

"Yes. Well, I'll have to take your word for that." Watson stopped and looked down at the single sheet of paper he held in his hand. "I brought this for you. I'm not sure I should be talking with you."

"What is it?" Ivan asked.

Watson let the paper slide across the table to Ivan. "It's a letter from Washington."

Ivan quickly read the letter and looked up. "You're kidding?"

Watson laughed. "No. It's perfectly serious. They're forcing me into retirement. I'll be gone in two weeks." He smiled. "I shouldn't be talking with you. You should talk to Sasha Karpov, but I think she agrees with Washington that we've both sunk into some sort of counterproductive state of permanent paranoia." Watson made the word "Washington" sound almost poisonous. "I think my continued interest in the Nunavik situation may have been the final straw."

Watson smiled slightly as he said, "Times are changing for us, Ivan. Time is leaving us behind." Watson looked across at Ivan, his old adversary and finally, after many years, his friend. They had been through so much together. In some ways they had both failed. Each had ensured that the other failed simply by surviving, himself.

"What will you do?" Ivan asked simply.

Watson looked away. "I don't know. I don't want to go into the security business." Watson turned back and spoke again. "Anyway, perhaps there's still something we can do together in the little time I have left."

Watson could see that his retirement had caught Ivan by surprise. Watson realized that Ivan was already trying to find a polite way to cut this meeting short. *Shit*, he thought. *Ivan too will find me useless.*

"You may be disappointed by what I tell you today," Ivan said. "It isn't much, only a name: Helmut Fankhauser."

"Am I supposed to know the name?"

Ivan shook his head. "I'd be quite surprised if you knew it. Helmut was a rather obscure computer programmer in our missile program, from the former East Germany. His specialty was programs for the guidance and targeting systems for our missiles. Like many others, his job disappeared with the cuts in the program." Normally Ivan talked with animation, but today his hands were still, folded quietly on the table. "Helmut is on the second ship to Wakeham Bay, with the supplies and materials for the Randal Lake mine. There's another man, too, a man who goes by the name of Igor Luchenko. It is an assumed name. It turns out he's one of our best missile engineers. He was instrumental in the design and construction of many of our intercontinental missiles. He had the lead position in the design team for the Topol-M."

"Probably they're ordinary crew members," Watson stated with a small dismissive wave of his hand. "Stranger things have happened. Men have to survive and feed their families." Watson had a sudden and unpleasant realization that he was sounding exactly like Andy Boyles in Washington, finding ways to explain away unpleasant possibilities.

"Yes. Indeed, stranger things have happened." Ivan cocked his head to one side, and with a half-smile he continued. "I suppose they could be looking after the mining equipment, or potatoes maybe, but I wouldn't bet on that. Would you?"

Watson looked across the table at Ivan. "So you still believe, in spite of everything, that an ICBM was on the ship to Wakeham Bay?"

"Yes."

"And you still think Zakhar Rostov controls it?"

"Yes. Randal Lake is Rostov's project."

"Do you think he plans to sell it or use it?"

"I don't know, but I'm pretty damn confident it's headed to where there's a ready-made missile silo."

Watson thought for a moment. "Tell me, Ivan, how long do you think it would take these guys to put a missile back together, in condition to sell it or use it?"

Ivan took his time to respond. "It depends on how carefully it was taken apart, how well it was handled in shipment, all of that.

Perhaps two months, maybe less. Fankhauser and Luchenko have the expertise, and probably the people, to do it, do it well, and do it quickly." Ivan stopped and looked at his hands.

The two men sat in silence, neither looking at the other. Ivan continued to look down at his hands, and Watson stared past him at the blank walls. Finally, Watson spoke again. "No one in Washington believes us. They're all convinced that you're telling me a bunch of bullshit to make me look like a fool. I guess we've been playing this game too long to start to really trust each other now."

Ivan looked up. "Why do you still listen to me, then?"

"I don't know the answer to that question," Watson replied, turning to face him with a smile. "I just have a bad feeling. I don't know about you, but I've never thought that the game we've played for so many years is a game of logic. It's a game of feelings. It's about getting inside someone's head. It's also about experience, about knowing what people like Zakhar Rostov are really capable of doing to us. Perhaps it's because I know from direct experience that at least one man has already died because of this story you've told me." The two men looked intently at each other. "Perhaps it's only that I'm an old fool."

Softly, "Thank you for your belief in me."

"Don't thank me, Ivan. You could use a stronger man than me. I'll be gone soon. Already I have no credibility in Washington, but there may be a couple of things I can do." Watson leaned forward, closer to Ivan. "I leave for Washington this week, to prepare for my retirement, all the debriefings, signatures, mind bending, all that stuff. I'll stop in Toronto along the way. I had several programs where I worked closely with the Canadians in the Arctic. I still have good contacts in the Canadian intelligence community. They're a small group, but they're very dedicated. Have you heard of a man called Richard Durban?"

Ivan nodded. "I've heard of him and know something about him. I haven't met him."

Watson sat back in his chair. "Richard's a good man. In spite of some of his personal choices, I trust him completely. When I stop in Toronto I'll talk to him. I think I'll be able to convince him to arrange for an examination of the Randal Lake site and the second ship's cargo when it's unloaded at Wakeham Bay. If the Canadians do that, we should know whether to be worried or not." Watson ran his fingers through his hair. "It should at least give us fair warning."

"I would greatly appreciate that. Let me know if you find out anything more, and tell this Durban to keep me informed." Ivan pushed his chair back and stood up. "There is one more thing. I believe that Rostov has someone, maybe several people, in place in Canada."

"Is there anything you can do about Rostov?"

"The President and I will handle that, but it will take time. The military is not entirely reliable in such matters these days. There are many in the military, or recently removed from it, who sympathize with and actively support people like Rostov." Ivan continued, "Anyway, I don't think that anything we do here in Russia will stop Zakhar Rostov's intentions, even if his entire organization in Russia is annihilated. He will have some sort of failsafe plan in place." Ivan paused. "Be careful. Trust no one."

"I'll be careful."

"Please keep in touch if you can, and let me know what Richard Durban thinks."

Watson jumped up with surprising agility and took Ivan's hand in both of his. "The world is changing, Ivan. Try to stay well."

"And you as well."

"One more question. You must know more details of Rostov's plans. You have to give me more."

Ivan stood quietly for a moment, then said, "I must go."

"Yes." Watson opened the door. "Try to tell me while there's still time."

Ivan looked directly at Watson but remained silent. Then he turned, gestured to the guard, and the two of them walked quietly down the hallway. The bitter taste of fear that Watson had first felt in Copenhagen rose again. He asked himself, *Is it too late already, Ivan?*

22

TWO DAYS AFTER THE MEETING WITH IVAN, WATSON SAT IN ONE OF the exit rows in the tourist section of an Air Canada 747 as it touched down at the Toronto Pearson International Airport. Watson didn't believe in wasting taxpayers' money, and he refused the extra cost of business class. As the plane came to a stop at the gate, he waited patiently as the tourists gathered their Russian dolls and souvenirs and made their way off the plane. When he finally came up the jetway, he could see Richard Durban standing to the side, waiting for him.

"Hello, Watson," said Dick. "Still traveling cattle class, I see. I have someone picking up your baggage. They'll bring it to the hotel. We'll take a shortcut to my car." Watson realized with considerable regret that this trip would likely be the last time he would enjoy the luxury of bypassing customs and immigration.

"So, are you looking forward to retirement?" Dick asked.

"You surely know the answer to that question," Watson growled with some irritation. "How are you doing these days? Your choice of lifestyle hasn't made your keepers show you an early exit?" They walked quickly, and Watson strained to keep up with Dick Durban's pace.

Dick looked at Watson beside him with a trace of a smile, but Watson continued to look straight ahead. Dick could count on Watson being blunt and direct. "Ah, we're a bit more tolerant here than in the United States, though I have noticed that you are catching up with us." Dick continued, "Why are they pushing you out so early? I thought you had at least a couple of years left."

Watson grunted. "Well, Dick, they think I'm past it, over the hill, scared of my own shadow, an obstructionist, you name it. Basically, they find me inconvenient. To be honest, I'm beginning to think they may be right."

They came out of the building into bright sunlight and a secured, guarded parking lot for VIPs and government officials. Dick got into an unobtrusive four-door sedan and unlocked the door for Watson. Unobtrusive as the car might appear, it had many similarities to the high-tech and heavily armored car Watson had used in Moscow. As he pulled away from his parking space, Dick asked Watson, "What do you know about what's going on up at Randal Lake in Nunavik?"

Christ! People are starting to read my mind, thought Watson. *I hope to God I'm not that obvious.* He pushed away the sense of irritation. "Strange you should ask that. I'm not sure I know anything, but it is one reason why I wanted to talk with you. The truth is, it's probably the main reason I've been forced into retirement. Someone has not appreciated my interest in that place." Watson paused and looked over at Dick as he drove. "We should wait to talk until we have a secure place to do it."

"That's fine. I'll take you to your hotel first. Get cleaned up and get a bit of rest, then come over to my office."

A few minutes later, Dick pulled up to the front entrance of the old and rather venerable Royal York Hotel. Old, solid, and traditional, the Royal York was a lot like Watson. Though it had once been the largest hotel in the British Empire, like Watson's career, its prominence had declined over time. Recent renovations had buffed up the old lady to a pleasant state of experienced modernity, but if the hotel was full Watson knew that the elevators would be as slow as ever.

Though tired from his trip, by long habit Watson would not sleep until after nine at night, local time, after crossing so many time zones. After a long shower, a shave, and a change of clothes he felt much better. He ate a light lunch and walked over to Dick Durban's office.

Dick had alerted the gatekeepers, and they let Watson in with a minimum of fuss. A guide took him to Dick's outer office, a kind of waiting room. Shortly, Dick appeared at the door and ushered him in to his inner office, which occupied a cement cube in the interior of the building. The lack of windows was a simple and cheap security precaution. Only two photographs adorned the walls. In one, Dick posed with the Prime Minister, and in the other he escorted Queen Elizabeth on one of her state visits to Canada.

Dick placed his hands on the desk. "So, what really brings you here, Watson? The little projects we're working on could be sorted out over the telephone. What has you interested in Randal Lake?"

"Dick, this has to be strictly off the record. You know I'm not allowed at this stage to talk about anything and certainly not to an agent of another country."

Dick settled back in his chair. "I know," he smiled. "We share a border, but we never share our secrets."

Watson, too, relaxed and settled into his chair. "No one in Washington believes I'm making sense, and I'm beginning to wonder myself. Whatever's going on, it appears to be on your turf."

Dick smiled and gestured for Watson to continue. "Well, fire away. I'll listen, and then I'll tell you what we have at this end."

Watson sighed. "Dick, I still believe that this has the potential to be something extremely bad." Watson took a deep breath and began his story. It took a while. He finished with Ivan's warning about Rostov's man in Canada. When he stopped, there was a long silence in the room. Watson looked at Dick, who was staring at the wall, deep in thought. Finally, Dick broke the silence.

"You can be sure I won't simply dismiss what you've told me." Dick ticked off the reasons on his fingers. "First, we've been seeing a lot of strange activity around Randal Lake recently. We've known from the beginning that Serg Ochenko was sent to Canada by the KGB. We've been watching him closely for a long time. It's possible he's Rostov's man, but he's always behaved himself. However, recently, a Russian pretending to be a German contacted him to set up a joint venture on Randal Lake. The deal was made and signed in short order, and this is quite uncharacteristic for World Nickel. Third, a geologist working near Randal Lake intercepted an impressive cache of weapons near his camp: assault rifles, machine guns, even surface-to-air and antitank missiles."

Dick leaned forward with a smile. "Two rather unpleasant ex–KGB types attacked the geologist, by the way. They quickly regretted their rashness. The geologist is one of your ex–Navy SEALs." Dick returned his attention to his fingers. "Fourth, a friend of mine was attacked by the man who contacted Serg about the deal on Randal Lake. She sent him to the hospital, rather badly damaged, I might add. Before we could even interview the guy, an assassin broke the guy's neck. Right under our noses, in the hospital. So now, counting your man in Copenhagen, we seem to have four bodies on our hands, all related in some way to Randal Lake."

Watson held up his hands in a gesture of frustration. "So what can we do about it? I can't get any help for you from the CIA." He continued more pensively, "I might still be able to talk to Ivan. In a strange way, we've actually become good friends. I'm convinced he's holding back on something, and I think it's something pretty important."

Dick turned quiet. "You know that the Russians asked us to check on the cargo of a ship that left Hamburg harbor?" Watson allowed himself a small smile. "We could check only the ship that was destined for Canada and Wakeham Bay. It all looked like legitimate cargo for the mining and rehabilitation operation at Randal Lake." Dick looked intently at Watson across his desk. "Now, you and I can make some guesses, and we can believe firmly in the validity of those guesses. The politicians can't or won't accept that. They have to know something is one hundred percent correct, without risk. You know our Prime Minister. He doesn't want any international incidents."

Watson thought about what they had to go on. Nothing really, no hard evidence. This wasn't going anywhere. Watson began to feel depressed again.

"I do have one person up in Nunavik, in a little geological exploration camp. I put him up there after that geologist found all the weapons and had his run-in with the ex–KGB guys. My man is a trained helicopter mechanic, so I sent him up there to 'work' in that capacity. He's already checked on the first shipment of materials and equipment for Randal Lake. I'll ask him to make an official inspection of that last shipment." Dick shrugged. "If all he finds is a few big pipes and mining supplies, I guess we ought to be able to relax."

"How confident are you of your man in Nunavik?" Watson regretted asking the question almost before it came out of his mouth.

"You mean, do I think he might be Rostov's man in Canada?" Dick shook his head. "No. I'm one hundred percent sure of Charlie Sturm." Dick smiled as he studied Watson. "He's young, enthusiastic, a real patriot, intelligent, speaks four languages, and he hasn't had a blemish on his record the whole time he's worked for me. We can trust him. I'm sure of it."

Watson stopped short of pressing the issue. He took a deep breath and responded, "That's good enough for me. Give me a call in Washington when you have the results of the inspection. I'll still be on board for another ten days or so."

"No problem. I'll call Charlie tonight and set it up." Dick grinned across the desk at the somber Watson. "Cheer up. After we're done today, I'll take you out to dinner at one of our great restaurants. You remember Watson's? The name is a good recommendation, I think."

"I'm not so sure that's the case anymore," Watson replied with a sad smile.

23

FOR THE NEXT FEW DAYS, PETER TRIED TO FOCUS ON HIS TASKS FOR the mining company. As he and Maria worked on the geological maps one evening in the office tent, the telephone rang. Dick Durban identified himself.

"Is that you, Peter?"

"Yes. What can I do for you? I trust things have calmed down in Toronto?"

"Uh, not entirely. Is Charlie around?"

"Yeah, I think he's in the cook tent. You want me to get him for you?"

"Yes, please."

Peter hesitated. "Can you tell me what it's about?"

"He needs to make a visit to examine the cargo that's being unloaded at Wakeham Bay. It needs to be an official RCMP visit."

"You know we made a visit already and examined the cargo?"

"Yes, but there's a second ship now. I want to be sure the cargo is what they say it is."

"I'll get him," Peter responded. He walked the few feet to the cook tent and roused Charlie from a cribbage game with the cook. "Dick

Durban's on the phone, and he wants to talk to you." They walked back to the office tent. "You can take the telephone down to the lake and call him back if you want some privacy."

"Shouldn't be a problem, Peter." Charlie picked up the telephone. "How are you, Dick? What's up?"

Peter sat on the edge of his bed and watched Charlie's broad back. "No problem," Charlie concluded. "I'll get a report back to you in a day or two." After a pause, "Sure. I'll talk to you then." Charlie stood up and turned around.

"What's up?" Peter asked.

Charlie looked down at Peter. "My boss wants me to make an official visit to the landing site for the two ships that unloaded at Wakeham Bay. I'm supposed to check on the cargo." He lowered his voice and continued, "I'll have to put on my uniform for the visit. That should be a bit of a surprise to those guys." Charlie grinned. "I think I'll get myself together outside of the camp. I don't want to make a big show of my official capacity."

"You mind if I tag along?" Peter thought he already knew the answer.

Charlie shook his head. "I think I'd better make this trip on my own. It's all supposed to be official, you know, and the fewer civilians along the better, don't you think?"

Peter didn't say what he was thinking, but he was relieved that Charlie had at least told the truth about the phone call. "Yeah, I suppose you're right. Anyway, I should get on with my work. NorthGold doesn't pay me to play policeman. Let me know your plans." As Charlie was about to leave, Peter sat down at the table again. With a gesture at the maps, he said, "I want Arnie to set me out on one of the grids tomorrow morning, and I don't want to get stuck out there all day unless I have enough work to keep me busy. I'll try to keep close to camp. That way I can walk back if I have to."

"It's probably a good idea if you, Maria, and the others stay close to home tomorrow. I expect this little exercise might take me most of the day," Charlie said. With a nod in Peter's direction and a smile for Maria, Charlie let the door close behind him and left to return to his cribbage game.

"Well, that's interesting," Maria commented as she got up from her bunk.

"Yeah, I guess it is," Peter said as he looked up from the table. "Let's see if we can get these maps up to date before we turn in for the night."

The next day Arnie flew Peter, Tom, and Maria a few miles south to their work area for the day. Peter and Maria would spend the day mapping and sampling several promising zones of quartz veins in iron-stained outcrops of sheared and broken dark volcanic rocks. Tom would spend most of the day with the portable pneumatic drill, preparing to blast three trenches across the most promising outcrops for more sampling. After Arnie refueled at the camp, he took off with Charlie to the east. Peter briefly watched the helicopter in the distance, and he wondered whether Charlie's inspection would be as thorough as Dick Durban expected. He shook his head. *Not my job,* he thought. He pulled out his maps and he and Maria got to work.

"Set down at Esker Lake for a couple of minutes," Charlie told Arnie as they flew to the east. "I have to get into uniform for this visit." Arnie looked over at him but said nothing. "This shouldn't take too long." Arnie selected a flat spot at the shore of the lake, set the helicopter down, and set the fuel flow to an idle as Charlie pulled his duffle bag out of the back seat of the helicopter. Charlie changed at a distance to keep his clothes from blowing away.

When he was finished, Charlie looked quite official and dapper in his uniform. He wore the standard issue, regular-duty gray shirt, with dark pants with their regulation broad yellow stripe. He had the standard, constable-style hat with the yellow band and a fully equipped belt complete with the standard-issue pistol. Arnie had to admit that it was a somewhat startling transformation from his slightly grease-stained khaki pants and shirt. Once Charlie got back into the helicopter, he took off his hat and put his flight helmet on again as Arnie powered up to take off.

Charlie looked at Arnie. "I'll need to set down for a while at Randal Lake before we go to Wakeham Bay. I have to look at what's already arrived at the mine site, besides what's on the beach at Wakeham Bay."

"No problem, Charlie. I'll shut it down for as long as you like. I've got my book to read, and I need to do some cleaning anyway. My mechanic doesn't always keep the Plexiglas clean," he said with a grin at Charlie. Charlie ignored him.

As they flew east, the headframe at Randal Lake, at least what was left of it, rose above the horizon. Charlie leaned forward, subconsciously urging the helicopter forward. The sooner this task was over, the happier he would be. He hoped he'd find Shawn Schmitz at the Randal Lake site. Presumably, Arnie would exhibit his usual complete lack of interest in anything other than his books and the helicopter. Shawn knew his role, and Charlie didn't want any screwups on this trip. They had to set this up and execute it properly.

As they approached the headframe, Charlie looked at the small group of men who left their work. A new windsock flapped in the gusting wind. *Arnie will appreciate that*, thought Charlie. Wind direction was always a challenge in this barren land. There was no room for their helicopter to land on the smooth, cement landing area where the two large Russian helicopters were parked. Arnie pointed at them. "Next to those things, I feel like I'm flying a mosquito."

Charlie breathed a silent sigh of relief when he saw Shawn lead the way to where Arnie was coming in to land. Arnie made a last-minute turn, headed into the wind, and landed quickly and smoothly about a hundred feet away from the bigger machines. As soon as the skids were down, Charlie had the door open. He bent over and half-ran over to Shawn Schmitz, holding his hat.

"Mein Gott!" exclaimed Shawn in German with a broad grin as he extended his hand to Charlie. "Have you lost your sled dogs?" The men with Shawn laughed at his joke.

"Very funny," Charlie responded in English. "Look, this is an official visit, and you and I need to go somewhere to talk in private."

The grin quickly faded from Shawn's face. "Not a problem. Follow me to my office." He made a few remarks to the other men, and they turned to get back to their work. Charlie could see that they had been busy. The entire top of the headframe was cut away, but close to the ground, most of the original structure remained in place.

Shawn looked over at Charlie as they walked. "You're wondering, perhaps, where we are in our plans?"

Charlie pointed at the headframe. "At the moment, I'm wondering if that thing is about to fall down."

Shawn looked over at the headframe. "Oh, it'll stand up fine. Anyway, once we're done with it, I don't know if it will ever be used again."

"So, the schedule? How are you doing?"

"We'll be done by the end of July or early August. I want to make sure that all of us are out of here on time. I don't want to be around here when they pull the damned trigger." Shawn opened the door to a small building near the headframe, and they walked into his empty office. "Now, what's so secret that we have to hide to talk about it?" They stood facing each other in the small construction office.

"Like I said, my visit is official. My boss in Toronto has told me to do a thorough inspection of the cargo, particularly the cargo from the second ship at Wakeham Bay." Shawn raised his eyebrows at the news. "We both know what's down there. I want to make sure I inspect the right packages. If it's done right, I shouldn't have to examine all of them, at least not in detail, but it has to look good for the sake of my pilot."

"Can't we just leave him here and go down to the bay ourselves?"

Charlie shook his head. "No, I don't think that's a good idea. It can't look like I'm afraid of having a witness watch me."

Shawn nodded. "I suppose you're right. Anyway, it's easy for you to select the right package. It's down by itself, closer to the water than the rest of them. The other three are farther away from the beach. Two of them are already on flatbed trucks, ready to be moved up here." Shawn paused a moment in thought. "I'll call the foreman at the beach. I'll tell him to act upset about the time required to help you with your inspection. That should make for a convincing inspection for your pilot."

"That's a good idea."

"Your pilot doesn't speak German does he?"

"Not that I know of."

"Good. We'll speak only German then." Shawn took the few steps to the desk in the small office and picked up the telephone. The satellite connection would be a long one to call a few miles, but it was relatively secure. He still had no ground line between the bay and the mine site.

The conversation in German was simple enough "There's an RCMP man here who needs to inspect the cargo from the second ship. He has to look at one of the large packages, the one down by the water. You understand?"

"Sure. I understand."

"Well, he'll say he wants to look at all of them, but this is a pain in the ass. It's interrupting our work. You understand?"

With some impatience the man answered, "Look, it is a pain in the ass. We have two of them loaded and ready to travel. You should get them on-site tomorrow. You ready for them?"

Shawn laughed. "Yes. We'll be ready. Just get them up here in one piece."

"Don't worry. I'll see you tomorrow with the shipment."

"No, I'll see you in a couple of hours. I'll be there for the inspection."

Shawn turned to Charlie after he hung up. "I presume you need to do a walk-through here as well?"

"Yes. I have to appear to be thorough. Besides," he said with a grin, "I'd actually like to see how things are going."

"Follow me," Shawn responded, and the two left the office.

Arnie watched Charlie and Shawn progress on the inspection tour. First they went into a small building next to the shaft. Then they progressed to the shaft, looked around at some new cement construction at the base of the old headframe, and then walked in and out of most of the buildings around the shaft itself. They were taking their time. There was lots of gesturing at some of the stops.

Charlie walked with sure, quick steps, his uniform clearly setting him apart from the rest of the workers. Shawn, heavyset and muscular from years of construction work, walked with shorter steps but with an aggressive purpose that left no doubt that he was in charge.

Charlie and Shawn were putting on a good act for Arnie's benefit. Charlie figured Arnie would be his normal bored and uninterested self, but he couldn't be sure. Arnie was a veteran from the Gulf, and Charlie knew that someone like Arnie never completely forgot his training. A little bit of a show wouldn't hurt anything.

After two hours, Charlie and Shawn walked over to the helicopter. "Time to head down to Wakeham Bay, Arnie. This is Shawn Schmitz. I think you met him on our first visit. He's the project manager here, and he's coming along with us."

"Pleased to meet you," Shawn said with a heavy German accent, extending his hand to Arnie.

Arnie nodded, shook his hand, and said, "Well, hop in, buckle up, and we'll be on our way. Shouldn't take more than a few minutes."

None of them spoke on the short trip to the beach, where most of the cargo lay in apparent confusion. Shawn told Arnie where to land, and Shawn and Charlie were out of the helicopter as soon as he touched down, talking to the foreman. As Arnie shut down, he noticed that the foreman was not happy about the inspection, protesting in loud German. In the end, though, the foreman stalked off with Charlie and Shawn to wander through the jumble of equipment and containers on the beach.

The helicopter sat on a small hill to the side of the beach, about a hundred yards away from any of the equipment. Dozens of containers littered the beach area. Piles of fuel drums and heavy equipment were interspersed with the containers. Four large cylinders, covered with a heavy tan fabric, stood out in the confusion. Two were already on flatbed trailers. A third lay in a cradle of timbers beside the trailers, and a fourth was separate from the others, closer to the helicopter and close to the water's edge.

Charlie walked up to the closest of the four large cylinders. "I want to inspect this. You need to remove the covering to let me see it," Charlie said to the foreman, still speaking in German.

"Christ almighty! Do you know how much work that is? We've got a deadline to meet here."

Charlie thought the foreman's show of reluctance was convincing enough. Charlie didn't think Arnie could hear any of their conversation, and being in German it probably didn't matter, but he also knew they had to produce this little play as realistically as possible. "Look, I'm sorry, but I have my orders, and I have to inspect all of the cargo here."

After much gesturing, the foreman gathered a number of workers, and they began the laborious process of removing the fabric covering. Actually, they removed the covering only from the end facing the helicopter, but that still took a significant amount of time. Even from a distance, it was obvious that the partially uncovered object was a large, empty pipe.

Charlie walked up the hill to the other three cylinders. He pointed to the one on the ground. Eventually, after an extended conversation, Charlie walked over to the large cylinder, walked around it, ran his hand along the fabric covering, and peered inside through a small opening. The foreman gave him a flashlight. Charlie stepped back, showing he was satisfied. Charlie looked back at the helicopter. Arnie was cleaning the Plexiglas.

Late in the afternoon, Charlie finished looking at all the material on the beach. He had looked under tarps, opened boxes, opened storage containers, and examined most of the equipment on the beach. Charlie had generally made quite a pest of himself. They had stood for some time at one large crate, set aside from the rest of the cargo. Even though they made no effort to open or examine the contents, it captured their attention for a long time.

As Charlie climbed into the helicopter, Shawn Schmitz commented in English, "Sorry about Rolf. He isn't usually so hard to get along with. He's got a tight schedule to get all this stuff off the beach and up to the mine site."

Charlie shook Shawn's hand. "Oh, I understand. I know my visit wasn't exactly part of the plan, and I hate being a pain in the ass. We'll get out of your hair and get back to camp." Charlie smiled broadly at Shawn. Then he turned to Arnie. "Let's go home, Arnie." As Arnie started the engine, Shawn shut the door. He would make his own way back to the mine site later.

Back at the camp that night, Peter listened as Charlie sat at the telephone in the office tent and gave his report to Dick Durban. "Arnie and I went over to Randal Lake and down to the bay," Charlie reported, "where they unload the equipment. It all looks pretty normal to me, a bunch of mining junk."

Peter listened to the one-sided conversation with considerable interest. Maria lay back on her bed. She, too, carefully considered what Charlie was saying.

"Look, if they're doing something weird over there, it's sure not obvious," Charlie said. "From all I can see, they're just refurbishing the road and the shaft and reopening the buildings at the mine site to prepare for the next phase of development. Nothing to worry about there."

Charlie was silent again, listening to Dick. The canvas on the tent slapped lightly against the plywood wall with the evening breeze. The different winds all had their own voices in the camp. This light wind had a low whistle as it tested the corners of the tents. Peter and the others didn't really hear the wind anymore. It was just part of the background noise of the camp.

"Sure. No problem," Charlie said as he ran his already sunburned fingers through his curly blond hair. "I expected to stay a while anyway, but this sure looks like an easy job." He continued to listen to Durban. "Yeah, sure. I'll call if I see anything suspicious. Talk to you later."

Charlie disconnected from the call and turned to see Peter watching him intently. He smiled. "Well, that takes care of that. I think we can relax."

Without smiling, Peter responded, "Good. I do need to get some actual work done around here. That's what they're paying me to do."

"Yep. Well, I'm going to see if I can beat Roland at cribbage tonight."

After Charlie left, Maria didn't move. "Well?" she asked.

"Well, what?"

She raised herself up on one elbow and hissed not much above a whisper, "For Christ's sake, what do you think?"

Peter shook his head as he got up from the bed and walked over to the little worktable. Softly he responded, "It sounds a little pat to me, but it's not my job. I need to do some mapping, and if I can do that in peace and quiet, that's exactly what I plan to do."

The CIA computers ran for twenty-four hours a day. Andy Boyles might forget his instructions, but the computers would continue to follow them, day after day. They would sift and sort, as they tried to find the one communication that would bring down a terrorist cell or prevent an attack, or in this case find anything that had any relevance to activity at Randal Lake in Nunavik. One of the communications systems that the computers routinely reviewed was the satellite telephone systems, including the one used by Shawn Schmitz when he called Rolf at the beach. Nothing in the conversation would have triggered the selection program, except for the low-level flag on Nunavik and Randal Lake, placed there by Andy Boyles.

Several days later, a translated transcript of the conversation reached Andy's desk for his review. He glanced at it, not understanding at first why he had received this piece of information. After a moment of thought, the location clicked in his mind, and he took another look.

The conversation sounded like a discussion with a manager who was frustrated at governmental interference in a project with a tight schedule. Andy Boyles picked up the phone and called to remove the alert. With a quick flick of his hand, Andy dropped the sheet into the shredder. He promptly forgot about Nunavik and moved on to his other work.

People generally hear what they want to hear. Dick Durban was no exception. He found it convenient to let his concerns slip away. He had a reliable man on-site who reported that all was quiet and that a normal development program was underway at Randal Lake. The Prime Minister believed in the inherent goodness of all people. Dick knew he didn't want to hear anything more about the Nunavik affair. In his monthly security report to the Prime Minister, Captain Durban reported on the alert from Watson and the deaths of Leonid Andropov, Vladimir Kazakov, and Gregori Borodin. In his conclusions he indicated that the RCMP man on-site had conducted a thorough examination of the mine site and the cargo shipped to Wakeham Bay. The man had found normal supplies for a mine development program, including four large, steel pipes to be used as shaft liners. It had been a lot of commotion over a bunch of empty pipes.

Harold James branded all of Watson's ideas as both crazy and unsupported. With that, Harold ensured that Watson's ideas found little audience in Washington. No one in the CIA bucked Harold without giving serious thought to the consequences. Harold made sure that what evidence Watson had gathered quickly disappeared as soon as he retired. In this case, with some special help from Harold, the disappearance was a little quicker and more thorough than normal. Watson and his concerns, having no champions in Washington, disappeared from view.

Ivan lost access to the President. His old allies in Moscow and the rest of Russia were abandoning him. A series of carefully planted and cultivated reports and complaints made Ivan appear to be out of touch and a bit incompetent. Ivan suspected that Zakhar Rostov was in excellent spirits. Ivan was not without assets within the Kremlin, and he survived. In spite of the rumors he continued to probe the edges of his suspicions.

24

ROSTOV PRESENTED AN EVER-PRESENT AND EVER-GROWING DANGER to the Russian President's position, even if the President didn't entirely believe Ivan's concerns about him. Rostov also represented an overwhelming danger to the country and to the government, but that was a secondary matter. Eliminating the man would present its own set of risks. The Russian legislative assembly, the Duma, might unite against the President, but the President thought that was unlikely.

Zakhar Rostov had advance warning of the raid on his office, in spite of every precaution. He had little time, though, and he was lucky to escape to his dacha, only a few miles outside of Saint Petersburg. There his personal security forces prepared for the inevitable.

General Khabarovsk had gathered his most loyal forces carefully. He didn't expect serious problems, but he made sure he had sufficient equipment and personnel in place to respond to any possible reaction from Rostov. From another nearby dacha, the general ordered the assault.

The first squads approached the dacha in armored personnel carriers. They raced up the rutted road, dodging only the largest of the potholes. The two vehicles came to a squealing and clanking stop at the top of a small rise on the road, about one mile from Rostov's dacha, and the soldiers made a last check of their equipment. They looked forward to exiting the vehicles. Already the smell of sweaty bodies and other, more unpleasant odors, mixed with the diesel fumes from the engine. It formed a cloud in the vehicles that was fast becoming almost unbreathable.

The general listened as the lead driver calmly reported on his view of the outbuildings and a portion of the dacha ahead of him. He reported no movement or activity. Then the radio crackled to life with the scream from the driver, "Shit! Missiles!" The noise that followed marked the elimination of the first squad of his best soldiers.

The young driver of the second vehicle screamed into his mouthpiece as he jerked back in his seat with the noise and force of the explosion. "Damn it! They're fucking gone!" He slammed the vehicle into reverse, and the general listened as debris rained down on its metal roof. The soldiers in the second vehicle, surprised by the sudden explosion and movement, sprawled painfully on the floor, tangled with their equipment and shouting curses. Within a few seconds, with the shelter of the small rise between him and the dacha, the driver stopped the vehicle with another jerk.

"The bastards have antitank missiles," the second driver shouted. "They took out Anatoli's vehicle right in front of us."

The general grabbed the communications officer's mouthpiece, "Where did they come from?"

"Hell! I don't have any fucking idea of where they came from. I never saw them. All I heard was Anatoli screaming, and then he was hit. We're dead meat if we go in on this road."

"Pull back a mile and get off the radio."

The general's cell phone rang. It was the squad leader in the second vehicle, and the general smiled at his resourcefulness.

The squad leader said brusquely, "We're getting out of the vehicle. We'll see what the hell is going on." The general could hear the fifteen other soldiers cursing the driver as they gathered their equipment together. Then he heard the driver, almost frantic to respond to his orders, shout, "They want me to pull back a mile."

"Just shut up, soldier, and stay put," the squad leader responded. Then, speaking directly to the general, "Sir, we'll report to you by telephone."

"Good. I'll be there shortly. I'll bring up some heavy support."

The general was furious. He cursed the loss of surprise and cursed his overconfidence. With some disgust, he considered that Rostov's soldiers were probably much better paid than his own, and from the looks of this first contact, they might be better equipped. He was confident that he could still outgun Rostov. This had to be quick. The President demanded that. With a grimace, he accepted that the time for subtlety had passed, and he turned sharply to his aide.

"Tell the tank crews to move up. For the moment they are to stay behind the cover of the last rise in the road before the dacha. The artillery stays here. Open fire on the dacha immediately. Move the rest of the men and the artillery spotters up to the same hill, and tell the Mi-17 crews that I want them ready to fly. Get my damned driver. I have to get up there and see what's going on." The general grabbed his coat.

The general found the squad leader at the lip of the small hill. He flopped down in the mud beside the man and looked toward the dacha with his binoculars. Artillery shells were already falling on and around the dacha. The ground shook, and the explosions were deafening. The squad leader, lying in the mud, tried to salute but gave up on it. The general smiled slightly. *A good man*, he thought, *a man with some initiative.*

"Tell me what you know," the general shouted above the noise.

"They are well prepared. You can see some cement bunkers."

The general scanned the open ground before him. It had been carefully cleared. No place for the attackers to hide. Scattered around the dacha, low, barely visible cement slabs marked the individual bunkers. "Yes. I see them." He continued to examine the ground in front of him. "This won't be easy." *It will cost too many lives*, he thought. He turned to his aide. "Get to the artillery spotters. Tell them to finish off the dacha and then focus on the bunkers they can see. I want the artillery to cease in fifteen minutes."

The general moved the rest of his men into position. A small group quickly maneuvered through the woods to position themselves behind the dacha. When the artillery ceased, the helicopters moved in to systematically strafe any defensive positions. A surface-to-air missile greeted the first helicopter. The pilot jigged the machine violently and fired off a series of flares. The missile exploded harmlessly. The second helicopter turned its attention on the source of the missile and the strafing continued. The general winced as a missile hit one helicopter. With a gaudy explosion it fell like a crippled bird to the ground. Gradually, the return fire from the dacha's defenses began to die out. The general brought six heavy tanks up over the rise, confident that any missile threat to them was already minimized. The tanks quickly completed the job of eliminating any effective resistance.

Within an hour, it was over. Only a few smoking remnants marked the location of the dacha. His men moved into the bunkers, searching for survivors among the defenders. The general didn't expect to see any. By that evening it was apparent that Zakhar Rostov was not among the many corpses in and around the dacha. Without a body to prove otherwise, General Khabarovsk had to assume that Rostov had escaped, probably only moments before his forces had arrived. He was not pleased.

It was a difficult report to bring to the President, and the general sighed. In the old days he would have already been on his way to Siberia, or executed. *I guess there are some benefits to the new regime*, he thought. The door opened and the President's administrative aide beckoned for him to enter. He got to his feet reluctantly and heavily, but he walked erect, stiff-backed as an old and proud soldier into the inner room. A tall, powerful man, he carried with him the assumption of command.

"Ah, General Khabarovsk, come in. Sit down." The President had a small smile on his face and gestured to a chair in front of his desk. "I gather from your reports that we did not do as well as we had hoped. We have to assume that Rostov is still alive."

"Yes, he was well prepared, Mr. President." The general sat stiffly in the hard-backed chair. "The attack cost me forty-five good men, loyal to me and to you. You never told me why we attacked the dacha or what to expect as a defense." He was sounding belligerent, he realized. It was not a good way to start with the President, particularly after a flawed mission. "I apologize, Mr. President. I have no right to talk to you in this manner."

The President, a smaller man than the general, sank back into his chair. The depth of his fatigue showed clearly on his face. "It is I who should apologize to you. You and your troops have shown true loyalty to the government, and I have come to trust almost no one these days." The President got up from his desk and walked over to the window.

The President turned back to the general, his hands clasped behind his back. He spoke softly. "It's a long story, General Khabarovsk, and I'll try not to bore you with details. You can find them in the reports I will give you. Essentially, Ivan Dinisovich discovered that someone has stolen a fully operable Topol-M ICBM and the warhead to go with it. The more Ivan looked into all this, the more he saw the signs of Rostov's involvement. Zakhar Rostov is a powerful and wealthy man. You know his views, and you know that he has a strong following, particularly in some of the old guard in the military."

The general did not change his hard expression. Little could surprise him now, not after so many years of surviving the intrigues of the Kremlin. "Yes. They all want us to return to the good old days, so long as they're the ones in charge. I can only imagine what he might do with his own nuclear threat." He paused. "Is it actually operational?"

"We believe so."

"How could this happen?"

The President stared grimly at the general. "Money, enough of it, can buy almost anything in Russia. Rostov has plenty of money and enough supporters all through the government and the military."

"Well, you raided his offices, and we destroyed his dacha. He's either dead, on the run, or in hiding. So what can he do now?"

"Rostov is no fool. We think the missile is installed in a mine shaft in the far north of Canada, but Rostov has put many layers of deception in place. His operatives eliminated anyone who got close to critical people or got too close to discovering the truth. The Americans and Canadians don't believe we have any reason for concern. Up until very recently we haven't been able to give them evidence strong enough to counter Rostov's deceptions."

The President stepped back to his desk and sat down heavily. "That's where you come into the picture. I had hoped to eliminate the entire scenario by eliminating Rostov, but I fear I have done nothing of the kind. I'm convinced now that Zakhar Rostov plans to use that ICBM, and I now believe that it will be used, whether Rostov is alive or dead. He had to assume that we might eliminate him or most of his organization here in Russia."

The general waited until he was sure the President had finished. "I don't want to believe this." He paused momentarily, wondering how he should proceed. "What do you have? What do you have that's solid, that supports this whole, crazy concept?"

"We don't have much that's solid. We have a lot of bits and pieces, lots of worrying circumstantial evidence. We have no hard evidence that the missile wasn't recycled as usual. However, with a second in-depth audit of the plant in the Urals that recycles our warheads, we finally determined that the warhead for that same missile is missing. It was replaced by a beautifully crafted, counterfeit warhead. We still have no absolutely solid evidence of who has the warhead or where it is, but we have enough information that we're convinced that the ICBM and the warhead are together in northern Canada, and that Zakhar Rostov controls them both. Something like this was bound to happen eventually, I suppose. We lost control of the military." The President made a dismissive gesture. "Please don't take that comment personally. I believe in officers like you, and you have been loyal beyond any question, but we haven't maintained the pay, the discipline, or the motivation, have we?"

"No, we haven't," the general responded, knowing it was never good to press too hard for an answer in the Kremlin. He hesitated, then he continued. "So I'll ask again. What hard evidence do you have that Rostov actually has an operable missile and a warhead?"

The President laughed bitterly. "The short answer is, not much, but we have enough that I am a believer. If you connect the dots, the resulting picture is extremely frightening."

The President took a deep breath and continued. "We did find records of Rostov's contacts and supporters. We have arrested all of them here in Russia, at least all that we know of. I hope, though I doubt it, that Rostov is quite alone in the world."

"I assume that's why so many old-line military men were suddenly arrested?"

The President nodded. "Yes. I'm sorry I had to use such heavy-handed methods, but there is no time left to be subtle. The only way we can prove this is to have someone on-site, someone absolutely uncompromised, to clearly demonstrate that the missile and warhead are also there on-site. The Americans choose not to believe us. They are busy with other things. The Canadians asked the Germans to clear the ship's cargo prior to leaving for Canada, and they found nothing. We asked the Germans to check one of the ships for radioactive sources, and they found nothing. The Canadians have a man on-site in northern Canada, and he has confirmed that there's no problem, no missiles, no warheads, that it's a normal mine development program."

The President paused. "We had several people in Canada working for the KGB, one in the heart of the RCMP counterintelligence group, but we think he works for Rostov now."

The President picked up a small envelope and leaned forward to hand it to the general. "These are your orders, General Khabarovsk. You are now in command of the entire armed forces of all of Russia. You report directly to me, and to me alone. You must convince the Canadians to take control and destroy or disarm the missile, or confirm beyond any doubt that there is no missile in place. The Canadians will have ten days to comply. If they will not do so, you must be prepared to attack the missile site with whatever force is required and appropriate. From what little we know, we don't think there's much time left." He reached down, picked up a large binder, and handed it to the general. "This is a compilation of information from Ivan Dinisovich. It sounds crazy, but read it with an open mind. I was misled by many who claimed that Dinisovich was crazy, disloyal, and untrustworthy. I know now that I was a fool."

The President sat back in his chair. "We are all depending on you. You must not fail, General. There is no time."

The general stood up and faced the President. "Thank you for your trust in me. I will not fail you."

The President sighed. "I believe you will do your best." Spontaneously, the President got up from his chair and walked around the end of his desk. He stepped up to the general and embraced him. Stepping back, the President said, "General, the world is in your hands," and then he waved him out.

As the doors shut behind him the general stopped and took a deep breath. "Amazing," he muttered. He looked down at the envelope and binder in his hand. This was the first time he'd ever heard anyone in the Kremlin admit to being a fool.

25

THE GENERAL SPENT THE EVENING ABSORBING THE INFORMATION IN Ivan Dinisovich's report. After overseeing the disaster at Rostov's dacha, it was not hard for him to believe the conclusions. By the afternoon of the next day he had his plans defined. It was more a matter of finding the units he could trust, rather than defining how to deal with the situation itself. A large part of the military, particularly the younger officers, remained loyal to the country and believed in the new direction for Russia. They believed, in spite of the hardships those changes had meant for them and their families. These men were so idealistic that there were times that the old general had a hard time not laughing at them, but he did not laugh. Getting old gave him no pleasure, but he doubted that he would find much pleasure in being young in Russia in these times. He shivered even in the warmth of the summer evening as he walked across Red Square on his way to visit Ivan Dinisovich.

Normally, he liked to walk through the great square. He liked the ponderous feeling of the place. History seeped out of the old buildings. The leftover intrigue and viciousness of Lenin and his far-too-excellent student Stalin, the drunken stupor of Brezhnev, the failed attempts at reform started by the bellicose and little-understood Nikita Khrushchev, all that history permeated the great square. What an opportunity Khrushchev had presented, if only the West had been ready. If only Russia had been ready. Lost opportunities and overwhelming distrust filled this place with a melancholy, but there had been greatness here too.

He showed his identification at the door, returning the salute of the young soldier with a smile. He passed through security quickly and climbed the stairs to Ivan's office. He was shown into the office immediately.

"Ah, General Khabarovsk, please take a seat." Ivan's face was without expression. The thin and almost bloodless lips pressed tightly together. "It's good to see you. The President tells me that you are fully briefed regarding my crazy ideas and delusions. Shall we go into a more secure room for our discussions?"

"That would be an excellent idea." Ivan's appearance shocked the general. Ivan had always been thin, but now he looked haggard and drawn. He had grown a ragged beard, and his eyes seemed to withdraw into their sockets. The general couldn't help but think that if the beard were a little longer the resemblance to Rasputin would be quite striking. As they sat down in the bunker-like room, its plain, gray cement walls broken only by the obligatory photograph of the President, General Khabarovsk asked, "How secure is this room?"

"I have no idea, General," Ivan replied with a dismissive wave of his hand. "In any case, you have come to take the measure of my sanity, General. This will take some time. Are you prepared to be patient?"

"I am a soldier. If there's one thing you learn as a soldier it is to be patient," the general replied with a hint of a smile.

Dinisovich took a deep breath and began his tale. "I'm convinced that Zakhar Rostov is behind all of this, and I'm convinced that he plans to use the missile." Ivan brought up the first image on his computer, and he jabbed his bony finger at the screen. "I first became suspicious with this image." He was careful to provide the general with all the details. The general listened intently, looked at the satellite images carefully, and occasionally asked a pointed question or two. As Ivan finished his story, he called for an aide to bring them coffee.

The general took a swallow of the bitter coffee and asked, "Why can't you convince the Canadians they have to do something? After all, it's on their land, not ours. A close look would resolve this one way or the other."

Ivan laughed. "We have no reliable eyewitness to the site in Canada. The Canadians have done their inspections and believe all is well. It was only very recently that we confirmed that a warhead is missing. I had a hell of a time convincing the President to insist on that independent audit of the Ural plant. Those results finally convinced him, but it may be too late."

General Khabarovsk took his time answering. "The whole thing is preposterous, of course. What you say in your report, what you think Rostov plans to do, is idiocy, madness." The general shook his head in wonderment. "Such destruction he plans, and mostly targeting innocent people. Of course, we Russians have been experts at mass destruction, particularly of our own people." The general put his coffee down and looked directly at Ivan. "His plan is so crazy that it will probably work. I guess it already has, except for the final act. Rostov thinks he has the people in place in the military to make sure we don't react in time, but I think he's wrong."

"If you don't succeed in Canada, General, our President may have ten minutes to talk to the President of the United States, to try to stop what might become the first major nuclear war, and perhaps the end of the world, at least the end of any world I want to live in."

The general got up from his chair, stretching. "I have spent too much of my life in rooms like this," he said, looking around at the bleakness of the place. "Most not as interesting. No, I should take that back. Most times were quite interesting, but most times were also extremely unpleasant." He turned around, taking in the whole of the room, as if remembering. Turning at last to Ivan, he said, "I will need all this," he gestured at the memos and miscellaneous data, "and the digital data for the images."

"Yes, I know. These are all duplicates. Most of this was also in the hands of the American, Watson MacDonough, and he passed it on to a man named Richard Durban, of the RCMP of Canada. I think if we are to stop this you must go to the Canadians, and the sooner the better. The Americans will do nothing. They don't believe me or Watson MacDonough. On my worst days I'm actually convinced that some part of the American government is working with Rostov, that they actually want this to come to pass." That comment shocked even the general. "The CIA forced Watson to retire because he believed me." Ivan paused. "We have very little time."

"I expect you're right. I'll contact the Prime Minister of Canada directly, after warning Richard Durban." As the general started to gather up the papers, he asked in an offhand manner, "Is it true, what you say in your reports, his homosexuality?"

Ivan nodded. "Yes, it's true. Though to be honest he's really bisexual."

"And his lover? The one who works for him? What you say about him is true as well?"

This time Ivan laughed. "Yes, that's just as true. In that case it appears we did our work a little too well for our own good."

"That's amazing. Some governments are even less responsible than our own. Having a homosexual, or a bisexual, as head of your national security is unforgiveable."

Ivan laughed again. "You are showing your age, General. Times have changed. If they're not forced to hide their preferences, how can we use those preferences against them? It's not so easy as in the old days at Cambridge."

The general frowned. He was old-fashioned, and he knew it. He collected the last of the papers and stood up. "I can let myself out."

The two men faced each other. "Will you risk the results of an air strike, General?"

"I will if I must. Using an adequate force of ground troops would be much better, and far safer. We will have a strike force in place, both air and ground troops." He sighed. "Let me know if you have any better luck with the Americans." He turned and left the room.

The general had a strange mixture of emotions as he walked down the halls to make his way out of the old building. *Too many painful memories here*, he thought, as he made his way out into the square and across to his waiting car.

Once inside his headquarters, the general sat at the well-used oak table in his office for a long time. Perhaps they would be able to stop this insanity. Perhaps. *If we fail, it could be the end of everything.* "This is not how I wanted to be promoted to head of all Russian forces," he said softly. Finally he got up, went to his desk, and placed a call to Richard Durban.

After the general left the conference room, Ivan sat silently in contemplation for a long time. He had done almost everything he could, and he was worried that it was not nearly enough. He had one more task to complete.

Ivan picked up the telephone and dialed. When she answered, he said, "You are working late. It is the price we pay for this life, no?" He smiled at the response. "I need to meet with you tomorrow. Early. I know that I'm being something of a pest, but we need to talk one more time. It's quite urgent. It will be the last time for a long time. I promise that." There was a pause before she responded. "Eight in the morning will be fine," he said. He hung up. *Time to go home*, he thought. *There's nothing more for me to do here.*

26

ALL THE EXPLANATIONS HAD NEVER FULLY SATISFIED DICK DURBAN. Yes, a close examination of the Bombardier did identify a number of valid scientific instruments. Yes, again, there was a proposal for the Russians to do some research in northern Nunavik, and the initial contingent was entirely Russian. The weapons? The Prime Minister didn't even want to hear about them. The Prime Minister told Dick Durban that he didn't want an international incident. The "leftover" Russians? Dick was told to quietly drop them off on a Russian ship that happened to be in the area. And the ex–KGB men who died in the snow? Well, they were dead. Let them stay dead. Even the Kremlin was strangely silent. No one came to claim the Bombardier.

It was all too easy. Dick sat at his desk in an outer office, looking out at downtown Toronto. He could feel the presence of something dark in Nunavik, but he glimpsed only the edges. His best man had checked all his doubts and put them to rest. His beloved government simply wanted to forget all about it. Dick thought it would be so much nicer to work for the CIA, for a government that wasn't afraid to flex its muscles. Then he thought about Watson, and he thought that he was better off with the RCMP after all. Anyway, he'd never be able to work for the straitlaced CIA.

He missed Charlie. He'd call him tonight to see how things were going. Charlie had come along at the perfect time. He was like the first warm day of spring after a long, gray winter. At first Dick had been suspicious. He checked Charlie Sturm's background extremely thoroughly. It was clean as a whistle. Not even an overdue parking ticket. It was so clean that Dick had to check it again to believe it. Dick smiled.

The ringing telephone roused Durban from his thoughts. "Captain Durban here." He recognized Watson's voice immediately. A few days earlier he had sent Watson a series of satellite images of the mine site at Randal Lake. Though he had never had any formal training, image interpretation was one of Watson's specialties. "So what's up, Watson?"

"I'm glad I caught you, Dick. I've noticed something interesting with these images you sent me."

Dick sighed. Would he regret sending those images to Watson? "Fire away, Watson. There may not be much I can do, you know. My bosses are about as interested in causing an international incident as stepping on dog shit."

Watson laughed dutifully. He stood on the outside now, out in the cold, living in his small home on the shore of a lake in upstate New York. Watson had sent a picture of the house to Dick, with Watson sitting on the front porch. Dick thought that the rough log construction of the house and the Adirondack furniture suited Watson's nature. Watson continued, "I don't know about the safety of this phone. I think my old employers are watching me."

"I hate to tell you, Watson, but I don't think they give a damn."

Watson laughed. "I suppose you're right, but if it's not them, I don't know who it is." Dick heard him take a deep breath. "Anyway, you remember those images you sent me, the ones showing the construction crew up at Randal Lake lowering giant pipes into the mine shaft?"

"Sure. What about them?" Dick's chair squeaked as he leaned back from his desk.

"Well, at first glance everything looks fine. It looked like the pipes were still wrapped in tarps until they were lowered into the shaft, but something bothered me. I couldn't put my finger on it. It drove me crazy. Then last night, just before I was ready to fall asleep, I suddenly realized what it was. If you look at those pipes, the shadow on the inside of the pipes doesn't change, regardless of their angle to the sun. In some of the images the pipe casts a long shadow, when the sun is fairly low on the horizon. In others, the pipe casts a much shorter shadow when the sun is higher. But the sun never shines on the inside of the pipe." Watson paused before giving Durban his conclusion. "Those pipes aren't open on the ends. They're covered on the ends, and the covering on the ends is black to make them look like empty pipes."

Dick waited. Watson's news seemed to be rather anticlimactic. "They always had them covered up, Watson, probably to protect them from the weather. Wouldn't it be natural to cover the ends with, say, black plastic?" Dick leaned forward, waiting for Watson's response.

"Jesus, Dick. You're as crazy as the rest of them if you believe that. Have you ever been to a mine?"

Dick laughed. "Uh, no, actually."

Dick could almost hear Watson's mind lurch into full speed again. Dick knew what he was feeling. Back in the harness, feeling the texture of the puzzle, pulling at the edges, pulling it apart bit by bit. "Hell," Watson said, "a mine is one of the wettest, dirtiest places in the world. There's water and muck everywhere. If these pipes have to be protected from a little inclement weather, you can be sure they won't last long in a mine."

Watson pressed home his arguments. "Look, it's obvious that they're trying to hide something." Watson paused. "I accept that we don't know precisely what's going on, but it could be a missile they're hiding. The longer I look at this mess, the more I believe Ivan Dinisovich. You know he sent me copies of some of the Russian satellite images. He said I'd understand if I looked at them. Their images are pretty good too." Watson paused. "I'd bet almost anything those aren't empty pipes up there."

Dick sighed. "You're reaching, Watson." Dick shook his head. Watson simply wouldn't let it go, but Dick had never been ready to let go either. "I have a guy up there. You know that. He looked at everything they shipped up there, and he said those things are empty pipes. That seals it, as far as I'm concerned."

Watson was silent for a long time. Dick exhaled. He knew what was coming, and he didn't like it at all. At last Watson asked, "How confident are you of this man of yours, Dick? Are you absolutely sure of him?"

"Look, I couldn't be more sure of anybody. I know him personally, and I've had him checked out in detail. He's clean, Watson, squeaky clean." Dick's voice was too loud in his denial.

Watson was silent again, but then he added, "You don't have to answer this if you don't want to. Do you have more than a professional relationship with this guy in Nunavik?"

Dick barked back, "Watson, you have no right to ask that, and you shouldn't expect an answer." *And that probably tells him the whole truth,* Dick thought.

"Dick, you've got to consider the possibility, however slim, that you're getting bad information."

The silence was thick, and it grew longer and more painful. Finally Dick spoke. "Okay, Watson, I take your point. Are you at your house in upstate New York?"

"You know I am." Dick could feel Watson smiling.

"Get over to the Rome, New York, airport at seven tomorrow morning. I want you to fly to Toronto and show me and my staff exactly what has you so worried about those images. I'll send one of the RCMP jets down to get you."

"I'll be there," Watson responded immediately. "And thank you, Dick."

Dick Durban sat back and shook his head. "Don't thank me yet. I haven't done a thing, and I don't know if I can." Dick hung up the telephone, not wanting to talk any longer. With any luck he'd be able to judge those images himself, but he'd have his own expert take a look, too.

He made one more call, to voice mail of course. Exasperating. "Warren. Dick Durban here. You remember those images we sent out on that Randal Lake site in Nunavik? The guy I asked to look at them has seen some things he doesn't like, and I've asked him to come to Toronto. He should be here by eight or so tomorrow morning. Make yourself available. I want you to look at what has him worried and give me your opinion." Dick trusted Warren Goodkin's judgment. He was a geek, and his perspective would be a good check on Watson's more intuitive approach.

Dick felt a little sick, like he'd just betrayed his lover. "That's just this fucking business," he muttered to himself. Watson had been right, but Dick didn't like the potential implications. It wouldn't be the first time a clever young man had made a fool of an old fox. *Damn,* he thought. *If Watson's right, I'm finished.* "Damn, damn, damn," he said softly. It was the oldest game in the business. Maybe, just maybe, he'd fallen for it, hook, line, and goddamned ass.

27

THE NEXT MORNING, WATSON THREW A CHANGE OF CLOTHES AND HIS toilet articles into a small bag. The telephone rang as he started for the door. He thought briefly that he ought to let it ring and leave, but out of habit he picked it up. "Yes?"

"Watson, is that you?"

"Yes. Who is this?"

"It's Sasha Karpov."

"Sorry I didn't recognize you, Sasha. Bad lines, I guess. What's up? Right now I'm in a hurry to get to the airport."

"This should take only a couple of minutes." Her voice was more subdued than Watson remembered. "I shouldn't be talking to you, but you need to know this. Ivan Dinisovich came to talk to me today. He's absolutely convinced that there's an operational ICBM at Randal Lake. He insists it's ready to go."

"Well, that's nothing new," Watson said.

"It's not the first time he's come to talk with me since you left. He says it's all tied up with that guy Zakhar Rostov, who's disappeared by the way, along with a bunch of old-line Communists." She hesitated and then continued. "He was ranting. He's getting desperate. He was starting to sound a little crazy."

"Yes, I know. He called to talk to me a few days ago." Watson shifted in his chair, anxious to leave. "What did he say to you? Did he finally admit that there's a live nuclear warhead on the top of that missile he's so worried about?"

"No, he still hasn't said anything to me about a warhead." A pause. "Did he say something to you?"

Watson laughed. "No. Think about it, though. What else makes any sense? Why else would he be so worried?"

"You have a point, Watson, but until they admit it, that idea's going nowhere." Sasha cleared her throat. "There's another reason I called. Rostov has powerful friends, and Ivan has powerful enemies. Ivan came to the embassy in a small car today. His regular car was in the shop. Someone attached an explosive device, and when he left, he didn't get more than a half mile away before it detonated."

"Christ!" Watson was fully alert now. "Did he survive?"

"Yes. He survived, and the hospital says he should recover, but it will be a long and painful process." Sasha paused. "He was careless. He should have known better than to be so exposed, but I'm not sure he cares anymore."

Watson was silent, numb. He thought about the people already dead. Everyone who believed there was anything wrong was either eliminated or disgraced. He knew someone was watching him. For a moment, Watson didn't realize that Sasha was talking again.

"He said two things that were particularly interesting," she was saying, "two things that I thought you ought to know. You know those mysterious explosions that were reported outside of Saint Petersburg? Turns out there was a pitched battle at Rostov's dacha outside Saint Petersburg. It was the most elite of the old-line military making the attack, a unit that's solidly loyal to the government. Ivan told me that the President had finally decided to take action against Rostov."

Even more alert, Watson asked, "What was the result of the attack? Did they capture Rostov?"

"I inferred that they didn't capture or kill Rostov, though they've made a major roundup of old, hard line, conservative Communists in the last week."

"What was the other thing he mentioned?" Watson's impatience increased with each passing moment. He wasn't sure he would hear anything more that was new from Sasha. She had always held her information quite close.

Watson waited as Sasha hesitated. She was putting her career on the line just by talking to him. "Ivan told me that anyone they haven't arrested, anyone who's even remotely associated with Rostov, has left Moscow. He's sure that means that the missile will be launched within days. With the Duma in session and all the government in Moscow, it's perfect timing for what Rostov wants to accomplish. Ivan can't get the President to take any action to remove the government from Moscow. He was quite depressed about that."

Watson stood up. He had to leave, but he couldn't pull himself away from the telephone. "There must be a warhead for him to be so worried. Did he give you any more information? Why is he so convinced that the missile will be fired so soon, and that the target is Moscow?"

"He asked me to give the information to you. He said you'd know what to do with it."

Watson was silent. Then he growled, "Shit. What the hell am I supposed to do with that?" He knew he should feel a huge rush of pleasure, that special thrill of finding himself in the key position to resolve an important case. He had been right all along, when all the others had been wrong and had dismissed him as a nutcase. He should feel fantastic, but he felt no rush. It was all too late, much too late. He was an old, tired, worn-out, and discarded relic of the Cold War. He sighed and said, "Okay, Sasha, I'm going to the airport. Dick Durban of the RCMP sent a plane down for me. He wants to see my interpretation of some satellite images he sent me. I'll see what I can do. Jesus Christ! Ivan still can't bring himself to give us everything we need. I have to tell you, Sasha, I'm starting to get really tired of this."

Quite softly but emphatically, Sasha said, "Don't crap out on us now, Watson, not when I'm finally starting to believe you. I've been no more successful than you were with Washington, and with me, the years ahead in this career are important. I can't take the risks you did."

"Do you think I wanted to throw away what was left of my career? Don't worry, Sasha, I haven't given up, not yet. I'm too damn stubborn for that, but I can't promise any action these days. You know that."

Quietly, "Do what you can. It may be more important than even we can imagine."

"I'll do what I can."

For a moment Sasha said nothing. Then, "I know you will. Thanks."

Watson hung up. *Yeah. I know exactly how important this is.* It might not be World War III, but it was getting bloody well close to it. Watson didn't want to be around if and when the new, or rather the old, order was back in control again in Russia.

Watson grabbed his bag and went out the door to his car. Out of habit, he checked the area and took an alternate route to the airport. He kept on checking as he drove to the airport. He was quite sure someone was watching him, but he didn't know who was watching. They were good, but they weren't perfect or he wouldn't have known they were there. For the second time in as many months he felt the deep chill of fear. Strange how it would come back so strongly so late in his career.

28

A FEW MINUTES AHEAD OF THE WORST OF THE MORNING RUSH HOUR, Richard Durban drove his car to the Toronto Pearson International Airport with grim determination. "Paranoid," he muttered. "Goddamned paranoid." Watson just couldn't let go of it. He'd accuse anybody of anything to make his point. Dick drove angrily, switching highway lanes recklessly. He raced through his own emotions. Anger, first at Watson for his accusations, then at himself because he recognized the dangers of his own weaknesses.

As he approached the airport he pushed the anger down. *Enough. This is not professional*, he thought. He had to deal with the surprise visit from General Khabarovsk today. He had no idea how explosive the visit might be, but he assumed it had something to do with the Nunavik affair. Quiet and remote Nunavik was suddenly taking on life again. He glanced at his watch. He wanted Watson at the meeting.

He pulled his official car into a space by the curb, in a no parking zone, locked it with his identification in plain sight, and walked briskly into the terminal. Dick looked across the terminal as he entered and immediately saw Watson and his police escort exit the main customs door. He smiled. Watson always looked as though he'd slept in his clothes. Watson was walking briskly. *He's actually looking enthusiastic*, Dick thought, and he shuddered to think of the implications behind Watson's enthusiasm.

They shook hands, both smiling. With careful control, Dick asked, "You had a good trip?"

Watson gestured toward his already disappearing police escort with a smile. "Well, it's nice to have your own private jet and the special customs and immigration service you provide. I'm a little surprised you're here to meet me, though."

Dick grunted. "I drove myself because I want some time to talk with no interruptions, and my car is about as good as it gets these days."

An airport policeman stood at Dick's car. He knew better than to make any complaint, considering the rank and position of the driver, but he didn't have to look happy about it. Dick waved at him, opened the trunk, and threw in Watson's carry-on bags. The two of them piled into the front and Dick pulled abruptly into traffic, leaving the annoyed policeman behind.

Watson looked across at Dick and asked, "So, anything interesting on this end that you can tell me about?"

"Well, I have a meeting in thirty to forty-five minutes with a General Khabarovsk from Russia." He looked over at Watson. "This meeting is a complete mystery. I didn't know anything about it until I got a phone call yesterday." Dick looked straight ahead as they merged into traffic on busy Highway 427.

"I know that name," Watson said. "Wasn't he one of the cadre of officers who was pushing the Russians to get out of Afghanistan? I thought he retired or was booted out years ago."

"I did too, but here he is. I looked him up. He has quietly advanced up the chain of command, but he's stayed almost entirely out of the spotlight." Durban stopped talking long enough to concentrate on the traffic as he changed lanes. "It turns out he played a very quiet and low-profile role in cleaning up the mess from the first war in

Chechnya. Anyway, he has a message for me from the President of Russia, extremely urgent, very high priority. He didn't tell me anything more, but I have a nagging suspicion that it has something to do with Randal Lake. If it does, I want you there at the meeting." Durban glanced over at Watson and smiled.

"Do you want to talk about the images before or after?"

"That depends on how much time we have. I expect it'll have to be after."

Dick glanced at Watson. He was looking out the side window of the car as the two proceeded in silence down the 427 to the busy Queen Elizabeth Way and on toward downtown Toronto. The hazy, warm summer air lay heavily on the city. The CN Tower stood out only vaguely in the distance. Dick waited for Watson to say something. Finally, Watson asked, "Have you heard from your man in Nunavik lately?"

Dick glanced at Watson. "No. I haven't heard a thing for some time." Ever since Watson had raised the issue of Dick's sexual relationship with his own agent in Nunavik, the relationship between Dick and Watson had taken on a completely new tone. Dick knew that Watson considered the relationship extremely unprofessional of him and damned dangerous. Dick also knew that Watson was right. They continued on in silence and drove into the underground garage of the building that housed Dick's office.

As they exited the elevator, the receptionist indicated with a nod a large gentleman in the waiting area. He was not young, and he had the ramrod-straight back of a career soldier. He sat still, looked straight ahead, and exuded patience and determination. His right hand rested on a small, brown leather briefcase that sat on the next chair.

Dick walked over to him and extended his hand. "General Khabarovsk?" The man looked up and rose out of his seat ponderously, gathering a sense of strength about himself as he did so. His large hand completely engulfed Dick's hand as he shook it. His suit did little to disguise the general's physical power, and without a word he dominated the room.

In mildly accented English the general said, "Yes. I am General Khabarovsk, and you are Captain Richard Durban, correct?"

Dick smiled. "You are correct, of course. Please follow me. I'd like to start our meeting as soon as possible."

"Thank you."

Dick leading the way, the three men moved down the corridor, through double security doors, and into a windowless, interior conference room. Dick Durban closed the doors softly behind them.

"You speak excellent English, General," Dick commented. "Did you spend time in the United States or Canada?"

"Yes, I spent several years as assistant military attaché in Washington, and I traveled extensively in North America at that time." He turned to Watson. "And you are? You look familiar to me, but I do not know your name."

Dick quickly answered for Watson. "I'm making an assumption that this meeting is about some activities at Randal Lake in Nunavik in northern Canada. This man is formerly of the CIA. I've asked him to sit in on our meeting." The general's expression indicated mild surprise, but he said nothing. "To be frank," Dick continued, "he was forced to retire from the CIA because of his deep interest in the Randal Lake developments. He was a bit too insistent."

"Ah. That's why I recognize you. You must be Watson MacDonough. I saw your photograph in the files. Ivan Dinisovich spoke highly of you before his unfortunate accident in Moscow. So you, too, have paid a price for your beliefs in this … this pending disaster?"

"It was time for me to leave," Watson responded.

The general shrugged his shoulders. "I have no problem with you being present in the meeting. We have little time, and I need all the help I can get."

"Do you need a projector or computer?" Dick asked.

"No, thank you." He turned to Watson. "I will be blunt and to the point. We are absolutely certain now that Ivan Dinisovich was right. Someone stole a fully operable ICBM with a nuclear warhead. We're confident that it has been installed in a refurbished mine shaft at Randal Lake. We still don't have much hard evidence, but we gained confidence when we attacked a dacha outside of Saint Petersburg and raided an office in the same city. We have also interrogated a large number of old-line Communists who appear to be involved in the plot."

"The office you raided was Zakhar Rostov's?" Watson asked.

"Yes, it was Rostov's office and dacha." The general gritted his teeth. "Unfortunately, the man himself and most of his key operatives appear to have escaped the destruction of his dacha. We have, however, put together the framework of the operation through our interrogations of Rostov's many supporters." The general took a deep breath. "They are fanatics, you know. We have many in Russia. We always have."

The general paused and then spoke again directly to Dick. "We have to get an independent observer on-site as soon as possible. We can't do it, but you can, and you can do it quickly."

Dick considered his guest. The general had just rather casually and bluntly confirmed all of Watson's unbelievable story. It was an astonishing statement. He looked over at Watson. "We had suspicions, as you know. We checked them out. The Germans checked the ships before they left Germany. I have a man on-site in Nunavik. He looked at all the shipments and assured me that what some people think may be pieces of an ICBM are nothing more than large, empty pipes to line the shaft, and everything else is normal mining equipment and supplies."

"And the weapons you found in the Bombardier earlier?"

"General, we can find no connection between that Bombardier and anything to do with Randal Lake."

The general spoke softly, sounding almost sad. "You say you have a man in Nunavik. His name is Charles Sturm. The KGB recruited him some years ago, when he was a field officer in Berlin. He works for Zakhar Rostov now."

Dick and Watson looked at each other. Watson didn't say a word. He didn't have to say anything. Dick already knew what he was thinking. *I'm finished,* Dick thought, *because of the oldest game in the business.* Dick did not respond to the general immediately, but eventually he turned back to him.

"I need some hard proof to take to the Prime Minister if I'm to have any possibility of doing something about this." Dick frowned. "So far I have a pile of weapons in a Bombardier that the Prime Minister doesn't even want to talk about. Then I have what most will regard as the crazy statements of a Russian general and the wild conjectures of a former CIA agent forced to retire under a cloud. It's a little hard to cover my ass with that, you know."

"I only ask that you send a security force to do a thorough examination of the Randal Lake mine site. That's all, at least for now." The general opened his small leather case and withdrew a thin, bound report. In addition, he withdrew a sealed envelope, addressed to the Prime Minister of Canada. "This report contains a summary, in English, of everything we have." He dropped the report on the middle of the table. "The envelope contains a personal note to your Prime Minister from our President. I am instructed to pass it to the Prime Minister or read it to him directly. I can summarize it for you. We believe the missile is ready to be launched, and we believe the target is Moscow."

The general looked intently at Dick Durban now. "Since it will be launched from Canadian soil, the act must be interpreted as an act of war. We have given you everything we know. We ask you to confirm what we've told you or clearly show that it's not true. We will give you seven days to determine whether the missile is or is not in the mine shaft at Randal Lake, and if it's there, to remove the threat yourself or with our help. We offer any help you need. If, however, you decide to not heed our warnings and if you do not thoroughly inspect the Randal Lake site to confirm or deny the presence of an armed ICBM, we will have no alternative but to attack the site ourselves." The general paused for emphasis. "We may be too late, even then."

For a moment Durban was speechless. Then he said, "You'd actually attack Canada? You must be as crazy as Rostov himself. You'd start the next world war. The United States and NORAD would be bound by treaty to defend us. The United States would consider the attack to be aimed at itself, not Canada."

The general shook his head. "We will not start a world war. We will send a small number of ground troops and their support vehicles and helicopters. We'll send only three or four Backfire bombers with a fighter escort and tanker support, and we'll send them only if required. If required, they will make the strike with laser-guided bombs and withdraw immediately. Our President will be on the hotline with the President of the United States. We will succeed, and we will not be attacked by the United States. We're already moving the necessary forces into place." The general's voice assumed a hard, metallic tone. "We will not take the risk of having Moscow and the entire Russian government destroyed because of Canada's inaction. I assure you that we will attack Randal Lake if we must. If you silence me or ignore these warnings, the attack will go forward regardless."

The general paused and then continued in a softer tone. "Captain Durban, we do not wish to make such an attack on Canadian soil. We especially do not want to attack the missile site with bombs, no matter how smart the bombs may be. We all know that such an action is fraught with many hazards and potential for deadly, unintended consequences, including a completely unwanted nuclear explosion. Please look at what I have given you. It should convince you to act on your own. We do not have much time."

While they were talking, Watson had skimmed the report the general had dropped on the table. There were some new, more revealing images. For the first time the Russians presented the satellite evidence of the removal of the warhead and the substitution of the counterfeit warhead. Then there was the inventory of the weapons site in the Urals, showing that the warhead was actually missing. A few key files from Rostov's office gave details of receipts for shipments, the hiring of experts in certain fields of missile maintenance and targeting, and all the connections between Rostov and the various salvage and shipping companies in Germany and Denmark. The most damning of all, though, were the contact reports between Rostov and Charlie Sturm and many summaries of brutal interrogations of Rostov's associates.

Watson looked up from the report to Dick. "From my quick glance, this report is pretty comprehensive, Dick. I think you should have your people analyze it, and maybe check some of it against our own satellite imagery." He handed the report to Dick.

Dick scanned the report quickly. The transcripts of conversations between Rostov and Gregori Borodin in Toronto were of particular interest. He needed to look at the report much more thoroughly, but he had seen enough to know that the situation had changed.

Dick picked up the telephone. "Cathy, please get Warren Thomas in here right now." Turning back to his guests, he explained. "Warren is our best man with satellite imagery. I'll ask him to get something close to real-time coverage of the Randal Lake area. We have to keep a close watch on what's going on up there."

The general spoke again. "We have some satellite coverage in place, if you need it. I can put your man in direct contact with our center in Moscow." The last was said with a rare smile. "I think, though, you need to prepare your Prime Minister. I may have to move up my timetable. We have wasted far too much time already."

This was starting to move much too rapidly. Dick Durban could feel the pressure building, and his right eyebrow twitched involuntarily. "General, I appreciate your offer of assistance. We may need it. Warren can deal with that better than I can."

Warren opened the door softly and walked into the room. "You need something from me, Dick?" Warren was a small man with a pinched, intense expression. He looked like a man who would run marathons for fun, and in fact he did so on a regular basis. Dick introduced him to Watson and General Khabarovsk. If Warren found it strange to see an ex–CIA man and a Russian general in the inner sanctum of the RCMP headquarters, he did not show it.

"I want you to get some satellite coverage over the Randal Lake area in Nunavik, as close to real-time coverage as we can manage, fed into this room. Take Watson with you in case you need some help with the CIA. General Khabarovsk will help you with anything you might find useful from the Russians."

Dick had made up his mind. All the pieces had come together. When that happened he always took quick and decisive action, regardless of personal risk. For that reason alone the RCMP had promoted him to his current position, in spite minor concerns regarding his lifestyle. He looked at the other three men in the room. "Now, gentlemen, if you could leave me for a while and get the coverage organized, I need to make a few phone calls." The three exchanged glances and got up without a word and left the room.

Once alone, Dick picked up the telephone and quickly called a familiar number.

"Prime Minister's office."

"This is Richard Durban of the RCMP. I must talk to the Prime Minister immediately. It's a matter of extreme and urgent importance to national security."

"Yes, Mr. Durban." Dick was a familiar caller. "He's in a meeting at the moment. Do I need to get him out, or can you talk to him from the telephone in the meeting room?"

"Put me through to him in the meeting, as long as it's not a speakerphone." He waited for the transfer.

"What can I do for you, Dick?" The Prime Minister's normally smooth and cultured voice sounded slightly concerned. Though they talked often enough, Dick never interrupted the Prime Minister when he was in a meeting unless the Prime Minister had reason to be worried.

"Do you remember my earlier concerns over a possible missile up in northern Nunavik, Quebec?"

"Yes, I remember. I thought that was all resolved."

"Well, a lot's happened in the last day or so, and I think we've got an extremely serious problem. I have a Russian general visiting my office with a confidential letter to you from the Russian President. We may need to take some aggressive action, including military action, in northern Nunavik, and I'll need your direct authority. Can you talk with the Russian general and me sometime in the next hour? I'd also like to set up a video conference call tomorrow to lay out all the details and planning. Can you be available early tomorrow afternoon?"

There was a moment of silence, then, "I can be available in about half an hour for the first call."

"That will be fine, sir. I'll probably have General Max Worthington sit in on the second part of the call as well, after you've talked with Russian General Khabarovsk. I expect Max will begin the initial planning today. And tomorrow afternoon?"

"I'm told that one in the afternoon will work for me."

"That should be fine. I'll get organized at this end in the meantime."

"All right. Thank you for the call."

"Thank you, sir."

Dick quickly called another number. "Max Worthington, please. This is an urgent call from Richard Durban, RCMP." He paused, waiting for the connection. "Max! Dick Durban here. We have an emergency, general. We may need you to undertake some air and ground action in northern Nunavik within a day or two. Can you set up for a conference call in about thirty minutes? This one's to give a summary of the situation to the Prime Minister, and to you as well. We'll have a more detailed video conference call tomorrow at about one in the afternoon."

"No problem, Dick. I'll get my staff looking at what resources we can deliver and the timetable for delivery."

"Good. The usual connections into our secure conference room. We'll be meeting with the Prime Minister, a General Khabarovsk from Russia, and probably a former member of the CIA. This is an extremely sensitive matter, and it must be kept under wraps, permanently."

"What about General Jacoby? Should we bring NORAD into this discussion?"

Dick thought for a moment. "I think we should have our first call, at least, before we make that decision. If I know the Prime Minister, he'll want us to handle this one on our own if we can. Jacoby is head of NORAD, but he's also an American general. He'll have to pass the information along to the Americans. I'm not sure we want to do that."

Max laughed. "Yeah. I understand that, for sure. I'll keep it tight on this end."

"Good. Just as a cautionary note, we may need most of our air force, including our tanker fleet, most of the Hornet squadrons, and perhaps one hundred troops or so, battle ready and equipped to handle a week in the field in northern Nunavik. I'll give you all the details you need after the first conference call, but I suspect that you may want to stage out of the airstrip at Kuujjuaq."

"All right," General Worthington responded. "I'll get things together on this end. We'll talk soon."

Dick hung up the phone, shut his eyes, and held his head in his hands. "Oh, Christ!" he said softly. "What the hell have I done?"

29

A MONTH AND A HALF HAD PASSED QUICKLY AT RANDAL LAKE, AND Shawn Schmitz had driven his crews relentlessly. Though to the casual observer not much had changed on the surface, the mine site had a purpose very different from the one it had before Shawn and his crews had arrived. Right under the eyes of the most sophisticated satellite observations, next door to the CIA and the most powerful military in the world, and in the backyard of the curiously uninterested Canadians, Shawn's crews had done their work well.

Igor Luchenko had led the design team for the Topol-M, and he had seen it deployed throughout Russia. He had never had one to call his own, and though this one, in the neat and cement-lined mine shaft at Randal Lake, had come to him courtesy of Zakhar Rostov, it effectively belonged to Igor now. Shining, gleaming in its body of carbon fiber, the Topol-M ICBM was a truly ingenious creation. As a "cold launched" ICBM, a special booster, a gas generator, would push the missile out of its silo—in this case, out of the mine shaft. The first stage of the Topol-M would ignite once it was in the air. Igor actually had to pat the side of the missile when it arrived at Randal Lake. It was his child.

Igor designed the Topol-M to carry multiple, independent reentry warheads, but, like most, this one carried only a single nuclear warhead and six decoys. The delivery system was accurate and designed to defeat any known or planned antimissile system in the United States, or in Russia for that matter. Simple, solid-fuel engines were almost failsafe and easy to maintain. A crew could keep the missile on alert for prolonged periods, ready to launch it within minutes.

The missile stood silently, nearly ready to do Rostov's bidding, and it was all because of Igor. Only a few critical systems tests remained, and those were Helmut Fankauser's job.

Occasionally, in spite of his sour disposition, even Igor managed a small smile at the status of the project. Igor and Helmut had suffered through delays and near disasters, but now they could see the missile actually poised in the shaft. Soon they would change the world. They would excise the cancers of modern Russia. Soon they would be part of the new world order.

Helmut and Igor were a strange pair. Helmut was chubby, with rosy cheeks, blue eyes, and wavy blond hair, which was somewhat thinning on top. He looked like the caricature of a rural German burgermeister. Except for being overweight and out of shape, he could have been a poster boy for Hitler's ideal Aryan man. Above all else, though, he was a dedicated Communist. He felt betrayed by the united Germany and by the modern Russia that had walked away from East Germany, leaving him behind, feeling alone and abandoned.

Beside him, Igor, with his thin, translucent skin, looked like a corpse. He seemed to grow thinner every day, and his skin grew tighter across his bones. Perpetually somber and taciturn, he seemed annoyed with everyone around him. The old Communism was a religion with Igor, and he was fully and devoutly dedicated to its revival. Helmut and Igor were a strange pair, but they shared a common cause.

Though habitually morose, Igor did become somewhat more animated as the days passed. "We are nearly there," he would say over and over.

Igor's enthusiasm always annoyed Helmut. "We're not there yet," he would answer each time Igor repeated his remark. "We have many tests to run before we can launch."

His response would always produce the same comments from Igor. "You and your tests. You should do it right the first time."

Helmut had to admit that they were finally nearly ready. The Germans had done their usual excellent job, and the mine shaft and control room were both equipped nearly as well as they had been in the original missile silo in Siberia. Actually, the computer systems were better. At depths of thirty, seventy-five, and one hundred feet, small tunnels, part of the original mine workings, led away from the shaft. The engineers enlarged the first two, lined the area close to the shaft in each with cement, and equipped the seventy-five-foot level with the test and control equipment. The ICBM sat on a reinforced cement plug in the shaft immediately below the seventy-five-foot level. All the cables, connectors, sensors, and little bits of hardware that were needed in the shaft for a successful launch of the missile were in place.

A small, internal-access shaft, a short distance from the main shaft, connected the separate levels and provided ventilation and access to the surface. Heavy, reinforced cement barriers sealed off each level from the main shaft. Two thick, steel doors controlled access from the surface, one at the top of the access shaft and another immediately above the control room. In the face of any threat, the crews could secure the doors from the inside. Once the crew completed targeting and prepared to launch the missile, the entire assembly could be locked down and secured.

Rostov had sent a small but effective security force of twenty-two men, including the pilots and mechanics for the helicopters. The ground force was by no means impotent. Their equipment included an assortment of assault rifles, light machine guns, and several small mortars. In well-prepared defensive positions, and with the support of the helicopter gunships, they still presented a formidable opposition if anyone were to attack them in the flat and open country.

Igor had only a few concerns and fears. His worst fear was that the ICBM would be vulnerable for a few minutes immediately prior to launch, when they opened the massive cement cover over the shaft. If undefended for that brief time, a small force could attack and easily destroy the missile, even with well-placed small arms fire. The security team expressed little concern for this tiny window of vulnerability. The overall defense plan was built around the two Mi-17 helicopters. Well-armed with rocket launchers and heavy machine guns, they could effectively neutralize any advantages that the minimal local cover could provide for a ground attack force. They could also effectively engage other attack helicopters or low-flying aircraft.

A major attack from the air was another matter, but only a direct hit on the mine shaft would cripple the missile launch. Furthermore, any direct hit could have seriously unpleasant consequences for Canada, including a huge problem of nuclear contamination, or worse, a nuclear explosion. Rostov counted on caution on the part of the Canadians and Americans.

A month and a half at the camp at Nuvilik Lake had passed quickly and quietly for Peter. Both Maria and Tom worked as his assistants. Peter found that his days alone with Maria were the more interesting, if less productive, despite the fact that the hungry mosquitoes kept them fully clothed most days.

Peter noticed that Charlie tried to be a conscientious mechanic and maintenance man for Arnie, and with Maria around he kept his hands off Peter. Everything at Nuvilik Lake seemed quiet and normal. Beneath the surface, though, Peter was not entirely happy and content. He continued to feel a barely perceptible sense of misgiving.

This particular workday had been a long one, one of many for Peter. As was their custom, Peter and Arnie sat in the cook tent, having a snack before they headed off to bed. Arnie polished off a piece of pie as he read. He looked up from his book and asked, "You think we should take another trip to Randal Lake, Peter?"

Peter put his fork down and turned to look at Arnie. "What made you ask that right now?"

Arnie shrugged his shoulders. "Well, I can't help but wonder what's really going on there."

"I thought Charlie took care of that with his last inspection trip." There was a barely perceptible edge to Peter's voice.

Lowering his voice to not much more than a whisper, Arnie continued. "Some things about that inspection didn't seem right. You know, Charlie never actually checked some of the equipment and containers." He held up his book. "This book I've been reading got me thinking." He had the embarrassed look of a teenage boy who's been caught masturbating. His book was one more of the endless series of spy-versus-spy thrillers he enjoyed reading.

"What do you mean? What didn't he check?"

Arnie made a small gesture with his hands. "Well, you know, he was a real pest. He looked into almost everything, but there were four big cylinders covered with tarps of some kind. He had them take the tarp off the end of one of them. It was sitting off by itself. Even from where I sat in the helicopter I could tell it was an empty pipe. Two others were on trucks ready to go to the mine site, I suppose, but he never checked them. He walked around them, but the crew never uncovered either of them. I couldn't hear, but the foreman appeared to raise holy hell at the concept of taking the tarps off. Even if I could hear them, they were always speaking in German. Then there was this big crate, way off to the side and away from everything else. Charlie never looked inside that crate." Arnie paused and shrugged. "The omissions seemed strange."

Peter felt an unwelcome prickling sensation as all his buried misgivings began to rise to the surface again. Then he heard the soft sound of footsteps outside the canvas walls of the tent. He put his finger to his lips and said, "I think you're reading too many spy thrillers for your own good, Arnie. Pretty soon you'll think there's a spy under our cook tent." Peter laughed just as Charlie opened the door and came into the tent.

"Hi, guys. Time for my midnight snack."

"Yeah, well, I think I've finished mine," Peter commented as he got up and took his plate to the washbasin and picked up his papers. Turning to Arnie, he said, "I'll be going to that grid south of the Povungnituk River tomorrow, Arnie. I'll take Tom and Maria with me. You'll be busy pushing the geophysical crew around. They should finish their surveys tomorrow. We've got a flight planned to take them out in a couple of days."

"No problem, Peter. I'll be ready to take you out whenever you want," said Arnie with his usual good-natured smile. "See you in the morning." Arnie left for his bunk shortly after Peter, leaving Charlie alone for the moment with his piece of chocolate cake.

When Peter returned to his tent, Maria was reading, and Peter decided to read for a short while before turning in. After a few minutes, though, he put the book down. With the quiet month and a half at Nuvilik Lake, Peter had relaxed, but his brief conversation with Arnie was winding him up again. Had Charlie heard Arnie's comments? Did it matter if he had?

Peter's mind raced through the previous six weeks, focusing mostly on Charlie. All his suspicions, all his worries, all his fears were roaring back to life. *Time to put your guard up again, old boy,* he thought. More than that, it was time to play dumb and shut his mouth, and it was time to be prepared for anything. Peter looked over at Maria. *No,* he thought, *I'm not going to say a thing.* He stood up and started to strip down for bed. Maria looked up from her book and smiled. When Peter next looked up, she was standing in front of him, stripped to the waist. He reached out, and they held each other.

30

OVER BREAKFAST, CHARLIE TURNED TO PETER. "I THINK WE SHOULD make another visit to Randal Lake. Maybe you and Maria could come along with me. It shouldn't take more than a couple of hours." Charlie glanced over at Maria and Arnie. "We can do it after Arnie puts the geophysicists out on their first grid."

Peter tried to hide his surprise. "Why do you want us to come along? Isn't this another official visit?"

Charlie shrugged. "Well, to be honest, I wouldn't mind a couple of extra eyes. I'm not all that familiar with the mining business. The last time I went I didn't see anything unusual, but the two of you might see something I missed." Charlie turned his attention back to his eggs. "Anyway, I didn't have the time to do a complete examination of the cargo, and the foreman at Wakeham Bay wasn't all that cooperative."

"That's for sure," Arnie laughed.

"If you don't mind," Peter responded, "I'd like to take Tom along as well. It'll make it easier to drop us off at our work site on the way back."

"No problem," replied Charlie and Arnie, almost in unison.

Arnie finished his breakfast and turned to the geophysicists. "You guys ready to go? It sounds like you're first on deck today." With the usual swearing and muttering, the geophysicists prepared for the field. Ten minutes later Arnie took off with the first helicopter trip of the morning.

Peter didn't believe in coincidences, and this trip to Randal Lake was coming too soon after his strange conversation last night with Arnie. *How much had Charlie overheard? Time to be prepared.*

Peter went to the office tent to gather what he needed for the day. The gray day, cold and windy, brought a foretaste of the winter that would arrive in little more than a month. As usual, he wore Andropov's old vest as an added layer for warmth. He reached for his loose-fitting field jacket beside his bed, paused a moment, and unlocked his trunk.

Peter considered the risk of discovery and what that might imply. Then he picked up Andropov's revolver, loaded it, and slid the holster and pistol onto his left shoulder. When he donned the loose field jacket, the pistol wasn't obvious, as long as he kept the jacket buttoned. Maybe he was crazy, but he didn't care. *It's always good to have a secret equalizer.*

He grabbed his pack and jogged the short distance to the helipad. Charlie, Tom, and Maria were already there, and Peter could hear Arnie returning from his first trip. Charlie carried a small bag.

Charlie spoke to Peter. "I won't need to top off the tanks. We can get right in and take off." Peter nodded, and the four waited in silence as Arnie landed and they all climbed in. No one said anything until Charlie asked Arnie to land at Esker Lake so he could change.

Arnie set the helicopter down softly on the gravel beach. Charlie hopped out, walked around the front of the helicopter and opened Arnie's door. He reached into his bag and pulled out his RCMP pistol. "Shut it down, Arnie. If you try to take off, before the skids leave the ground I'll splatter what little brains you've got all over your nice, clean Plexiglas. You aren't the only one who can fly this thing." He waved the pistol at the three in the back of the helicopter. "The rest of you, don't move. We've got a change of plans." Charlie took a small step back. He had to shout to be heard. "Now, if you all behave yourselves, you might live to tell this story to your grandchildren."

Shutting down the helicopter, Arnie glared at Charlie in disbelief when he could look away from the dials. "So what are you planning to do, Charlie? This is crazy."

"Just shut up, Arnie," Charlie shouted. "I'm tired of sharing a tent with you, tired of your worn-out jokes, and tired of being around you. You pilots are all the same, all cock and no brains. Just shut it down." Arnie looked shocked at Charlie's outburst, but he kept silent and focused on shutting down the helicopter.

Peter sat in the back, weighing his chances. He unzipped his heavy jacket a bit. It'd be one thing if he were alone with Charlie, but there were three others to consider. Tom had turned slightly pale, but he looked calm enough. He looked more angry than terrified. Maria looked angrier. She clenched her teeth. *I have to be patient*, Peter thought. *Just wait for an opening.* He knew he had to do something quickly, though. Charlie would never leave them all alive to find their way back to Nuvilik Lake.

Finally the engine and the main rotor stopped. "Get out of the helicopter, Arnie," Charlie said as he backed away from the machine a few more steps. "The rest of you get out on this side, very slowly, and stand next to Arnie." He pointed his gun at Peter. "And don't try to be a hero, Peter."

Tom stepped out of the helicopter first, and Peter followed. He turned to give Maria a hand, and she put her hand on his jacket where it covered his shoulder holster. Their eyes met and Peter gave the slightest of nods. "Get moving, you two," Charlie shouted. "I don't have all goddamn day."

Peter glared at Charlie. "To hell with you, Charlie." He and Maria moved away from the helicopter and stood next to Arnie and Tom. Charlie was wound up tight. He was starting to move with jerks and twitches. *Is he high on something?* Peter wondered. If he was really high, it might give Peter and the others an edge, but Charlie might be even more dangerous for his nervousness. Peter needed to have Charlie drop his guard for a moment. "So who do you really work for, Charlie? I'm curious. I guess you don't work for the RCMP, at least not exclusively."

Charlie laughed nervously. "You never quit, do you, Peter? You think you're so damned smart." He laughed again. "Well, it'll do no harm to tell you now. Sometime today, maybe in a few hours, we're going to change the world. There's nothing you or anybody else can do to stop it now. I just need to make sure you don't complicate matters."

"So you're going to kill us all?" Peter asked softly.

Charlie's laugh was almost a giggle. "No. You're wrong again, Peter. If I leave you guys out here, with no transportation, it doesn't really matter. I guess I do have to kill you, though. You're just too dangerous." He raised his gun, pointing it at Peter. "I'm actually a little sorry about this," he said with a smile.

Maria spoke up. "So you'll fly away to Randal Lake to rendezvous with your buddies? Is that it?"

Charlie glanced over to her, but he kept his pistol aimed at Peter. "Yes. You'll have a long walk back to camp. By the time you get there, if you get there, we'll be done and out of here."

"Well hell, Charlie, if you're flying away, and if I'm facing a long walk back to camp, I'm getting my pack out of the helicopter." Maria turned and started back toward the helicopter.

Charlie yelled at her. "Stay where you are. Don't go near that helicopter, damn it."

She kept walking. "Oh piss off, Charlie. Shoot me if you have to. I don't think you have the balls to do it, anyway."

"Damn it, stop right there." Charlie turned toward Maria and moved his aim away from Peter.

Peter didn't hesitate as he saw the opening Maria made for him. He quickly shoved his hand inside the partially unbuttoned jacket and pulled out the .44 Magnum. Charlie saw the movement and turned back quickly, but not quickly enough. Peter got one shot off, but the pistol had caught on his jacket, and even at close range he had managed a clean miss. "Shit!" Peter muttered.

Charlie completed his turn and brought his gun to bear, a standard .38. Charlie didn't miss. Though the caliber of the gun was not large, Charlie's shot felt like a hit with a sledgehammer. It hit the right side of Peter's chest at his shirt pocket, where he carried his field notebook. Andropov's vest stopped the bullet, and the notebook absorbed and distributed some of the force of the bullet. Nevertheless, the blow staggered Peter. He fell to his knees, momentarily unable to breathe or respond.

If anyone had asked Charlie before he took his shot, he would have said that of course he knew Peter was wearing body armor and that he should shoot him in the head, but his quick reaction was to aim for the biggest target. Now Charlie aimed the pistol at Peter's head. He took his time, with a smile on his face, as he prepared to finish Peter off.

"You fucking bastard!" Maria screamed. She leapt at Charlie. Peter watched in disbelief as Maria deliberately drew Charlie's attention toward her. As Charlie again turned toward Maria, his pistol turned with him. Gasping for breath, Peter raised the .44 in both hands and fired a second time. The force of the .44 sent Charlie stumbling backward. His pistol slipped from his hands, and he fell to his knees with an astonished look on his face.

Maria took a couple of quick steps, picked up Charlie's gun, and turned to him with his gun in both her hands. Charlie looked up at her with a mixture of surprise and fear. "I should finish this right now, you bastard!" she shouted at him.

Charlie continued to look up at Maria, and a grin slowly spread across his face. Clutching his lower abdomen with his hands, Charlie looked at the blood oozing through his jacket and fingers. "Shit," he said softly and slowly slid onto his back on the ground.

"Are you all right, Peter?" Maria shouted. "Arnie, Tom, check him out." She kept the pistol aimed at Charlie.

"He's all right, Maria," Arnie responded. "He had his stupid vest on."

"They'll come for you," Charlie said softly. "They were expecting me. So have your fun. It won't last long." He coughed and instantly grimaced from the pain.

Peter stood up, supported by Arnie and Tom. He searched for the slug and finally pulled it out of the vest. "Not such a stupid vest." Then he pulled out his notebook. "Not a bad notebook, either," he said with a smile. Finally, Charlie's last comment registered, and he turned to Charlie. "What do you mean, they'll come for us? You mean those guys at Randal Lake?"

Waves of pain cascaded over Charlie's consciousness, but he managed something between a smile and a grimace. "And they have enough firepower to take care of all of you, no sweat." He grunted with the pain from his wound. "Oh, Christ! I knew you were trouble, Peter."

Peter took a deep breath. It hurt. He knew he'd be sore for a long time, but a surge of adrenaline blunted the pain. He walked over to Charlie. "I always wondered about you, Charlie. I never trusted you, not really. You must have fooled your boss completely."

"More than you know," said Charlie.

Peter carefully placed his right foot on Charlie's gut wound. "I want to know exactly what's going on over there. What's happening today?" Peter pressed a little harder on the wound. Charlie let out a low moan.

"Is this really necessary?" Maria asked quietly.

Peter glanced at her. "Look, I don't think we have much time, and we sure don't have enough time to be subtle." He looked back at Charlie, and he pressed down a little harder with his foot. This time Charlie screamed and flailed weakly at Peter's leg before Peter backed off. "You have a choice, you son of a bitch. You can tell us right now what's going on, and we'll get you to medical help, or you can die alone, right here on the ground." He pressed down on the wound again with his foot, and Charlie screamed again. "Right now I'm getting damned impatient." Peter hoped Charlie thought he was tough enough to go through with his threats of torture.

Charlie gasped, "Okay." The noise from his labored breathing was impressive. "If I tell you, where the hell do you take me?" He tried to laugh, but he failed. His voice had declined to a rasp.

He's probably going into shock, Peter realized. If they didn't get the information from him soon, it would be too late. "We'll get you to Asbestos Hill. That's the best we can do. The medical technician there should be able to keep you alive."

"How do I know you'll keep your word?" Charlie grunted.

Peter laughed. "You don't, Charlie, but you're hardly one to question my word. Anyway, you don't have much choice."

"Yeah." Charlie managed a hoarse chuckle. He was looking intensely at Peter. Peter knew Charlie was dealing with an intense mixture of fear and pain and that Charlie's thinking would already be slow and confused. Charlie knew, though, that if he didn't get help fast, he'd be dead within an hour. "Okay. There's a missile in that mine shaft ... a Russian Topol-M ... they'll launch it today ..."

"Damn! So that's what the other big pipes were," Arnie said, disgusted.

Peter turned sharply to Arnie. "What do you mean?"

Arnie stepped closer to Peter. "It's what I was telling you last night. There were four big, pipe-like things that came on that last ship to Wakeham Bay. They were all covered. When Charlie made his inspection, he looked at one, an empty pipe. I'll bet those other three were the missile. He never looked at any of them. The pipe was just a decoy, and I bet that big crate thing was the warhead."

Listening, Charlie croaked out a shallow laugh. "You ... were observant." Arnie glared at Charlie but remained silent.

Peter considered what Arnie had just said. He had overlooked so many clues. Charlie had managed his inspection well enough that no one had caught the obvious. "All right, Charlie, just who's behind this missile, and where do they plan to send it?"

"It's Russian … A guy named Rostov's behind it, old KGB." Charlie grimaced with pain. "Jesus! Get me some help."

Peter made up his mind. It didn't matter what the target was, he realized. He had no intention of sitting on his butt waiting for someone else to take action. He turned to Arnie. "Get the chopper started. Take Maria and me to the camp, and pick up Roland. Then come back here to pick up Tom and Charlie and take Charlie to Asbestos Hill. Maria, give Charlie's pistol to Tom, so Tom can watch over him until Arnie gets back. Tom, shoot the son of a bitch if he so much as twitches." Peter walked toward the helicopter. "Let's get moving. I don't think we have much time."

"Time?" Maria asked. "What are you planning to do?" Arnie was already starting the engine.

"If those bastards really are coming gunning for us, we have enough firepower to give them an exciting reception. I have no intention of making it easy for them."

Arnie looked back at Peter and Maria. "Shouldn't we take Charlie to Asbestos Hill first? He could bleed to death before I get back."

"You won't need to spend too much time at the camp. We need a couple of the Stinger missiles, a few other items, and the telephone. Then you need to get us into position on the other side of the lake."

As Arnie lifted off, Peter looked back at Tom on the ground. He looked quite lonely. The red stain on Charlie's shirt was growing. Peter didn't expect Charlie to survive for more than a few hours. The damage from the .44 Magnum shot to the gut would be massive. Asbestos Hill wasn't set up for serious surgery. *I guess that's Charlie's problem*, Peter thought. He'd given them the information they needed.

Peter looked over at Maria. "I think you'll get a chance to see if you can fire a Stinger missile at a moving target."

Maria looked back at Peter with raised eyebrows. "You know I've only fired it once."

Peter took her hand in his. "Don't worry. Like Charlie said, they're simple enough that any GI is supposed to be able to use one with almost no training. I need all the help you can give me. I haven't had any training on them for a while, myself."

The camp came into view as they flew over the east end of the lake. Peter's mind raced, trying to sort out all the issues and options. He knew they'd probably have only one chance. He hoped both helicopters came at the same time. To accomplish anything at Randal Lake, they had to eliminate those helicopters. Whatever they could do, they'd be doing on their own. No time to call in the cavalry.

None of them had put on their flight helmets, which had built-in microphones for communication, so Peter leaned forward and shouted, "Arnie, when we get to the camp, get a radio. You'll need to fuel up, set Maria out across the lake, and then take care of the others. I'll give you a call when you should come back to pick us up. If those bastards are coming for us, I hope they come right away. It'll sure make life a lot easier if we don't have to worry about their damned, big helicopters." Turning back to Maria, "Maria, you and I will set up an ambush."

"What about the geophysicists?" Arnie shouted back.

"Oh, Christ! I forgot all about them." Peter looked to the south, toward where they were working. "I don't know what to do about them." He shook his head. "Leave them where they are for now, Arnie. They have a radio to call for a move, and I don't think they'll be ready for a couple of hours."

Arnie set the helicopter down at the helipad. Roland came to the door of the cook tent, wiping his hands on his not-too-clean apron. "Let's get moving, Maria. We've got a lot of work to do and not much time to do it." Peter climbed out onto the ground, and Arnie moved quickly to shut down and top up the fuel tanks. Peter shouted back to him, "Fill in Roland while you fuel up."

31

PETER AND MARIA WORKED AS QUICKLY AS THEY COULD IN TOM'S bunk tent, sorting the weapons and ammunition. The sense of urgency was almost overwhelming. Peter was still hurting, but he was angry enough and pumped-up enough that he was functioning just fine. He gave Maria a quick refresher lesson on the Stinger missile. For what he had in mind, she had to be able to use it right the first time. They loaded the canoe and together piled a small stack of arms next to the helipad.

As Arnie finished fueling the helicopter, Peter rattled off his instructions. "Arnie, take Maria and this load east down the lake. She needs to be on the back side of the hill, near that little esker we use for a garbage dump."

"Sure," Arnie replied.

During this exchange, Maria looked carefully at Peter. "Exactly what do you expect me to do?"

Peter talked quickly. "We don't have time to be neat and precise." Peter turned and pointed east, down the length of the lake. "My bet is that they'll send both helicopters straight down the lake, one hanging back half a mile or so, playing tail end Charlie to support the lead helicopter if he's needed."

He turned back to Maria. "We have to assume that both of them will be armed to the teeth. They have all the mountings for machine guns and missile pods. I figure we have to take one out right here in front of the camp. When that happens, the one holding back will come in loaded for bear, and I want someone covering my ass." He shrugged his shoulders. "It may not be perfect, but it's the best I can think of."

Maria looked hard at Peter. "I hope I know what I'm doing."

Peter smiled with a reassurance he was not sure he felt. He spoke calmly, "You should be fine. All you need to remember is to expect them to fire off defensive flares to confuse the heat-seeking targeting of the Stingers. If they fire off a set of flares, fire your next Stinger as soon as they start to fade. At least we're dressed for action today," Peter concluded with a wry smile. Their light-tan field clothes were effective camouflage in the Arctic. "I'll be across the lake with my rifle. If we both miss with the missiles, I may need it."

Arnie loaded the weapons as Peter and Maria talked. Even Roland, caught up in the sense of urgency, put on his jacket and pitched in to help. Once the helicopter rotors reached full operational speed, Arnie shouted out the window, "Let's go, guys. You said yourselves we might not have much time, and this buggy doesn't do too damn well against gunships. Can't out run 'em, and sure as hell can't out gun 'em."

Peter turned to Roland. "You ready?"

Roland laughed. "I guess so."

Peter smiled and shook his head. "If what I think is about to happen actually happens, I sure don't want you in the camp. Head out with Arnie. When Arnie picks Charlie up and takes him to Asbestos Hill, stay with him and make sure they treat him well, okay?"

"I guess so," Roland laughed. "Since I don't know what's actually happened, I can play dumb pretty easily." He produced a nervous smile and climbed into the helicopter. Peter didn't blame him for being concerned. He shared the feeling.

As Maria started to follow Roland into the helicopter, she turned to Peter. "Just one last thing, Peter. How will you be sure when those helicopters show up that they're the bad guys and not a bunch of innocent bystanders?"

Peter leaned into the back seat. "Well, after what Charlie did and said at Esker Lake, I think it's a pretty good bet that we don't want to get to know these guys up close and personal. Anyway, if they come in fully loaded and firing, it'll be easy to know. If they don't have their full weapons load, I suppose I'll have to let them land and see what happens." Maria did not respond.

Peter shifted his focus to Arnie. "Keep your radio on, both of you, set on channel three. We don't want to screw this one up. Arnie, when you take Roland, Tom, and Charlie to Asbestos Hill, don't hang around. I don't want them to hold you there once they find out Charlie was shot. Fly over with Tom to the other side of that fjord on the west side of Asbestos Hill, set down, and wait for my call." Looking over at Roland, he said, "I'm counting on you, Roland. Charlie may be a son of a bitch, but he still deserves the best care we can get for him."

Peter shut the door and stepped back from the helicopter. As he watched it lift off and fly up the lake, Peter thought about what Maria had said about innocent bystanders. The thought had been eating at him since his last conversation with Charlie.

"Good luck to all of you," he said softly. "This could be an interesting day." Peter looked at his watch. Over an hour gone since they had left Charlie and Tom behind. He hoped they still had time.

In the mine shaft, the missile stood like a giant and gleaming arrow. Igor turned to Helmut. "All the systems for the stages on the missile are in order. What are the test results on the guidance systems and targeting?"

"I'm nearly done. I see no problems so far. We should be ready either late today or early tomorrow." Helmut looked up from his work, frowning. "I still worry about the emergency power. It never has worked properly. I don't think there's enough fresh air circulation."

Igor glared at him. "You worry too much. We have a reliable generator. Besides, once the command to launch is given, the missile is totally autonomous."

Helmut returned to his work. The tension between the two of them was just part of their lives. Without looking up, Helmut asked, "I know we have the big generator, but we both know it's vulnerable if there's an attack on the camp."

Igor grunted. "Who's around here to attack? We've gotten this far without any interference. Besides, we have an excellent security force."

Helmut did not look up. "That may be so, Igor, but we both know the security force is small. The larger weapons and the missiles were lost from the Bombardier." Helmut cocked his head slightly and glanced at Igor. "Perhaps the one who attacked Andropov and his men will show up again. We both know he's still around."

Both were silent after Helmut's comment. Neither liked to think about the fact that two men as fundamentally vicious and well trained as Andropov and Kazakov had been eliminated by a single man. Rostov refused to listen to their concerns. Rostov was either afraid of the attacker or was confident that he would not strike again. All the weapons Andropov had carried with him in the Bombardier had simply disappeared into the hands of the attacker.

Finally, without looking up and with some nervousness, Helmut asked Igor, "Do you know if Charlie Sturm has arrived yet? I haven't been in touch with the surface for several hours now."

"Let's see what they say," Igor replied and stepped over to the telephone that connected to the surface. As Helmut listened to Igor's conversation, it became obvious that Sturm had not arrived. "Then he is at least one or two hours behind schedule, no?" Igor asked. "And no messages at all?"

"That's right," the guard replied.

Igor didn't hesitate. "Send the helicopters over to the camp. Perhaps he's been delayed by a helicopter failure. If nothing's wrong, it can be a quick social visit." Igor paused and listened. "No. Send both. Only one is fully armed. Send a security force with them. Nothing must go wrong now." Another pause. "No, Charlie never told us anything about weapons at the geologists' camp. The weapons were at that camp, but we have no idea of where they are now."

Igor turned to Helmut. "Charlie hasn't arrived. There's some problem. I sent the helicopters to Nuvilik Lake to check."

Helmut looked at Igor for a moment. Igor watched as he started to say something but changed his mind. Finally, Helmut commented, "Well, we'll soon find out why he's delayed, won't we?" He turned back to his tests and continued with his work. As the launch grew closer, nervous worry and anxiety had overcome Helmut's normally placid manner.

On the surface the guard roused the two helicopter pilots and the mechanics from their bunks and quickly told them Igor's orders. As he gathered his helmet and slipped on his flight suit, the lead pilot asked, "What about weapons? What are we flying into?"

"Igor says he doesn't know."

The lead pilot, Genadii Seleznev, swore. "Just like a bunch of damn engineers. First they lose all the Stingers, and then they don't know who the hell has them." He zipped up his flight suit.

As he put on his flight helmet, Genadii continued, "Look, Valentin, your machine is fully armed. Follow about a mile or so behind me. Be ready for anything. I'll go in with the security force, unarmed, and land at the camp. When I land at the camp, set down east of the lake and watch and listen." By the time they reached the helicopters, the mechanics had both machines ready to fly. The security force, six well-armed men, waited beside the machines.

In spite of their complaints, the flight crews and the security force were happy with any change in the endless routine of Randal Lake. The second helicopter would fly empty except for the crew of three. In both cases, the copilot also served as the weapons officer. He would fire whatever weapons were necessary, if any were indeed required. Genadii's young copilot gave little thought to any risks they might face. "About goddamn time we had something to do."

Genadii glanced at him and with considerably less enthusiasm responded, "Yes. Goddamn time." They lifted off with the six heavily armed guards in the back and headed westward. Valentin's helicopter followed.

After Arnie left with Maria, Peter jogged down to the loaded twenty-foot freighter canoe, untied the rope, and flipped it into the front of the canoe. He pushed off with a paddle and started the small outboard motor. The lake was narrow, less than half a mile wide at this point, and the wind remained calm. Halfway across, he looked to the east to see Arnie's helicopter lift up after dropping Maria off at the esker.

She had four Stinger missiles and two AK-101 rifles with four hundred rounds of ammunition. He had about the same, plus his Weatherby. *Should be enough for now,* he thought. *If it isn't, we're both in more trouble than we can handle.* He breathed a sigh of relief when he saw no strange helicopters on the horizon and turned his attention back to the shore of the lake. He aimed for a spot with more large rocks than were normal along the shore. The dark-green color of the canoe stood out sharply in the drab universe, but he had grabbed a small camouflage tarp from the supply tent. The canoe bumped up against the shore. Peter quickly jumped out onto the rocks.

He worked quickly but deliberately. First he unloaded the canoe and removed the outboard motor. Then, with considerable effort, made more difficult by the effects of his earlier encounter with Charlie, he hauled the heavy canoe up onto the shore and turned it over. He unfolded the tarp, covered the canoe and much of the equipment, and weighted down the edges with rocks. It wasn't bad. Unless someone looked closely, they would never see the canoe from the air.

He looked up. "Christ," he said. He could feel the adrenaline pumping as his body prepared for action. As his thinking gathered speed, the rest of the world began to slow down, at least as he perceived it. He greeted the sensations unhappily, as old and somewhat unpleasant friends. They had served him well before, and whether he liked them or not he knew he needed them today.

Peter left the two assault rifles and their ammunition beside the canoe, under an edge of the tarp. With two Stingers and his Weatherby rifle, along with a small amount of ammunition, he started off at a quick trot to the top of the low ridge. Peter looked around and identified two large rocks, positioned side by side and divided by a cleft. The rocks overlooked the lake, providing a view to the camp on the other side. They would provide protection from hostile fire and shelter from prying eyes.

He dropped the rifle and the two Stingers into the shelter of the rock cleft and took a quick look to the east. Did he hear a helicopter? Sounds carried well in this land on calm days. It had to be Arnie. The sound didn't have the characteristic deep and slower beat of a gunship. Peter ran down the hill to the remainder of the equipment. He picked up one more Stinger and one of the AK-101s, with two extra clips. He had planned to bring the satellite telephone across the lake, but in his haste he had left it in the office tent. He barely made it to the top of the hill when Maria's voice startled him, loud, on the radio.

"Peter, this is Maria. Over."

Panting and hurting from his second jog up the hill, Peter answered. "Go ahead, Maria. Over."

"I can hear a helicopter, due east of me. I'll call when I see anything. Over."

Peter clicked the mike. He had to hope that their radio conversations were relatively private on this particular channel. He got up on his knees, his head barely above the cover of the rocks, and listened. He could hear it too, and it didn't sound like Arnie. He looked around to be sure all the weapons were well hidden but close at hand. He felt naked and exposed. He was in full combat mode now. *This is crazy,* he said to himself. *It'll never work. They'll see one of us right off, and that'll do it for sure.* Peter found some comfort in the fact that he was well armed. The people in Afghanistan had done well against these same helicopters in their war, with older, less reliable Stingers.

Even knowing that someone had hijacked the Bombardier, would the pilots realize what he and Maria had at their disposal? Could they even imagine a geologist and his assistant setting up an ambush? *Charlie knew about my time with the SEALS, and he knew about the weapons,* Peter thought. *They have to know.* "Jesus Christ," he said out loud. "We're in for it." He could hear the lead helicopter quite clearly, and in spite of the coolness of the day, he was sweating. "Too late now, you fucking idiot!" he said. He took a deep breath and then he added, much more softly, "We're ready for you, you bastards. Just come and get it."

32

PETER HEARD MARIA ON THE RADIO. HE DISPENSED WITH RADIO etiquette. "What is it?"

"I see two helicopters coming from the east, one behind the other. The first doesn't look like it's carrying any missiles."

"Keep a close watch on the second. Let me know if it looks armed. Remember, Charlie knew all about our weapons. We could be in for quite a show here if they're ready for us. Hold on and keep out of sight."

Maria felt no need to respond. Peter pulled out his binoculars as the first machine approached his position. He tried to blend into the ground, to become invisible. He knew from experience how hard it could be to see someone from the air in the Arctic. The land was too big. Right now, though, he found it hard to convince himself that he was invisible.

The first helicopter came into view. Even at a distance, the black machine loomed large and ugly. Except for machine guns, it was unarmed. The water from the half-frozen clay between the rocks began to soak into his clothes, and Peter shivered. He cursed softly and watched closely as the helicopter approached the camp. The pilot circled the tents slowly. Would they take the elementary precaution of setting a guard down on top of one of the hills, perhaps next to him? They didn't. When its arrival sparked no activity at the camp, the helicopter headed slowly toward the open space to the west of the helipad. The radio beside him came to life. *Christ, it's loud,* he thought, and he quickly turned the volume down.

"Peter! The second helicopter landed on a small hill about a half a mile east of me. I don't know what's on board, but there's lots of stuff hanging off the sides."

"Okay. Keep out of sight. I want to see what they do at the camp." He watched as six men got out of the helicopter. Each was in full battle dress and carried an assault rifle. One went up to the cook tent and kicked the door in. The door gave way easily, and Peter laughed softly. The soldiers' approach was a serious case of overkill. The same man went systematically from tent to tent, searching each one. When he got to the office tent, he spent some time inside, then he signaled for one of the other soldiers. Shortly afterward, the two of them emerged from the tent carrying all the radios, along with the briefcase loaded with cash from under Peter's bed. They gave them to another soldier, who put them into the helicopter.

One of the soldiers carried the satellite telephone to the helicopter, and a second ripped the antenna off the tent and took it to the helicopter. "So much for communications with the rest of the world," Peter muttered.

Peter watched with increased interest as the lead soldier finally got to Tom's bunk tent, where they had stored most of the weapons from the Bombardier. By now the security force knew that no one was in the camp. The men held a hurried conference, and they looked around at the hills. Peter smiled at their obvious discomfort. He understood the way they felt. The soldiers carried the missiles from Tom's tent back to the helicopter, both the Stingers and the Dragons. After they finished, one man carried a small package to the supply tent. Peter was pretty sure he knew what would happen next.

Peter reached down for the radio and thought better of it. He had to be careful with radio communications as long as these characters had all those radios. Peter put down the binoculars, lifted up one Stinger, and began to prepare it.

The man left the supply tent, jogged quickly back to the helicopter, and hopped aboard. It lifted up, backed out over the lake, and started to turn to head down the lake to the east. Before the pilot completed his turn, Peter fired the Stinger. At close range, the impact was almost instantaneous. Attracted to the heat from the exhaust, the missile exploded. The helicopter erupted into a blossom of flames. In only a few seconds, a quickly dissipating whiff of smoke and a shower of what looked like hundreds of burning leaves hung in the air where the helicopter had already sunk into the cold, dark waters of Nuvilik Lake. Peter saw no survivors. The soldiers would not last in the cold water more than a few minutes in any case.

He could already hear the second helicopter coming toward him, and he quickly reached for the radio. "Take him out now!" he shouted. Peter worked quickly to get the next Stinger ready to fire. He stole a glance up the lake to the east. *Oh, shit! Here they come.* The helicopter popped some flares, not many, but enough to make the first of Maria's Stingers miss the target. "Oh, Christ!" was all he could say as the machine turned slightly and aimed directly at him.

As the flares burned out, Peter fired his second missile. More flares flew, and the helicopter pilot took violent evasive action. Peter's missile missed. *That pilot's good*, Peter thought. The helicopter was moving fast, but the evasive maneuvers gave Peter a few extra seconds. He threw down the launch tube and picked up the Weatherby. The flares wouldn't distract the flight of a bullet. The helicopter came on at full speed. A burst of fire erupted from the machine gun in the nose. Little splatters of mud and chips of rock erupted around Peter.

The pilot and copilot tried to focus all their attention on Peter, but the rocks hid him, and he was a small target. They couldn't ignore the threat from the rear. Peter scrambled along the cold, wet mud to the other side of his rock shelter. Freezing water and mud soaked his clothes, but he didn't notice the wet or the cold. He could see the pilot clearly in the rifle's scope. He aimed at the pilot and fired a single shot. Though he was prepared for the massive recoil, it nearly knocked him over. The helicopter wavered. It struggled to maintain even flight. With the pilot dead or seriously wounded, the copilot and flight engineer would be very busy. He ejected the casing and prepared for a second shot.

The helicopter was directly over the lake and nearly upon him as Peter took aim with the Weatherby. The remaining crew had popped flares one more time, but they were dying out. Peter aimed at the copilot and took his second shot. As he absorbed the recoil, Peter saw that Maria had fired another Stinger, and he ducked down behind the rocks again. He looked up again when he heard the explosion. Like the first helicopter, the second fell clumsily into the lake, leaving behind a thin trail of smoke. Peter stood up to take a good look.

The sudden explosion from Tom's bunk tent staggered him. Peter dropped behind a rock for cover. Most of the ammunition and explosives in the tent went off all at once. Whatever they'd put into the tent had done a good job of destroying what was left of their weapons. It also wiped out some of the other tents in the camp and set a number of the fuel drums ablaze. After a few moments, he took a cautious look at the camp, or what was left of it. There were still a few small explosions, probably from leftover ammunition and hand grenades. He realized for the first time how fast his heart was beating.

He leaned up against a rock and keyed the mike. "Thanks, Maria. I owe you one."

After a short silence, "What's going on down there?"

Peter got to his feet and looked across the lake. "They put a demolition charge in Tom's tent. We may have destroyed their air superiority, but we don't have a hell of a lot to throw at them anymore. We've got another problem, too. The satellite telephone was on the first helicopter, so we've lost any reliable contact with the outside." Peter stopped to catch his breath. "You hear all that, Arnie? Over."

"You bet, Peter," came the quick response. "What do you want me to do? Over."

"Fly down to the esker where you left Maria. I wouldn't go too near the camp for now. Watch your fuel. I don't know how much we have left. I'm going across the lake to see what's left and what I can salvage. I think the worst of the explosions are over. I'll meet you at the esker with the canoe. Over."

"No problem. See you there. Over."

Peter collected what was left of his weaponry and began to walk down to the canoe. He carried his Weatherby rifle, the AK-101, and one Stinger. A sense of calm began to flow over him, almost a sense of depression after the adrenaline rush.

Maria Davidoff stood on the esker, the discarded launch tubes on the ground beside her, trembling in the aftershock of what they had done and thoroughly embarrassed by the almost sexual sensation she felt as adrenaline continued to surge through her body. All her martial arts training had been for fun, as well as for a sense of empowerment after the abuse at the hands of her husband. Other than that one night, when her ex-husband nearly killed her, she'd never considered killing anyone. Now it all seemed much too easy.

As she watched, far down the lake, Peter started across to the camp in the canoe. She could barely hear the sound of the small motor, and she thought about what Dick Durban had asked her to do here. "Get close to him," he had said. Well, that was easy. She didn't want to think about the rest of Durban's request.

A vivid anger, mixed with bitterness, began to rise within her. She didn't know whether to laugh, cry, or scream. Gregori's attack in her apartment had convinced her to go along with Durban's request. She shook her head. Why had she agreed? "You can just go fuck yourself,

Dick Durban," she muttered. *I've finally made a decent decision about a man. I'm going to bury what you asked me to do so deep nobody will ever find it.*

At Randal Lake, Igor listened as the radio operator made his report by telephone. "Genadii landed at the camp and reported it was empty. Valentin landed nearby." He rapidly related what happened. "Genadii lifted off from the camp, and Valentin screamed that Genadii was shot down by a missile. Valentin flew toward the camp, attacking the source of the missile. Then there was an explosion, and nothing more." The radio operator paused, near to an emotional breakdown. He and the pilots had been good friends. "I've tried, but I can't raise either one."

Igor let the telephone hang from his hand at his side. "How long before we can launch the missile, Helmut?" he asked in a monotone.

Helmut stared at Igor. "I haven't finished the final tests of the programming yet."

Coldly, "That's not what I asked. How long before we can get this thing into the air?"

Helmut threw up his hands. "I don't know. If everything's right, we could move to alert status in a few hours, five or six, maybe less. Once in alert status, you know as well as anyone that we can launch in a few minutes. I just have to finish reviewing the last of the arming and targeting circuits, and I should test them one more time."

Igor said harshly, "We'll have to go without all your tests. We'll have to trust that you and your people did your job right the first time."

Igor brought the telephone back to his mouth again. "Tell the technicians to get down here at once," Igor told him. Though Igor knew that Helmut, with a single computer, could target and fire the missile himself, the additional five technicians made the process far smoother and more reliable.

Igor called the security force, or what was left of it. "Evgenii, we've lost the helicopters. I expect we'll be attacked within the hour. We're going to code red, and we'll seal the area as soon as the technicians get down here. Get all your remaining men in position." He hung up.

He turned to Helmut, who stared at him. "Now it's time to earn that great pay you've been making. It's time to change the world. Get this goddamned missile ready to fly!"

33

PETER LAUGHED AS THE CANOE CUT A WAKE THROUGH HALF-BURNED hundred dollar bills on its way across the lake. The briefcase full of cash must have burst in the explosion, and what had looked like burning leaves had actually been burning hundred dollar bills. Bits and pieces of cushions floated on the lake, but most of the helicopter appeared to have sunk to the bottom of the lake, taking the pilots and soldiers with it, leaving a sheen of oil and the smell of jet fuel behind.

Peter cut the motor and the canoe bumped up against the rocks. The explosions appeared to be over, but multicolored flames still danced from the remnants of Tom's tent. Some of the fuel drums still burned, but the small pile near the helipad remained intact. The geophysicists' bunk tent had partially protected the office tent from the worst of the blast. It survived largely intact. Peter entered it, unlocked his metal locker, took out the remaining ammunition for the Weatherby, and stuffed it into his jacket pocket. He quickly searched the remains of the cook tent and found some cheese, sandwich meats, and bread. The rest could wait.

He heard Arnie coming in to land at the east end of the lake. He jogged to the shore, jumped into the canoe, and headed east toward the esker. Then he heard another sound over the noise of the small, outboard motor. Peter turned and looked up to see an old, single-engine Otter floatplane gliding in for a landing from the west. "Christ, just what we need," he said. He'd forgotten about the grocery delivery. The pilot was probably his old friend Tommy Francis. Tommy's father had run a fishing lodge near Kuujjuaq for years. Half Inuit, Tommy had started flying when he was old enough to see over the controls, and he'd seen just about everything in Nunavik. Peter laughed. *He probably hasn't seen an exploration camp that's been bombed.* Peter continued with the canoe to the esker. The old Otter would follow him.

The floatplane pulled out of its glide, made a lazy turn, and began a second, slow descent to the lake. As the canoe arrived at the esker, the plane glided to a stop about twenty feet away. The pilot gave the engine a little throttle, then cut back and lightly bumped the edge of the gravel bank as the engine stopped. Tommy Francis opened the hatch above his seat and stood up, looking over the big rotary engine with his round, freckled face.

"You sure picked a great time to stop by for a social call, Tommy," Peter said with a smile.

"That's not much of a welcome for the grocery delivery man," Tommy laughed. "I was planning to stop at the camp, but it looks a little worse for wear."

"You might say that," Peter responded.

Tommy climbed over the jumble of groceries in the plane, opened the side door, and jumped to the shore from the float. "What the hell happened?"

"It's a long story. I'll fill you in as we walk up to the helicopter." By the time they reached the helicopter, Peter had finished with his abbreviated account.

"Holy shit, man," Tommy said in amazement. "You need to call in the troops or something."

"I don't know how we can. We have radios to talk to you, to Arnie, and to each other, but we can't talk to anybody else. The satellite telephone's at the bottom of the lake. We could go to Asbestos Hill, but we left Charlie there shot in the gut, and he could be telling them almost anything. If we hang around there, we're not getting out, and I don't think we have much time to lose if we're going to do anything about this mess."

Arnie spoke up, "What about his radio?" He pointed to Tommy Francis. "We can talk to him, and he should be able to raise his base back at Kuujjuaq. Give him a message to pass along."

Tommy looked at Peter and shrugged. "I'd be happy to try to get a message out for you, Peter. I'm not sure anyone will believe what you've told me, and I'm not sure I want to put that out over the radio anyway. I can be back at Kuujjuaq in about three hours. Will that be soon enough?"

"I doubt it," Peter responded. "I half expect at any moment to see a missile contrail rising up into the sky from Randal Lake." He thought for a minute. "Let me write a message for you to radio in when you get high enough to make contact with Kuujjuaq. Then you can make a telephone call to the RCMP when you get in."

Peter pulled his field notebook out of his shirt pocket. He held it up. "A bit bent out of shape, but I don't mind that." He wrote, "To Richard Durban, RCMP." He added the telephone number. "Emergency. Nuke launch at Randal Lake imminent. Will try to stop or delay. Peter Binder." He ripped it out and handed it to Tommy. "Tell them it's extremely urgent. They can use my name to get through to Durban. Okay?"

"No problem at this end," Tommy replied with a grin, "but you know it can be hard to get anybody excited at the Kuujjuaq base unless their ass is on fire."

"Yeah, I know. Just do the best you can."

"So what do you want me to do when I get back to base?"

"Call the same number, and tell Durban what I told you. Make sure you add that his man, Charlie, tried to kill me. Charlie's wounded. We sent him to Asbestos Hill, and Durban shouldn't believe a damned thing he says."

"Well, that should be an interesting conversation," Tommy responded with a bemused smile and raised eyebrows. "You're going over to Randal Lake to try to stop this yourself? You've got to be crazy, Peter. They must have a bunch of people just waiting for you."

Peter gestured at the empty landscape. "I don't see anyone else around, do you? We may be a small group, but I'm pretty sure we have the only air force around at the moment." He laughed at the thought. "Would you be willing, Tommy, to do a little long distance reconnaissance on your way back to Kuujjuaq?"

Tommy laughed. "Well, the old Otter isn't exactly a modern fighter, but as long as you promise no jet fighters or missiles, I guess we can give it a try."

"I can't promise no missiles, but I don't want you to get too close. Just look at the mine shaft with your binoculars and see if you can tell if the cover they installed is open or closed. Let me know if there's any diesel exhaust coming from the low building immediately east of the shaft."

"I'll give it a try. You want me to get the radio message off first?"

"Get that off as soon as you get high enough." Peter looked at his small group. "Okay. I'm in the middle of this, and so are you guys, whether you like it or not. Any of you can get in the Otter and fly out with Tommy. No hard feelings anywhere." Peter shrugged his shoulders. "God knows what we'll find when we get to Randal Lake, but you can bet it won't be a welcoming party." He looked at each in turn. "What do you say?"

No one spoke for a few moments. Finally, Maria said, "Peter, I don't think any of us wants to leave you to handle this on your own. I think we'd better get on with it."

"Who agrees with Maria? Tom? Arnie?" Peter asked.

Tom nodded and said, "Look, I don't know what we can do, but I'll do what I can to help."

Arnie spoke up next. "Let's stop talking. Tell us what you've got in mind."

Peter knew Arnie was the only one who had a clue about what he was getting into. "Okay. First, let's unload the groceries. Who knows when we'll need them? Once that's done, Tommy, take off and do your fly-by of Randal Lake. We'll be busy picking up some supplies at the camp. Don't get too close to the mine site."

"Don't worry about that," Tommy laughed. "I'll keep my distance. The old Otter's been around for a long time, and I hope to fly it for a few more years."

"I don't want you to talk to us on your normal frequency, Tommy. Arnie, give him the radio frequency we're using."

They moved as a group down to the plane and quickly unloaded it, with help from Tommy's copilot. Pausing in her work, Maria turned to Peter and said, "I thought you said that all the weapons in Tom's tent had been destroyed."

Peter looked out over the lake. "When I don't completely understand what's going on, I generally don't put all my cards on the table until I'm sure of the bets all around. I hid a few things up behind the camp. I hope they're in good shape." He turned back to the stack of groceries. "They damn well better be in good shape."

Maria laughed. "Peter Binder, you're one suspicious bastard."

Peter smiled at her. "Not everyone appreciates it as one of my better traits."

"I think you can count on a few people around here appreciating it right now."

They stashed all the food under the canoe. Tommy and his copilot climbed back into the plane, started it with the usual bangs and minor explosions, and headed out into the lake to take off. The rest of them didn't bother to watch the takeoff. They trotted up to the helicopter. Carrying what was left of the weapons and ammunition, they piled in.

As Arnie powered up, Peter leaned over and shouted, "Land at the ridge behind the camp. You'll see where I stashed the box of dynamite in a crevice in the rocks. What's left of the weapons should be there too. While we sort out what we want, you'd better fuel up. I think most of the drums by the helipad are still okay." Peter's mind raced as he frantically tried to piece together a sensible plan. The helicopter couldn't carry all the gear and people he wanted, in one trip. He'd have to ferry in the weapons, along with Maria and himself, and bring the rest in later, assuming they and the helicopter survived the first try.

Visions of the buildings at Randal Lake flickered through his mind. He tried to remember the details. What would it be like as a battleground? His mind searched for advantages. A few small hills could provide some limited cover, but any approach was pretty barren of cover near the mine site itself. How could they possibly get from the landing site to the mine alive? Maybe the range of the Weatherby would be an equalizer. The night at this time of year in northern Nunavik wasn't dark enough to provide much cover. Had the Germans or the Russians changed things much? How could this small group have a chance to cripple the carefully laid plans? Peter's mind jerked back to the present as Arnie bumped down next to his hidden cache of weapons.

Peter leaned forward. "Arnie, when you're down at the camp, take a quick look in my office tent, under the work table. Grab the roll of duct tape I got from the Bombardier, if it's still there."

"Duct tape?" Arnie laughed. "Why do you want duct tape?'

"Arnie, you should know better. You always need duct tape," Peter said with a grin.

Once his passengers had offloaded, Arnie immediately returned to the camp to refuel. Peter scraped the dirt and grass off one end of the tarp. He and Tom pulled the first tarp off the pile and unwrapped the orange tarp to reveal the plastic bags with the assault rifles, a few hand grenades, a large amount of ammunition, and the handheld missiles. Peter had to admit that it didn't look like enough to take on a bunch of crazy Russians and a stolen ICBM, but it was all they had.

"What should we take?" Maria asked. Peter could sense her growing nervousness. He didn't blame her for it. Still, he was sure she wouldn't back out now. Of course, now that the Otter was gone there weren't too many options anyway.

"We should take as much as we can manage. I have no idea of what we'll need. Maria, you and I will go over to Randal Lake with as much of this stuff as possible. Arnie will come back for you, Tom, and whatever else we think we need." Peter looked at Tom and took in his obvious discomfort.

"If anything goes wrong with this, Tom, you'll have to find your way to Asbestos Hill. There's enough food up at the esker for a while. You've got your GPS, and I'll have Arnie leave his flight map with you, just in case. You can make it to Asbestos Hill with hard walking in two or three days." Tom was in good shape, and he was dressed for the walk. He would survive. Peter wasn't so sure about himself and Maria after they landed at Randal Lake.

Peter turned back to the task at hand. "Okay. Be sure we've got twenty-five sticks of dynamite, about thirty feet of fuse, and five caps. Then we need four of the AK-101 assault rifles, five of the thirty-round clips for each one, and a few of the hand grenades. That's all but one rifle and about half of the ammunition." Maria and Tom began to sort the dynamite and ammunition. There was probably no air force left at Randal Lake, but Peter put two Stingers aside anyway. He selected all four of the antitank Dragons. "Let's see, we already have two Stingers on the helicopter. Right, Maria?"

"No. We've got four left from this morning."

"Good. We'll take along two more of the Stingers. We may need them if I'm wrong about the helicopters. Maybe we can bring down an ICBM with them if we have to." He chuckled. "I very much doubt it, but it might be worth a try." Below them, in the camp, the sound of the helicopter rotors rose in pitch and volume. Arnie was returning to pick them up.

Arnie set the helicopter down beside the trio and their small pile of weapons and dynamite. He opened his door and signaled to Peter, handing him the roll of duct tape with a smile. "I found your tape, and I've got Tommy on the radio," he shouted. "You want to talk to him?"

"Yeah, sure." Arnie handed his headset and mike to Peter. "Tommy, this is Peter Binder. You got anything for me? Over."

"I took a look around. It looks very quiet. I didn't see anyone moving around. The shaft still looks like it's covered, and I did see some diesel smoke coming from the exhausts on the building east of the shaft. Over."

Peter smiled at the news. They had a little time left, and he could see the edges of a plan taking shape in his mind. Imperfect, but they might have a chance. "You didn't see anyone around at all? Over."

"Not a soul." Tommy paused. "Listen, Peter, you be careful over there. It looks like someone's waiting for something to happen, and I'll bet my last dollar you're the happening. Over."

"Don't worry. I intend to be careful. Did you send the message? Over."

"No problem. I told them it was important. They promised to pass it along right away. You watch your ass over there, Peter. I'd like to see you again up here and still in one piece. Over."

"Have a safe trip home. Over."

The Otter's mike clicked once. Peter handed the headset and mike back to Arnie. "How much fuel do you have on board, Arnie?"

"I topped off the tanks. We have enough for about three hours of flying."

"We might be able to squeeze all of us in, plus all the stuff we're taking, but it'll be a really tight fit."

Arnie looked a bit dubious. "I think we ought to take two trips, to be safe."

Peter laughed. "I think the term 'safe' is a bit relative today." He turned to Tom. "We'll load this gear, and I'll go over with Maria. Okay?"

Tom shrugged his shoulders. He was not happy. Peter knew he was asking a lot of Tom.

"Can you give me your chart for here and over to Asbestos Hill, Arnie? I want to leave at least that much of a map for Tom, in case he has to walk to the mine." As he waited for the map, Peter turned back to Tom. "Keep the rifle and ammunition with you no matter what happens. If anything happens and you aren't picked up, you know what to do." Tom nodded. Arnie handed the maps to Peter, who passed them to Tom.

"Now let's get loaded up," Peter said. They all pitched in and had the weapons and dynamite loaded in a few minutes. As Peter sat down in the helicopter, Maria touched him on the arm.

"Peter, this isn't exactly what I imagined for our time together when I came up here." She smiled.

"Don't say I didn't warn you. I seem to remember saying something like 'going to hell to stay away from the devil'." Peter grinned. "You'll be fine. You're tougher than any of the rest of us." Peter looked ahead as they pulled up and away. For a moment a wave of guilt for involving all of them almost overwhelmed him. *Damn! I hope I can handle this.* It had been a long time, and he'd made one big mistake at the Bombardier when he let the lookout see him first. That could have been fatal. He had to do better than that this time. He took a deep breath, and the moment of anxiety passed.

He put on his flight helmet, signaled Maria to do the same, and keyed the mike. "Arnie, I don't want you heading straight in. After Esker Lake, get down on the deck, head south for about four or five miles, and then head east. I want to come in from the south, below the top of the little hill about a mile south of the Randal Lake."

"You'll have to give me some help. You know that area better than I do."

"We should be able to see the headframe as we move east. When it's due north of us, turn to the north. I'll tell you when to stop. Stay as close to the grass as you can. We'll land on the south side of the hill for cover. We can unload there. Then get back as quick as you can to pick up Tom. Bring him back to where we unload." Still speaking to Arnie, Peter looked over at Maria. "While you're gone, we'll see if we can raise a little hell at Randal Lake."

34

THE HELICOPTER CREPT ACROSS THE LANDSCAPE, NEARLY GLUED TO the sparse tundra grasses. Arnie was taking no chance of being seen. Flying so close to the deck had its own risks, but Arnie liked nothing more than a challenge to his flying abilities. A low hill lay ahead, between them and the Randal Lake mine site.

"Arnie, I'm pretty sure that's the hill I want up ahead. Put down at the base of it, near that small patch of grass. We can unload there. Before you leave, I want to make a quick run to the top of the hill, to make sure we're where I think we are. Okay?"

"No problem. You want us to unload while you run up there?" Arnie maneuvered for the landing.

"No, both of you sit tight. I'll make a quick check on our position before we unload. If this is the right hill, it's the only cover we've got from here to the mine. If anything happens to me, get out of here as fast as you can. We're not dealing with idiots or amateurs here."

The helicopter touched down beside the grass, and Peter jumped out. He reached quickly behind the seat for an assault rifle and checked to be sure it was loaded with a full clip. With a second clip in his pocket, he started at a trot up the hill. Near the crest, he slowed his pace to a quick walk. In his heightened state of awareness, the world moved slowly, with brighter colors and louder noises. His nerves stretched taut, looking, watching, listening. The pain in his chest retreated to a background annoyance. He felt exposed and vulnerable as he approached the top of the low hill, a jumble of boulders and fragments of rock broken from years of frost. Most stood less than five feet tall, wide at the base and set firmly in the ever-present, half-frozen clay.

Peter maneuvered quickly, low to the ground through the maze of large boulders. He stopped next to one of the larger ones. The ground dropped away in a gradual slope in front of him. He was right where he wanted to be. The Randal Lake camp sat in full view about a mile to the north. It looked quiet and peaceful as he scanned it with his binoculars. He had momentary doubts. Then he saw the four figures who hurried south across the tundra toward the hill, his hill. He felt a new surge of adrenaline. Someone must have seen them arrive.

The approaching men, dressed in shapeless, camouflage battle dress, all carried a rifle, probably an AK-101, the same as his. They moved with the effortless trot of soldiers kept fit by constant training. Supremely confident, they took no action to hide their intentions or to make themselves less visible. Of course, there was no cover to hide them. Peter imagined he could hear their boots making little squishing sounds in the water and clay, though the low moan of the wind made that unlikely. Peter was aware of his heart beating hard again. The men had abandoned their prepared positions at the camp. They presented an easy target.

"Too bad you're a few minutes late," Peter said softly. He readied his rifle. They still had not seen him. They came quickly in a tight group up the nearly barren lower slope of the hill. Ground-hugging willows clung to the hillside. They neither hindered nor hid the advancing men.

Peter waited, forcing patience, stretched out between the rocks. He watched them through the sights, looking up from time to time to check on their position. *Bloody fools*, he thought, *bunched so closely together*. Finally, at a range of fifty yards, he opened fire. Outnumbered and outgunned, he gave no thought to a warning. He could not afford a protracted firefight. He caught the four completely by surprise, with no place to hide or seek cover. In no more than three seconds, Peter emptied the clip. All four men fell to the ground, unmoving.

Peter put the gun down and took out his binoculars again. He looked carefully down the hill and toward the mine. He saw nothing to disturb the quiet emptiness that had been broken only momentarily by what had been, essentially, an execution. The scene bordered on the surrealistic.

He put a fresh clip in the rifle, got up slowly, and stepped out from the rocks, still watching carefully. The rush was past, replaced by a growing sense of calm. He trotted quickly down to the four men, about fifty yards away, rifle at the ready. He saw no movement, though one man still lived, barely. Unconscious, the man bled profusely from several wounds. Peter could do nothing for him. He picked up the four rifles plus what ammunition the men had carried and ran back up the hill.

At the top, he took out his binoculars one more time to look more closely at the mine site. He still couldn't see any activity. Peter put the binoculars away, took out a small compass, and took one bearing on the headframe and a second one on the last building to the east. The headframe lay nearly due north of the small hill. Then he picked up his rifle, left the rest piled against a rock, and took a quick look around.

To the west Peter saw a low, dark line of clouds. It would be upon them quickly. He took a closer look. The thick, rolling fogbank moved slowly toward the east on the light wind. The unpredictable northern Nunavik weather was ready to make a sudden change from beautiful, bright sunshine to zero-visibility fog. Maybe they'd have cover after all.

He turned, pushed down the lingering pain in his chest and

started a quick jog back down to the helicopter. Maria was about halfway up the hill with one of the rifles. When she saw him coming toward her, Maria stopped and waited.

Maria panted slightly to catch her breath. "What the hell happened up there? We heard shots and you were nowhere in sight."

Peter continued toward the helicopter, and Maria turned quickly to jog along with him. "Four men were supposed to meet me at the top of the hill," he said. "They were a little late." He looked at Maria, his face set. "I've lost count, but I think that makes about ten down, not counting the advance team and the helicopter crews. We might be getting close to even now." Cold logic told him that now they had a much better chance of success.

At the helicopter, Arnie stared at Peter, but he asked no questions. "I had to get rid of some unwelcome visitors, Arnie. We need to get unloaded. We have a change in the weather coming in the next thirty minutes or so." Peter pointed to the west. "I can just see it from the top of the hill. It looks like ground-level fog with about zero visibility. We don't have much time to raise hell from a distance, so let's get moving."

All three of them took to unloading. In a few minutes they piled all the equipment neatly on the ground, about ten feet from the helicopter. Peter turned to Arnie. "With that change of weather coming so fast, take a chance and fly back the most direct way possible to pick up Tom. I don't want us separated. Stay on the deck, though. I can't guarantee no Stingers."

Arnie laughed and smiled at Peter. "You're always so reassuring. I'll get out of here and get back as quick as I can. If the weather gets so bad I can't fly, I'll set down until I can make it through. How will I find you when I get back?"

"I've got my flare gun with me. I don't want to use the radios unless we have to. I'll fire a green flare if it's safe to land near me, a red one if I don't think it's safe and you should keep your distance."

"Okay. Sounds simple enough." He climbed into the pilot's seat and started flipping switches to get the helicopter running again. "See you soon. As Admiral Farragut would have said, 'Damn the missiles! Full speed ahead!' I'll be back."

Peter laughed and shut the door on the helicopter. Arnie wasted no time moving out. Peter watched for a moment as the helicopter skimmed the ground at full speed, heading west. Maria spoke up, "Well? Shouldn't we get moving?"

Peter turned and said, "Yep. Let's get ourselves, plus our rifles and four antitank missiles, up to the top of the hill. It wouldn't hurt to take along two of the Stingers, too." Peter continued, "I have an idea of how we might get those guys excited and rather busy before Arnie gets back. We've got to stay on our toes, though. Obviously, they know we're here." Maria simply nodded and started up the hill with her share of the load. They made quick time of it. When they had the missiles collected at the top of the hill, Peter laid out his plan. Maria looked out at the four bodies lying fifty yards down the hill. She was very quiet.

"This first step is pretty simple." He took a breath and pointed at the mine site. "I asked Tommy Francis to look for exhaust coming from that building to the right of the headframe. You can see some now. That's the old generator building. They may have emergency power, but we can hope they don't, or that it's not enough to actually launch the missile. If we can knock out those generators, we may be able to delay the launch."

"Do you think a Stinger missile would lock onto the exhaust heat?"

"I'm not sure, but I think the Dragon antitank missiles are a better bet. They have a lot more punch than the Stingers."

Peter quietly took his time to examine the target. "The only problem is that we're at about maximum range. It's worth a try, though. If I remember right, there were two big generators, one in each half of the building. A direct hit on a generator with one of the Dragons will definitely destroy it."

As Peter periodically searched the sky around them for unfriendly helicopters, he continued to outline his plan out loud, as much for himself as for Maria. "After we take out the generators, I want to stir things up in a big way and set fire to the fuel tanks. The burning fuel and the heat of the explosions and fire should ignite a few more buildings. That should flush out some of the remaining defenders." Peter looked to the west. The weather front looked ominous, and it was moving closer by the minute. "What do you think? I don't think we have much time before the weather takes a turn for the worse."

"Give me your binoculars. I'll tell you what happens when the missiles hit their targets."

"Fine by me." He handed her the binoculars. "See if you can spot any people in or around the buildings, and watch any of the outside lights if they're on. If they go out, that should tell us if we've succeeded and knocked out the generators." He began to assemble and lay out the antitank missiles.

Maria scanned the camp. She noticed one small building that appeared newly built. Slowly, she trained the binoculars on the other buildings, looking for people, and eventually she spotted four. Two appeared briefly in windows high up in the mill building. One more crouched at the top of the headframe, and one showed himself briefly at the window of the new building.

"I can see four people. They're all close to the generator building or the fuel tanks. The next few minutes should be exciting for them." She wondered what the small building was, and then she thought she could see the shimmering of heated air. "Peter, if you've got a minute, look at the small building to the left of the headframe. Does it look like a lot of heat coming out of there?"

He took the binoculars and looked at the building. "Sure does. I don't think that building was there earlier in the summer. It's probably part of a ventilation system. They must have lots of electronics for the missile controls somewhere underground, and they'd need ventilation." Peter looked at the camp now without the binoculars.

"I guess we'd better stay focused. We should investigate that little building when we can." He handed the binoculars back to Maria and returned his attention to the missiles.

A few minutes later, Peter announced, "I'm about ready to fire the antitank missiles now. These are the new and improved Super Dragons. They're extremely accurate with their wire guidance." Peter figured that talking was a good way to keep him and Maria calm and focused, and he continued his commentary as he prepared to fire. "This one, though, you can't fire and forget. You have to keep sighted on the target until the missile hits. It should be quite a show." He had moved farther away, but they could still talk easily.

"Okay." Maria kept her binoculars trained on the lit bulb in its fixture on the outside of the mill building. The Super Dragon missile launch was not impressive, and from the perspective of those at the Randal Lake mine site, the only clue that anything important was about to happen was the contrail streaking toward the generator building.

The explosion, though, burst into an impressive ball of fire, combining the explosive power of the missile with the fuel and combustibles in the building. Maria watched the street light blink out. Within a minute Peter sent a second missile into the inferno, slightly farther along the side of the now-burning building. Maria saw several men, probably some of the ones she'd seen before, move out of hiding.

The fire they'd caused in the generator building paled by comparison with what happened next, when the third Super Dragon slammed into the large diesel-storage tank. The mushroom cloud of burning fuel spewed black smoke high into the air above an angry, seething mass of dark-red and orange flame. The intense heat from this fire, coupled with the flaming fuel that was scattered for hundreds of feet by the explosion, endangered all the buildings. Almost immediately, the closest outer wall of the big mill building erupted in flame. The men Maria had seen earlier were running from the flames. The shaft area and most of the other buildings were far enough away from the fuel tank to escape immediate damage.

Even Peter was a little shocked by what they had just done. He said rather quietly, "I don't think we need to fire another missile at the fuel tank. We may need it for something more important later." He could hear Arnie coming in from the west. They both turned and looked toward the sound. They could see the little MD 500 helicopter silhouetted against the billowing wall of dark-gray cloud. "Some days, even days like this one, do seem to go well, after all. We're going to have perfect cover." There wasn't much more to say.

In the background, the sounds of the helicopter grew louder, and the noise of its rotor blades mixed with the dull thud of explosions from the mill building. Peter reached into his jacket pocket and pulled out his flare gun. The flare flew high into the air, bursting in a bright green. Arnie came on and landed on the south side of the hill. The fog followed quickly and settled in with the suddenness of a desert night. As the helicopter grew quiet, and the fog muffled the sounds from Randal Lake, Peter listened to the low moan of the wind as it blew softly among the rocks. *Now*, Peter thought. *Time for the next move.*

35

ARLY IN THE MORNING, DICK DURBAN SAT IN THE ROOM WITH WATSON MacDonough and General Khabarovsk, on a video conference call with General Max Worthington to review the status of the Nunavik situation.

"General Khabarovsk, Max and I had a very satisfactory call with the Prime Minister yesterday," Dick said. "We gave him a brief summary of the situation, and he approved all of our initial planning."

Max continued, "Last night, we started to move assets to the airport at Kuujjuaq. Everything should be in place and ready to go later this morning."

Turning to General Khabarovsk, Dick asked, "I understand that you had the opportunity yesterday for a private conversation with the Prime Minister?"

"Yes. I read the letter to him from our President. I think he's prepared to support whatever action is needed."

With a soft knock at the door, a young woman quietly entered the room and handed a note to Dick Durban. Dick unfolded the note, read it, and then he read it again. He looked up at his visitors with a

275

strange, crooked smile. "Well, gentlemen, this may be the smoking gun we need, but I admit it needs some interpretation."

He handed the note to Watson, who read "To Richard Durban, RCMP. Emergency. Nuke lunch at Randal Lake imminent. Will try to stop or delay. Peter Binder." A note at the bottom said the message had been passed urgently from a bush plane near Randal Lake to the flight operations base at Kuujjuaq and then passed along verbally by telephone. The pilot would call as soon as he reached the base.

Watson looked up at Dick. "Doesn't he have any means of communication better than this?" He handed the note to General Khabarovsk.

"Well, he did have a satellite telephone, but who knows what's going on now." Dick turned to the general, who looked a bit confused by the note. "For your benefit, general, Peter Binder is a geologist working out of an exploration camp near Randal Lake. He's a decisive fellow. He eliminated an earlier reconnaissance force, probably sent by Rostov, the one with the Bombardier full of weapons. As I interpret this note, he believes that the launch of the ICBM is imminent."

Dick pressed a buzzer that summoned the secretary back. "Cathy, please call this bush plane outfit back and find out when the pilot's expected. I want to talk with him as soon as he arrives at the base." He looked up at the video feed and at the other men in the room. "Well, we all have a lot to do today to be prepared for the meeting with the Prime Minister. Let's plan on another call at noon, to make sure we're ready."

Dick headed back to his office. Shortly after he sat down at his desk, the telephone rang. "Dick Durban here."

The telephone line hissed faintly in the background. "Monsieur Durban, I am Pierre Couette of the Quebec Provincial Police. We have received a disturbing call from the Asbestos Hill asbestos mine in northern Nunavik. A helicopter dropped off an injured man from a nearby exploration camp. He has a serious gunshot wound in the abdomen. He claims to work for you and demands to talk to you immediately. His name is Charles Sturm."

Dick put his head in his hands as he listened. "What's his condition?"

"He is in very serious condition." The policeman paused. "He's telling us a strange story of a group of four or five men and women, about to go on a rampage and kill everyone at the Randal Lake mine site. He says they have some crazy idea that the people there are all Russian spies, and that they have a nuclear-tipped missile that they intend to launch with Toronto as its target. Do you know anything about this?"

Dick sighed audibly. "Can I talk to him?" As he talked he filled the memo paper on his desk with complex geometric designs and mazes.

"*Monsieur,* he is not in good shape," Pierre Couette responded, "but, yes, we can connect you. Do you wish to talk to him right now?"

At that moment a call came in on the second line. "Can you hold for a moment? I seem to have another call. I'll get back to you as soon as I can."

"No problem, monsieur. I will get Monsieur Sturm on the telephone while we wait."

Dick picked up the second call. "Who is it?" he asked, knowing that his secretary would be on the telephone.

"It's the bush pilot, Tommy Francis, from Kuujjuaq. He says he has an extremely urgent message for you from Peter Binder. I assume it's the follow-up for the one I gave you earlier."

"Put him through."

After a pause, "A Mr. Tommy Francis for you, Mr. Durban."

"Mr. Francis, I understand that you have an important message for me. The first one I received was a little garbled."

"I can imagine. I flew into Nuvilik Lake this morning on a regular grocery run to the camp, and the camp looked like it'd been hit by a bomb. Peter Binder asked me to relay to you what happened up there. Unfortunately, his satellite telephone ended up in the lake, so this is the best he can do for communication." Tommy proceeded to tell Dick what he had heard from Peter, along with some of his own observations.

"I have a hard time believing most of his, Mr. Durban, but I know Peter Binder really well. I don't have any reason to think he'd make this stuff up. He told me to be sure to emphasize what I told you about Charlie Sturm. That was confirmed by two others, the helicopter pilot and a lady, who were with Peter. They must be over at Randal Lake by now, and if I know Peter at all, those guys at Randal Lake have no idea of what's coming their way."

Dick thought for a moment. "Tommy, did you fly close enough to Randal Lake to see if anything was going on there?"

"Peter asked me to fly by. It looked real quiet. No people on the surface that I could see, but I didn't get too close. He asked me to check on exhaust coming from one building east of the shaft and whether the shaft was still covered. The place almost looked too quiet to me. Not like a mining camp at all."

"So what did you see? Was the shaft covered? Did you see exhaust?"

"Yes for both questions. The shaft appeared to still be covered, but I wasn't too close. I didn't think my old Otter should get too nosy. I don't think it'd do too well against ground-to-air missiles."

Dick laughed. "No, probably not. Can you get a message to Peter?"

"I can try to get through to the helicopter pilot. If he's on the ground I won't be able to reach him."

"All right. Tell him to sit tight and not to do anything stupid. Tell him reinforcements are on the way."

"No problem. Anything else?"

"No. Thanks for the help, Tommy, and give me a call if you get through to the pilot." Dick crumpled the page of doodles and tossed it into the wastebasket in the corner. He picked up the first line again. "Sorry to keep you waiting. Is Charlie on the line?"

"Yes. I'm on the line, Dick." Charlie's loss of blood and the morphine for his pain forced him to fight for the words he wanted.

"Peter Binder's gone crazy. He's going to attack Randal Lake. He's stuck on this nutso idea that it's a nest of Russian spies ready to launch a nuclear warhead on Toronto. He's gone crazy, absolutely crazy." Charlie paused, breathing heavily. "It's like something out of a bad novel. With all the weapons he has, he can do a real number on that camp, and he's convinced Maria Davidoff, Tom Grogan, and Arnie Ward to go along with him." Summoning a hidden reserve of strength, he raised his voice, "He actually shot me, the bastard."

Dick listened to Charlie's rantings, waiting for him to finish. Sadly, quietly, Dick responded with, "Charlie, when did you sign up with the KGB? Was it in college? First, second, third year? Or was it when you were in Berlin?"

"What the hell are you talking about?"

Dick shut his eyes and, bowing his head, squeezed his forehead with his left hand. "You know exactly what I'm talking about. Charlie, it's all over. There's a Russian general here who says he knows you. He came up with your name without any hints from me. He said you first started working for the KGB about the time you were in Berlin for us, and that a guy named Zakhar Rostov has been paying you recently. I've seen copies of communications between you and Rostov." The line dropped into silence, with only the soft hiss of the connection.

Dick thought it odd that all he felt was an intense frustration with his own weaknesses and stupidity. Taking his own agent as his lover? How could he have been that stupid? Did the lack of anger mean that he actually did love Charlie? He knew that the cop from the Quebec Provincial Police was listening to the conversation, but he didn't care anymore. "Charlie, I believed in you. I cared about you. Isn't there anything you can say to convince me that I'm wrong?"

After a few more seconds of silence Charlie asked, "What's the general's name?"

"General Khabarovsk. He's come with reports showing the relationship between you and Rostov. Your payments are even in the copies of Rostov's accounting records, for Christ's sake."

The voice on the other end of the line went quiet and cold. "They're pulling out all the stops. Well, I hate to tell you, but it's all way too late." When Charlie continued, he sounded bitter and angry. "You have no idea what happened in Berlin. No idea." Charlie continued, "If you must know, I never liked pretending to be your lover. It was my job. I did it pretty damn well, didn't I?"

Dick cut him off. "Goodbye, Charlie." After a short pause, Dick continued, "Officer Couette?"

"Yes. This is Officer Couette."

"I need to talk with you privately for a moment."

Dick heard Charlie say, "I'm dying, Dick. I'm dying." Then there was a soft click as Charlie was removed from the call.

"Monsieur Durban, it is just the two of us on the call now."

"I want to thank you for the call. I have now discovered that Charles Sturm has been an embedded agent for Russian interests. Please make sure that if he is moved that he is heavily guarded. Please keep me informed of his status."

"I will see to it."

After Officer Couette hung up, Dick held the telephone in his hand for some time. That bit from Charlie, about pretending to be his lover, stung. Dick shook his head. How could it be, when someone betrayed you this badly, that the greatest pain would be the loss of love?

Dick rubbed his eyes again, trying to rub out a sudden sense of absolute exhaustion. *I'm a fool, and worse*, he thought. He tried to get his mind around the enormity of what he had done. "Damn!" he muttered. Only one thing he could do now. He'd do what he could to put things right, if only there was enough time. He laughed bitterly. *I don't think a geologist can pull me out of this fire.*

36

I N TORONTO, CAPTAIN RICHARD DURBAN SPOKE TO A GATHERING
unlike any that that he had ever seen in this conference room. On
the previous day, the Prime Minister and General Khabarovsk had
reviewed the private letter from the President of Russia. Dick and
General Khabarovsk had given the Prime Minister a summary of
the situation, but they had waited until today to fill in all the details
and provide an update on the planning. An air of tension filled the
room, partly from the seriousness of the situation, but mostly due to
the extremely large egos of some of the people involved. There was
no room for distrust, but it lay quietly in the background, unstated.

After the Prime Minister's teleconference connection was
established, Dick began the discussion. "The purpose of this call is to
bring everyone up to date on the Randal Lake situation and decide on
our immediate course of action. I believe we need to send an effective
force to take control of what appears to be a totally unacceptable
situation at Randal Lake in Nunavik, and we need to send that force
as soon as possible. One thing we need to decide on is the makeup of
that force and whether we inform NORAD or handle it ourselves."

Dick pointed to Warren Goodkin. "I've asked Warren to arrange for the most recent satellite images of the Randal Lake area as we talk. The images will be updated as new ones become available. It's not quite real-time imaging, but for this part of the world it's as good as it gets." As the lights turned low, the large screen behind Dick showed a tranquil image. "What have you seen in the recent images, Warren?"

Warren tapped on the computer and the image changed. "You can see a helicopter here at the south end of a small hill." An arrow pointed at the little helicopter. "You can also see two people near the helicopter with a small amount of supplies of some sort. We think some of the items are handheld missiles, and there appear to be several rifles, but on short notice we can't be absolutely sure of the details with these images. You'll see from the next image that they carried most of the material to the top of the hill."

Warren tapped on the computer again, and the image changed again. "This is the most recent image. You can see the two people here." He pointed again. "This vantage point would give them a good, sheltered view of the Randal Lake camp. There are four bodies here. We don't have any images that explain what happened." He expanded the view of the image. "This weather line to the west is slowly moving into the area." He paused. "It's only a matter of time before we'll be essentially blind, and we'll remain blind for a long time. We won't be able to see anything."

Dick turned back to the small audience and the video camera, his back to the screen. The large display of the Randal Lake camp provided a dramatic backdrop. "I'll quickly review the situation as we know it." Dick had almost finished explaining the Russian understandings and the need for immediate action when he realized he was starting to lose the attention of his audience.

"Something happened up there, Dick," Watson commented softly.

Dick whirled around to face the screen to see the large image of the Randal Lake site. The satellite view of the boiling inferno of flame and smoke was impressive. "Holy Christ!" was all Dick could come up with as an immediate comment. "Warren, what's going on up there?"

Warren pointed at the two figures on the hill. "Well, I think the two people on the hill fired two, possibly three, handheld missiles at the camp, aimed at this large building and the fuel tank here. Whatever happened, the Randal Lake mine site has become a very unpleasant place. I'll need some time to analyze the images to provide more details."

"Watson?"

"I think somebody up there decided to raise hell. I'd guess it must be that geologist you were talking about." Watson continued, "He must be quite the remarkable fellow."

The Prime Minister interrupted. "Well, General Khabarovsk, I wish I could say that we have the situation under control, but it seems rather obvious that we do not. Would you agree that you can put off any action on Canadian soil by your forces, at least until we have a chance to sort this out?" The Prime Minister folded his hands on a small table in front of him.

The general responded, "I am worried that our time frame for decisive action may be closing rapidly." He smiled, revealing some metal dental work. "I'd say that your geologist has begun an effective attack with a rather small force. I hope your entire army is not geologists if we ever go to war against Canada." He laughed. "No. We'll do nothing for now. We're not ready and won't be ready for at least another few hours." He looked directly at the Prime Minister. "We will, however, watch this closely, very closely."

They all looked up as the image changed to show thick cloud and fog cover over the entire area of interest. "Well," Warren stated flatly, "my usefulness for this discussion is over. That muck is going to be around for a while. You can see that the cloud cover is disturbed in this area. That's from the heat of the fires at Randal Lake."

The Prime Minister looked at the cloud-covered image and then spoke to General Khabarovsk again. "I understand your concerns, General Khabarovsk. We will cooperate fully with you on this. I would like to keep the Americans out of this as long as we can, and that includes NORAD, Max. Our friends to the south already think they own our country. I'd like to see this handled by Canadians, if possible, with help from you and your people, general, if necessary. In one respect, general, our two countries have something in common. We both try to hold onto our national pride in the face of overwhelming American arrogance." The Prime Minister paused. "What do you want me to do, Captain Durban?"

Dick was astonished by what he had just heard from the Prime Minister, but he responded immediately. "I want you to give me and General Worthington a free hand to take whatever actions and to use whatever force is necessary to ensure that if there is a nuclear-armed ICBM at Randal Lake it never gets off the ground, regardless of its intended target."

"Fine. You, together with General Worthington, have that authority." The Prime Minister spoke to an aide barely visible at his side and then looked directly at the teleconference camera. "Max, I assume you can make sure all our defense forces know that. I'll need a good cover story for all this. It will have to be a good story to tell the U.S. President if I'm to have a hope of keeping his country out of this, and I need to talk with him sooner rather than later."

The Prime Minister paused. "Now, gentlemen, I must leave to attend to other matters. I want complete security, a complete blackout, on this. This could cause panic in Canada and around the world. It could also lead Rostov's people to launch the nuclear missile sooner than planned. Right now, what we need more than anything is time. If we need more forces than we ourselves are capable of providing, we will call on General Khabarovsk, and on the Americans only as a last resort. Understood?"

"That is perfectly clear, sir. Thank you." Dick maintained a somber face.

"Ah, this was my pleasure, I'm sure." There was no smile. "Make sure you and Max keep me fully informed." He stood up and his aide reached over and clicked off the video connection.

While Peter and Maria were destroying much of the surface facilities at the Randal Lake mine site and while the conference came to its foggy conclusion in Toronto, the work underground at the missile site was reaching a critical phase. In the underground control room, the muffled sound of the first explosion accompanied a brief flicker of the lights. Igor Luchenko looked up from his work and away from his instruments toward Helmut Fankhauser. Helmut was sitting closer to the computer monitor showing a video feed from the surface cameras. "What was that, Helmut?"

Helmut responded in his tenor voice. "I don't know. One of the video cameras on the surface is out of order. All I can see in the others is smoke. Can you still get in contact with the surface?"

"I can try." He picked up a telephone and dialed a number. He heard nothing, no ring and no answer. "The line is dead," he said calmly.

"I told you, Igor. I told you we were vulnerable. That emergency unit may be enough for lights, but is it reliable enough for the computers? For the actual launch? I don't know." At that, the muffled sound of a second explosion rumbled through the control room, and the lights went out. The screens on the three desktop computers blinked before the emergency power had a chance to come online. They had never installed a backup battery support system for the computers. No one had thought it would be needed.

Helmut threw his hands up again and swore. "Crap! This is fucking ridiculous! Now I've got to reset most of the systems before we can even think about a launch. You have to find out what's going on up there, Igor." They heard yet another explosion. "Send someone up there to find out." He pointed at one of the video screens. "That last explosion was the big fuel tank. We've got one hell of a fire up there."

"Will it threaten the headframe or the launch?" If nothing else, Igor was focused.

Helmut glared at Igor. "How should I know? If the headframe gets hot enough or if it gets jarred out of alignment by one of the

285

explosions, it could damage the missile when it's launched. It could fail. It could crash. It could explode. We need a careful surface survey and accurate measurements on the alignment of the headframe to make sure it's not a problem." Helmut continued to glare at Igor. "Right now we don't have the power to complete the launch, unless that miserable emergency generator runs perfectly for the first time ever."

With a parting glare at Igor, Helmut turned back to his work. Quietly, "Don't worry Igor. I will do my job, but I have no intention of launching this missile if it will simply explode and kill us all." He turned back to look at Igor, but the intensity of Igor's stare made Helmut turn quickly back to his computers.

37

"ELL, ARNIE, DO YOU REMEMBER THAT TEAM OF GEOPHYSICISTS you dropped off this morning?" Peter asked.

Arnie smiled. "I do seem to remember that sometime in the distant past I left a few of them on a grid south of the camp. What should we do with them?"

"Can you get in touch with them by radio?"

"I can try. I haven't had it on for a while." He turned it on and made a call. The response was immediate. The heavy fog had them worried.

"Let me talk to them for a minute." Peter calmed them down. He told them that Arnie would come for them as soon as there was a break in the fog. He assured them, a bit falsely, that these fogbanks usually broke up by the end of the day.

Peter handed the headset back to Arnie. "Arnie, I don't want to risk this helicopter or you in the next part of this exercise. It's the only lifeline we have back to civilization, and you're the only one who can fly it and pick up these guys, or us for that matter. How much fuel do you have back at the camp?"

Arnie responded calmly. "There are plenty of undamaged fuel

drums. There's no problem, at least not for now. Not much place to sleep at the camp, though."

"It looked like your tent and the office tent were still in reasonable shape, along with part of the cook tent. There should be some shelter, but it won't be a nice place to stay the night."

Peter looked at his little crew. The dense fog brought a damp chill, and they all bundled up against it with heavy jackets. The fog muffled all sounds and colored the landscape a featureless, matte gray, giving each of them a sense of isolation and disorientation.

"Okay," Peter said. "Tom, Maria, and I will head to the Randal Lake mine site. Frankly, I have no idea what we're walking into." He turned back to Arnie. "I want you to stay here, Arnie, and make sure those geophysicists are looked after." He gazed to the north, toward the invisible Randal Lake camp. "With this fog, we're on our own. We can't expect any help, not right away. If we're successful in stopping the launch of a rogue ICBM, or at least delaying it, one of us will come back to this hill to meet you, Arnie. If you leave to take care of the geophysicists, return as soon as you can. Don't land unless you clearly recognize one of us. If I can, like this time, I'll fire another green flare if it's safe to land, but you'll have to use your judgment about safety and landing. Okay?"

Arnie nodded. "That's clear, but are you sure you don't want me to go along with you? You could use another set of eyes and another rifle, I think."

"Yes, I could." Peter laid his hand lightly on Arnie's shoulder. "I want to be sure we have a way out of here, though. Keep one of the rifles and be prepared for anything, but most of all try to keep yourself and this machine in one piece."

Arnie threw a mock salute. "As you wish, general."

Peter smiled and turned to Tom and Maria. "Okay. You said you saw four people, Maria, before we fired the missiles?"

"Yes." She counted off on her fingers, "One was in the little building and one in the headframe, up at the top. Two were in the mill building. They went outside when the first missile hit the generator building. They ran like hell when the fuel tank went up in flames."

Peter peered into the fog again. "Well, they may not be in great shape now, but we don't know. The fellow in the headframe should be okay, but maybe a little toasted." He turned to face Tom and Maria. "We have excellent cover, which is an incredible gift, and I know the camp pretty well. We have plenty of firepower. Those are our advantages. Our disadvantages are that we don't know how many we're up against, and we don't know where they are."

I've got to be crazy, Peter thought. He began to summarize what they had to accomplish. "We have three objectives. First, eliminate or at least neutralize the last of the security force. Second, jam or destroy the mechanism to open the cover on the top of the mine shaft. Third, destroy the control system, or ensure that any power supply is out of commission. Comments?"

They were silent. Finally, Maria spoke up. "It sounds logical enough, Peter. Since you're more used to this kind of work than we are, I guess you're in charge." She laughed. "So here we are, your vast army of well trained and loyal soldiers, ready to go into battle."

"Thanks, Maria, I guess." *Well, at least they're willing enough*, he thought. "Let's grab what we can easily carry and head into the camp. We have to work closely together. We won't use the radios, and we won't be able to see much." Peter gestured at the equipment on the ground. "First priority is the assault rifles, one each with two full clips. Second is the dynamite. I'll pack extra ammunition in a backpack for each of you." They promptly began to pick up their equipment.

"Arnie, please review the basics of the assault rifles with Tom and Maria again. I have a feeling we don't have much time."

Peter worked quickly, loading the backpacks as Arnie reviewed the operation of the AK-101 with Maria and Tom. He made sure they traveled light. He trusted that they had no further need for the handheld missiles or his Weatherby. They were moving into what was effectively urban warfare. They'd leave the food on the hill and carry no water. Water lay in small pools everywhere in this land, and they could drink that if they got thirsty. In addition to his rifle, Peter continued to carry the pistol. The main items in the packs were additional ammunition and the twenty-five sticks of dynamite with fuse and caps. He took the time to tape the sticks together into one bunch, using three strips of duct tape. Twenty-five sticks would make a pretty good bomb if he needed one.

After he had finished packing and Arnie had finished his review lesson, they shrugged on their backpacks. Peter turned to Arnie. "Wish us luck, Arnie. We're going to need it. Take care of the geophysicists, and we'll see you soon."

At that, the army of three turned to head north to the Randal Lake mine site. Peter took out his GPS unit. He had the location of the headframe from a topographic map. He also took out a small compass and set a heading for the last building to the east. They moved toward the north at a deliberate pace, and the three of them disappeared into the fog.

"Good luck," Arnie said softly as he watched them disappear. "If these are the saviors of the world," he said to himself and the fog, "Lord, you sure make your choices in mysterious ways." He turned back to the helicopter, climbed in, and closed the door.

Cloaked by the fog, Peter, Tom, and Maria moved slowly to the north. Peter aimed the little march to arrive at the east end of the buildings, hopefully at the last bunkhouse. Thanks to the GPS, he knew he wouldn't miss the camp altogether, but he didn't want to walk into the middle of the camp, either. He assumed that when they got close they'd see, smell, hear, or feel the fires, but the fog was a danger as well as a friend. It gave cover for everyone, not just the good guys.

They walked on silently, the gray fog swirling around them. Tom and Maria mutely followed Peter. After about twenty minutes, Peter stopped and held up his hand. They heard faint sounds of crackling and popping. It had to be the fires. He squatted down, and the others did the same. He spoke softly to them. "All right. We're getting close now. We've covered nearly a mile. I plan to walk us to the last bunkhouse to the east. We need to be careful, in case it's occupied. We'll check each bunkhouse to make sure it's empty. I don't want any surprises behind us. We'll figure out our next moves when we get to the last bunkhouse."

They got to their feet again. "Keep about six feet between you. Make sure you keep the one in front of you in sight. When I put my hand up, stop. When I beckon you forward standing still, move up to me. When I beckon you to follow and start walking, keep your distance. Maria, you follow me. Tom, you take up the rear, and don't forget to look behind you once in a while. Keep your eyes open and keep quiet. Clear?" They nodded. "Okay then. We have a good chance of pulling this off, but only if we're careful, good, and damn lucky." Peter smiled. "Let's go."

Peter listened to the sound of the fire and continued to the north. The sound came from northwest of them, as it should, but he knew that sounds in the fog could be profoundly misleading. He took a deep breath. *Christ, I hope we can manage to pull this off.* He looked behind him, nodded, turned, and set off at a slow walk toward the invisible buildings. His eyes hurt from the strain of trying to see something in the fog ahead of him. He'd glimpse images only to see them fade away, phantoms of his overly active imagination.

In the next five minutes the faint image of a low building appeared in front of him, and he put up his hand and crouched down. All three waited, silently. An orange tint colored the fog to the west-northwest.

Peter got up silently, signaled to Tom and Maria, and moved slowly toward the foggy apparition of a building. Slowly, the outline clarified and took definitive shape. A second building gradually materialized in the fog, another bunkhouse to the east of the one ahead. Moving more confidently, Peter turned toward the western entrance of the easternmost bunkhouse. He held up his hand and moved to the side of the outer door. Peter signaled to Maria and Tom and pointed to the side of the building. They moved to crouch at the side of the building.

Peter turned back to the entrance. The outer door squeaked on its hinges, but the noise of the fire masked the sound. Peter slid into the cramped entryway. Cautiously, he stood up and looked through the window of the inner door. He saw no one. He used the barrel of the gun to slowly open the door. Empty. He closed the door slowly, exited the entryway, and crouched down next to Tom and Maria.

"Empty," he said softly. "Let's hope the rest are." They moved cautiously westward to the east end of the next building, and Peter repeated the process. It, too, stood empty. They moved along the south side of the building, westward. At the west end of the building, Peter crouched close to the ground. He crept forward to a point where he could see around the edge of the building. He saw no one.

He sensed that the heat of the fires was shredding the solid curtain of the fog. He hated to lose the advantage of the fog as cover. So long as they were not detected, improved visibility could work both ways. He stood with his back against the building and signaled for Tom and Maria to come up to him.

He spoke softly. "So far, so good. I don't see anyone around, but the fog is starting to thin, probably because we're getting close to the fires. This next building should be the last of the bunkhouses. When we cross this space, let the person in front of you make the entire crossing. When I signal, move across quickly, but as quietly as possible." Tom and Maria nodded. Tom was sweating, in spite of the cool fog. Maria cloaked herself in an icy calmness and intensity that Peter had seen before. He always found it a little unnerving.

Peter got into a crouch and peered around the corner of the building again. Nothing in sight. He took off in a crouching run across the opening between the buildings and stopped beside the end of the final bunkhouse. He waited for a moment before he signaled for Maria and Tom to follow. When the three were back together, he moved to the east entrance.

With his first glance through the window he could see at least one person in the building, at the far end of the large, open room. He chanced another look. One man stood at the far end, about seventy feet away. Three others lay on simple, metal-frame beds. White bandages covering much of the face and hands on each of them. *Burn victims,* he thought. The one stood, or rather leaned over, one of the victims, with his back toward Peter. Several rifles lay against an empty bed. Through the windows, an orange light from the burning mill building lit the scene, and small explosions punctuated the constant snapping and crackling of the fire. Peter moved back to the side of the building and signaled for the others to come to him.

Almost in a whisper Peter said, "This one's not empty. It looks like three seriously wounded on beds and one looking after them. Probably burn victims. There are a couple of rifles nearby."

Peter looked at Tom and gestured toward the west end of the building. "Tom, go down to the other end of the building. Make sure no one gets out that door. Take my backpack, but be careful. It's loaded with the dynamite, caps, and extra ammunition. If all goes well inside, I'll bang on the wall four times before I come out. Answer with three if it's okay to come out. Be patient. This may take a while." Peter put his hand on Tom's shoulder. "Stay out of sight as much as you can. We still don't know how many may be left around here." Turning to Maria, "You come with me." With a nod, Tom got up and moved off in the fog, to the other end of the building. Peter watched Tom take up his position, barely visible in the thick fog.

Peter turned to Maria. Softly he said, "Okay. Here's what we're going to do. I'll lead the way into the building. When I go in I'll move to the left and get down on the floor. You follow and go to the right. Get down prone on the floor as soon as you can. Let me take the lead if there's a firefight. Back me up if I yell for you. Otherwise, fire only if fired on. Got it?" Maria nodded. "I want to leave these guys alive if

I can." He shook his head. "Too much killing already." They crept into the tiny entryway. "On the count of three," he whispered.

They burst into the room. Peter rolled to the left, and Maria flattened herself on the floor to the right. They both trained their rifles at the far end of the room. The attendant jumped up, startled at the sound, and started to run toward the weapons. "*Nyet! Nein!*" Peter shouted. Beside him, Maria yelled at the attendant in Russian to stop and put his hands up, lacing her command with a spice of Russian expletives. The man hesitated and then he slowly raised his hands, facing Peter and Maria. Peter slowly got up, his rifle at the ready. "Thanks, Maria. I'd forgotten about your Russian. Keep your rifle trained on him. If he makes any move, shoot him. I'll have to put my rifle down to search him and tie him up. If there's any question, don't hesitate. Just shoot him."

"Okay," Maria replied softly as she got to her feet as well.

They walked watchfully toward the man, who kept his hands raised in the air. To Peter, in the dim, orange light, he looked vaguely familiar. As they moved closer, Peter recognized the uninjured man as Pyotr. "Jesus Christ, it's Pyotr," he said. "This is one of the guys from the Bombardier, Maria. How the hell did he get here? This is amazing."

Pyotr was grinning broadly by the time Peter and Maria arrived at the three occupied bunks. "You tie up again?" Pyotr asked.

"Yes, Pyotr. I tie you up again." Peter motioned with the rifle to another bed, and Pyotr went over to it, lay down on his stomach and stretched out his hands so Peter could tie them to the side of the bed. *Well trained*, thought Peter.

Peter turned briefly to Maria. "Keep a close watch on those injured guys." Then to Pyotr, "Is one of these guys Yegor?"

"Yes. Yegor is there. Bad burned. All bad burned."

"Maria, bring over three or four of those rolls of medical tape." Maria brought them over and stood nearby, watching the three injured men, as Peter bound Pyotr's wrists to the head of the bed and then his ankles to the foot of the bed. "How many more soldiers are there?"

"One more, up high in …"

Maria broke in with a question in Russian. "He says the guy is up in the headframe. He's the last one on the surface."

"The headframe," said Peter, remembering Maria's earlier comments about seeing someone in the headframe. If the fog cleared, he had to be eliminated, and quickly. Close to the fires, the visibility from the top of the headframe might be too good already.

Peter finished taping Pyotr to the bed. "No more soldiers? No more men?" Maria repeated the question in Russian.

"No. No more here. More down."

"Where's the control center, Pyotr?" There was no answer. Peter poked Pyotr in the ribs with the muzzle of his rifle. "I don't have time, Pyotr. Where's the control center?" Maria again repeated the question in Russian.

Pyotr sighed. "Small building, near …" He turned to Maria and continued in Russian.

"He says there's an access shaft in the small building near the headframe. The control center's down in the mine," Maria said.

"How many in the control center?"

After more discussion in Russian, Maria said, "He says there are nine people down there."

Poor bastard, Peter thought. *I almost feel sorry for him. I wonder how Charlie arranged for him to be sent back here.* Aloud to Maria, Peter said, "Go check on those other three. See if you think they'll survive with no one to look after them."

He turned back to Pyotr on the bed. "Listen, Pyotr. We have to stop the missile. We'll get help for your friends as soon as we can."

"I understand."

Maria returned to Peter's side. "They're all badly burned, but I think they'll live. They don't look like much of a threat. I don't think we need to tie them down."

Peter turned away from the bed, walked over to the wall, and hit it four times with the rifle butt. He heard the three answering thuds. "Let's go." As they left, he picked up the three rifles that leaned against an empty bed, and he wondered how many more were lying around. *We don't have the time to search*, he thought, and they walked out the door into the fog and joined Tom.

38

THE DIM GLOW OF A FEW EMERGENCY LIGHTS INTENSIFIED THE closeness of the underground control room. To save on power consumption, they had reduced the ventilation. As a result, the temperature rose, and the smell of sweat and unwashed bodies pervaded the atmosphere. Igor paced the floor, back and forth, and he cursed Helmut on a periodic basis.

Helmut mostly ignored Igor, which only made Igor's cursing expand to new levels. Helmut had considerable difficulty getting the computer systems back online. The destruction of the main power plant must have included a power surge. He was bringing backup systems online. "Igor," he said, "I'm trying to get this system together again." Igor continued to complain. Finally, Helmut pushed back from the table, stood up, and confronted Igor as he turned back to face him in his pacing.

Normally round and soft in appearance, Helmut now stood more like a bulldog. "Have you sent anyone up to see what's happened?"

Helmut's defiance astonished Igor. "No, Helmut. Isn't it obvious? We've been attacked by Andropov's killer. No?" Igor stared at Helmut.

"Probably you're right," Helmut responded, "but there's a lot of damage on the surface. Most of the video cameras are out of commission, and with those few that still work we can see almost nothing because of the fog and smoke." Helmut's voice rose in intensity. "We cannot launch the missile until we know it will clear the ground. If debris covers the shaft or the shaft cover cannot open, everyone here will die when the first stage engine ignites."

Igor replied with disdain. "It makes no difference. We will all die anyway. We will launch the missile as soon as you're ready."

Helmut stood his ground in front of Igor and replied defiantly, "Igor, I will not take that chance with all these people."

Igor's face contorted in an ugly grimace. His usual icy demeanor was slowly being chipped away, replaced by a boiling anger. "What do you mean you will not take the chance? You will do what I tell you to do. I ought to have you shot."

Helmut laughed, which only increased Igor's anger. "Shoot me if you wish, but there are only two rifles in this room, and you are far away from both." He laughed again. "And if you shoot me? Who will launch your missile, then? Not you and not anyone else. Not unless I have the systems working perfectly, and then only if I give you all the codes. I have not said I won't launch the missile. I only ask you to make sure we won't kill ourselves in a futile effort to complete an impossible mission."

Igor glared at Helmut. He barely controlled himself. "If we fail in this mission, we have little choice but to kill ourselves."

"That should be each man's choice, and his alone." The two men glared at each other in silence. Helmut finally spoke again. "So, what's your decision, comrade?" Helmut's defiance stunned Igor. "Do you at least send someone to look," Helmut continued, "or do we admit failure and simply wait to be executed or to suffocate here? It's your choice. You're in charge, as you so loudly remind me."

Igor leveled his icy gaze at Helmut and said coldly, "If you're so damned concerned, send one of your men. Until you do your job, they have nothing to do anyway. I will not waste the security guards."

Everyone in the room, including the five technicians, had witnessed the confrontation. A tense silence filled the darkened space, broken only by the hum of the electronic equipment. Helmut turned away from Igor and walked over to Arkadii, the youngest of the technicians. He put his hand on the man's shoulder and said softly, "I want you to climb to the surface and look around. It will be dangerous. Obviously, we've been attacked, and we can't be sure we can open the cover on the shaft unless someone goes up there and takes a good look. If we launch the missile when the cover is still closed, we're all dead men." Helmut waited for an answer.

Arkadii looked up at Helmut and put his pen down on the table in front of his blank computer display. Even in the dim light, Helmut could see the mass of freckles on his smooth face. Arkadii got up from his chair and asked, "What exactly do you want me to look at?"

They walked over to the ladder and the hatchway together. "The main thing is to check if there's any wreckage on the cement cover, or any damage to it or the old headframe. Take these." Helmut handed Arkadii a small pair of binoculars. "Stay out of sight as much as possible. As long as you're up there, we will not seal this hatch, but get back as quickly as possible."

Arkadii nodded his head. Without another word he put the binoculars in his pocket along with a flashlight and started up the ladder. He pushed the hatch open, climbed through, and lowered it back in place. One of the guards turned to lock it, but Helmut touched his hand and shook his head. The guard shrugged his shoulders and went back to his chair.

The lights in the access shaft were not connected to the emergency power supply. Arkadii climbed quickly in the dark, guided by the thin beam of the pocket flashlight. In his haste, the echoes of his steps on the metal rungs filled the shaft with a hollow, ringing sound. After a climb in the dark that seemed endless, he reached the intermediate level and stepped into the tunnel. It led to a now-sealed entrance to the mine shaft, the missile silo. He moved a few steps to the side and started up the next ladder, a shorter climb. At the end he would find the answers to Helmut's questions. Arkadii would not enjoy opening the top hatch. Perhaps debris had fallen on the hatch, leaving all of them trapped. Fear and darkness were Arkadii's uneasy companions on his climb to the surface.

Like chess players in a hurry, Dick Durban and General Max Worthington had pushed the required forces into place, or at least close enough to respond quickly once the fog dissipated. Now all they could do was wait. The satellite images still showed the disturbance in the cloud cover caused by the raging fire at the fuel tank, but it seemed to be growing less obvious with time. Perhaps the fire was dying down.

Dick spoke to the video image of Max. "General, do you have everything you need in place now at Kuujjuaq?"

"Do you want a full rundown or just a summary?"

Dick gestured at the satellite image of a fogbank and smiled grimly. "We've got some time, I think. Give us the full treatment."

"Okay," Max answered.

It was a long explanation. The Canadian Air Force had activated three C-17 Globemaster military transport jets and positioned them at Kuujjuaq, along with fifteen of their CF-18 Hornet fighters. That left enough of the Canadian Hornets at Cold Lake and Bagotville to cover the Canadian commitments to NORAD. One hundred troops with full battle gear and all their equipment were ready to go in one of the Globemasters with provisions for about five days of operations. Two light-armored personnel carriers and one Bombardier tractor accompanied those troops. Those men and their equipment would be the backbone of this operation. Boots on the ground, as usual, presented the most precise and effective response.

Of the two remaining Canadian C-17 Globemasters, one carried fuel for the operations, and the other held four Bell 412 helicopters.

The helicopters would be the main transport and fire support for the troops on the ground. They were equipped with a Dillon Gatling gun in one door with a rate of fire of about three thousand rounds per minute. The Hornets carried laser-guided, air-to-ground Hellfire missiles, along with air-to-air missiles just in case they ran into some unfriendly airplanes or helicopters. At least initially, none of the aircraft in the air carried any bombs. Any bombing support had to be precise. Unless they were left with no other choice, they had no intention to target the silo itself, even with precision-guided smart bombs. The risks of a nuclear incident were simply too great. They would have a small number of aircraft loaded with laser-guided smart bombs in reserve, just in case, but those would remain on the ground at Kuujjuaq.

A rotating group of Hornet fighter jets was already in the air, supported by tankers. They'd be the first eyes on-site and would give a report on the status of the situation as soon as the fogbank dissipated. One of them carried equipment to test for radiation contamination. The troops would land at the airstrip at Randal Lake if the reports and observations from the Hornets were favorable. Otherwise they'd land at the Asbestos Hill landing strip. In that case, a small number of men would head for Randal Lake immediately in the Bombardier tractor, a three- to four-hour drive. Once they had been unloaded and were operational, the helicopters would ferry the remainder of the troops to Randal Lake.

"Why can't you send in the troops by helicopter right now, without delay?" Dick Durban asked Max.

"There are a couple of problems, Dick. First off, these helicopters aren't set up for zero-visibility flying. They'd have to pick their way along, slowly and at low altitude. They couldn't carry many men, and they'd be close to their maximum range. The other problem is that we know somebody up there has a bunch of handheld missiles, and I want to be sure we know what we're getting into." He paused, looking at the image of Dick Durban. "We need to get our fighter planes up there to take a look around and neutralize any anti-aircraft defenses, and we can't do that until this fog clears up a bit."

"And you, General Khabarovsk? Are you are ready to respond if needed?" Dick asked.

"We have twenty-five fighter bombers in place in our forward bases in the Arctic. Frankly, hearing General Worthington's plans, I very much doubt we will be needed."

The Russians had some of the same concerns about bombing the mine shaft while it still contained a nuclear warhead, though perhaps they were not quite as worried as the Canadians. In General Khabarovsk's opinion, it was far better to risk nuclear contamination in a remote location of northern Canada, rather than risk the destruction of the city of Moscow.

General Khabarovsk spoke to Watson MacDonough and Dick Durban. "We intend no hostile action against the United States. I assume your Prime Minister, Captain Durban, is also prepared to talk to the President of the United States if we are required to launch an attack on Randal Lake?"

"Yes. We'll keep the United States out of this if we can."

"Probably shouldn't be all that hard to do," muttered Watson.

Dick Durban laughed. "I don't know, Watson. Ever since Pearl Harbor, a sneak attack is one thing your government takes seriously, and these days there seems to be an eagerness to rush into military action by the residents of your White House." Dick turned back to General Khabarovsk. "If any Russian planes come into Canadian airspace, we will have to keep our partners in NORAD fully informed. We do have Americans at our control center in North Bay, and we can't screw around with that mutual defense agreement."

Max Worthington spoke up. "I've prepared a little cover story for this operation. It reports that we're conducting the first Arctic emergency response exercise in cooperation with the Russians. The exercise is designed to improve our response to a major disaster at one of our mining operations in the Arctic."

"And the Americans are buying that?" Watson asked incredulously. After a brief pause, Max continued. "We shouldn't have any problems with the Americans, but they'll be nervous, and, obviously, NORAD will be tracking the activity. I've sent a report with the details to you, Dick, and to the Prime Minister, and you can discuss them with General Khabarovsk."

They sat in silence, looking at the useless satellite images. Breaking the silence, Dick summed up the situation. "All we can do is wait until the weather clears and we have our forces in place."

"Maybe your geologist will take care of it all for us," Watson said flatly. The men all laughed mirthlessly.

Ignorant of the meeting in Toronto, Peter, Maria, and Tom were hard at work at Randal Lake. Peter carried the three extra rifles as they exited the bunkhouse and joined Tom outside. Their rifles hung loosely at their sides. "You won't believe this, Tom," he said quietly. "Pyotr is in there, one of the guys I brought into camp from the Bombardier."

Tom laughed. "You're kidding me."

"Nope. It's him all right, and his friend Yegor is one of the injured. No wonder they were smiling when they left camp." Peter continued. "Okay. We've got to get moving. According to Pyotr, there's one more armed man at the top of the headframe. I guess I'll believe him. That means we can forgo searching all the other buildings, but let's still keep a close watch for more men. We've got to get close enough to the headframe to take that man out. The fog may be thinner there, so be careful."

The noise from the fire had slowly diminished during the time they searched the bunkhouses, but it still provided an abundance of background noise. Speaking softly, Peter had little fear of being overheard. "We'll spread out, like we were before, and head over there." He pointed in the general direction of the headframe. "We have to at least try to jam the cover over the shaft, or maybe drop part of the headframe on it. If they can't open it, I assume they can't launch the missile." He looked at the extra rifles he was carrying. "I've got to find some place to get rid of these. I don't want to leave them just lying around."

Peter shrugged on his backpack, turned, and started forward. He looked back and saw that Tom and Maria moved out exactly as they should, about six feet apart. *They learn fast*, he thought. *They must have watched way too many combat movies.* Then he concentrated on his own movements, trying to remember where different buildings were located and the exact location of the headframe. As he recalled, it was west of the still-burning mill. Close to the mill and the fuel tank, but far enough away that the guy had most likely survived the explosion. He must be feeling lonely.

Peter came to a corner of a building. He looked around and then upward. For a moment he thought he could see the outline of the headframe ahead and above them, but then the shape vanished in the fog. He crouched and started to jog across the space between the administration building and the maintenance building, the last structure still standing before an open space to the base of the headframe.

As Peter started, the fog layer momentarily broke. In the sudden, brief clearing, a man high above them in the headframe spotted Peter. He immediately opened fire, and Peter dropped the extra rifles and broke into a full run for cover. Behind him, Maria jumped out from behind the building and fired a long burst at the top of the headframe. Peter looked up in time to see the man drop his rifle and slump against the guardrail. Slowly, he slid down to the narrow walkway, slipped over the side, and fell in a long, gliding tumble onto the concrete shaft cover. He lay on his back in the center of the cement cover, his arms and legs spread out. His blood began to pool on the cement.

Maria shouted, "Peter are you all right?"

Peter jogged quickly back across the opening. He put his hand on Maria's shoulder. She was breathing hard. "Thanks, Maria. I owe you for that one." Maria relaxed a little, and Peter hugged her to him.

After a while, with a strong hint of exasperation, Tom said, "I hate to interrupt, but shouldn't we get moving?"

Peter laughed. "Yep. You're right, Tom." He looked over at the shaft cover, dimly visible in the fog, with the dead Russian spread out on its surface. *Christ almighty.* With renewed determination, he spoke. "Okay. First, let's see if we can jam the shaft cover or drop debris on it. Then a couple of us have to find our way to the control center and see if we can shut down the launch system completely."

Peter picked up the extra rifles and began to walk toward the mine shaft, and Tom and Maria followed. A light rain had started to fall, but they didn't notice.

39

MAX LAUGHED AS HE TOLD DICK DURBAN AND THE OTHERS IN Toronto about their military's move into Kuujjuaq. They created more noise and commotion than the old airport had seen in an extremely long time. The local Inuit residents watched with some curiosity, along with the local charter airline employees. They were quickly ushered away if they came too close to any of the soldiers or to any of the airplanes.

The airport hadn't seen this many military aircraft since the Second World War, and even then the airstrip was no more than one of many emergency strips and potential refueling stops for ferrying airplanes from the United States to Europe. The CF-18 Hornets sat on a taxiway off to the side. Periodically, fresh pilots took off to relieve the ones on station to the north, and the relieved pilots landed to take a break and catch up on sleep.

The three Globemasters filled up most of the remaining space to the side of the main runway. The troops did what soldiers do in all armies most of the time. They waited for their moment of action.

The flight crews, like the soldiers, all had their own approach to preparing for action. Some smoked and avoided thinking about what lay ahead. Some rehearsed their role in their minds and checked their equipment. Some told stories and jokes. Some played poker. Some slept.

In flight over the North Pole, the Russian bomber crews and the Russian soldiers put in place by General Khabarovsk faced a significantly higher level of anxiety. They were part of a potential attack on a foreign country. The Russian transports, filled with one hundred and fifty bored but battle-ready soldiers and all their equipment continued to fly in large, lazy circles just outside of Canadian airspace.

Dick Durban, Watson MacDonough, and General Khabarovsk waited in Toronto and General Max Worthington waited at his base. They watched the satellite images in vain, drank coffee, and listened to the routine communications between the various attack and support groups. The next move lay with the weather, over which they had no control. In truth, when the action began they had no more real control over it than they had over the weather.

In Ottawa, the Prime Minister continued a difficult telephone conversation with the President of the United States, who sat with Harold James, director of the CIA, and General Weston, the chairman of the joint chiefs of staff. "Regardless of what you think about this, Mr. President, this is sovereign Canadian soil and sovereign Canadian airspace, and this is a decision of State. We will undertake the joint disaster response operations as planned with the Russians."

"This sets a dangerous precedent."

The Prime Minister paused. "We are restricting all activity in this exercise to north of sixty degrees latitude and east of eighty degrees west longitude. NORAD has been instructed to understand that any flight activity by any of the participants outside of those boundaries, other than by the Canadian Air Force, will be considered hostile and open to attack."

"There's been some unusual activity by the Russian bomber fleet in some of their Arctic bases. Is that part of this exercise?" The voice of General Weston, the chairman of the joint chiefs of staff, boomed over the speakerphone.

The Prime Minister sighed audibly, and the President smiled. The President knew that this conversation would be almost physically painful for the Prime Minister. "It is my understanding that these forces are not airborne and are not actively approaching our airspace. To my knowledge, the only Russian air forces near our airspace are a small group of cargo planes carrying Russian forces to assist in the practice response to the emergency, along with some air tanker support."

"You know that we'll happily assist in any disaster. Why do you suddenly want to get the Russians involved?" the President responded.

"Mr. President, we always welcome your assistance, and we appreciate your help in the past. We're just trying to ensure a robust plan to react to a disaster in the Arctic as we bring more development into the area. We're particularly concerned when your resources are stretched by activities elsewhere in the world." The Prime Minister smiled as he completed that last remark.

The President was annoyed. He was fully aware of the Prime Minister's enduring opposition to America's constant involvement in warfare around the world, and he certainly recognized the thrust of that comment.

The chairman spoke up again. "We'll increase monitoring activity and our flight operations in our eastern sector. We'll be sure to keep NORAD informed."

"Thank you. I understand that you don't like this, but it is a simple test exercise of a mutual assistance and response program for our holdings in the Arctic." Both sides hung up without much ceremony.

"Now, what the hell is all this about?" the President asked, nearly shouting. "What's behind this? Why are they doing this?" He directed his complaint at the urbane and aristocratic Harold James.

Harold took his time responding. "It is our opinion, sir, that the Canadians have identified a group of renegade, ultranationalist Russian Communists in Nunavik. That's essentially northern Quebec. The Canadians now fear that these Russians may have stolen a Russian ICBM, a Topol-M, complete with a nuclear warhead, and that they may have installed it in an unused mine shaft. I should emphasize that we do not believe there is any danger to the United States at this time."

The President exploded. "What in God's name are you telling me? The Canadians think a bunch of crazy, nutcase Communists may have simply walked into their country with a fully loaded nuclear missile, aimed who the hell knows where, and you 'do not believe there is any danger to the United States at this time'? Jesus H. Christ! I demand a full explanation. Now!"

"That could take some time, sir." Harold responded more quickly this time.

The President pounded the table with his fist. He shouted, "I don't give a damn how much time you think it should take. I want your explanation right now, for Christ's sake!"

"Yes sir. I understand that." He paused. "To start at the beginning, we were presented with a set of unsubstantiated rumors that the Russians had lost a missile, not including a warhead, just a missile. These rumors first came to us some six or eight months ago."

"I gather you decided to keep this information to yourself? You didn't think it was worth bothering to tell me? Jesus Christ!"

"Let me emphasize, this was an unsubstantiated rumor. To make a long story short, we now believe that our people may have been wrong in their evaluation of the information. It is possible, only possible, that there really is a missile up there, potentially with an operational warhead. We have no direct confirmation one way or another. Our satellite coverage shows a lot of activity at Randal Lake, an old mining development site, but it shows no direct evidence of the installation of a missile in the old mine shaft. However, if it really is there it could be fully operational by now."

"Jesus Christ!" growled the President. "And tell me, what's the lucky destination for this little gift of Russian ingenuity?"

"We don't know the target. We don't have any direct knowledge of the target," Harold stated flatly.

The President almost lost his voice in his anger. "You don't know? Don't you even have a goddamned guess? That's what you're paid for, Harry, isn't it? To make guesses?"

Harold ignored the insult and plodded on at his own pedantic pace. "This is such a fantastic story that it's really hard for even me to believe any of it. Assuming for a moment that there really is a missile there, and remember, that's a big assumption, at first we thought the target would have to be the United States. But this isn't the Russian government undertaking this exercise, or why would they have leaked enough information to make us take a hard look at it? If it's really there, we believe the missile is part of a scheme undertaken by an extremist, right wing, old-line Communist cabal. They're a bit like the extreme, right-wing Patriot groups in this country, but considerably more virulent and deadly. They're dedicated to the elimination of the current government in Russia. According to the rather dubious information provided to our contacts in Moscow, the Russian government believes the target is Moscow."

An astonished silence greeted the conclusion of Harold's monologue. Even the President was speechless.

Finally, the chairman of the joint chiefs responded. "That's nuts. Why would they do that?"

Beads of sweat appeared on Harold's forehead. "You just have to think like an old Communist. Even with the current President, they hate every bit of what we see as democratic progress in Russia, anything that moves away from the old style of centralized, Communist control."

Harold continued, "With the Duma in session, you engineer a nuclear explosion over Moscow, and in one blow you wipe out the entire government, a big chunk of the Russian wealthy upper class, and probably a good chunk of the Russian mafia. You leave the industrial and agricultural centers of the country essentially untouched, and you blame the whole thing on the United States, because the missile was launched from North America. It would be hard for us to convincingly deny any involvement. How many other nuclear powers are there in North America? The old-timers reestablish the old order, with themselves in charge. Quite neat, if you ask me, and it's almost crazy enough that I think it could succeed."

"Jesus Christ!" from the President again. He turned to the chairman of the joint chiefs. "Do you have the assets you need in Canada to make absolutely sure the Russians don't violate the boundary zone that Canada has identified?"

The chairman had the stiff-backed demeanor of all career soldiers. "Our main assets in Canada are with CANR, the Canadian arm of NORAD. With the unusual activity of the Russians just outside of Canadian airspace, we asked our commander, General Jacoby, to check into it. The Canadians, including the deputy commander for NORAD, are feeding us the same line that the Prime Minister just gave us."

Rather grimly, the President interrupted. "You haven't answered my question. Do we have the assets in place to keep a fence around the Russians?"

"Yes, we do. They're already in place in Maine and farther north, just offshore of Canada's airspace. They will stay in place indefinitely with tanker and relief support."

"Is there anything we can do to stop this missile? Can we kill it?" The President spoke more calmly, but an edge of venom colored his voice.

"We don't know that there is a missile," Harold reminded him.

"Christ, Harry, I know that, but for Christ's sake, even you admit that it might be there." Turning back to the chairman, he asked again, "Can we kill it?"

"We can use cruise missiles, but without Canadian approval,

doing so would be considered to be an unprovoked attack on a friendly neighbor. In any case, the accuracy of cruise missiles is not actually good enough for this sort of mission. It would take a laser-guided smart bomb to do the trick. The most serious risk of a direct hit on the mine shaft is, of course, a nuclear explosion. The risk of creating a major, long-life nuclear contamination issue is extremely high."

"And the risk of doing nothing might be a nuclear explosion that destroys New York City."

"The Russians tell us the target is Moscow," Harold said softly.

"Oh, for Christ's sake, Harry, just shut up." The President turned back to the chairman. "So, can we put a stop to this mess?"

"Understandably, sir, with our concerns based on nothing much more than unsubstantiated rumors, Canada won't be eager to approve of us making a direct strike on the missile or mine shaft. To be honest, the only completely reliable approach for us to take, other than landing a significant force on the site itself, the only approach that would guarantee to take the missile out of action right now, is a nuclear attack on the site. Canada, to put it mildly, would not be particularly enthusiastic about that."

The chairman paused and then continued. "I've been in some discussions with their military. Their main contribution to this, quote, emergency-response exercise is to deliver a military ground force of about a hundred fully equipped and battle-ready ground troops to secure the site, along with several support helicopters and ground vehicles. They're providing a number of their jet fighters for air cover. This is a pretty powerful force for an emergency-response exercise." The chairman shook his head. "I think they're in about the same situation as we are. They don't know what's going on up there, but they're doing everything they can to neutralize whatever it is. There's not much more we could do."

"Can we do anything once the missile is launched?" the President asked.

"Can we shoot it out of the sky? No. We don't have anything in place to handle that situation. Once the missile is launched, it quickly reaches a speed of over twenty times the speed of sound. At that point, there's little we can do except pray for the victims and the survivors. The Topol-M, if that's the ICBM that's at Randal Lake, is one of the best the Russians have. It reaches full speed very quickly. The boost phase is so short that even our dedicated, infrared-detecting satellites have a hard time spotting the launch. The Topol-M usually carries a single warhead with a yield of about eight hundred kilotons. That's forty to fifty times the size of the bombs we dropped on Japan. There are also six or eight decoys to confuse any defense systems. The warhead is shielded against any radiation, even from nuclear explosions at distances over half a mile, and it's almost impossible to get closer than that when the target is moving so fast. The missile and warhead are designed to be immune to any current or planned missile defense we have. The Topol-M has an autonomous flight control, tied to the Russian version of GPS, and can hit a target with an accuracy of about six hundred feet. We don't have anything to stop this missile once it's launched, and the Russians sure as hell don't."

"So you're telling me there's nothing we can do?"

The chairman smiled slightly. "For a moment before ignition, when the silo's open, and even for the briefest of instants after the first stage is ignited, the missile is vulnerable, even to small-arms fire. It's a cold launch missile, which means it has a gas generator that boosts the ICBM out of the silo before the main stage ignites in the air. If you had people on-site, and if you had the time and opportunity, you could probably make a successful launch impossible by destroying the cold launch part of the system. I'm sure the Canadians are thinking about all these scenarios, but at the moment they aren't talking to us or even to their own representatives at NORAD."

"This whole thing is absurd, gentlemen." The President, fuming, looked from one man to the other. "I want a full alert of all our forces. If the Russian bastards step one millimeter out of line, I want their fucking heads on a platter. Meantime, if we have any indication that we're running out of time, we will make a strike ourselves, whether it's requested or not and whether it's welcome or not. Understood?"

"Clearly," said the chairman.

"Can we put some drones up there? If our neighbors are giving us a one-fingered salute, we can damn well throw a few unmanned drones in their direction."

"If the Canadians find out about them, they'll be really pissed off," Harold responded quietly.

"Quite frankly I don't give a damn about Canadian sensitivities at the moment. I want to make sure that, if the missile exists, we use every possible resource to prevent the launch. You haven't answered my question. Can we put some drones on-site?"

The chairman and Harold exchanged glances before Harold responded. "We have one over the site already."

The chairman spoke up. "It's armed with two Hellfire air-to-ground missiles. They're really tank killers, but they'd do a number on an ICBM in an open silo."

"Right now the whole area is obscured by thick clouds, but once they clear we can get a good look at things and decide whether to take any action or just get out of there." Harold looked steadily at the President.

"Christ almighty!" The President glared at Harold for a moment and then stood up. "All right, then. Our meeting is over. I would appreciate it if you would start thinking to inform your commander in chief before you make command decisions. I want no significant hostile action without my direct approval, but I want us ready to move instantaneously, if needed." The President turned and stalked out of the room, followed by his aides. Harold and the chairman exchanged glances and left the room shortly thereafter with their aides. "POTUS is not amused," General Weston commented dryly.

40

ETURNING TO HIS OFFICE AFTER HIS MEETING WITH THE PRESIDENT, Harold quickly entered its interior, secure conference room. The three men at the table were talking softly. They stopped talking and looked up as he entered and sat down. "I'm sorry I'm a little late. The meeting with POTUS did not go well. The Canadians are aroused, and they're cooperating with the Russians. Rostov has lost control and is on the run. There's still a chance, but Randal Lake will likely fail."

G, with his heavy German accent, responded, "How can it be that one man can wreak such havoc?"

Harold shook his head. "We thought we had him neutralized. We were wrong. This geologist is very resourceful and destructive. Single-handed, it appears he's taken out two helicopters, Rostov's security force and his mole in the RCMP, and destroyed much of the Randal Lake site."

BD laughed. "That's quite impressive. It appears that we underestimated the man."

G glared at BD and then turned back to Harold. "You were wrong about Ivan Dinisovich and Watson MacDonough, too, Harold. Those are fundamental failures."

"I will not deny that, but I will remind you that your faith in the strength of Rostov and his group was equally incorrect."

BD smiled again as he watched the two men. After a pause, he spoke in his polished English, "We all knew the risk from the start. Zakhar Rostov was always a shaky proposition. Personally, I'm amazed that we got this far." He looked at the others and then back to Harold. "Can we rescue the mission?"

"We have few assets to deploy. We have a drone in the air with two Hellfire missiles, but the weather's terrible. We can't see a damn thing. The Canadians will destroy the drone if they see it, and they will see it eventually."

BD again, "Does the President know about the drone?"

"Yes. I was skating on very thin ice. I had to give him something."

G growled gutturally, "You can keep it there, then. Eliminate the geologist if you can. He is getting very annoying. POTUS won't target the missile directly."

"I'm not so sure. He will hesitate, yes, but he's very angry. When he's this angry, as we all know, he can be very unpredictable."

G again, "Well, it was a good try. Eliminate the geologist, and it might still be possible. Other than that, just let it be. Make sure you keep our fingerprints off this mess." He shrugged his shoulders. "Too bad. We might have finished what Churchill wanted to do at the end of the Second World War. We might have managed to have the Russians destroy themselves as a world power for well into the next century. Too bad."

"I'll order the drone to try to eliminate any armed groups, hopefully including our annoying geologist, and then order it back to base. Agreed?" Each of the men nodded silently. "POTUS may order a strike directly on the missile. If we fire both Hellfire missiles at armed groups, the order will be moot." Harold turned to the silent man. "You'll handle General Weston?" The question elicited a small nod of agreement.

"I can reach you all at the usual numbers?"

Each man nodded in the affirmative, and G commented, "I'll be heading back to Wyoming tonight. I'll be out of contact for several hours. You can connect through the satellite, but I do not recommend it."

"Okay. We're done, then." Harold rose from the table, and the other men did as well. Then Harold commented, "There is one more thing. You should all be prepared to implement your plans in the case of my dismissal."

"Indecisiveness will rule the day. You'll be safe in your position," was G's heavily accented response.

BD laughed, and Harold said, "You're probably right." The four men left the room without further discussion. *I'm beginning to like this geologist,* Harold thought as he walked back to his office.

Back at Randal Lake, Peter, Maria and Tom stood under what was left of the headframe, and Peter leaned the three extra rifles against one of the main steel supports. Two slabs of cement came together over the shaft. They projected under a cement housing on either side of the shaft.

"It looks like the two sliding cement slabs are hooked to some sort of pulley or hydraulic system under the cement housing," Peter commented. "It wouldn't withstand a direct hit from a nuclear bomb, but it's tough enough to keep us out with what little dynamite we have."

Peter got down on the slab and looked closely at where it disappeared into the housing. "There's only about an eighth of an inch gap between the slabs and the housing. It'd be nice to sabotage this, but we can't get any explosives in there unless we have an air hammer and a lot of time. We'd need a pile of ANFO or some other explosive if we're to make a dent in this setup."

"Well, at least now we know why they were taking the headframe apart," Tom responded, looking up at the open space above them. "Maybe we could collapse part of what's left of the headframe and drop it over the shaft. We would just need a good cutting torch."

Peter looked around at the headframe. "I don't know, Tom. The main supports are pretty heavy-duty steel beams. You'd have to do a lot of cutting to get this to fall down."

"Well, I can't think of anything else, can you?"

Peter shook his head. "No, I can't, except to try to get underground and shut down the whole launch process." Peter looked at the steel beams dubiously. "Give it a shot, Tom. Maria and I will check out the little house over there and see if we can find the way down to the control room."

"Okay. You guys have fun while I do the dirty work," Tom replied with a grin.

"I'll leave the dynamite and extra ammunition with you," Peter said, taking off his pack. "I need another clip for my rifle and one for Maria." He rummaged through the pack and dropped the additional clips of ammunition into his jacket pocket.

Peter and Maria started toward the building, approaching it slowly and carefully. They eased around to the back and checked the interior through a small window. They saw no sign of anyone, but some large piping and electrical machinery obscured the view. Moving silently, close to the outside walls of the building, they approached the door and cautiously opened it. Nothing. Peter stepped in.

"There's no one here." He pointed to the floor. "This looks like a hatch cover. I'll bet anything it leads to the control room below." He pulled on the handle to no effect. "It must be locked from below." He looked around. "This looks like some sort of ventilation system. We saw hot air or exhaust coming from this building before. It doesn't sound like it's working. If that's the case, it must be getting pretty hot and nasty down there."

They heard a squeaking noise, and they both searched for the source. The intermittent sound came from the metal hatch in the floor. A set of hinges on one side clearly indicated the direction of opening. Peter motioned to Maria to step with him behind some pipes in back of the hinges. They crouched there as the squeaking sound continued. Finally, they saw the lip of the hatch rise slightly and go back down with a metallic thud. A moment later it rose a full foot and then opened completely, slamming down on the floor almost at their feet. Peter and Maria withdrew into the maze of pipes.

They heard footsteps on a metal ladder as Arkadii climbed out, followed by silence. Then footsteps again, leading away from them. Peter put his finger over his lips, then signaled Maria to slowly step out with him into the room. They saw a short, red-haired man, apparently unarmed, looking out the window. He was studying Tom, who had his back to the building. Silently both aimed their rifles in his direction, and they waited.

When Arkadii turned and saw them, the look on his face was one of sheer terror. He immediately wet his pants. Peter jerked the barrel of his rifle up a couple of times, and the man understood and raised his hands. They walked nearer to him, and Peter, with a circular motion of his left hand, again indicated for him to turn around. Peter pushed him roughly toward the wall. Arkadii stumbled but caught himself with his raised hands. Peter pushed his legs apart and frisked him quickly. No weapons, but he did retrieve the small flashlight and binoculars.

"You speak English?" Peter asked. Arkadii gave no response. Again, "Do you speak English?"

"Let me try Russian," Maria said. She spoke quickly to him, and he answered her in Russian. "Do you want me to ask any questions?"

"No. I won't know whether to believe him or not. See if you can find something here to tie him up. Whatever he says, we still have to go down and find out what's going on. Just in case Tom can't sabotage the shaft cover and keep it from opening, we need to stop the launch some other way. The best opportunity has to be in the control room, and I'll bet that's where this guy came from." Peter looked down the narrow shaft. "It looks pretty quiet down there. I hope there aren't any other locked doors or well-armed security guards along the way."

Maria pointed at Arkadii's boots. "I think his bootlaces should be good for something."

Peter leaned his rifle against the wall. "Okay. You cover him and I'll tie him up. Just tell him what I'm doing."

Maria spoke to Arkadii softly, and he responded. "He says he understands."

"Okay, but please keep a finger on the trigger." Peter knelt down and started to unlace Arkadii's boots. The strong smell of sweat and urine made Peter grimace. When he finished, he took off Arkadii's belt. As his pants started to fall down, Arkadii looked at Maria with a pained expression. She smiled, shook her head and said a couple of words. "I told him to lie down," she said to Peter. Arkadii looked over at Peter. He nodded and pointed to the floor. Arkadii slowly backed away from the wall, held his pants up with one hand and lay down on his back on the floor. With Maria standing over him, Peter turned him on his side and bound his hands tightly behind his back with the rawhide bootlaces. Then he took the belt, wound it tightly around his ankles, and fastened it with the buckle. Peter dragged him to the wall and helped him into a sitting position.

"That should hold him until we get back." Peter stood up and looked at the open shaft. "I think we've got to climb down the access shaft, but I'd better tell Tom what we're doing." Maria nodded, and Peter ducked out the door and jogged over toward the shaft. While he and Maria had been dealing with Arkadii, the rain had faded into a light mist. Tom was heading toward what had been the maintenance building and truck repair shop. Peter gave a shout, and Tom turned and waited.

"What's up, Peter?"

Peter explained his immediate plans. "So we're about to climb down and see what we'll find."

"Okay. I'm still on a hunt to find a cutting torch."

"Okay. See you soon." *I hope I will*, Peter thought. Peter turned and jogged past the body still lying on the shaft cover and back to the small building over the access shaft. Tom continued on his search. When Peter got back to Maria, she was sitting, back against the wall across from Arkadii, with her rifle lazily aimed at him. The two of them were chatting away in Russian like old friends.

"Tell him to keep tight. We won't be long," Peter said. Maria spoke to Arkadii, and he shrugged his shoulders.

"Leave your pack here, Maria. Take an extra clip of ammunition with you. This is probably a fairly long climb down, and I have no idea what we're going to find when we get to the bottom." Peter looked at the shaft and took a deep breath. He didn't like the close quarters, and he didn't like the darkness. It would be far too easy for even a single defender to finish them off. *Maybe we've killed off enough of the security force that there's no one left to defend this access shaft*, Peter thought. *I hope so.* Then he stepped onto the ladder.

41

PETER AND MARIA SLUNG THEIR RIFLES OVER THEIR SHOULDERS AND began to climb down the ladder in the dark access shaft. The warm, humid air smelled strongly of electronics and unwashed bodies. The cold of the permafrost created a constant dripping condensation along the walls and on the metal rungs of the ladder. Peter led the way, using the flashlight occasionally. They climbed blindly and slowly down the slippery ladder, with barely enough room in the narrow shaft for one of them to fit at a time.

Peter had never experienced any feelings of claustrophobia, but he had to admit that climbing down this pitch-black shaft could do it. He wondered how it was affecting Maria, but then he just concentrated on the task at hand. Finally, Peter stepped onto the rock floor at the end of the ladder. He breathed a sigh of relief and called softly up to Maria, "Just a few more steps and you're down." He lit up the base of the ladder with the flashlight, and she stepped down the last few rungs. Peter looked at her sweaty and shining face, and in a quiet voice he said, "This is really bothering you, isn't it?"

She held onto his shoulder to steady herself. "I hate to admit it, but you're right. It's the closeness, and I guess the darkness. I've felt claustrophobic only once or twice before." She took a deep breath. "My ex used darkness when he was being particularly violent. That doesn't make this any easier."

"Well, the good news is we're about a third of the way there, I think. The bad news, of course, is that we're only about a third of the way there."

Maria sighed. "I'm sorry, Peter, but I'm not sure I can go on, knowing I have to climb out too."

Peter considered for a moment. "You stay here. I'll go on alone. They'll be expecting their man to return soon. I doubt they've got many security guards left." He led her away from the base of the ladder.

"I feel terrible about this, Peter. I should go with you."

"If it's bothering you this much now, you could get into real trouble going deeper. Stay here. I can't give you the flashlight, but if you come over here to the top of the next shaft, you'll be able to see my progress and get some idea of what's going on. If you feel better in a bit, you can always head down after me."

Peter led her to the second shaft and sat her down beside it. A guardrail surrounded the opening, except at the ladder. He squeezed her hand and started down the ladder. He could feel time slipping away. This next shaft was a straight ladder, down about fifty feet. He couldn't see the bottom clearly. He still wore his field jacket and carried the rifle over his shoulder. Progress was slow. He was tired, hungry, and still hurting from the impact of Charlie's shot earlier in the day. Only the conviction that it would all be over soon, one way or another, gave him the stamina to continue.

When Peter thought he was about halfway down the ladder, he thought he heard steps on the metal ladder above him. Maybe Maria had decided that sitting in the dark was no better than being in the shaft. Peter kept on going at a steady pace until he reached the base of the ladder, where the shaft widened slightly into a small room.

In the center of the floor, he saw the heavy, steel door, similar to the one at the top of the small shaft. He looked around with his flashlight, but he couldn't see any obvious control to open it. There was a crude metal handle opposite some hinges. He reached down, his feet on either side of the steel door, and pulled on the handle. The door opened slightly. He lowered it again, careful to not make any sound. He took his rifle off his shoulder and held it in his right hand. He braced himself and pulled the heavy door open.

Only dim emergency lights lit the room below, but the lights seemed bright after the total darkness of the shaft. Peter blinked his eyes and looked straight down at a man standing at the base of the ladder calling up to him in Russian. A security guard after all. Recognition of the situation was instantaneous and mutual. The guard started to unsling his rifle to swing it upwards at Peter, but Peter already had both hands on his rifle, aimed at the guard, and he pulled the trigger. The noise of the five shots was deafening in such close quarters. The security guard collapsed in a heap on the floor of the room below, and Peter wasted no time in jumping down on top of him, falling to one side in the process.

The sudden gunfire stunned the inhabitants into inaction, at least momentarily. Peter jumped up. He faced a large, open room, about fifty feet long and twenty feet wide. Three desktop computers and two small laptops lined a bench against one of the walls at the far end, monitored by four attendants. He was close to one end of the room, and one man stood in the middle of the room, staring at him. Another security guard, at the far end of the room, had already laid his rifle down and raised his hands.

"Does anyone speak English here?" Peter asked loudly. His ears still rang from the sound of the gunfire.

"I speak some English," Helmut Fankhauser replied from the middle of the room. "What do you want?"

Peter almost laughed at the question. He stepped forward a few steps into the room. In a voice that sounded far calmer than he actually felt, he said, "You will slowly shut down everything in this room and climb out, one at a time."

The German laughed. "You are only one man. How can you hold off all of us?"

Peter waved his rifle slightly. "Maybe I can't, but I can kill most if not all of you, and do a lot of damage to the equipment at the same time."

"Do not move," came the voice behind him in heavily accented English. At the sound of those three words, a wave of overwhelming despair washed over Peter. He had failed. Everything he and the others had done was a complete waste. They might as well be dead. They would be soon enough, that much was certain.

Igor had crept out of the shadows behind Peter to silently pick up the rifle from the dead security guard. "Do not move or I kill you." Igor jabbed Peter in the back with the dead guard's rifle, and Peter raised his hands and his rifle over his head. In Russian, Igor continued, "Helmut, come over here and take his rifle. I think we may have captured our phantom of the north. Perhaps we can find out what's happening up above us before we kill him."

Just then, Peter heard Maria shout in Russian from the access shaft. "Hey, you Russian pig!"

Igor jerked his head back and looked up at the source of the shout. He swung his rifle up toward Maria. She squeezed the trigger, and Igor went down in a shattered heap. At the far end of the room, the second security guard had a sudden surge of bravery and picked up his gun. In the confusion, Peter almost didn't see him, but he and the guard fired at the same time. Peter's shots hit the man in the chest, and he fell against the wall. One bullet from the guard caught Peter in the left arm, ripping through the fabric of the parka and jerking his arm violently backward. The shock hit Peter like a hammer blow, instantly followed by a searing pain.

Helmut, who had thrown himself onto the floor, watched as Peter sat down heavily, swearing. He dropped his rifle and grasped his left arm. The two men were about thirty feet apart. Helmut didn't know who or what was up in the shaft, but it sounded like a woman. Perhaps he could even the odds. He jumped up and started toward Peter. With a grunt of pain, Peter reached inside his jacket, pulled out Andropov's pistol, cocked it, and aimed it at Helmut in one motion. Peter's hand trembled slightly from the pain, but even Helmut could see his aim was accurate enough. Helmut stopped and slowly raised his hands again.

"That's better, you bastard," Peter growled. "Now back off." Helmut backed away toward the center of the room. "If anyone goes near that other rifle, they're dead." The four technicians were frozen at their positions, wide-eyed, with their hands over their heads. They were Russian geeks, not soldiers.

"Maria, I need you down here. I've been shot. Watch yourself on the ladder. There are a couple of dead guys at the bottom."

Maria climbed down the ladder and stepped on Igor's chest. Though he was dead, he let out a little grunt as Maria stepped on him. "How badly are you hurt?"

"I'm shot in the arm, but I'm not bleeding badly. I can deal with the pain for now. See if you can bandage it up while I keep my eyes on these guys. You'll need to make a sling out of something." As he spoke, his eyes scanned the room. "By the way, thanks. That's twice today."

Maria shook her head. "I'd prefer to not make it a habit." She helped Peter out of his jacket, took a small pocketknife out of her pants, and quickly cut the shirtsleeve off his left arm. She ripped the sleeve into strips and bound up the wound as best she could. "I'll make a sling out of a shirt from one of them," she said, pointing to the bodies at the foot of the ladder. Then she whispered, "What do we do next? It looks like we've got five guys still alive down here. What do we do with them?"

Peter motioned his pistol toward the man in the center of the room. "What's your name? Are you in charge here?"

"My name is Helmut Fankhauser." He stared malevolently at Peter and Maria and shouted angrily, "I am in charge here, now you murder Igor."

Peter looked at Helmut in disgust. "Man, you're an odd one to use the word 'murder'. A Russian missile aimed at some major city, I suppose, where you plan to kill maybe a million people? You call me a murderer?" Helmut was silent. "Move to the far end of the room, along with your technicians." Helmut didn't move. Peter was getting impatient. "Move, damn it! Stay away from that guard and his rifle."

After a moment Helmut spoke to the technicians in Russian. They gradually got up with their hands raised and moved to the far end of the room. Helmut joined them. Peter watched them closely.

"So, you murder us now?" Helmut asked with a sneer.

Peter grimaced as Maria moved his arm into the makeshift sling. "No, Helmut. That's not the way I do things, though I guess that might surprise you." Maria finished arranging the sling, fashioned out of Igor's shirt, and Peter got up, using his right hand for support. "Put another clip in your rifle and keep a close watch on all of them, Maria. If anyone so much as twitches, shoot him."

Maria spoke to the technicians in Russian. They were still surprised to hear fluent Russian, even though they had heard her shout and curse at Igor. *Now, how do I make sure all this equipment is inoperable?* Peter wondered. He walked down the bank of computers. Where was the power coming from?

After a quick examination of the entire room, he ended up in the area behind the access shaft. There had to be a secondary generator somewhere, he thought. That end of the room narrowed down, probably to one of the original exploration levels off the main shaft, and it ended in a concrete barrier. As he drew close, he could hear the faint sound of a diesel motor. He took out Arkadii's little flashlight. Heavy electrical cables ran through an opening in the concrete barrier up to a large, gray switch box secured with a heavy padlock. He turned back to the main area of the room and grabbed the two large flashlights he'd see there. He handed one to Maria. "Hang onto this. I'll tell you to turn it on if I try to turn off the electricity. I think they're running on a backup generator." Peter turned back to Helmut. "Where's the key for the electrical switch box? Do you have it?"

Helmut remained silent. Peter raised his pistol and fired it just above Helmut's head. The bullet slammed into the cement wall just behind Helmut. "Scheiss!" he shouted as he fell to the floor.

"If I have to do that again, Helmut, you're dead. So where is the key to the switch box?"

Glaring at Peter, Helmut pointed at Igor's body at Peter's feet. "Igor has it."

Peter looked down at Igor. The guy was a bloody mess. He started to pat down Igor's bloodstained pants to find the key. In the right pocket he found something hard, but when he pulled it out he saw that the brass key had been hopelessly deformed by one of Maria's bullets. He held it up in the dim and flickering light. "I guess that finishes that idea."

Maria couldn't help but smile. "Sorry about that. One too many shots, I guess."

"I could argue with that estimate," Peter laughed, but it hurt to laugh. "I'm going to walk down along the computers. I'll see what happens when we unplug this little operation. Keep a close watch on our buddies."

Peter holstered his pistol and walked slowly over to the first of the shiny, new, Japanese laptops. Peter assumed that if he unplugged all the computers and destroyed their hard drives, it would probably be impossible to launch the missile. He unplugged all the cables on the first computer with his right hand and held down the power switch. He heard the hard drive shut down as the screen went blank. He repeated the process with the other computers. Then he gathered the five computers into a corner of the room, against some heavy timbers that must have been part of the original mine workings. The more he thought about it, the less he relished the idea of shutting off the power with a room full of mad Russians.

Peter looked at Helmut for a moment. *The man has the look of madness about him,* Peter thought. Peter bent over and picked up the dead guard's rifle. "Maria, you might want to cover your ears. I'm going to kill these computers." He stepped back from the computers and, using the fingers of his left arm as little as possible, emptied about half the clip into them. Bits and pieces of computer flew around, and the computers jerked and jumped as the shots hit them. Peter winced from the pain of his left arm.

He turned back to Helmut. "Now, Helmut, I hope that I've managed to murder the brains to this operation and that we don't have to worry anymore about some poor city being annihilated."

Helmut looked at Peter with pure hatred. "We would have changed the world, you bastard. You've ruined everything."

"Why Helmut, that's the nicest thing you've said to me yet." Peter walked back to Maria's side, near the ladder.

"Okay, Helmut. Sometime, if we have time, perhaps you can tell me why you were doing all this. For now, though, let me tell you what we're doing next. Maria will leave first, and then all of you will follow, one at a time. We'll all stop on the next level up, and then we'll do the whole thing over again to get to the surface." He turned to Maria. "Will you translate that into Russian for the technicians?" Maria spoke briefly.

"So, all that's clear, Helmut?"

"Yes. It is clear." *He'll do anything to kill me,* Peter thought.

"Maria, tell them to stay where they are until I signal for them to move, one at a time, to the base of the ladder. Helmut will be last." Maria again spoke briefly to the technicians.

Peter picked up his rifle again and tried to replace the spent clip. Maria gave him a hand. "Thanks, Maria," Peter said with a smile. "I want you to go first. Stop at that intermediate level. Hold them there until I come up to that level too. Don't trust any of them, particularly

Helmut. I won't send anyone up until you yell down that you're ready. Yell again when Helmut arrives." Peter looked at Maria. "You up to this?"

She looked at him. He was starting to look worn down. "Don't worry, Peter, I'm fine now. How will you get out of here?"

"I'll manage to get up the ladder somehow, but I'll be slow. We've got to get out of here. We don't know for sure if we've shut this down, and if we didn't, and if Tom has the shaft cover permanently shut, I don't want to be here when the engines ignite." He pointed down at his jacket. "Help me get into this before you leave."

After the painful process of getting into his jacket and adjusting the sling, Peter looked at the group of men at the other end of the room. The four technicians had lowered their hands. Two of them rested their hands on their head. Even Helmut, to some degree, looked resigned to his fate. Peter stepped back and leaned his rifle against the wall, along with the two from the dead guards. "Okay, Maria. You go first."

Maria hesitated. "You're going to be all right?"

"The longer we talk the tougher it'll get. So we should get moving. This shouldn't take very long."

She took four steps over to him and touched his cheek. "Take care of yourself." Then she turned, stepped over the bodies, started to climb, and disappeared out of sight.

Peter sat down next to the rifles with his pistol in his right hand and waited for Maria to call. *Well,* he thought, *all we need is for the generator to keep working, for Maria to keep her nerve, and for me to keep functioning reasonably well.* He could feel the edge of his profound exhaustion. The deep fatigue from the emotional drain, plus the wound, even the bruise from Charlie's shot, it all started to settle in and envelope him. *Somehow I'll stay awake,* he told himself, *and alert.* He watched the men in silence until he heard Maria's call.

"All right, Helmut. Send them over one at a time." Helmut spoke to the men, and one separated himself and walked to the ladder, stepped on the bottom rung, and started to climb. After Peter figured he was about ten or fifteen feet up the ladder inside the access shaft, he signaled for the next one. He repeated the process until only he and Helmut remained in the room. He waited. After about fifteen minutes he heard Maria shout that she was ready for Helmut. "Okay, Helmut, it's your turn. Try not to do anything stupid."

Helmut glared at Peter and started to walk toward the ladder. Suddenly, the generator faltered. The lights dimmed almost to the point of complete darkness. Peter heard Helmut start to run toward him in the darkness. Peter fired at the faintly outlined, lurching figure. The muzzle flash briefly illuminated the room as the sound of the shot echoed. The shot struck Helmut on the right side of his chest. He fell backward in a twisting motion, as the generator came back to life and the lights returned. Peter listened to Helmut swear in several languages as he sat up on the floor. Awkwardly, using his left arm as little as possible, Peter ejected the two spent shell casings from the pistol and replaced them from the supply in his pocket. Helmut was still swearing.

"Well, Helmut, that was a really stupid thing to do." Peter stood up and looked at him closely. *I ought to kill him now*, Peter thought, *but I guess he can't get into too much trouble now that all the technicians are gone and all the computers are dead*. Out loud he said, "I don't think you're getting to the surface right away."

"You fucking bastard," Helmut grunted. He was holding his hand over his wound, and blood already soaked his shirt.

Peter holstered the pistol again and reached into his jacket pocket for the flashlight. "I'm heading up the shaft to the surface. As soon as I can I'll send someone down here to help you get out."

"Just drop dead, damn it."

"I'll try to avoid that, Helmut." Peter leaned over and picked up the rifles. He cradled them one at a time in his sling and removed the magazines. He made sure the chambers were empty and dropped the two magazines in his parka pocket. After he dropped the empty rifles back on the floor, he turned back to Helmut. "I'm on my way, Helmut."

"Fuck you."

Peter shook his head, turned to the ladder, and started to climb. Before he entered the shaft, he looked back at the control room. "What a fucking waste," Peter muttered, and he climbed up into the shaft. He slammed the metal door shut behind him.

In the dim light of the control room, Helmut watched Peter disappear. He looked down at his hand. It was covered with blood. It hurt him to breathe, and the gunshot had obviously punctured one lung. He started to smile. He struggled to his feet and staggered over to the corner where they had all stood while Peter destroyed the laptops. He swore at the pain as he bent over and picked up a small briefcase. Unsteady, he made his way over to one end of the small table where the technicians had sat, put the briefcase on the table, opened it, and pulled out a laptop computer. In spite of the pain, he smiled again.

42

PETER DESPERATELY WANTED TO REST ON HIS WAY UP THE METAL ladder. In the narrow shaft he could lean back against the side. That freed his right hand to take out the flashlight to see how far he had to go to get to the top. He was sweating heavily in his jacket and breathing hard, but he continued to push himself. He stopped about five feet from the top. "Maria! It's Peter."

"What happened down there, Peter?" Maria asked.

"Helmut decided not to make the trip. Everything okay up here?"

"Everyone's acting like perfect gentlemen."

"Okay. I'm on my way up and out." He finished his climb, made the transition from the ladder to the guardrail with difficulty, and lurched out into the tunnel. Maria had placed the flashlight on a pile of rocks, aimed at the four men. "Give me a moment to catch my breath, and you can make the next ascent. Take my flashlight and leave yours where it is." He handed his flashlight to her.

"What actually happened down there?" Maria asked softly.

"Well, the generator quit, and Helmut made a rush for me in the dark. Unfortunately for him, the generator came back to life. He's still sitting down there, hopefully bleeding to death." She could hear the fatigue in his voice. "Now let's get these guys moving," he said. "Just in case we didn't shut everything down, I don't want to be down here or anywhere near the mine shaft."

Maria spoke to the technicians, and they began the whole process again. The small group quickly progressed up the access shaft to the surface. In about twenty minutes Peter, soaked in sweat and breathing heavily, peered over the edge of the access shaft in the little building. The four technicians, with the addition of Arkadii, sat quietly on the floor with their hands on their heads. They were by the window that looked out toward the headframe. Maria sat on the floor and leaned up against the door with her rifle across her lap.

Peter pulled himself up and out of the shaft, stood up, and looked out the window. While he and Maria had been underground, the rain had stopped completely. He could see Tom working with a welder's torch on one of the main steel support beams of the headframe. Though Peter didn't know it, Tom had already cut nearly through three of the four main supports, and he was nearly done with the fourth. The headframe was still standing, but it was certainly fragile. A good shake would send it crashing to the ground. Tom was wearing a welding helmet and was completely absorbed in his task.

Peter caught some movement, beyond the headframe. He moved closer to the window, stepping between the technicians. He watched. Then he saw them. Pyotr led the way around the side of the old maintenance building, followed by the three wounded men from the bunkhouse. Each carried an assault rifle. "Christ!" Peter shouted. "Maria! Tell these guys to lie flat on the floor. Those four guys from the bunkhouse are headed our way, and they're all armed."

Maria shouted at the technicians in Russian, and they all went down on the floor.

"God damn it, this looks like the attack of the zombies." Peter took his rifle off his shoulder. With his right hand, he smashed the butt into the glass of the window. "Maria! They're coming right at Tom. Get out the door. You should have a good shot from there, but try to keep some cover along the wall." Peter took a quick look at the technicians. They were all flat on the floor.

At the sound of the breaking glass and Peter's shouts, Pyotr and the three burn victims hesitated. Pyotr saw Tom at the same time, and as Peter set the muzzle of his rifle on the window sill, Pyotr got off a couple of shots in Tom's direction. One of them hit the top of Tom's welding helmet. Tom dropped the welding torch as he fell over, and he whipped off the helmet. Peter heard him shout, "What the hell?"

"Tom! It's the guys from the bunkhouse!" Tom looked over and saw them coming. He scrambled over to his rifle and raised it up as Peter and Maria opened fire on the advancing group of four. Without effective use of his left hand, Peter used the windowsill to help steady his aim. He knew he wouldn't be accurate, but he hoped that he'd help some. Tom joined in about a second later. The four men were caught out in the open, bunched together and about twenty feet in front of the maintenance building. With the combined firepower of Tom, Peter, and Maria, the four men were immediately hit multiple times. They staggered backward and fell to the ground. It was over in less than five seconds.

Peter whipped around as he heard a sound behind him. One of the technicians was sitting up looking at him. Peter aimed his rifle at him and yelled, "Get down!" The technician quickly lay flat on the floor again. Peter turned back to the window. "Tom," he yelled. "Put in a new clip and make sure those guys are dead."

Peter turned to see Maria coming in the door. "I don't believe it. Attacked by the walking dead," Peter said, shaking his head.

"I'm sorry Peter. I shouldn't have left them on their beds like I did."

"Don't worry about it, Maria."

While Peter and Maria were climbing up the shaft, and while they and Tom were involved in the firefight on the surface, Helmut had his laptop up and running in the control room. He typed in a code and connected to the guidance and targeting system on the Topol-M. He was losing a lot of blood. When he began to feel faint, he stopped to let the feeling pass. He knew he didn't have much time. Still, he smiled as he confirmed the connection and entered the first password. He tapped in the coordinates for the center of Red Square. He smiled again as the program confirmed the target for the eight hundred– kiloton warhead. It would vaporize the center of Moscow and obliterate most of the city. Helmut could barely focus. After a few minutes passed, with a surge of determination he continued.

As far as targeting was concerned, the missile was now completely autonomous. Helmut opened the program that would initiate the firing sequence. He typed in the passwords, and the program asked if he had opened the sliding cement doors on the top of the mine shaft. Helmut punched in the necessary passwords and noted with satisfaction the blinking response that the doors to the missile silo were opening.

On the surface, Peter said, "Help me get a new clip in this rifle, Maria. I'm not very accurate, but I feel a little naked without this thing loaded and ready. Remind these guys to stay on the floor, too."

Maria spoke to the technicians and stepped over to Peter. He handed her a new clip from his pocket. As she finished, they felt a vibration and heard a heavy scraping sound.

Tom was running back. "The doors over the shaft are opening!" he shouted.

"Jesus Christ!" Peter shouted. "Get these guys out of here, Maria. Get down to the other side of the hill where we landed with the helicopter, and move it. We don't want to be around here if that damn missile lights up."

Peter ran out the door. "Tom, go with Maria and those technicians and get out of here as fast as you can." He saw his backpack by the headframe and ran over to it. Maria was already exiting the small building with the five technicians. Peter started pawing through his backpack. "What are you doing?" Maria shouted.

"Get out of here. I'll be right behind you." Peter grabbed the taped bundle of dynamite and the fuse and caps. He pulled out his pocketknife and used it to dig a hole in one end of a stick of dynamite. He hastily cut off a length of fuse about three feet long. That would give him about a minute. He didn't have time to find the tool to crimp the end of the cap onto the fuse, so he used his teeth to crimp it down as best he could. *Christ*, he thought, *the safety officer wouldn't approve of that technique.* He smiled briefly at the thought. He got out the remaining duct tape, and after he stuck the cap in the end of the dynamite, he ran the fuse up the side of the bundle and with some difficulty taped it to the three strips of tape that held the sticks of dynamite together.

Peter looked over at the shaft. It was completely open now. He thought he had a few minutes at best. He found the matches in his pack and carried his improvised bomb over to the edge of the shaft, lit the fuse, and dropped it in. Then he turned and started running. He left everything behind except his rifle. He could see Tom, Maria, and the technicians running ahead of him.

Peter could feel the pain in his chest, and as he ran his arm throbbed with each step. It hurt to breathe, and it hurt to run. His heart pounded. "One more time," he shouted to the wind. He called on his body to use every last ounce of energy, every bit of reserve. He heard the explosion behind him, but he didn't stop and look. He kept running. A faint sun was starting to burn through the fog as he started up the north side of the hill. Soon the fog would disappear. He was running on empty, but like a marathon runner he called on reserves he no longer had, and somewhere his body found them.

The impact of the explosion of Peter's dynamite shook Helmut into consciousness. He had fainted and fallen out of his chair onto the floor. He blinked his eyes. After the explosion he heard a scraping sound. He lay on the floor trying to recover full consciousness, but his brain was starved of blood and oxygen. He heard a loud beeping noise, but he couldn't seem to focus on it.

In the mine shaft, Peter's improvised explosive device had destroyed the gas generator that was designed to boost the Topol-M missile out of the shaft before first stage ignition. The explosion pushed the gas generator to one side of the shaft, along with the base of the missile. It also broke the nozzle assembly at the base of the first stage, and damaged the casing and lower seals. Now the Topol-M was no longer vertical, had no ability for a cold launch, and had a severely damaged first stage. It leaned to the side, and the top rested on the side of the cement liner to the shaft. All this damage created an impossible situation for a launch, but Helmut couldn't know the severity of the damage. In any case, he knew he'd be dead in a few minutes, and he really didn't care.

Helmut sat up. He blinked his eyes again. He had tunnel vision. His one functioning lung was filling with blood, and his breathing was shallow. After several minutes went by, he managed to pull himself up and sat on the chair in front of his computer. He strained to focus. The computer was beeping loudly. The screen displayed a bright-red, flashing message: "WARNING – LAUNCH COMPROMISED."

Helmut could barely keep his head up, but he tapped at the keyboard to override the warning and get back to the launch program. He typed in the word "yes" to initiate the launch sequence. Another warning flashed on the screen: "DANGER – ABORT LAUNCH." "Fuck you," Helmut muttered as he minimized the warning screen. The timer on the screen ticked down. Under five minutes to go. Helmut smiled, passed out, and slid off the chair onto the floor.

As Peter approached the hill, he began to hit a wall. He watched the technicians disappear over the hilltop. Maria stopped for a moment, looked back at Peter, and then disappeared over the hilltop as well. Peter slowed down. The slight uphill grade didn't help any. He pushed on. He wanted as much distance as possible between himself and the mine shaft. He assumed, he hoped, there would be a major explosion. He didn't think a nuclear explosion was possible, but perhaps the warhead would break apart if the missile exploded on ignition. He didn't want to be close to any of it. If there were a nuclear explosion? Well, he didn't think he could run far enough or fast enough to escape that.

He passed the four bodies and continued his exhausted run to the jumbled, frost-broken rocks at the top of the hill. He stopped next to the remaining Dragon and Stinger missiles, dropped his rifle, and risked a look back. The fog was starting to clear, and in the stillness, above the sound in his ears of his pounding heart, he thought he heard something above him. More from instinct rather than thought, he fell to the ground, grabbed a Stinger and fumbled to prepare it. With his wounded arm, the task was daunting.

"What are you doing?" Maria asked from behind him.

Peter was starting to breath normally again. "Get down beside me. Somebody's got a drone up here, and I won't be surprised if they try to kill us. I want to be able to fire back if somebody fires at us." Peter tried to find the source of the low sound, but the clouds still obscured much of the sky. "Grab the other Stinger and get it ready to fire. If the missile lights up before we take out the drone, and if it starts to rise out of the shaft, we've got to fire both Stingers at the missile. They'll probably have no effect, but we've got to try."

At that moment they heard a roar and looked back at the mine shaft to see a tower of flame erupt as the first stage of the Topol-M ignited inside the mine shaft. Peter was torn between sheltering behind the large rock and watching what happened next. He compromised and crouched behind the rock, mostly protected but still able to watch. Maria handed him one of the Stingers.

Because Helmut had overridden all the safety measures, the first stage ignited in the shaft. The cement barrier between the control room and the shaft failed immediately. The explosive force of the exhaust roared into the control room, neatly cremating Helmut, Igor, and the two security guards, and roared up the access shaft. When it reached the surface, the small building exploded into splinters and flying bits of pipe, roofing, and metal siding.

As Peter and Maria watched, the ICBM began to rise out of the shaft, but the pressure and heat from the ignition in the shaft, coupled with the severe damage to the first stage, exceeded the engineered strength of the carbon fiber body of the missile. In less than a second, the main stage exploded, followed instantly by explosions of the second and third stages. The explosions launched the warhead and decoys neatly into the air, tumbling in an arc above and away from the boiling inferno. The warhead had been designed to arm itself for detonation only when well on its way to the target. The outer shell of aluminum honeycomb, reinforced by an epoxy resin covering, protected the radioactive core. The outer heat shield, designed to protect the warhead during re-entry, shielded it from the flames. The warhead and the decoys landed, relatively unscathed, on the third bunkhouse, collapsing most of the roof and parts of three walls.

A giant ball of fire and smoke billowed high into the air from the explosions as the headframe collapsed over the mine shaft. The force of the explosions destroyed the old maintenance building and the administration building behind it and severely damaged the first bunkhouse and several other small buildings. Immediately after the explosions above the shaft, Peter dropped down to join Maria behind the rock. They laid down the Stingers, and they both covered their ears only a moment before the shockwave and sound of the explosion hit the top of the hill.

After the shockwave had passed, they stood up and looked back at the mine site. "Holy Christ!" Peter muttered.

"Jesus!" was all Maria could manage in response.

Peter looked up in the sky again. The roar of the explosion had faded, and he listened for the sound of the drone. The sky was nearly clear now. Just as he glimpsed the drone, flying a bit to the north of them, he saw the contrail streaking toward them. "Get down!" he screamed, and he and Maria fell on the ground again behind the large rock. The missile exploded, a direct hit on the four bodies fifty yards away.

"Now I'm starting to get really pissed off," Peter said, and he picked up the Stinger lying at his feet. He and Maria fired both Stingers, almost simultaneously, at the drone.

"I'm at least as pissed off as you are," Maria responded. They watched the Stingers streak into the air as the drone turned to fly away from them. The drone was a small, slow target, and as the Stinger missiles exploded, pieces of the drone fell to the ground.

"You're getting pretty good at that, Maria."

"Well, I'm getting really tired of people shooting at me."

"Me too." Peter shook his head in disgust. "We were damn lucky. Somebody made a strange targeting decision."

The fog had cleared quickly. There were only a few puffy clouds in the sky now. Suddenly a group of four CF-18 Hornets flew up from the southern horizon, only a few hundred feet off the ground. The jets thundered over the hill, over the mine site, and beyond. "I think the cavalry has arrived," Peter shouted. They could clearly see the Canadian markings on the jets.

"About bloody time," Maria shouted back. "I hope they know we're the good guys."

The jets flew rapidly out of sight, but they quickly turned and made another pass overhead, a little higher this time. One flew over the hill, did a quick barrel roll, and flew south with the rest.

43

BACK IN TORONTO, THE GENERALS, ALONG WITH DICK DURBAN AND Watson MacDonough, watched the first clear satellite image of the devastated mine site with relief. They could finally see something. "Warren, tell us what you see," Dick said.

"Well, you can see that the mill building and the generator building are both gone, as is the main fuel tank, but that's no surprise considering what we saw before the clouds moved in. There must have been a major explosion. Most of the buildings close to the shaft are destroyed. Lots of damage to the more outlying buildings as well. The shaft is open, but the headframe appears to have collapsed. You can see a small group of people here." The arrow pointed to the south side of the hill where the technicians were gathered. "There are a couple more people here at the top of the hill." He paused. "It doesn't look like there's any missile to worry about. If there was one, it seems to have vaporized. Literally."

General Worthington picked up his telephone. After a pause, he spoke. "Please tell the troop commander to find a man named Peter Binder, probably with that group south of the mine site. Get him on a satellite telephone call to Dick Durban as soon as possible."

General Max Worthington looked up. "The fighter pilots confirm just about everything you just said, Warren. They see no evidence of a missile in the shaft. Their measurements of background radiation show no anomalies. The fighter group was a little cautious initially. They detected a ground-to-air missile firing just prior to their arrival over Randal Lake. We're not sure about the target, but the Hornets drew no fire, and the transports are on their way to land at the airstrip at Randal Lake. The Hornets will continue to fly cover."

As the last of the fog burned off, Peter and Maria watched Arnie's little helicopter come into view. After Peter fired a green flare, Arnie landed on the south side of the hill. Peter looked back at the Randal Lake site. He felt exhaustion washing over him. Everything hurt. He turned to Maria. "I'm beat. Can you check on Tom and how he's doing with those guys?"

Maria stepped over to Peter. She held his head in both hands, leaned forward, and kissed him. "I'd hug you, but I guess it'd hurt too much. I'll check on Tom, but I'll be right back."

Peter slumped down and leaned against one of the rocks at the top of the hill, where he had a good view of the Randal Lake site. The four now mangled bodies lay where they'd fallen a few hours ago. The enormity of what they'd done was beginning to sink in. Except for the smoking ruins, the mine site looked remarkably peaceful. Maybe they'd saved the world. Peter laughed at the thought. "Shit, that hurts," he said.

"Then why do you do it?" was the soft response from Maria, who had already returned and stood behind him.

In response to Peter's questioning look, she said, "Tom's standing guard, and Arnie brought bread with ham and cheese. He's making sandwiches." Maria laughed. "It looks quite domestic." Maria sat down beside Peter. "How are you doing?"

"I feel like I've been run over by a truck, but I'm still alive." He paused and looked over at her. "You know, Maria, I think we actually did it."

"Yeah, I think we did. It's amazing. I know we did the right thing, but I guess I'm not entirely sure I know what it is." She turned to Peter, gently put her arm around his shoulders, bent forward, and they kissed. They looked up when a new sound became apparent, and they watched the first of the Canadian Globemasters approach for a landing on the gravel strip.

"Christ! That's got to be the biggest plane that strip's ever seen," Peter commented.

They watched in silence as the plane came to a stop and the rear ramp opened. A stream of soldiers exited and took up positions around the airstrip. They were followed by two small, armored personnel carriers and a Bombardier tractor. Eight soldiers jumped into the Bombardier, and it headed straight for the little hill where they sat.

Peter and Maria didn't move, but Maria said, "Like I said before, I hope they know we're the good guys."

"If they think we're the bad guys, I don't think there's much we can do about it except put our hands up, which isn't a bad idea when they get closer." Peter could already see the second Globemaster getting ready to land, and he now counted six Hornets flying around at altitude. "Christ, they really are sending in the troops."

The Bombardier came at the hill at nearly full speed, but it slowed as it climbed the side of the hill. It turned to a stop about fifty feet from Peter and Maria. An officer with prominent Canadian insignia jumped out, along with seven other soldiers. Maria raised both her hands in the air, and Peter did the best he could by raising his one good arm. The soldiers spread out with their assault rifles at the ready. The officer called out, "Mr. Peter Binder?"

"That's me," Peter said.

"Mr. Binder, I'm Captain Mercur, and I have orders for you to speak with Captain Durban of the RCMP." He held out a satellite telephone. "And you can put your hands down if you like."

"If you don't mind, could you bring the telephone up here? I'm a little worse for wear."

"Oh, sorry sir," Captain Mercur responded. "I'll be right there." He turned and spoke softly to one of the other soldiers. Turning back he asked, "You have some people on the other side of the hill? Can you tell us about them?"

Maria spoke up. "They're Russian technicians. We've got two men guarding them."

Peter watched a third Globemaster land. The airstrip was getting crowded. They were already pushing helicopters out the back of the second cargo plane.

The captain spoke to the second soldier again and then to Peter and Maria. "We'll take over guarding the Russians, and we'll have some medical help over here as soon as we can get it." The seven soldiers jogged up and over the hill. They found the Russian technicians calmly eating ham sandwiches and chatting among themselves.

Captain Mercur walked up the hill and handed the satellite telephone to Peter. "Captain Durban is already on the line."

"Peter Binder here."

"Peter! Peter! Good to hear your voice again. Maria's with you?"

"Yes, Maria's here. You want to talk with her?"

"Later. Later. First, tell us what's happened. What's the status of the missile and the warhead?"

Peter laughed. "Damn," he muttered. "It's a long story. You got a few minutes?"

When Dick Durban finally hung up the speakerphone in the conference room, he sat back and muttered, "Holy crap!"

They all looked at the latest satellite image on the screen. With a clear note of admiration General Worthington said, "That guy's a bloody one-man army."

"Actually it appears to be an army of three, two men and one woman," Dick corrected him.

"You're right," General Khabaarovsk commented, "but it's still amazing."

In Toronto General Hospital, Peter's visitors included Dick Durban, General Khabarovsk, General Worthington, Harold James from the CIA, the Prime Minister of Canada, Watson MacDonough, and of course Maria, Tom, and Arnie. The congratulations from Harold James seemed a bit strained. Canada and Russia both honored Peter, Maria, Tom, and Arnie with medals, none of which would ever be announced. A grateful Russia also arranged some impressive financial awards. The United States was strangely silent on what the Canadians referred to as the Nunavik Affair.

World Nickel reported the entire incident at Randal Lake as a tragic fire and explosion that killed several workers, destroyed the headframe and many critical buildings, severely damaged the shaft, and would delay the nickel development project indefinitely. Their partner withdrew from the joint venture. Charlie Sturm's death at the asbestos mine was never publicly reported. Dick Durban managed to save his job.

Zakhar Rostov simply disappeared.

44

A MONTH LATER, IN THE FAINT, GRAY LIGHT OF THE WARM, EARLY morning, Peter stood naked, looking down from the balcony of Maria's apartment in Toronto. Dimly, the light shimmered on the waters of Lake Ontario. He could feel his body healing. He knew the nightmares would continue for at least another few months. He would survive them. Maria was the best medicine for him, and maybe he was helping her heal as well. Some of her wounds were old, and some still hid stubbornly in the shadows. No problem. Peter was learning to be patient.

Slowly, the pale light grew stronger. Peter was losing the privacy offered by the darkness before the dawn. Soon he would have to leave the balcony. Peter heard the door open and shut softly, and Maria stood behind him. She was naked too in the warm morning breeze. She put her arms gently around Peter's waist and kissed his neck. Her breasts pressed softly into his back. Peter sighed as she moved her hand below his stomach and he began to respond to her attention. "Come back to bed, Peter Binder. I need a little more loving before the day begins, and I think you do too." She laughed lightly.

Peter looked out over the city, where the buildings were slowly taking shape in the early morning light. He knew he should relax, give it up, but he couldn't. *There's something still out there,* he thought. *I can feel it, but I don't know what it is.* He exhaled softly. Then he turned to face Maria and kissed her. "Yes. I think you're right," he said with a smile. He took her hand, and they stepped back into the bedroom. They left the balcony door open to the morning air.

The muscular man watched from an apartment across the courtyard. When Peter and Maria returned to the bedroom, the watcher sat back from the spotting scope. It wasn't light enough to see into the bedroom. Rostov had been quite insistent, but the watcher never thought revenge was worth the risk. In this case, the risk was high, and the ultimate rewards were worthless. This was much higher risk than the hospital. Perhaps he should refuse the job, but he didn't think Rostov took refusals well. He sighed and started to assemble the sniper's rifle, silencer, scope, and stand. He was paid to take risks.

At the same time a tall, thin man standing at another window put down his binoculars and called a number on his cell phone.

"Captain Durban here."

"It's Sam. I don't like where this is headed."

"Well, it's too early to reel him in. They want us to leave the bait out there to see if we can catch the big fish."

"I don't like it. Neither of them has any idea of the danger they're in. For what they've done, they deserve better. We know where this fish is, and we know what he can do."

Dick Durban thought about Maria and the unpleasant discussion they'd had when she returned to Toronto. He smiled. "No. We're not bringing anybody in. Not yet. I don't like it either, but that's the way it has to be. Just do your bloody job."

THE END

Printed in the United States
By Bookmasters